A PLUME BOOK

GLAMOUR

LOUISE BAGSHAWE is an internationally bestselling novelist and screenwriter. *Glamour* is her second novel for Plume, following *Sparkles*.

Praise for *Sparkles*

"With a Jackie Collins–ish flair for soapy melodrama, Louise Bagshawe stylishly imagines pretty young things consumed with money, power, and romance." —*Entertainment Weekly*

"[An] internationally flavored fantasia on love, lies, and shopping." —*Publishers Weekly*

"Louise Bagshawe's characters are vivid and memorable. It is easy to see why this author's works are international bestsellers." —www.curledup.com

"Bagshawe immerses readers in the world of the fabulously wealthy with this engaging tale of a diamond heiress and her captivating life." —*Romantic Times*

"Mouth-wateringly addictive." —*OK! Magazine*

"Throbs with vitality from the first page." —*Daily Express* (London)

GLAMOUR

LOUISE BAGSHAWE

A PLUME BOOK

PLUME
Published by the Penguin Group
Penguin Group (USA) Inc., 375 Hudson Street, New York, New York 10014, U.S.A. •
Penguin Group (Canada), 90 Eglinton Avenue East, Suite 700, Toronto, Ontario, Canada
M4P 2Y3 (a division of Pearson Penguin Canada Inc.) • Penguin Books Ltd., 80 Strand,
London WC2R 0RL, England • Penguin Ireland, 25 St. Stephen's Green, Dublin 2, Ireland
(a division of Penguin Books Ltd.) • Penguin Group (Australia), 250 Camberwell Road,
Camberwell, Victoria 3124, Australia (a division of Pearson Australia Group Pty. Ltd.) •
Penguin Books India Pvt. Ltd., 11 Community Centre, Panchsheel Park, New Delhi – 110
017, India • Penguin Group (NZ), 67 Apollo Drive, Rosedale, North Shore 0632, New
Zealand (a division of Pearson New Zealand Ltd.) • Penguin Books (South Africa) (Pty.)
Ltd., 24 Sturdee Avenue, Rosebank, Johannesburg 2196, South Africa

Penguin Books Ltd., Registered Offices: 80 Strand, London WC2R 0RL, England

First published by Plume, a member of Penguin Group (USA) Inc.

First Printing, March 2009
10 9 8 7 6 5 4 3 2 1

 REGISTERED TRADEMARK—MARCA REGISTRADA

LIBRARY OF CONGRESS CATALOGING-IN-PUBLICATION DATA
Bagshawe, Louise.
  Glamour / Louise Bagshawe.
    p. cm.
  ISBN 978-0-452-28942-0 (trade pbk.)
  1. Female friendship—Fiction. 2. Department Stores—Management—Fiction.
3. Hollywood (Los Angeles, Calif.)—Fiction. I. Title.
  PR6052.A317G57 2009
823'.914—dc22   2008025124

Printed in the United States of America
Set in Bembo
Designed by Eve L. Kirch

This book is dedicated to Kathleen Brooks,
the best mother-in-law in the world. No joke.

Acknowledgments

I'd like to thank my wonderful editor Signe Pike, who picked up *GLAMOUR* and ran with it in record time; she made editing easy and was a joy to work with. It was one of the most painless edits I've ever done and greatly improved the book. I'm grateful to my U.S. agent Emma Parry of Fletcher Parry for an excellent deal with a wonderful house. Thanks are also due to the entire team at Plume, particularly Kathryn Court and Cherise Davis Fisher. Abigail Powers turned production of the book around at lightning speed and Nadia Kashper heroically entered every change (and there were lots—I am a copy editor's nightmare) and got the MS to production. I'm lucky to have such a strong team of colleagues, and every one of them a woman. That's real girl power for you!

GLAMOUR

PROLOGUE

The name was written in brass letters, each one sixteen feet high, polished like a mirror. They glittered on the front of the store, sparkling in the California sun like a permanent firework.

What a store! In Hollywood, the city of the stars, GLAMOUR said it all. A landmark attraction since the day it first opened, the new building was a must-see on every tourist itinerary. All-American razzmatazz; a monument to luxury, money, and power.

The flagship store was ten stories high. Dwarfing Harrods in London and Saks in New York, L.A.'s GLAMOUR was the ultimate shopping temple. Sleek and modern, it had been fronted with glossy black granite, so that the golden letters shone even more brilliantly. The trademark uniformed doormen and valets, both men and women, stood to attention behind the huge glass front doors, waiting for opening time. At GLAMOUR, shopping was an exquisite pleasure. Once you entered those doors, the cares of the day fell away. You were in another world: soft carpeting underfoot, exquisite fresh flowers at every corner, assistants to wait on your every whim. Every shopping trip was a vacation, and around the world, women with money just couldn't get enough. If you bought so much as a hairband in GLAMOUR, somebody would wrap it in the iconic triple-G tissue paper, tie it with mint green ribbons, and carry it to your car—should you so desire.

The clothes were fabulous. The scents adorable. The shoes haute couture. The jewels must-have.

L.A.'s glitterati loved it. And the women who had founded it were set to become among the wealthiest in the world. Everybody knew their story.

Three women. Beautiful, powerful, and rich.

And, it seemed, absolutely ruthless.

Once, they had been the closest of friends. Once, they had all suffered. And together, they had triumphed.

So how had it gone so wrong?

CHAPTER 1

"It's the princess!"

The little girl tugged on her mother's coat sleeve, jumping up and down with excitement as a sleek black limo eased by.

"Look! Momma. It's her. There she is!"

"You're right, baby!"

Her mother, Coco, a bank teller in her mid thirties, leaned over the thick velvet rope flanking the long red carpet that swept across Rodeo Drive. Keisha's childish enthusiasm was infectious. Coco hoisted her daughter up on her shoulders so the girl could get a better look.

Across the street, forced back by security, was a gaggle of media reporters, cameramen, and boom-mike holders, the reporters all talking intently to their cameras. Two local TV news choppers whirred overhead.

Normally you only got this sort of turnout for the biggest stars. A-list actresses, the First Lady, the Lakers. But these three young women were legendary. America—and the world—was watching this meeting.

Coco felt her stomach knot with anticipation. She was going to be late taking Keisha to school, late for work. But it was worth it. She'd pushed her baby into the crowd, determined to show her three of the most sizzling, famous businesswomen in the world.

The American dream. Anyone could make it. It could be

you in that limo. Never mind school—*that* was a lesson Keisha should learn. Coco turned toward the car as the L.A.P.D. officers shouted, motioning for everybody to get back. Keisha squealed in delight.

The security men swarmed around the gleaming black vehicle. There were olive-skinned soldiers, lean and dangerous looking, the palm tree of Ghada emblazoned on their uniformed chests. Mingling with them, brawny Americans with dark suits, shades, and earpieces—the Secret Service.

A man stepped forward and opened the back door of the limo.

The Arab security men snapped to a salute.

A slippered foot emerged from the limo, swathed in gorgeously embroidered gold thread. It was followed by the swish of a long dress, a floor-length robe in butterscotch silk, well-cut and covered with ornate stitched designs; modest, self-assured, and beautiful. The woman stood up; she wore a simple veil across her hair, secured with a solid semicircle of polished gold; her aquiline face was calm and confident.

"She's so beautiful," Keisha gasped. "Can I get a dress like that, Mom?"

"I don't think it would fit you, baby," Coco replied.

The crowd recovered from its fit of awe.

"Princess! Princess!"

"Princess Haya!"

"Haya, over here! Highness!"

The gold-robed vision smiled and waved; to the dismay of her handlers, she strode up to the barriers, shaking hands and greeting the crowd. They cheered and shouted; Haya chatted graciously.

"I want to meet her!" Keisha squealed.

"There are hundreds of people here, honey," Coco said, not wanting her daughter to get disappointed.

But then four black-suited men brushed past her—and all of a sudden, there was the princess, standing before them, resplendent in her traditional gown; gleaming, as golden as the sun, like something out of Coco's childhood fairy stories.

Keisha clapped her hands.

"You're a real live princess!" she shouted.

And as Coco watched, Princess Haya laughed, reached forward, and gave the little girl a big hug.

"And so are you," she replied. Then she looked down at Coco.

"Ma'am, you have a beautiful daughter."

"Th-thank you—Highness . . . ," Coco stuttered.

Haya smiled and winked at the amazed mother. Then she turned and walked up the red carpet, past her bowing security men, her silken robe fluttering in the light breeze.

"Oh, my gosh!" Keisha was saying. "She hugged me! Oh, my gosh!"

"Come on," Coco said. "We got to get you to school, honey."

Normally this would have provoked instant moaning. But Keisha allowed herself to be drawn along meekly, lost in her own little world.

To be honest, Coco had a buzz as well. That was cool—*way* cool. When they reopened the store, after the big meeting, she would pop in—buy herself a little something. Not that she could afford much. But just entering GLAMOUR made you feel like you were living the dream.

As she hustled her happy daughter toward the car, Coco stole a glance back over her shoulder. The crowd was still there, adrenaline up, chattering as they awaited the other two.

❧

"Miz Nelson."

"Yes?" Sally shouted back. She had to shout—the whirring of the chopper blades was just too loud.

"If you look to your left, ma'am," the pilot bellowed, "you can see the store. We'll be landing in just a second."

"Great!"

Sally gave him a thumbs-up, and the pilot smiled at her momentarily before turning back to the controls. Like all men, he was flirting with her.

Sally shook her long blonde hair smoothly down her back. Expensively and expertly coiffed on Fifth Avenue by Rolande himself, owner of the famous line that she had discovered, it was a shimmering curtain of platinum. She snapped open her Hermès Kelly bag and removed a compact mirror. Too fabulous for words! No wonder it had been the hit of spring's accessory line. She ran through the numbers in her head—five hundred dollars times how many? Ten thousand? Why, she'd made millions just from this *one* product. Customers couldn't get enough of that Sally, GLAMOUR magic. And whatever the other two said, *she* was the one who knew how to give it to them.

Sally examined her beautiful face critically, looking for flaws. But there were none. Her skin, helped along by the very best facials and professionally applied Lassiter makeup, was glowing. She looked ten years younger than she was. Her body was buff and lithe—a personal trainer worked it out daily—and her dress was French Riviera chic, a Pucci print with a white silk jacket over the top, designed just for Sally. Sassy, cool, and irreverent, she carried it with her Kelly bag and trademark Manolos—throw in a large pair of tortoiseshell glasses and she was the living spirit of summer.

Sally knew she looked like a star. But then again, she *was* one. She leaned across the soft leather seats of her personal helicopter and looked down on the seething crowd milling alongside the GLAMOUR red carpet. They were her fans—the fans of the dream. The other two girls, well, she shrugged to herself, still angry—they'd just helped with the mechanics.

Sally Nelson was the star here. She was Barbie. She was Lady Liberty. The all-American icon, blonde hair, tanned skin, healthy Cali lifestyle, and oh yes, the small matter of a billion dollars or two to boot. She had appeared in more ad campaigns than she could count, and the public ate her up. GLAMOUR. That was her, wasn't it? Not cold, bookish Jane, or regal Haya—who, let's face it, had taken herself out of the game.

When they thought glamorous, they thought Sally. She smiled triumphantly. It was her store, her dream. They had named it after Sally!

Of *course* GLAMOUR should be hers.

"Please remain seated until the airplane has ground to a complete halt," said the steward.

Jane Morgan didn't even look him in the eye. She had already unbuckled her belt and jumped to her feet.

"Ma'am—please take your seat," he said uncomfortably.

"Please get out of my way." She turned to him, her famous black eyes cool. "This flight was delayed for four hours."

She snapped open the overhead locker and retrieved her laptop bag, oblivious of the other first-class passengers' stares.

"You're defying FAA regulations."

"Correct." She shrugged. "I don't pay ten thousand dollars for a first-class ticket in order to be prevented from doing my job."

"We tried to make you as comfortable as possible, ma'am," he began.

"I don't need to be comfortable. I need to be in Beverly Hills. I have a meeting. And I'm *late*."

Jane Morgan made that sound like a terminal condition.

Every fancy businessman, society wife, and ruddy-cheeked CEO in the first-class cabin was now watching the show.

He remonstrated with her, almost pleading . . .

"It'll just be a minute . . ."

There was a small shudder, and the plane docked with the exit tunnel. The pilot, perhaps sensing the trouble, switched off the seat belt signs, and with that little ping, all the suits were up, fumbling around their laps, trying to get their bags.

Jane Morgan was already standing by the exit door. First in line and ready for business.

~

"Highness, I must advise against it."

Ahmed al-Jamir, the embassy's special adviser, leaned across the table, his dark eyes intent on Haya's. "Your position . . ."

"I am a member of the board," Haya said mildly.

"I meant your *royal* position," Al-Jamir persisted. "This busi-

ness stuff can be left to others. You should simply sell your stake.
What is the point?"

Her dark eyes raced across the figures on the packet in front
of her; finally they lifted and regarded him.

"The point is that GLAMOUR is *my* company. It's *my* store.
And I haven't forgotten that."

Even if the others had.

Al-Jamir was ready to weep. The princess would be queen
one day, maybe one day soon. Her husband controlled countless
billions, a major army. Even before the inheritance, Haya had her
pick of no less than sixteen separate palaces, more jewels than she
could wear.

For all its high-profile branding, this company was nothing.
Nothing!

He lowered his voice and said as much. They both knew what
he really meant. It was unseemly for a princess of Ghada to be
playing around in American business. Look at the Englishwoman,
Jane Morgan. Famous across the world, although Al-Jamir did
not dare voice the thought, for being one *hell* of a ball-breaking
bitch.

He did not want *Siti* Haya mentioned in the same breath as
Jane Morgan! It demeaned her, it demeaned Prince Jaber. It lowered the very royal house!

Haya closed the company report and turned her gaze to the
security men and civil servants.

"Leave us."

"But Princess—"

"You can wait outside the door."

There were a lot of reluctant bows, and then they all trooped
meekly out. Haya gazed at her ambassador.

"When I married His Highness, I told him I had no intention
of surrendering my past life."

"But events . . ."

"Yes. We all know what happened." She would not refer to the
change in their circumstances. "Nonetheless, Ahmed, I founded
this company. I began its spirit. I began its ethos. Something Sally
and Jane apparently want eliminated. You need not fear; today

will be the very last day I spend engaged in the world of business. I know my duty."

She tugged her silken robes a little tighter around her shoulders, and the diplomat was impressed. Indeed, whatever her origins, Haya al-Yanna bore herself as though the crown were on her dark head already.

"But you and everyone else need to understand something. *I will not let them destroy this place.* Today is the last meeting. And I'm going to make it count."

He was silent in the face of her anger.

"You may call them back in," Haya told him regally, dismissively. She turned back to the report.

⌒

Sally blew one last kiss to the cheering crowds, waving just the tips of her manicured fingers at them. "Thank you all *so much!*"

She crossed the red carpet to where the hungry media were waiting. Flashbulbs popped like fireworks; a forest of microphones jostled toward Sally's face. The Arabian princess had cut them dead, and that was lame, but so what? Sally was the real golden girl, America's sweetheart! The reporters shoved forward, yelling questions at the star.

"Sally! Is it time to get your revenge?"

"Who owns GLAMOUR?"

"Are you here to take control?"

"Is this an American company?"

"What do you have to say to the fans?"

That last one was a perfect softball. Sally stopped smiling for the photographers and turned to camera.

"I want to thank them for their love and support! I couldn't do it without you guys!" she purred.

"What're your plans, Sally?"

"You know how much I love GLAMOUR! I'm just here to set things straight." She gave America that famous wink. "Now don't y'all worry, because I'm here to see everything works out *just fine.*"

"But Princess Haya! Jane Morgan!"

"I looooove those ladies," Sally said brightly. "But everyone knows that GLAMOUR *is* Sally Nelson! Now, if you'll excuse me, I have to get to work."

She blew another kiss, direct to TV land, pirouetted on her Manolos, and sashayed up the red carpet while the doormen saluted.

The reporters buzzed.

Sally Nelson knows how to give good coverage.

Sally is such a star.

She is gonna kick those other girls' asses.

None of the paparazzi had any doubt.

⌒

"It's coming up ahead, Miz Morgan."

"I know where the store is," Jane said shortly. She examined the letters from her bankers. Every word of the legal document mattered. Sometimes lawyers let things slip; she didn't trust them.

"Shall I take you out front?" Her driver peered ahead. "There sure is a big crowd. Look at that turnout!"

"No. Make a left here."

"A left?"

Was he deaf? "Yes," she snapped.

"But GLAMOUR . . ."

"We're not going to GLAMOUR. We're going to the storage warehouse. There's a closed parking lot between the warehouse and the offices."

"You don't want anybody to see you," he said, slowly clocking on.

That's right.

"I can't stand fuss."

In the rearview mirror he watched the chestnut hair, wound tight into a neat bun as tight as she was. Damn! He'd seen porcupines with less prickles.

But Jane Morgan paid good, real good, and at Christmas his

bonus could run into thousands of dollars. His colleague's son, the one with the gimpy leg, had gotten bullied at school and Miz Morgan had paid for private Catholic school. Now that the kid had maxed out his SATs, Rafael thought he might be going to get a scholarship to the Ivy League.

He swallowed and shut up. So she didn't fraternize. That was okay. Everybody who worked for Morgana, Inc., knew who the boss was.

"Yes, ma'am, you got it," he said.

Two minutes later he had dropped America's toughest new businesswoman, queen of the Dow Jones, at the back of the warehouse. He watched as she swung her neat legs in their court shoes out the back of his car and marched off, between the enormous trucks full of GLAMOUR goodies, through the parking lot.

So she was arriving on the down low. Jason figured she had some calls to make, last-minute deals, something like that.

Most thought this was her last stand. That it was all over.

Not him.

He'd never bet against Jane Morgan.

The boardroom crackled with energy.

The long, glossy table was surrounded by rows of men and women in dark suits—high-priced lawyers, investment bankers, and M&A sharks, all toying with their pads and Montblanc pens, or pretending to examine their figures.

Behind them, the view was fabulous. High over Beverly Hills, the floor-to-ceiling glass walls showed every billboard, every limo wavering in the smoggy haze hanging over the city. But nobody was distracted.

Around the head of the table were the three women of the hour. On the left sat Princess Haya, her security men hanging back behind her chair, cradling their guns.

Directly opposite her sat Sally Nelson, her famous blonde hair cascading glossily down her back, her baby blue eyes steely and hard, revealing the businesswoman behind the star. She was more than a figurehead, and she was here to let them know it.

And in the center, having insisted on her right to the chairman's seat, sat Jane Morgan, all in black. Dressed for her own funeral?

Three powerful women. Once best friends. Now deadly rivals. Each of them determined to control the world's most famous store. A global icon.

Its fate, and theirs, would be determined today.

Jane Morgan stared down the length of the table; she nodded coldly at Haya and Sally. Most people in this room thought all her plans were about to be ruined, but her voice, that famously cool English voice, betrayed no fear.

"Good morning. The meeting will come to order."

CHAPTER 2

LOS ANGELES, TEN YEARS EARLIER

You've got to FIGHT
For your RIGHT
To PAAAARRRTTYYY...

The boom box in the corner of the playground was pumping out rap, the Beastie Boys blasting into the still air of a muggy fall day in Beverly Hills. It was the start of a new term, and the teachers smiled to each other and looked the other way. Already the overprivileged girls of Miss Milton's Academy were settling back into their tight little cliques; Julie Manners, the queen of eighth grade, had her new toy out and she was showing off. Julie and her friends wore their white socks around their ankles, hitched up their skirts, pinned their hair back with Ray-Bans, and wore badges with heavy-metal bands on them. They banged their heads, long hair flying, to show just how tough they were.

The teachers, milling around the registration booths outside, pretended to be deep in conversation, ignoring Julie and her clique. Her dad was a movie director, and that made her powerful. This was the eighties; fame and celebrity counted for a lot in this town. And everywhere else, for that matter.

Most of the girls, younger and older, were already forming

knots around the queen bee, pretending to like the music, complimenting her on her hair, her Lee Press-On nails, the cloud of Dior Poison she liked to swan around in. Julie eyed them all with a nasty sneer, her hair tossing, as though deciding where to dispense her favors. It was social death to be disliked by the most powerful clique in school.

And the staff had learned to fear her, too. Teachers Julie's dad didn't like tended to have short tenures at Miss Milton's. They shut their ears to the deafening music, pretending it was no big deal. Heavy metal and rap were *in*. So was Julie. And everybody wanted to be just like her.

Well—almost everybody.

~

A dark, slender girl sat in the opposite corner of the playground, next to the oh-so-hip Zen garden the school board had planted over the vacation; raked lines of gravel, flat stepping stones, square pools, bonsai trees, and flourishing patches of bamboo. She sat on the lawn, reading a book, her neat leather satchel beside her.

Unconcerned with Julie's court. Waiting for someone.

"Limey," hissed Maureen Smith, kicking at her as she passed.

"Do sod off, Maureen," the girl replied equitably. She wasn't much to look at: neat hair in a severe ponytail, black-rimmed glasses, no makeup. But there was a certain resilience to her.

Maureen Smith was one of Julie's cronies.

"Jane Morgan. The bookworm's at it again. What's this?" She snatched up the slim volume. "*Ariel* by Sylvia Plath. Hmm . . . studying up on laundry detergent?"

Maureen snickered. Jane Morgan didn't suck up. And she didn't fear bullying. Two reasons to hate her. The girl wasn't pretty, yet she didn't seem to care. She was all around *weird*.

"It's poetry. 'Course, you'd have to actually be able to read to know that. How was summer school?" Jane asked coolly.

Maureen flushed; she had indeed been forced to take summer school to catch up on her grades. Everybody knew Jane was a superbrain.

"Great," she lied. "And you know, there were *boys* there. Not something you'd know a lot about."

"Not interested," Jane replied.

"That's right. They aren't." A rather smart insult from Maureen; she tossed her hair proudly. "You never sent Julie a birthday card, Miss Fish 'n' Chips. People notice these things."

"That's because I can't stand Julie."

Maureen bridled. "You'd better watch yourself. We can make life very hard for you in this school. If you want to be picked for any teams, or sit with anybody, or get a part in the play, or go to parties . . ."

"Yeah, well, I don't." Jane Morgan snapped the book shut. "That's what you don't get. So tell me again why I should give a damn what you think?"

"Watch yourself, weirdo," Maureen repeated, and stalked off. Damn! That ugly Brit. She was so arrogant. Every year she managed to survive the worst they could throw at her. She should have been hounded out of Miss Milton's by now. Of course, Maureen, Julie, and everybody else knew why it hadn't happened. One word.

Sally.

Sally. The country bumpkin. The dumb blonde with the stupid Texas twang, Barbie hair, and outrageous curves. A few more years and she could be starring in *The Dukes of Hazzard* as a blonde Daisy. There was nothing hip about Sally, nothing cool. She didn't listen to the Beastie Boys or Mötley Crüe. She always had that boring-ass country and western playing. She didn't wear the right clothes—no black leather jackets with metal studs, no fingerless black lace gloves, no tights in exotic spiderweb patterns.

But Sally had two things in her favor (at least, Maureen only admitted to two). First, she was rich. And not just film-biz, garden-variety Beverly Hills rich like most of them, with their daddies working producers, driving Mercedeses and flying business class. No, Sally's family was Money with a capital *M*. Her pa was in the oil business, and had long ago stopped counting his wealth in millions. Estimates in school varied from one billion to four.

One thing was definite. Her daddy could buy all their daddies ten times over and still have plenty to spare.

Insults to Sally Lassiter were muted. Even the daughters of studio heads had to mind their manners.

And two—even worse—Sally was *gorgeous*. You could sneer—and they did.

Dumb blonde.

Texas rose.

Bimbo.

Cheerleader.

Yet their own reluctant eyes, and their brothers' admiring stares, confirmed that Sally Lassiter's looks were devastating. Her skin glowed, warm and tanned. Her long, rich-girl blonde hair was glossy and smooth like a Timotei commercial. She had coltish legs, slender arms, large, bright blue eyes, and, over the whole package, a white-toothed, milky, all-American wholesomeness. She was always smiling, always upbeat; narrow waisted, but with large breasts and a tight, curvy butt that suggested she was fit and healthy, and someday would make a good-looking mom of good-looking babies; when she laughed, she lit up the entire room.

Sally made sophistication and cynicism seem like a waste of time.

She was the best-looking girl in the school. Some thought she was the best-looking girl in the city.

So she wasn't a brainiac. So what? She was an only child, heir to a vast fortune. And it seemed so unfair, Maureen thought, absently touching her own rather bulbous nose, that she wouldn't even have to waste any of it on plastic surgery.

It was hard to condescend to a girl like Sally. Richer and prettier than you, of course she had confidence. Buckets of it.

Yeah, she was a dumb hick; they all thought that, sometimes even dared to say so. But Sally just smiled. She knew she was untouchable, Maureen thought, knew she was better than all of them. It was so unfair! She didn't even work at being popular; she didn't have to navigate high school politics. Instead, she just went her own sweet way. And they had the uncomfortable feeling that all the time they were laughing at Sally Lassiter, the Texas honey was laughing right back.

And of course, if she wasn't smart, she had a friend who was. Jane Morgan.

They made such an unlikely duo. Best friends as long as anybody could remember, yet totally different. Jane was, in Miss Milton terms, a nobody. Her folks had no cash; her fees were all paid by the British Embassy. She was doing this on the taxpayer's dime. She wasn't pretty, either, no style, no hipness to her whatsoever. Jane was a real little bookworm; unsuited to the sun, sea, sex of L.A., the hot, dusty city of perfect bods and shiny cars. She lived an internal life, always in the library, studying; no crushes on actors, no gossip about boys—like they'd be interested in her. She was Miss Ice Maiden.

Jane Morgan *would* have made an easy target. She didn't have Sally's weapons. Status, sure; her daddy was practically royal, and the cars that picked her up sometimes had little fluttering flags on the front, which was cool. But this wasn't Washington. It didn't count for a whole lot, not like having a movie with boffo opening numbers, owning a magazine, or being a top-notch sports agent, like Maureen's father.

Yet they could not touch her. Sally protected her. And as long as they stayed friends, together those two girls were so much more than the sum of their parts. Julie Manners said— damn, all the time—that Sally and Jane were like a jigsaw puzzle. They made no sense on their own, but together they were unstoppable.

Jane had the brains.

Sally had the looks.

Jane had that smart mouth.

Sally was loaded.

Maureen had to admit they made a hell of a team.

❧

Jane watched, carefully, as Maureen's tense back receded into the distance, joining the throng of girls hanging around Julie. It wasn't till Maureen was safely out of reach that she could breathe a sigh of relief.

Not that she would let it show. No way; never. Jane Morgan had no truck with weakness. But she *was* unhappy, even depressed.

Another bloody term, stuck in this shithole. With no decent teachers and no good courses. Girls went to Miss Milton's for one thing—social cachet. How the hell would she get into Oxford or Cambridge after studying at this dump?

She shut her book with a snap and buried her dark head in her hands.

Trouble with being clever, it was harder to deceive yourself. Of course the lack of academic standards was a problem for an ambitious student. But that wasn't why she was unhappy. . . .

Jane looked wistfully at the laughing, jostling crowd surrounding Julie Manners and wished she was the other girl. Just once. What would *that* be like? To be popular . . . to have people fighting for your attention. She had never had that, never, not as long as she'd lived.

She looked at the front gate, her knuckles tightening on her book, hoping to see a limo pull up. She had never wanted to see Sal as much as she did right now. The warmth of that smile, the native happiness, might pull her up a little. As long as she had Sally, it wasn't all black.

But Sally wasn't here yet. And as she sat by herself in the courtyard, pretending to be absorbed in her reading, young Jane Morgan felt a wave of loneliness crash over her. It was a wretched feeling, and she lifted her head, jutting her chin up, as though she were in danger of drowning.

Her dad. His Excellency, the Hon. Thomas Morgan. Jane thought of him, smiling that politician's smile at her. As she tried to persuade him to stay with her, to want her close . . . to love her, just a little, the way she loved him, always had; a child's needy love, that was still unrequited.

"But Daddy . . . I really hate that school."

She'd been hovering on the landing, at the top of the stairs, her suitcases all packed and in the limo already.

"We all hate school, darling." He gave her an absentminded kiss.

"But I want to be with you." Jane's words tumbled out, eager, desperate, although she'd promised herself she wouldn't beg. "I want to stay here—in Washington."

"No, you should mix in other surroundings. The political hothouse . . ." He waved his hands vaguely. "Not good for teenagers. And I'm so busy, you'd never see me. Going away to school is best. We did it in my day."

"I live in a rented house, with Consuela."

"Same thing," he lied. "Now run along, darling, your driver's been waiting ten minutes already."

"But . . . Dad." Her voice was already pleading, whiny. "If I were here, you could see me more. And you'd like that, wouldn't you?"

"Of course I would." His voice softened, just a fraction, and he leaned over and kissed her on the forehead; a brief touch, but manna to Jane. She wanted desperately to hug him, but he pulled back, and his clear gray eyes regained their professional detachment. "And I'll see you this summer, sweetheart."

Sweetheart. Darling. If only that were true.

But Jane Morgan squared her slim shoulders and pasted on a smile, as brisk and impersonal as Daddy's always were.

"Okay. See you then," she said, and gave him a hug; he patted her stiffly on the back. "Love you, Daddy."

"Love you, too, Jane."

As she walked down the stairs, she heard him turn and go back to his office. He didn't even wait to wave good-bye to her.

❧

The memory was bitter. And she had chewed on it, like a foul herb, all the way to the airport, and then all the way to the smart, lonely rented house she lived in when she was at school. There was a mixture of longing and loathing when she thought about the school; bleak despair at yet another term of being the outsider, the outcast; her life sometimes seemed like one long story of rejection. And yet, that bright spot, her best friend; Sally, who was the closest thing, Jane sometimes thought, that she had to real family; Sally, who was almost a sister.

There was a sound; a large limousine rolling over the speed bumps in the drive. Yes—that was Sally's car, straight out of Texas, a large, gleaming white monster; Jane would know it anywhere.

Her blues temporarily banished, she scrambled to her feet.

The car parked; the driver, neatly dressed in an immaculate uniform, got out and held the door open for his young passenger, like she was a princess. Jane hovered; behind her, she was aware of the rock music being lowered, the general drop in the hum of voices—everybody was looking this way, everybody was waiting for Sally. For that matter, they were looking at her, too.

Her friend was one of life's stars, brilliant and dazzling. And yes, those legs, slim and tanned above the white bobby socks, tumbled out of the car's chocolate brown leather seats; her skirt just that touch shorter, her long blonde hair blowing around her shoulders in the breeze, designer sunglasses holding it back, her eyes thick with mascara in defiance of the no makeup policy—there she was, and the school collectively exhaled at the sight of her.

She gave a whoop of joy and ran to Jane.

"I'm so glad to see you," she cried, flinging her arms round Jane and enveloping her in a cloud of scent. "It's been so boring while you were in D.C."

"Me, too." Jane felt awkward; she always did when Sally first appeared. Sometimes she was a little jealous; she was the moon, pale and serious, while Sally blazed like the sun; other times she felt all her vulnerabilities crash in on her, and agreed with the rest of them; why would Sally even be her friend?

But slowly, she relaxed. They would be chattering away by lunchtime.

"What's going on? 'Bye, Jake. Y'all take care." She waved to her chauffeur, who tipped his cap. "Is that Maureen talking to Julie? Horrible haircut. She looks like a boy."

"Tough is in this year," Jane answered wryly. "Haven't you seen Julie's black leather jacket? She's all over Whitesnake. And she had platinum highlights put into her perm, and it's gone all crispy."

"No!" Sally squealed with delight. "I gotta see. That girl has no style."

"Knows a lot of movie stars, though," Jane observed.

"Whoop-de-do," Sally said. "They're ten cents to the pound around here."

Her pretty face reflected such total unconcern that Jane instantly felt lightened. And slightly ashamed. How could she have let Maureen Smith get to her? Sally and she were unbreakable. The in crowd could do their worst.

"Can you help me with my vacation project?" Sally asked, lowering her voice. "I think I got the Tudors muddled up. I could use an A—Daddy's kind of bothered about my SATs."

"Sure." Jane was on her own ground now. "I'll write you something at lunchtime, you copy it out, hand the project in tomorrow."

"Thanks." Sally blushed. "I know I should have gotten it right by now."

"Don't worry about it. I'm always here."

Sal squeezed her arm, and they walked off into the playground, chattering away like starlings.

"... which wraps up assembly for this morning," Miss Milton concluded. Her gray hair was neatly wound in a steely bun, her doughy body encased in a couture Dior tweed suit, as she surveyed the room full of her well-heeled charges. "Orientation for the new girls we welcome into the school this year will continue at first period."

Jane glanced, without much curiosity, at the gaggle of new girls standing off to one side like sheep waiting to be herded into a pen. Most of them, with an unerring sense of social accuracy, had tried to glom on to the crowd surrounding Julie.

There was one latecomer. Dark-haired, average height, slim without being skinny, her socks raised to maximum calf-length, no makeup. A pretty enough girl, but rather shy looking. Understandable. Unlike Jane, she seemed to make an effort: whitened teeth, plucked eyebrows, neatly brushed hair worn loose instead of scraped into a convenient ponytail, no glasses. She looked uncomfortable, and twisted her fingers around as though wanting something to do.

The English girl felt a pang of empathy. Very tanned, though, and pretty enough not to be an obvious target for bullies; not like Jane, with her thick glasses and disregard for fashion.

"We will now stand for the Pledge of Allegiance. Foreign citizens are excused."

There was a rustle of cotton as the room got to its feet; Sally stood, her blue eyes fixed patriotically on the Stars and Stripes displayed at the front of the room; she always meant it, when some of the other girls sneered and rolled their eyes; another reason to love her—Sally didn't have a cynical bone in her body.

"I pledge allegiance to the flag of the United States of America . . ."

Jane, from her chair, cast her eyes around the room, picking out the other diplomats' daughters.

". . . and to the Republic for which it stands, one nation, under God . . ."

Cecile Perron wasn't here, then. Stuck in Paris, or had Papa been reassigned? That would be great; Jane couldn't stand Cecile.

". . . indivisible . . ."

Wait. The new girl wasn't standing, either. One lone chair had been provided for her, and she was sitting in it, sticking out. The other new girls were casting sidelong glances . . . sneering at her. Jane looked closer; that wasn't a tan, she was from the Middle East. Large dark eyes, an aristocratic nose. Israeli?

". . . with liberty and justice for all."

The bell rang, and Miss Milton left the stage.

"I got art history first period. You?"

"Math," Jane responded, still looking at the new girl. She was being jostled. Another wave of empathy broke over Jane; it was almost exactly the same as what had happened to Jane when she first got here—before she'd found Sally. "Hey, Sal. See that new girl over there? They're picking on her."

"They always do."

"Let's go and say hi," Jane urged. "Come on, it'll be your good deed for the day."

Sally sighed; art history was the one lesson she enjoyed, and the teacher hated it if she was late. All those glorious dresses they wore back in history. Fashion meant something then, it was more than a Donna Karan bodysuit or gray Armani dress. She liked color and style, gold cloth and lace.

"Sure, why not?"

Jane was her conscience. And Sally knew there was a streak of iron in Jane, something she respected, even feared at times. Jane would go over to that girl whether Sally came or not.

Sally scrutinized the object of her friend's attentions. Modest, shy, a clever look about her; disturbingly pretty . . .

She felt a moment of misgiving. She'd never felt dwarfed by Jane's formidable intellect, because Jane, let's face it, *wasn't* attractive. Both of them had strengths, but not in the same areas. This new girl was looking threateningly gorgeous, and also had a sharp light in her eyes that Sally recognized from a long association with her English friend.

What if she wanted to be real friends? She might be clever enough to rival Jane and pretty enough to steal Sally's thunder, too. Not right now, but with a little work . . . some caramel highlights, a pair of heels, some berry lip gloss . . .

Sally blushed. Those were mean thoughts, worthy of Julie or Maureen, not her. The new girl needed help. And Sally Lassiter, even though she schemed and gossiped and loved her own reflection almost as much as everybody else did, was fundamentally kind.

"Hey!" she called out, waving brightly to the new girl, who was heading toward the door. "Hold up, hon! We want to talk to you."

The other girl hesitated and nodded.

Jane fell in behind her friend, slightly annoyed. Now Sally was marching over there, taking the lead, like she did in everything. Jane sighed and followed her, smiling softly at the new girl.

⌒

"So what's your name?"

Sally Lassiter flicked her curtain of blonde hair over her shoulder and treated her to that patented, dazzling smile. Behind her, Jane Morgan grinned. One thing you could say about Sally, she was no snob. She had no need to play cliques, or make anyone earn her friendship.

"I'm Sally, Sally Lassiter," she encouraged. The warm Texan tones matched her mahogany tanned skin. Sally was a hot little butterfly, and even the sedate uniform of Miss Milton's couldn't disguise that.

The new girl's dark eyes swept over the blonde, drinking her in.

Sally was a million miles away from her own long hem and high socks. Sally wore her gray pleated skirt hiked up an inch or two, with her socks down to her ankles. Her cream shirt had an extra button undone, revealing a tiny glimpse of bountiful, all-natural breasts. The boys all stared, and some of the men, too, when Sally walked by.

That was the way she liked it. Such brassy confidence!

"Helen," the new girl muttered. "Helen Yanna."

"I'm Jane." Jane moved forward, adjusting her glasses up the bridge of her nose. They were thick, and made her eyes disappear behind them. Helen pegged her as English, at once. She had unkempt hair roughly tied back in a ponytail. Not a likely companion for this Sally Lassiter.

And nor, Helen thought, *am I.*

Olive-skinned with an aristocratic, aquiline face, Helen had hazel eyes flecked with green, and lush, black hair, glossy and sleek. Where Sally's shirt was undone, Helen's was buttoned up, the extra button under the chin tightly drawn. Her thick hair was loose, and her dark eyes peeked shyly out from under her bangs. But, like Sally, Helen's frame had dangerous curves that no amount of buttons could hide.

"How do you do?" Helen replied, formally. Warily. Were they about to start teasing her like the other girls had done? She already hated this school. When she got home tonight she'd beg her father to reconsider.

But Helen was a realist. Baba was a bit of a social climber. He was thrilled when his daughter was accepted at Milton—they weren't ambassadors or princes, after all, just mildly successful businesspeople.

And whatever her differences with the other girls, they all had that one vital thing in common—cash.

It required *mucho dinero* to make it here.

Everybody tried to get their kid in. The school had an unofficial policy against the Biz—only the finest directors, Oscar-winning actors, and truly determined studio execs and producers managed to get past admissions. Miss Milton's Academy preserved its cachet by attracting a better class of girl. The daughters of congressmen and senators, the mayor and the governor. Senior lawyers, major player bankers, and real estate moguls. And huge amounts of girls from the diplomatic community. They liked exotic—French, European, Israeli, Arab. Once there had been a couple of genuine Russians. Sending your girl to Miss Milton's Academy guaranteed her an instant shot of culture.

Of course, the Americans still ruled the roost. This was their home turf, and they knew all the unspoken rules from day one.

Helen had already suffered from that.

"You're new," Sally observed. "We figured maybe you'd want somebody to show you round. Help you fit in."

The olive-skinned girl nodded shyly. "That would be very kind."

Jane noticed at once she spoke in full sentences, didn't use contractions or slang.

"Where are you from, Helen? Israel?" she guessed.

The girl didn't take offense. "Jordan. It is very close by."

"You're an Arab!" Sally said, blue eyes widening.

Helen nodded, and Jane noticed her back stiffen. "Does that upset you?"

"Of course not," Jane said quickly. "We have people in the school from all over. I'm English; my dad works in Washington."

Helen made a face. "How sad, to be separated from your father."

"Not particularly." Jane tried to harden her heart to match her words. "My father's a diplomat. He mostly thinks of politics. I don't think he'll be winning Father of the Year anytime soon."

"Your mother, then."

The English girl shook her head. "She died when I was three. Car crash."

Helen looked horrified. "I'm sorry."

Jane shrugged. She sometimes wondered about that night. Her father had been driving, and had emerged almost unscathed, apart from one long scar on his back. Who knew the truth? Maybe he had been drunk.

Her mother would have loved her. As it was, Jane had nothing but herself and her friend. She had learned to be self-sufficient, and books and studying were her salvation. Every time she got an A, it soothed her, deep inside. Intelligence was the one area where she was more than good enough. She was outstanding.

Jane had big ambitions. Oxford or Cambridge. A Fellowship of All Souls. After that, tenure somewhere in an Ivy League school. Permanent respect, a job for life, and worth that did not depend on something unreliable, like a man, or something ephemeral, like looks.

She knew her best friend felt sorry for her. In her turn, Jane felt sorry for Sally. Beauty fades; brains endure.

"Well, anyway," she said shortly, "I'm a day girl here. And I have a nanny in our place by the beach."

"I'm day, too. Daddy has a house in Bel Air," Sally said artlessly. "Right next to Aaron Spelling, but twice as big. We're in oil."

"My father is a businessman."

"What business?" Sally zeroed in.

Helen spread her hands. "Many." It was true, her father had his fingers in many different pies. "He arranges contacts, meetings, for Americans who want to work in the Middle East. They build roads, apartment buildings, water facilities. . . ."

"That's swell," Sally said, losing interest. "He's not in oil?"

"Jordan has no oil."

"So he's not a sheikh or a king?"

Helen smiled. "I'm afraid not. Just a businessman."

"Oh, well, never mind." Sally was too bubbly to be put out for more than a few seconds. "Come with Jane and me and see the school. We'll introduce you *way* better than orientation."

Helen looked behind her; a bossy-looking matron with white hair in a stiff bob was taking the rest of the new intake toward the labs. Rebellion was not her strong suit, but the enthusiasm of the American and the friendliness of the English girl intrigued her.

"Why not?" She tried out her practiced English vocabulary. "That sounds like . . . fun!"

The three of them went round the school grounds. Jane watched Helen as she soaked it all in. It was nice, she realized, to have somebody else there. Good to have more backup. On days that Sally was sick, or traveling, it was not particularly pleasant to be in this school.

And of course, Helen Yanna was a foreigner, too. That made her even more of a target. It was something she'd have in common with Jane. Plus, she could tell at once that the girl was clever, brighter than Sally. It might be nice to have somebody around she could chat with about the stuff that didn't interest Sal. Like her exams.

Jane found herself nervously hoping that they'd hit it off.

"That's the fountain." Sally beamed. "Impressive, no?"

"No," replied Helen, thinking the question was serious. "We have much better in our garden in Amman."

Jane bit back a smile.

"And the statue . . . it's old. *Real* old. Victorian, imported from San Francisco. Almost *two hundred years*." Sally was determined to show off. "A genuine antique."

"I think she's seen older." Jane smiled at their new friend. "Have you ever been to Petra?" she asked, with a touch of envy.

"Yes, of course." Helen returned the smile. "One day you can come with me. On a visit."

Jane glowed. "Really? I'd love to."

"And here's the pool." Sally wasn't interested in archaeology or ancient sites. She waved her hand, her enthusiasm infectious. "Olympic size, and it's got a current. The gym is fully equipped. Rock-climbing walls . . . TVs on stands while you work out . . . treadmills . . . free weights. Even kick-boxing."

That did it. Helen's eyes roamed excitedly over the massive pool. Yes, this was fun. Kick-boxing! Why not? This was an all-girl's school. She'd *love* to do that.

"And come on in." Sally strode commandingly through the steel-door entrance to the architect-designed school building. It was modern, clean, everything brand new. Helen saw rooms full of new personal computers. A theater, with a real lighting rig.

"Room 102—drama—the aspiring movie stars love that. Right next door is crafts. They do pottery and all that stuff. Computers—you have to get with the program, right, Jane?"

Jane snorted.

"Sometimes I have to physically drag her out of there."

"There are the classrooms." Sally's pretty mouth made a moue of dislike. "Gotta say, I still hate class. It's such a waste. Learning about General Custer and stuff. When are you gonna use that in real life?"

"History teaches us about the future, too," Jane said.

"Deep. Teacher's pet." Sally winked at her friend. Helen looked at Sally enviously. She wished she had that American confidence. And she secretly wished for beautiful golden hair. Would Baba let her dye hers?

Probably not; that would be a Western step too far.

"And this is the chapel," Sally continued, gesturing at a long room with benches, an altar, and stained-glass windows. "Nonde-nominational. I pray there—"

"When?" Jane snorted.

"Sometimes," Sally lied. She turned to her new protégée. "Want to go inside?"

Helen shook her head. "No, thanks. I'm a Muslim."

Sally stopped walking. "Huh?" she asked, really amazed.

"Of course she is," Jane swooped in quickly, to cover the faux pas. "She's from Jordan—what did you think she would be, Sal?"

"That's okay." Helen was amused at the blonde girl's discomfiture. Didn't they understand not everybody was like them? "Actually there are lots of Christians in Jordan. More than five percent. But my family is Muslim."

Sally made a good recovery. "That's cool. There are lots of Jews here anyway. And here's where we eat lunch. Do you want to sit with us and eat lunch?"

Jane looked at her best friend, and felt a rush of warmth. Really, asking somebody to sit with you at lunch was a big deal. She was offering to support Helen Yanna, in public, in the full view of all the nasty, cliquey, bullying teenage girls that otherwise could make this shy young Arab's life a perfect misery.

And Sally was doing that for a girl from the Middle East with no connections, no cool factor, nothing that indicated she'd do Sally any good.

Sometimes Sal aggravated Jane, despite their friendship. That blinding beauty and the huge wealth, the careless, confident dismissal of academic things. But deep down, she was a really big-hearted southern belle.

Jane was proud to know her, and proud to be her friend.

"I'd like that, too," Jane said softly.

"I'd love to sit with you." Helen felt nervous for the first time that day; she peered in to see the refectory full of loud, noisy American girls, already bonded into their little groups. She wanted to cling to her two companions. "But . . . I can't eat the food . . . it isn't *halal*. . . . My father made an arrangement. They will bring me my food especially."

She hesitated. Was that too weird for them? If they left her, she would be the new, strange Muslim chick, and the brash American students would bully her. Helen felt the butterflies crawl in the pit of her stomach.

"I *dig* that!" Sally Lassiter sensed the fear, and hastened to reassure her. "See? You're special. Like waiter service, right in hall!"

"Thank you. *Shokram*." The Arabic slipped out, from habit. "Do you two have other friends?"

"Sure! Plenty. But we're *best* friends," Sally said, confidently, squeezing Jane's arm. "We're our own group."

"And can I be in your group?" Helen asked artlessly.

Jane Morgan smiled warmly at her. "Absolutely! We'd be delighted."

"Thank you," Helen said again, with a grateful smile. She loved it. This was a great school.

And these two were nice girls.

The ache that had been in her heart since their family had left Amman started to dull, just a little.

It was so great to have friends.

The first year seemed to blend into itself. Every day was packed. The girls made a tight group, and they could handle themselves. Jane Morgan could cut down any mean girl with a withering quip, Sally Lassiter was simply too rich and too pretty to fight, and Helen, well—Helen was exotic. These were the eighties; heavy-metal bands were rocking the Sunset Strip and money was gushing everywhere. Reagan was president, life was good.

In lessons, Jane did best. Her brain was like a machine and, with her incredible dedication, only Sally and Helen could tug her from her books. Sally, well, average was the best she could hope for. But that didn't bother Mom and Pop, so why should she care?

Helen did fairly well. Despite her admiration for Jane, her brain was not quite as sharp. And she still found herself struggling with the language at times. She could never be as pretty as Sally; her father forced her to keep her hair as it was, and she was never allowed to layer on the makeup, just a little tinted moisturizer and mascara, occasionally lip gloss. Not that it mattered; Helen's skin was luminous and clear, her eyes limpid, her lips full. And she had a place in school now. If Sally was the beauty and Jane the brains, Helen was the all-rounder.

Best of all, she had people to rely on. Two friends of her own.

And the three of them were a tight, loyal group.

⌒

"What are you doing, freak?"

Helen touched the mat in front of her with her forehead and tried to concentrate on her prayer.

"I *said,* what are you doing?"

There was a sharp kick in her ribs. Helen flooded with anger and fear. She knew that voice. That was Julie Manners. Queen of the cliques. And first-class bitch.

"I don't like Ay-rabs," Julie announced.

Helen gritted her teeth and raised herself, sitting back on her heels, praying for forgiveness. Especially for the fact that right now she wanted to smash Julie Manners's teeth in.

"You ignoring me? You better *not* be ignoring *me.* Towel-head!"

"Allahu Akbar," Helen whispered. She knelt down again, putting her head to the ground, toward Mecca and the holy shrine.

"Look, girls. Little Miss Sand Nigger here thinks she can act all hoity-toity in the U. S. of A. . . . *oof!"*

There was a gasp and Helen, her eyes closed, heard shouting. She continued to pray. There was the sound of a sharp slap and a howl of rage. . . .

"Y'all better back off *our* buddy." That was Sally, Helen thought, with a rush of gratitude. "You're a fat ugly waste of skin, Julie. They ain't made the surgeon in America who can turn you into a babe. You'd best get to prayin' somebody puts a padlock on your refrigerator."

"Leave me alone!"

"Let her *go!"* Julie's groupies, chiming in.

"I suggest you leave Helen be. Permanently. Otherwise I will go directly to Miss Milton and report what I saw. You'll be expelled." Jane Morgan, speaking with that proper British accent. Daring them to continue.

"Screw you, you limey bitch! And *you,* you redneck slut! The whole world knows that Jimmy Quiznos turned you down last Saturday!"

"Yeah, like I'd give Jimmy the time of day. He's so ugly even you could go out with him!" Sally retorted.

"Bitch!" Julie shrieked again, but Helen could hear it was from farther away.

"*Allahu Akbar,*" she whispered again, a little more fervently, and stood up, finished. She opened her eyes and saw Julie and half her gang skulking off to the other end of the playground. Julie stuck up one manicured finger.

"Don't you mind her. She's ignorant," Sally said, as Helen rolled the prayer mat up.

"Did she hurt you?" Jane touched her friend's ribs through the gray jumper.

Helen winced. "No," she lied.

It would make a pretty fair bruise, that was for sure. But the insults kept ringing through her head. *Sand nigger. Towel-head. Weirdo. Ay-rab.* "Why do they talk like that?"

"Just showing off. They think you're strange because you never have any boyfriends."

"Nor does Jane."

"Ouch," Jane objected mildly. "You don't understand tact, do you, Helen?"

"What does it mean, 'tact'?"

"Never mind." Sally was full of beans. "You want to be accepted, don't you?"

"She has *us,*" Jane retorted, still mildly stung.

"But the other girls . . ." Helen had an outsider's longing to fit in. "The rest of them. You know."

Jane nodded and glanced at Sally.

"I agree. They never let up. Especially Julie and Maureen and company." She patted Helen on the shoulder. "I agree it can get wearing."

"Then we should do something about that." Sally stretched, her tanned schoolgirl body catlike in the sun. "Serve them out for what they just tried to do to Helen." Underneath her southern milk-and-honey tones, Jane heard real anger, and she half shivered; Sally might not be academically bright, but she wasn't dumb. There was a streak of steel to her. And now that they'd messed with Helen, she was furious.

"Let's throw a party," Sally said, after a pause.

"A party?" Helen asked.

Jane smiled. Subtle.

"Yes. A real party. Like, party of the year. Must-attend, social death if you don't show up. It's my birthday in two weeks—lets crack the whip a little bit over these girls. Prove to them that y'all really *are* my friends." There was a dangerous light in Sally's eyes. "And there are consequences if they mess with you."

Helen's dark gaze flickered over the loud, obnoxious gaggle of girls at the other corner of the playground; they were laughing, most likely at her.

"But they won't come to our party," she said. "I don't understand."

Sally smiled at her friend.

When it came to pure, glorious style, Sally Lassiter was in her element.

"Oh, they'll come," she said, coolly. "Right, Jane? They'll come. We just make the party big enough and hot enough and they'll be begging me for invitations. You can handle it just fine, if you've got style."

She reached out, patting the girls on their shoulders.

"You need to understand. Glamour is a weapon."

She winked.

CHAPTER 3

Helen Yanna stood in the kitchen of her house and carefully watched her mother fixing tea; she made it fresh, the Moroccan way, with mint leaves and lots of sugar, served in small, decorated glasses on an ornate silver tray. A slice of home, this was an afternoon ritual with them, and one that always made her feel comforted.

"Do you want some?" her mother said, speaking carefully in English. Baba insisted they use it, even at home.

"Thank you," Helen replied, politely. She accepted the glass and sipped carefully, wondering how to broach the subject.

"I found some beautiful peaches at Farmers Market today," her mother said, starting to chatter. Helen glanced around the kitchen; it was modern and stylish, but relatively small. Baba loved to move, wanting to be in the best areas the family could afford. This was her third house in six years. It wasn't yet Bel Air, or even Beverly Hills at all, but it was not far, on Third Street, near the Writers Guild building, and inside a prestigious gated complex. She knew her mother and sister loved the security; the manicured lawns, the little houses in the development all the same size, the community leisure center with its pool and gym. Everything was neat and clean here. Baba had bought them one of the smaller properties, and was spending the rest on school fees for Helen and her sister, Jasmine. That, and a really big Mercedes, a fancy TV, a home computer, and the right kinds of suits and watches.

With Baba, appearance was everything. Helen calculated; could she use that to her advantage now?

It was a strange way to grow up, living between two worlds. With loving parents, but hypocritical ones. Yes, Baba and Mama desperately wanted to fit in. And Helen knew all about that longing. She felt it, every day, at school. But they were also Muslims ... not very devout, hardly practicing, but still, it was one rule for them, another for her. To this day, she had not dared to bring Sally or Jane home. *Especially* not Sally. She was too Western, too determined. If Baba ever caught sight of Sally's deliberately shortened skirts he'd order Helen never to see her again.

Was it likely he'd let her go to a party?

Helen twisted her fingers around the glass. She didn't think so. And yet she wanted to go, oh, so, so badly. It wasn't like she'd do anything, she thought resentfully. She wouldn't drink alcohol or kiss some boy. She just wanted the chance to go, to be with her friends. To be at the heart of things. To get her own back on the bullies.

To see what it was like to be like Sally—just one time, one night.

"You know, Mama, there's a big party at my friend Sally's house in two weeks." Helen strove to sound casual. "She's very rich; her father owns an oil company."

"Your friend is too young for that sort of thing." Mama sniffed.

"Well ... there won't be any alcohol," Helen lied. "And Sally's parents will be there ... you know, as chaperones."

Mama turned to her daughter, her mouth drawn in a thin line.

"Absolutely not, Helen. It sounds forbidden, with boys and mixing. That sort of decadence is not for a good girl like you. Your father will say no. Put it out of your mind."

"But—"

"No," her mother said, then lapsed into Arabic, for emphasis. *"La-a."*

Helen shrugged as if she didn't care and finished the rest of her tea. The direct approach hadn't worked. A year ago, before

Sally and Jane, she would have accepted that quietly, resignedly, as she always had.

Tonight, she refused to give up.

The answer would come to her. Helen was determined.

~~~~⌒

Her father came home, kissed his wife, and started telling her about his day. Average . . . not too many orders. Possibly a deal importing cosmetics. Mama started gabbling in Arabic, which Helen was already starting to forget, as her memories of her old life in Jordan slipped through her fingers. . . .

She suddenly had a brain wave. She got up and went into the kitchen as though unconcerned, getting the cutlery out for dinner.

"Helen." Baba's voice was stern. "What is this your mother is telling me? About some party? You should know better than to even ask."

"Oh," she said lightly, taking water glasses out of the cupboard. "It's nothing, Baba. Just a grand affair at Sally's estate in Beverly Hills. Mama didn't understand—I would never be invited anyway."

"What?" He blinked.

"Well, you know." Helen shrugged. "Sally is nice to me in school, but of course she and Jane move in different social circles."

"Explain that," Baba said, darkly.

"Well, you know, Jane's father is an ambassador. And an 'honorable'—it's an English title; he is aristocratic. And Sally is one of the wealthiest heiresses in America. I mean, come on—*our* family can hardly hope to be seen in public in that company. Sally's party is very exclusive, strictly for the top girls in school. I don't mind."

Her father's cheeks had gone a nice shade of puce.

"You mean she is supposed to be your friend, but she didn't invite you?"

Helen shrugged. "Yes, she invited me—after I told her you

would never allow it. That way she gets to say she invited me but she knows I won't show up to mix with the important girls. All *their* fathers are major movie producers at the very least." Helen flashed a smile. "That's life, Baba. You know what this town is like. . . ."

"No. No way." Her father shook his head. "We are as good as any of them."

"The party will be chaperoned," Mama broke in. "Maybe the ambassador will be there. It would be good for our daughter to know such people."

"I have made my decision." Baba's voice was stern. "You will attend. Tell her I said you may go. Your brother will pick you up at half past ten. Of course you will be modestly dressed. And you will stay with your friends from school. All the girls."

"But Sally doesn't think—"

"She can hardly take back her invitation. No! *My* daughter is as good as any of them. As is our family. We are related by marriage to the Hashemites." He sniffed. "You will go, Helen. Do not argue with me."

His daughter turned aside so he could not see her triumphant smile.

"Of course not, Baba," she said meekly. "I wouldn't dream of it."

Green Gables. Named after the L. M. Montgomery novel. Mrs. Mona Lassiter was a big fan.

Green Gables. The biggest and most fabulous estate in Bel Air.

Paulie Lassiter loved it. It was his home, his castle, and the definition of his status.

L.A. ran on star power, the electricity that truly supplied the city grid. And Paulie had none of it—nothing but the thick black ooze that poured out of his desert wells in the Lone Star State. He'd grown up poor, and he wanted only the best for his little girl. In America, Hollywood was the best, and Paulie Lassiter, despite his lack of connections, was determined to be a big fish.

That meant one thing. Conspicuous consumption. The buzz-word of the eighties.

So what if his name was never mentioned in *Variety*? Mona, his wife, would be at all the right parties.

So what if he had nothing breaking out at the box office? He would have the biggest pad in L.A.

Sally was doing fine at Miss Milton's. And Paulie kept a fleet of six luxury cars. Ferrari Testarossa, Porsche, Rolls-Royce, Aston Martin . . .

Even the garage wing that housed them was specially made. Yeah, Green Gables was the greatest thing since sliced bread. A canny purchase of some sloping, dusty land in a good part of Bel Air, and unashamed bribery—make that "campaign contributions"—had gotten Paulie Lassiter, from Belmont, Texas, all the planning permission he needed.

And boy, had he gone to town.

Spielberg—in your face!

Lucas—fuggedaboutit!

The main house had twenty-two bedrooms—some he'd never gone into. There was an enormous heated pool complex, two kitchens, ten en suite bathrooms, eight dressing rooms, stables, an apple and pear orchard, and a goddamn maze. On top of that, the "guest wing" of the estate had tennis and squash courts, three guest bungalows—modeled after the famous Beverly Hills Hotel—a formal Italian garden planted with lavender, rosemary, and olive trees and dotted with fountains and statuary, and a vast enclosed private gym with full-time trainers on staff. And all that was before you counted the staff accommodation for his 'n' hers chauffeurs, the maids, the cooks, and the private barman. . . .

Green Gables had its own private golf course. Eighteen mani-cured holes.

Green Gables had a fully stocked poolside bar.

Green Gables had a helipad, a landing strip, and an aircraft hangar for Paulie's private jet.

No wonder he was delighted to show it off!

"Daddy." Sally put on her best little-girl voice. It was Saturday, and she was sitting in the enormous eat-in kitchen eating buttermilk pancakes with syrup and watching the fire blazing in the grate. Even in L.A. it occasionally got chilly in winter, and the Lassiters knew how to make the best of it. "Can I have a party?"

"What kind of a party, honey?"

Her father moved to the refrigerator to grab a glass of fresh-squeezed juice. It made him feel healthy, even if Momma was fixing him a pile of bacon and sausage for breakfast. Just chuck some fruit on top, get those vitamins. Right?

"A biiiig party," Sally wheedled. "For my best friends . . . Helen and Jane."

"I love Jane!" her mother said vaguely. An English diplomat's daughter was pure class, and wasn't that why they paid Miss Milton's the big bucks? "Who's Helen?"

"A new girl." Sally wasn't certain Daddy would love the whole Arab thing, so she kept it to herself. "She's real nice. But some of the others have been acting up, you know how uppity they get, the actors' daughters and all that. I thought it'd be cool to have a nice party . . . you know, all the works."

"The works, huh?" Paulie grunted. "Sounds expensive."

"I bet all the papers would write it up," Sally said winsomely. She knew marketing. "Party of the year! At Green Gables!"

"That'd be nice," Mona Lassiter mused. She'd missed making the society pages for the last four weeks in a row. It was hard for "civilians" to be anywhere in this town. What Paulie had was cash—and cash was made to be spent!

"I don't see why we can't live a little," Mona wheedled. She walked over to her husband and trailed her long nails through his thinning hair, scratching his skull and making him purr with pleasure. "You can't take it with you, Paulie. . . . It'd be nice to see all the young people enjoying themselves. . . ."

"Ah . . . my two best girls," Paulie said expansively. He shrugged in a hopeless gesture. "Guess I'm outnumbered!"

"Yay!" Sally squealed. Paulie looked at her fondly. He'd have liked a son, but really, Sally was pitch-perfect, his little honey, and he adored her. Since Mona wasn't able to have a second, he'd given everything to his baby.

And let's face it, he *liked* to spend money. Mona was one hundred percent right. Money was there to have fun with. First him, then his baby. Ever since they'd struck that black gold he'd had more of it than he knew what to do with.

"We'll definitely get the works." He grinned. "Mona, take care of it, will ya? A carousel . . ."

"A carousel!" Sally rolled her beautiful eyes. "Dad, I'm not *eight*. We need one of those flight simulators! You know, from the fairground, you strap in and take a rocket to Mars . . . and we need fireworks . . . a *huge* display. And candles all round the pool."

"Fairy lights . . . lanterns . . . a marquee, tented silk . . . we should get Chasen's to do the catering . . . or Zanzibar. . . ."

"Not Moroccan," Sally said hastily. Didn't want Helen to get upset. She was touchy sometimes. She ran over, kissed her mother and father exuberantly on the cheek. "Thanks, you guys! You're the best!"

They hugged her back. Yes, her parents were the absolute best, Sally thought happily. And so was her life. She was Queen Bee, and she was taking her friends with her!

⁓

Helen gulped down the tea her mother, Aisha, had prepared, and it was delicious, floating with fresh mint.

It scalded her throat a little, she was so fast. But nerves were twisting in her gut. Helen could tell her parents had bad news.

And she had a sinking feeling she wasn't going to like what came next.

"Haya. I'm having second thoughts about you going to that party," Baba said sternly. He glanced at his wife. "And there's something else."

"You tell her," Baba said to her mother.

"We found a nice man for you." Aisha stirred a sauce on the

stove, not looking at her daughter. Deliberately, Helen suspected. "He's family. . . ."

"Distant family," Baba interjected.

"My cousin Firyal—her son. Ahmed is his name. He's twenty-four. . . ."

Ugh. An old man. Helen's skin prickled with an urgent warning. She had a horrible feeling about where this conversation was going. . . .

Little Jasmine looked round at her big sister, then lost interest. *Fraggle Rock* on the TV held much more fascination for her than Helen's love life.

"He's a merchant, in Cairo. Has a very nice house—a large garden, like our old house in Amman. You'll like it. You'll like him." Aisha's back stiffened. "Baba and I are all agreed."

There it was. Her parents, her English-speaking, alcohol-drinking parents, wanted to push Helen into an arranged marriage. Tie herself for the rest of her life to a guy she'd never met, and tear her out of America as part of the bargain.

Helen burned with resentment. Her father was such a hypocrite! He wore Western clothes, gave his children anglicized names, and drank like a fish. She hardly ever saw him attend to prayers or go to the mosque. Baba made his friends call him "Al," because that sounded less foreign than Ali. She strongly suspected their family had settled in L.A. instead of New York because, with year-round tans on everyone, their Levantine skin stood out that much less.

"Well, isn't that nice." Helen was surprised to hear the bitterness in her own voice; rebellion wasn't her thing. But she was saying it, all the same. The words tumbled out of her. "But you forgot to ask me. I'm not agreed."

"You've always been a good girl," her father grunted. "You knew this had to be."

Knew this had to be? Baba had never mentioned it, just like he never went to the mosque. She gathered up her courage.

"Not now. Not anymore." Helen stood firm. "*I'm* going to decide who I marry, Baba."

"But Ahmed is a nice boy!" Aisha was scandalized. "It's a lot of money. An excellent match, a good family. Cairo is perfect for you! We've discussed it."

"You will obey me on this, Helen. I am your father," Baba reminded her stiffly. "Our family has position—reputation—to think of. Maybe I should pull you out of that school!"

Helen bit her lip. Leave Sally and Jane? Like hell! She was *not* leaving school, and what's more, she absolutely, definitely, one hundred percent *was* going to Sally's party! All his crazy schemes came second to that. She *was* going to the party!

Helen choked back her outrage. The faces of her parents, even Jasmine, stopped her. Her mother was looking at her pleadingly; her father's bluster concealed real anxiety. Her kid sister was chewing on her lip anxiously, brown eyes darting from Helen to her mom and dad, hating the conflict.

"You cannot let us down," Baba said heavily. "Ahmed arrives here in a few days, with his parents. They are your mother's cousin Firyal and her husband, Rashid. You would not make me look stupid before the family, I hope, Helen. They've all come thousands of miles to see you."

Helen sighed. Who cared? She could play along—for a while, anyway.

Mama and Baba had an arranged marriage themselves, and she knew perfectly well it had been happy. Maybe it wasn't *such* a contradiction that they wanted the same for Helen. But then, they never should have brought her to L.A., she thought.

Helen Yanna was of a different generation. The world had changed.

Yet she loved her parents, and she wanted to let them down gently. Of course she wasn't going to marry this guy. But if she played nice, didn't embarrass Baba in front of their cousins ... maybe there was an opportunity for her.

Sally or Jane would *work* this situation. She could, too. *To get to the party.*

"I tell you what, Baba." Her father was a businessman. They could do a little old-fashioned horse trading! "I'll think about it. So long as it doesn't interfere with Sally's party. It's going to be a major social event, you know. Paulie Lassiter is a billionaire, all from oil. There are going to be movie stars ... diplomats ... bankers ... and of course, Mrs. Lassiter is overseeing the entire thing. You should let me go; it'll be a feather in your cap."

His eyes narrowed. "And if I do? You'll marry Ahmed?"

"I'll *meet* him," Helen countered. "I'll *think* about it. . . . Certainly, why not? Cairo is very cosmopolitan ... and like you say, he has a good family. . . ."

"You're in no position to bargain!" said her father crossly. He marched to the dresser and took out his bottle of whisky.

Helen lowered her eyes. "Okay, Baba," she said meekly. "Whatever you think is best. . . ."

Perfect tactics. He shook his head, sorrowfully, and spread his arms.

"I suppose if there are chaperones, you can go. We want you to fit in. Ahmed will like it if you have friends here ... he can expand his business. . . ."

"What business is he in?"

"Carpets."

Helen looked away so Baba would not see her roll her eyes. Carpets, great. What a cliché. Did he have any flying ones?

"*Very expensive* carpets," Aisha announced. She was sharper than her husband, and knew something about the set of her daughter's back. "Priceless works of art. . . . Some of them, only the real Hollywood types could afford anyway."

"That's great!" Helen lied. She tried to give it some of Sally's cheerleader pep. "I'll see if I can collect business cards, Baba. Anyway, a woman has to think of her social position. For the family ... ours ... and his."

Yeah, lay it on thick. Was this a sin? Maybe. But she had no intention of marrying somebody she'd never met. And in her religion they couldn't make her.

But it didn't hurt to give them a little soft soap. Anything, as long as she could go to the party.

"That's very true. You'll make an excellent wife ... very well, you have a deal. You're a good girl," Ali pronounced smugly.

He watched his daughter, dark head bowed, turn back to her books. That had gone surprisingly well. Of course he loved

America, and the lifestyle here, but there were limits. He had not
been blessed with sons, and he had no intention of either daughter shaming him.

Helen was disturbingly beautiful.... Her body was ripen-
ing daily. When the family went out to restaurants, men looked
boldly at her.

She was ready for marriage. If they waited, like Western girls
did, it would be a disaster. Let her complain, Ali thought; she
will enjoy her life, once she has a husband, some babies, and
a fine house. He himself had grown up poor and had made it
through the sweat of his back. Things would be altogether easier
for Helen.

Yes, he had done well.

~

Jane sat in her favorite nook in the library. There was a comfy
window seat, padded with soft green cushions, and it looked out
over the lush lawn that sloped down toward the carp pond. There
was a great view of the permanently flowering garden—Miss
Milton's, like the rest of the town, was *big* into image. Best of all,
it was a tucked-away spot, near the reference shelves.

Hell, the library in general was pretty tucked away. The school
had cachet, sure, but not the academic kind. The glossy Angeleno
teens who populated it didn't care too much for books.

The ones who did use it were like her. Natural loners, a bit shy,
usually not so easy on the eyes. Fat Debbie Mitford was in here
a lot. And Soon-Yi Kiwasa, the Thai girl with the serious acne
problem. All of them using books as a get-out clause from life.

Because you had to have real motivation to study at this school.
It wasn't done. Grades. Who needed 'em? City College types that
would have to get *real* jobs when they went out into the world.
With its enormous fees and three-year waiting list, only greased
by additional massive donations, Miss Milton's was not stuffed
with girls who'd ever need to work for a living.

If your parents weren't worth upwards of ten mil you were
nothing in this school.

Jane Morgan knew she was the odd one out.

Her father—her bastard, unloving, selfish peacock of a father—he wasn't rich. Powerful, yes. Prestigious, sure. But money? He went through it like water. And he detested actual work.

They lived richly. Many would say better than Sally Lassiter, even. But they owned nothing. The sumptuous Washington town house, stuffed with antiques? The beach house in Malibu? The driver, and the glossy limo with the diplomatic plates?

None of it theirs. All provided by the state for its loyal ambassador.

His Excellency. A major international figure.

His Excellency—a worthless piece of crap.

Everything Thomas Morgan did in his life centered around himself. The wonderful, sparkling Thomas. Like her friend Sally, he was one of life's butterflies. Gaudy ties and waistcoats that were the talk of the town, always twinned with his famous green socks.

When she was small, there had been bewilderment. Why was Daddy always at work? Why was there a succession of nannies? Whenever Jane got fond of one, the woman was sent away.

She had always been bright, and worked the main fact out fast.

Her father didn't love her.

He was never overtly cruel. There were plenty of toys, outings, a smart nursery, the right parties with the children of other diplomats—Thomas even showed up to those. And Jane had used to glow, bathe in the magic of his famous smile and laugh, and hope things would change.

They didn't.

When she got old enough, she challenged him. Why wasn't he there? Why didn't he read her bedtime stories? Give her cuddles?

"I'm busy, darling," he'd replied, giving her a stiff, perfunctory hug. "I have to provide for you. You have lots of games and toys, don't you?"

"I don't want games. I want you, Daddy."

"And you've got me, so that's lucky." Her father was already absorbed in his press clippings. "Now run along, Daddy has to get to work."

Rejection.

It became part of her soul.

Too painful. Too much. Deep down she determined she would never suffer through it again. Jane Morgan withdrew into a world of books and figures. She would never wind up a cocktail-party-circuit feature like her father, a stuffed shirt whose only concern was his image, being seen in the correct circles. How he loved it when they promoted him to ambassadorial rank. The word "Excellency" dripping from everybody's lips. Next, they said, it would be that long-predicted knighthood. Eventually perhaps a peerage of his own. He'd rank with his elder brother, back in England. Jane knew nothing would please her father more.

But that shallow life wasn't for her.

Jane felt small. She couldn't engage the attention of her own father. What chance did she have with other men?

She decided not to compete.

Math—a serious subject. One her father knew nothing about. The only use he had for figures was for injections of cash.

She'd asked to be sent to a *good* school—since he couldn't wait to get her boarding somewhere. Out of sight, out of mind! The further the better. At least, Jane asked, could it have a brilliant college-placement record? Top SAT scores? Pupils who had their pick of Ivy League schools?

Instead, Daddy darling had picked Miss Milton's. Some surprise—he chose the one with the social status.

Jane learned not to complain. Never did her any good. Sure, Miss Milton's was lousy academically. All the more opportunity for her to stand out. It had bad teachers with good connections, but it also offered the raw materials. Computers. Books. A well-stocked library. Whatever periodicals she wanted.

By the age of eleven Jane Morgan was reading the *Wall Street Journal*. And the *Economist*. That was her idea of fun.

But she loved hanging out with Sally. Though golden and bubbly like her father, unlike him, Sally had a heart. To young Jane's amazement her early, tentative overtures at friendship weren't rejected. And if Sally saw her as a plain backdrop against which she herself could shine, so what? At least Jane had *somebody*. At least she had a friend.

She craved normality. Acceptance. Sally Lassiter offered her a slice of both. And when Helen joined the twosome, things got even better. It was easier to talk to Helen—she had the makings of a brain—and she was shy, made Jane feel confident by comparison. Plus, there was a fascinating background. It was great knowing somebody from a completely different culture—the anthropologist in Jane Morgan ate that up. Here was a girl even weirder than Jane! Somebody who needed protecting, the same way she did.

They were a strange trio. But a good one.

It was the closest thing to family that Jane'd ever had.

⌒

"Well, well, well."

Jane sighed. It was Julie. With her two sidekicks right behind her, Maureen and Kate, otherwise known as the Terror Twins. They delighted in bullying the new girls—forcing them to throw parties, then making sure nobody came—getting them to dye their hair strange colors. General nastiness. If you didn't suck up to Julie's clique, bad things could happen.

"What do you want? I'm studying."

"You're always studying," Kate Menzies piped up. "Lamebrain."

"Get out of here, or I'll go get a teacher." Jane brushed them aside. She was with Sally; untouchable.

"Ho ho." Julie looked triumphantly at her hangers-on. "Maybe *Miss* Jane Limey doesn't want to know our news."

They all smirked.

"Maybe I don't." Jane forced herself not to ask.

" 'Course, it isn't set. Just a rumor. But I do have *great* sources."

"Seems a certain fancy diplomat's getting himself into trouble."

"Like, *real* trouble."

Jane shrugged. "You should know by now, I don't care *what* my father does. Nice try, though, girls. Better luck next time."

"*Oooh,*" they chorused.

"I think you'll care about this one, babycakes. When it all goes down," Maureen said nastily. "Front-page stuff. I'd be using this library while you can. And make sure to say all your good-byes to Sally and the towel-head."

"I told you to get out of here. Don't speak like that about Helen. I'll report you, in a heartbeat."

" 'Course you would—sneak."

Jane made a supreme effort and lightly shrugged her shoulders. "Everybody knows how mad you are you can't get an invite to Sally's party, Maureen. So sad to be left out like that. Rob Lowe's coming—I hear you like him. But really, don't take it out on the rest of us. It just looks pathetic, don't you think?"

Maureen flushed a satisfactory shade of puce. "Bitch! Let's see how long Sally Lassiter hangs out with a *goddamn bum.* You're going to be on the streets. Maybe you could come to our house—we need a new maid!"

"Or you could sell oranges on the roadside. Like a wetback." Julie laughed loudly, and her companions snickered. "See ya, welfare girl."

Jane yawned and went back to her book.

Only when they'd left the library did she left her head. She wouldn't have wanted those cows to see the anxious expression on her face.

~

"So how did it go with your dad?"

"Fine! I can come," Helen replied happily. She had no intention of telling Sally about Ahmed and the arranged marriage.

"That's great. Julie was begging for an invite earlier." Sally smirked as she contemplated her party-throwing skills. Some of their enemies had thought they could get away by blanking her, but Sally had played it carefully. Stacked the party with rides and treatments until it sounded like paradise—manicure tents, masseuses on hand, fireworks displays, flight simulators, camel rides—then added cool little gifts, like necklaces specially designed at Frederick's of Hollywood, and lastly, added the killer ingredients—boys and stars.

Juniors and seniors from the *most* exclusive L.A. boys' schools were all invited before *any* invites went to the girls of Miss Milton's. And Paulie Lassiter knew actors. Mona was able to get several of the younger, hotter Hollywood set. Molly Ringwald was an acceptance. There were producers there, aching for some of Paulie's cash for financing. Actors followed producers—and in a feeding frenzy, like lissome teen piranhas, the girls of Miss Milton's followed the men.

Nobody tried to play it cool.

Sally was accosted.

"Hey, Sal. Where's my invite?"

"Sally. Can I come?"

"Hon—you haven't forgotten about me, have you?"

She enjoyed them all. Usually accompanied by a wheedling tone and a cajoling sort of smile. Anybody who thought they were too cool for Sally Lassiter had another think coming!

"We'll let her crawl a little while," Sally decided. "And then she's gonna be seated at the *worst* table—I'm talking Siberia!"

"Out by the tennis court?"

"Yeah, with my mother's tennis coach! And the guy who comes to teach Dad French."

Helen laughed. Yes, Julie would *hate* that. Plus, it would be the talk of the school.

"And Maureen nowhere . . ."

"She ain't coming. Baby, I gotta have me some standards."

"I can't wait," Helen said truthfully. She would be at the center of things for once, right at the epicenter. Top table and in the thick of it. That idea gave her a buzz. "And we have to help Jane. . . ."

"Of *course*." Sally lifted one perfectly plucked eyebrow. "That's what this whole deal is about! We'll bring her out of her shell. She'd be a *babe,* once she got introduced to the human race. And a pair of eyebrow tweezers. *You* know what I'm talking about. Grooming 101."

"Exactly," Helen responded. Thrilled that her friend considered her hip enough to help.

Make Jane Morgan in Helen Yanna's image. Wasn't that a kick?

⟵⟶

Jane turned the pages of her calculus textbook, trying to absorb the numbers. But outside her sitting-room windows, the path down to the clifftops beckoned. It was a glorious summer day, and she couldn't concentrate. Maybe she would drop the numbers and pick up one of her biographies instead. That was a hobby of hers—delving into the lives of others. She especially liked ones where the subject had made it after a tough childhood. She could relate to that.

Okay, so here she was in her luxurious little rented house in Malibu, with every modern convenience, a nanny/housekeeper, and a driver. But nobody who really gave a damn. As she reminded herself, you couldn't pay people to love you.

She wondered, with a pang, what her father was doing right now. Last time he had called, Thomas Morgan had sounded even more stressed than usual. She shouldn't care, but she did. The hope that he would love her one day never really went away.

"Jane!" Her nanny, Consuela, was calling from the sitting room where she was watching an *Arsenio Hall* repeat with a big bag of Doritos. "Your friends are here."

Jane jumped up, pushing the book away. What? Sally never came out here. There was nothing in her cottage that Sal didn't have ten times better at home—they always hung out on the estate. But sure enough, her personal white limo was pulling in at the front gate, or trying to.

"Make sure you're home by nine—remember the curfew," Consuela said, halfheartedly.

"Yeah, sure." She treated that with the contempt it deserved. Consuela wouldn't care if she jumped off a bridge.

"Hey, get in." Sally flung open the door. "We're going to a beauty salon. And an optician."

"What for?" Jane asked suspiciously, pushing her glasses up the bridge of her nose.

"Don't argue with me, honey. We're going to fix you right up."

Helen poked out her head, smiling. "I'm going, too."

"You both are. I won't take no for an answer," Sally said firmly. "Get in. Now."

⌒

"Try these."

The optician leaned forward and handed her another pair of lenses. "Don't worry. You'll get it; everybody drops them at first."

"Sorry . . ." Jane was embarrassed. She hated clumsiness. Any lack of control, in fact.

"On the tip of your finger . . . *there* you go."

"Ah." Jane gasped. But she could see! She blinked.

"Now the other one."

She put it in, blinked again. Her vision swam, then settled.

"What do you think?" the optician said.

"She looks hot!" Sally approved.

"You're very beautiful," Helen agreed. *"Very."*

"Don't be silly," Jane said gruffly. But she couldn't suppress a smile. Without glasses, her face was so . . . different.

Better. Prettier. Yes, almost beautiful, in its way.

"Thanks, doc. Messenger her lenses to our house, 'kay?"

"Sure thing, Sally." The optician smiled benignly. The billionaire's daughter got whatever she wanted. "A pleasure . . ."

"Come on." Sally was tugging Jane along by the hand. "We haven't even started with you yet."

⌒

"I don't know. . . ."

Jane shifted uneasily in her seat; the hairdresser was holding a large clump of her hair. She was still getting used to the lenses; as she blinked, her face swam in the mirror.

The hairdresser had swooped on Sally as though she were his long-lost best friend. Then when she'd presented Helen and Jane, there had been a lot of clucking and sucking air through the teeth.

Now he was prancing around like a circus pony, grabbing great fistfuls of her hair in exaggerated movements. Not that Jane really cared about looks, but still, she didn't want to come across as a nun.

"Of *course* you don't know. If you did, would you look like *that*?" Maurice snapped his fingers. "Nuh-uh! I'm the artist, baby, you're the canvas. Let's leave it to the experts. You got it?"

He drowned out her protests. "See your girlfriends, sugar?"

Maurice spun the chair—there was Sally, getting her golden mane blow-dried, and Helen, having her nails manicured.

"Now they got it going . . . Sally the most. The dark one's shy, but she's at least at first base. *You* need help. Major help. You do *know* that, right?"

Jane swallowed her pride. "Right."

It wouldn't do much good to go to the party of the year as guest of honor—to queen it over Maureen, for once—if she was also wallflower of the year.

No. No way. Like it or not, Jane Morgan was about to compete. In a new arena.

"Go for it," she said shortly.

"Really?" He beamed.

"You got it. Give me the works."

~

No pain, no gain. It took hours, long, and for Jane, boring hours. There was washing, combing, cutting, dyeing, and blow-drying.

"Does it always take this long?" she complained as Maurice wrapped the millionth piece of foil around her newly shorn head.

"You have to suffer for beauty," he sighed.

Jane returned to her shopping magazine. It was as dull as all hell.

Shopping! Who on earth would be interested in that? Green was in, was it? So what—there were only so many colors in the rainbow. Would anybody complain if she wore blue? 'Course not.

Were women really this moronic?

"Head back," Maurice commanded. "This is going to sting . . . a little."

"What's that?"

"Hot wax. You're way too cute for that unibrow."

"Aaaargh!"

◦───◦

"I'm giving you French."

"Excuse me?"

"Mani-pedi. No colors; you're not ready to graduate."

"If you don't use colors, what's the point?" Jane asked, staring at her hands. The other two had gone off for a coffee in the diner across the street. She was *still* stuck here, and that tyrant Maurice wouldn't let her see a mirror.

"You'll see," he said mysteriously.

◦───◦

Finally, it was over. Ten minutes after Helen and Sally sauntered back in, cradling their triple latte foam whips, Maurice flicked the switch off on his sleek steel dryer.

"Of course, I don't make her up yet," he said modestly. "And you understand she need clothes . . . colors. But still!"

He beckoned them forward, spun the chair around, and whisked away the black silk drape he'd placed over the mirror.

"Holy Toledo!" Sally shrieked.

Helen gasped.

"Oh, my goodness." Jane was reduced to childishness. She placed one hand over her mouth. "Oh, my goodness . . ."

Her hair, cut to just above the shoulders, was streaked with subtle lights of bronze. It was full of bounce and fullness, the lack of weight giving it a lift it had never had. Without that thick coil wound into a bun Jane felt as light as air. Her beetling eyebrows had vanished in favor of high arches that opened up her face. And the hand clasped across her mouth boasted neat, shiny nails with attractive white cuticles.

"Wait till we get some makeup on her." Maurice preened. "I am magician, no?"

"No—you had great stuff to work with," Sally said, smiling. "But you *are* good." She pressed forward and gave the outraged stylist a kiss on the cheek—and put five hundred dollars into his hand.

Maurice smirked back. "*Merci, chérie.* It was *un plaisir.*"

"Now we get you a dress," Sally announced briskly.

"You'll look fantastic," Helen said delightedly, beaming at Jane. It was so good to see her blossom . . . they had brought the beauty out from the shadows. Now who could bully Jane? What girl would even dare to try?

Her friend was transformed. Jane—prettier than Helen . . . but it wasn't in Helen's nature to be resentful. She was happy for her—after all, poor Jane. For all Baba annoyed her, at least she had family. Like Sally. What did Jane have? A useless father, not worthy of the name.

And Jane Morgan was so cold, so walled-off all the time. Angry at the world. At life. Helen, who was soft and gentle, hoped her friend would marry one day, but she wasn't sure. Sometimes Jane gave every indication of wanting to be a bright, crabby professor somewhere—a distinguished old maid. And that would be a pity, because if Jane needed one thing, it was family. A real family, of her own. Maybe loving her own children would heal her, Helen thought.

"Not just her—*you.*" Sally's warm southern tones interrupted her reverie.

"You can't get me a dress!" Helen was half-flattered, half-offended. Unlike Jane, her family had their own cash. "I'll bring my own."

"I want to style you," Sally wheedled. "Like Jane. Just imagine when we get the makeup girl on her!"

"Nuh-uh." Helen shook her head. "I don't do low-cut, Sally. I'm not like you."

"What? Are you calling me trashy?" Sally's eyes flashed. If she had a weakness, it was being laughed at. She just hated that. So what if she wasn't book-smart? She was *street*-smart.

"Of course not," Helen prevaricated. Her eyes slipped to Sally's tight white dress, which left very little doubt as to the impressive curves and golden tanned skin beneath. If Baba saw Helen wearing something like that he'd have a fit! "I just don't think we have the same style."

"Relax. I know that, I know what'll suit both of y'all." Sally nodded. "I'm throwing this party *for you*. Trust me."

"For us," Jane said, nudging her. Come on! Sally loved being the leader of the gang of three. The party was hers; it would only highlight her untouchable star status, her truly limitless wealth.

Whatever Paulie had would someday be Sally's. So what if the other girls' fathers were famous directors or noted producers? When Sally Lassiter grew up, she'd be able to *buy a damn studio* and hire—or fire—any of them.

This party was just Sally flexing her muscles.

"Okay, then. For us. The three musketeers!"

"Excuse me?" asked Helen.

"Never mind," Sally said. Impatiently, she tugged at the two girls. Making them over was like playing with grown-up Barbies. She adored her friends, and wanted them to look as hot as she knew they could. "Neiman Marcus. Now. I got a personal shopper waiting!"

Helen looked at Jane and shrugged. In this mood, Sally was a force of nature.

⟨⟩

"You ladies look wonderful," the manager gushed. Of course it meant sales for him, but Jane could see the light in his eyes; he really did seem enthused. "Truly, you are something else. You're going to *wow* them!"

"What do you think, ladies?" Sally didn't trouble to keep the triumph out of her voice. Her two friends had emerged from the chrysalis, and they had her to thank for it. "We make a pretty cute trio, don't you think?"

Their reflections in the mirrored wall opposite confirmed that diagnosis.

Sally—blonde, tanned, and stunning in a knockout dress of golden sequins, with a scalloped neckline, tiny fluted sleeves, and a fishtail. She looked like a mermaid from a fairy story.

Jane—newly beautiful, now made up by the counter assistant from Chanel, her hair bouncing with life, her delicate features enhanced with a natural, glossy makeup that emphasized her youth—was wearing a sheath of dark green velvet that picked up her emerald eyes and honey-highlighted hair.

Helen—exotic and aristocratic. Playing to her heritage, Sally had chosen her a long-sleeved gown with a dramatic sweeping trail, a satin and lace confection of pewter and gray, with a matching cape of lambswool, soft as thistledown. A collar of seed pearls was knotted around her neck.

Her friends had protested they couldn't possibly accept anything so expensive.

"Screw that," Sally said forthrightly. "Daddy doesn't count his money, girls, he weighs it. And if he wants to spoil me, I want to spoil *you*. We're friends, so don't be stupid."

Lots of people sucked up to her, but she knew these two really liked her; they would even if she had nothing. In Sally's position, that meant a lot. In fact, it meant everything.

"If you say so. Thank you." Helen kissed her on the cheek, thrilled. It was an exquisite gown, modest as well as stylish—even her parents would have no objection.

"Thanks, hon." Jane gave Sally a bear hug. Anything more, and her voice would have started to crack.

She could hardly believe how Sally had transformed her. Lose the glasses, get some makeup, color and cut her hair—she barely recognized herself. And the nasty bitches that tried to make her life a misery weren't going to, either.

Jane was big on brains. Not so much on self-confidence. After this party, that was all going to change.

⌒

"Jane."

"Jaaannnneee!"

Sally swooped down on her as she walked along, staring into the middle distance. Helen snapped her fingers in Jane's face.

"Hello? Anybody home?"

"I'm sorry." Jane snapped back to the world around her. "I was miles away."

She didn't mention her worries. Neither one would understand. But Maureen Smith's father was a lawyer—a very high-priced *criminal* lawyer. He had gotten countless embezzling billionaires and rich, murdering husbands a "Get Out of Jail Free" card. Okay, not exactly free—Mr. Smith's fees cost more than the president made in a year.

"Yeah, well, forget all that. What are you doing tonight?" Helen snaked a buff arm through hers.

"I have archaeology club . . ."

"No. You don't," Sally announced. "You're coming with us."

"I've got obligations. . . ."

"And *I've* got you an appointment at Fernando's." The most exclusive salon in Bel Air. "Just for starters. You can consider yourself kidnapped. You're coming with us."

Jane tried a small smile. "Party stuff?"

Despite being a brainbox, she was still sixteen years old. And the idea of being guest of honor at the hot party Maureen couldn't get into was delicious.

"Bet your ass," Sally agreed.

"Okay. I'll come."

Helen squeezed her arm reassuringly. "Don't worry, Jane. When we're done with you, you're truly going to be beautiful. . . ."

In the whirlwind of activity with her friends, she practically forgot the acid tongue of Maureen Smith.

\

"Baby, baby, baby," Mona said. She sighed with satisfaction, walked across the kitchen, and gave Paulie a hug. "You wouldn't *believe* the response I am getting for this party. Shelby Cusack's agent just called to ask me if we could squeeze her in!"

"That's great," Paulie said absently. Normally, he'd have been thrilled to bits that hot new starlets were paying court to his wife. But right now, his attention was fixated on the screen in front of him.

"We've got Feliz, too. You know, the Amazing Feliz? He's the big lion tamer from Vegas! It's, like, the most incredible act. And Maureen Ugoretz wanted him for *her* wedding anniversary but she couldn't afford him. . . ."

"How much is the party costing?" Paulie asked suddenly. The figures . . . they didn't add up. He suddenly had a dry mouth. His business brain was stuck, like a slow computer dragging—he just couldn't process this.

"Why?" Mona asked innocently. "We haven't had one this year. . . ."

"No. I know." It hit him that he didn't want to know the answer.

"Well, Feliz was a hundred fifty . . ."

"Thousand?"

Mona laughed. "I love it when you make a funny, baby, you crack me up."

"I like to see you smile," Paulie responded mechanically. What had he thought the party would cost? With fireworks fit for a county park, fairground rides, a private zoo, party designers on an 8 percent budget, and the best of everything, it would be plenty.

No way would he get out of this for less than a mil. Judging by past triumphs—one point five.

He didn't blame his wife. It was just her talent. She was a world-class expert on spending cash.

And up until two weeks ago, Paulie Lassiter had loved it.

"You okay, Paulie? You're looking kinda pale."

"I'm fine."

"If your tummy's bothering you again I can get you some Pepto-Bismol."

"Nah . . . I think I'm gonna go into the office," he said.

There had to be some mistake. What he needed was an hour with his accountants, and his lawyers. Maybe fire some of these dumb-ass executives, if they were dumb-asses. Starting to look like they might be crooks.

But he, Paulie Lassiter, was in the clear. He hadn't done anything wrong.

He tried to calm the churning in his stomach by reminding himself of that. And anyway, Saturday was the party. His wife would expect him to be upbeat. This was only the second major party he'd given for Sally—her sweet sixteenth!

It would be a golden moment and worth every damn penny.

The reckoning could come later. A couple days would make no difference, not right now.

Sally's party. Sally's day. Whatever he did in life, it was for her.

⁓

"Do you think we're doing the right thing?" Aisha asked nervously.

"Of course." Ali gave her a quick peck on the cheek. "She's ripe, you know it."

"But to force her . . . what if he's not the right boy? We brought her up here, darling. Sent her to that school . . ."

Ali's face darkened. He wasn't sure if that had been the right move. Helen was growing too bold, too rebellious. Of course he wanted a spirited daughter, but not one who would defy him.

"I never met *you,*" he reminded his wife. "Aya Muna set us up, if you recall."

She smiled. "Yes. And I didn't want to marry you."

He scooped her up and nuzzled her ear. "I wanted you, though."

"Because you came to my father's house and climbed up the olive tree by the garage."

"It's true." Ali was proud. "Had to scope you out."

She had been so beautiful, his young bride, her raven hair flowing loose over her beige cotton dress with embroidered sleeves, hanging out the wash on the line her mother had strung up. He had wanted her instantly, felt his destiny calling. "I won you over."

Aisha blushed, remembering her wedding night.

"That's right, sweetheart."

"The old ways are the best ways. We're not doing this *to* Helen, we're doing it *for* her. Think of that—her happiness. Why should young ones make their own choices? Who says they have any idea how to do it? All these American marriages ending in divorce . . . how many ex-wives do you know, stuck with babies?"

Too many. Aisha nodded.

"In the end . . . it is the solemn bond, the friendship that wins through. We are doing what's best for our little Haya."

Aisha smiled. He had rarely called Helen by her original name since they'd landed in America, six years ago.

"Ahmed lands tomorrow," she said, reassured by her husband.

"Good. That is the day of her big party."

"He can take her to it!" Aisha suggested brightly.

"I don't think that's the best idea." What if Helen had been wrong? What if there was decadence, after all? Ali had no intention of letting Ahmed see his daughter in any light other than that of a modest and suitable bride. He loved the idea of Helen, wife of a Cairo businessman, contentedly walking through her garden lined with trees, prosperous and—*insh'Allah*—pregnant. "But he can be here, waiting, the next morning. As soon as she wakes up. We will organize the meeting in the morning, and in the afternoon, the *nikkah*. What do you think?"

The engagement ceremony. Under Islamic law, they would be as good as married. It didn't matter then how long till the party and the wedding reception. Helen would be a married woman . . . all the rest, just so much paperwork.

"She might refuse," Aisha fretted. "You know her, Ali!"

"She won't understand what she is getting into. Her Arabic is fading." Ali had thought of a plan, and hurried to explain it to his wife, to show how clever he was. He had seen the reserve in Helen's eyes, and he didn't trust her one bit. "We will tell her it's a *friendship* ceremony. Old Egyptian custom. She knows no better! She'll sign, Aisha. And once she realizes . . ." He shrugged. "We'll have her in Cairo, and it will all be different. She will accept it—and be happy."

"She might sign the nikkah like that," Aisha conceded. "But sweetheart, how do you get her to Cairo? Signing a paper is one thing, getting on a plane . . ."

"Here's where the smart plan comes in." Ali puffed out his chest a little, because this was brilliant. He hadn't made almost four hundred thousand dollars in trading this year by being stupid. "We'll have to waste a little money, but it's worth it for Helen's happiness. We tell her we are *all* going to Cairo."

Aisha's eyes widened. "But why? The honeymoon is just for them."

"Not honeymoon." Ali grinned. "She won't even know she's married. Family holiday. I buy the tickets. We all pack hand luggage. Drive to the airport together. Check in, even. I ask her to sit with Ahmed, up front, for politeness. You know Helen is very polite."

"Go on," his wife said, doubtfully.

"Our seats will be in back. Of course, they will get on the plane first. We will make to follow them, but we will not get on the plane. We will hang back with Firyal and Rashid. Then she will be on a plane to Cairo, with her husband, by herself!" He clapped his hands together and grinned. "Don't worry, my darling. You've seen the photographs; Ahmed is very handsome. Helen will adjust. She will go to Ahmed's beautiful house, he has servants, he is wealthy. I expect she may come back here pregnant, *insh'Allah!*"

"Jasmine will miss her," Aisha sighed. She knew this was best, but the thought of sending her firstborn away made her want to cry.

"We'll all miss her." Ali hugged his wife. "But if we want her happiness, we will have to make sacrifices. Once she's pregnant and has accepted him in her heart, they can come here, and we will all be a family again."

Aisha nodded, but wept a little into his chest.

Ali stroked her hair fondly. His own marriage had been the most solid thing in his life, and he loved his strong-willed child enough to do right by her. Of course, at first she would feel betrayed, but soon she would understand.

CHAPTER 4

T he day of the party dawned bright and clear.

All over town, girls were getting ready for it. Half—
the lucky half—of Miss Milton's Academy. Daughters of
movie stars, studio heads, and other power brokers. Some models
and actresses, and wives of famous athletes.

Everybody who was anybody.

Maureen Smith was *not* on the list. And nor were half her
friends.

They sat in the walk-in closet of Julie Manners, watching her
try to pick between eight different outfits. Seething with envy.
Why couldn't *they* go to the ball? Where was a fairy godmother
when you needed one?

The Brat Pack were gonna be there! And maybe somebody
from Guns N' Roses. For heaven's sake!

"You think the blue?" Julie held up an electric blue minidress,
no longer than a T-shirt with pretensions. "Or the white?" Body-
hugging to the extreme, it was practically see-through.

"Either'll look great." *Tramp*, Maureen thought. Just because
they hung out together, didn't mean she had to *like* Julie.

"Don't know why you're bothering to go," Swan Cohen said
petulantly. "It's gonna be a real drag. None of *us* will be there."

"Oh, I only want to see how *lame* it really is, so I can report
back," Julie lied, smiling sweetly at them.

Miss it! The party of the year! Hell, no. Sally Lassiter was a real bitch and so were her two stupid friends. But if you weren't at this party, you were *dead* in this town.

Everybody in the room knew it.

"I heard that they got that Jane Morgan scrubbed up. You know, that she looks like a human . . . ," Swan said curiously.

"No way!" Julie was scornful. "Jane could turn milk sour. Crack mirrors. She's, like, a total nerd. What the hell could they do with her?"

"And Helen Yanna . . ."

"That towel-head just trails around after Sally. She's nothing to write home about. Don't think Rob Lowe's gonna be asking *her* for a dance." Julie was scornful. "If the point is to show off those two, Sally's gonna have wasted a whole lot of Daddy's dollars. . . ."

"Don't be so snippy, we all know you crawled to get that invite," Maureen snapped.

"Sweetie," Julie retorted acidly, "I don't *crawl*. I think it's gonna be fun to show the world that *we're* the stars of *Sally's* party. When all her hot dudes are asking for *our* phone numbers, Sally's gonna feel way dumb. You get it?"

"Oh, yeah," Maureen said sourly. "We" and "our" included Emma Lightfoot and Caroline Morse from their gang, but not her, Swan, Patsy, or Melissa. For the last two weeks they'd been at each other's throats. "I get it alright."

She wasn't going to give Julie that cool new video console she'd been planning to get her for her birthday. Not anymore!

"I'll have Emma take some pics to show you," Julie said in a mollifying tone. She held up a green silk dress with an obscenely plunging neckline. "What about *this* one? Should steal the show from Sally and crew, don't you think?"

"Whatever."

"Maybe."

The other girls chewed on their resentment, torn between wanting Sally's party to fail, and wanting Julie to get shown up.

"You better *hope* so," Julie warned, reading their minds. "Because we're *friends*—do you want that Ay-rab and the limey laughing at you on Monday morning?"

They all shook their heads. Hell, no. After all, Sally had the power. She was the one withholding the invites—all to prop up her little gang of three.

They didn't like Julie much, but they *hated* that lot.

"Go for the white," Maureen said, speaking for all of them. "It's *way* sexy."

She hoped Helen and Jane didn't get so much as a second glance from all the boys! Let this party be a disaster. Then, at school, they'd show them who was boss!

~~~

Green Gables was on fire.

Helen ran excitedly to the window of Sally's enormous bedroom. It had a walk-in closet that was bigger than Helen's lounge, its own bathroom, complete with Jacuzzi and stand-alone power shower, a separate dressing room, *and* a private kitchenette!

Wow. Helen wondered what it'd be like to have this much money. Her dad was comfortable, rich middle class, but compared to Sally they were nothing but paupers.

She wanted this kind of success.

"Look at that!" Another rocket arched into the sky and exploded, a fiery rain of stars and whistling comets descending on an awestruck crowd. The air was full of oohs and aahs. "Come on, Sal! We *have* to go down!"

The party had been raging—and that was the word—for two hours already. Mona kept popping her head in to report this movie star or that supermodel had arrived.

"Yes—let's go!" Jane was surprised at her own eagerness. Dressed in the gown Sally had picked out for her, carefully madeup by a pro and spritzed with a little rosewater, she looked astonishingly lovely, and she knew it.

"We want to make an *entrance*." Sally smirked. "This is our *moment,* ladies. We're not going to blow it."

"Aww, please . . . ," Helen said. She did not want to miss the fireworks!

"Five more minutes. Momma's getting them all ready." Sally was in her element, supremely confident. "You'll see."

⁓

"Damn," Julie Manners seethed. She was gyrating on the dance floor, but it was having no effect. Rob Lowe had been here, but hadn't even looked her way.

"That preppy kid from Beverly Hills High was checking you out," Emma suggested helpfully.

"Screw him!" Julie pushed her bangs out of her eyes. Who cared? He was probably some dentist's kid. . . .

She was frustrated. All the girls from school were watching her and Emma like hawks. It was a battle for supremacy. The party was supremely, awesomely great, so now all that remained was to see who was the most beautiful. Those three girls had been the talk of the school for too long. How dare they hang out just with themselves? They were freaks . . . but Sally Lassiter had been the protector. Julie did *not* want to see Helen and Jane Morgan making it by themselves.

She was possessed by the sudden, deep loathing of a bully who suspects she's about to see her victims succeed.

The music suddenly stopped, leaving Julie in mid grind. Emma sniggered. Julie scowled at her.

"Ladies and gentlemen," the voice of the Lassiters' real English butler came over the speakers. "Please welcome the birthday girl, Sally Lassiter, and her best friends, Miss Jane Morgan and Miss Helen Yanna!"

⁓

The glittering crowd, gathered around the dance floor, buzzed in anticipation. Everybody's eyes were fixed on the top of the stairs.

Julie Manners had a sinking feeling in the pit of her stomach.

And there they were. At the top of the stairs.

"Oh—my—*gosh,*" said Emma. "Oh, my gosh!"

There was a collective gasp.

Sally stood in the middle. Long blonde hair, va-va-voom body, illegal curves, in her form-fitting gold-sequined gown with scalloped neckline, looking like a Greek goddess—Aphrodite, the queen of love.

Holding her left hand was Helen Yanna in her flowing robes, statuesque as a model, makeup emphasizing her natural beauty, a diamanté circlet in her hair, her Arabian features exquisitely calm and confident. Golden slippers glittered on her feet.

And holding her right hand, glasses vanished, hair light and gorgeous, high cheekbones glowing under radiant skin, was dark-eyed Jane—perhaps the loveliest of all—the ugly duckling turned swan, with all the extra firepower of good old-fashioned shock.

The crowd froze for a moment. Sick with jealousy, Julie glanced around. She saw the men's eyes narrowing with interest and admiration, the girls from school staring as if starstruck.

Then the applause broke out—and the cheering.

The orchestra struck up "Happy Birthday to You," and the three girls started to walk downstairs, holding hands. Three babes. Three best friends. Unbreakable. Perfect.

Flashbulbs popped as the official photographers captured the moment. Julie knew just how that picture would look—a glorious capture of youth and a level of beauty that neither she, nor any of her friends, would ever be able to match.

Just before the well-wishers—and boys—swarmed in on the glittering trio, Julie saw Sally Lassiter scope the crowd and find her.

The birthday girl gave her an insolent, triumphant wink.

I hate her, Julie thought. I've got to destroy her!

But what could she do?

Those three girls—they were untouchable!

She saw that hot new movie star, the one from the serial killer flick with all the Oscars, go up to Jane Morgan—and ask *her* to dance!

It was just horrible.

Julie turned to Emma. "I'm leaving," she said.

But Emma was gone. She was pushing through the crowd,

shouting to get some attention. "Helen! Hey, Helen!" Julie heard her calling. "That's a great dress . . . who's the designer?"

There were two new queen bees in town. Furious, Julie stalked off to the cloakroom.

"I want my bag!" she yelled. "Like, pronto!"

Time to split. Seething, she stewed in her failure. Damn it all to hell. Would anything ever go wrong for these bitches? Well, when it did, she, Julie Manners, would be right there waiting.

She had no idea just how soon it was going to be.

Thousands of miles away, as his daughter partied, British Ambassador Thomas Morgan was lurching up the carved oak staircase of his official residence.

The house on Massachusetts Avenue. He loved it. It had been the scene of so many of his triumphs. The intimate party for the Princess of Monaco. The state dinner for Vice President George H. W. Bush. The negotiations—tremendously secret, but bugged by both sides—between the UK and Russia over the Ukraine. . . .

And more. The scene of his personal rise . . . and he did mean rise.

The Hon. Thomas Morgan took a last, unsteady walk through his house. It was like taking a walk through a film . . . of his life, starring him. And hadn't that been how it really was? He, the star? Emerging from the shadow of his oh-so-lucky big brother, James, the one with the title and the fabulous Elizabethan manor house. Second sons were awkward . . . James was the heir and he was the spare. In bygone ages they'd have shoved him into the Church. Right. He laughed wildly. Some priest *he'd* have made!

Ah, yes . . . the billiard room. He particularly loved it, because it had been the scene of so many great screws. Two of the sexy young nannies, right there on that table. A couple of desperate Washington housewives, longing to climb that social ladder. What a room! It was in there that he lived and breathed . . . there that he had his power.

Nobody more charming. Nobody more brilliant. . . .

The grip of the drugs subsided in his mind, and for a second melancholia swept in. What the hell . . . what the hell did it all mean?

The unwelcome thought arose that maybe he hadn't been *that* brilliant. Maybe he'd just been the best kiss-ass in town. A natural politician, one that could groom his lords and masters in London just as well as sucking up to the Yanks and assorted foreigners who comprised the social scene in America's capital.

Maybe that wasn't something to boast about. Fucking desperate women, poor immigrants without the right papers, nannies longing to keep their job and their shot at freedom . . . obsessed wives of other men, dumb enough to see the world through the same shallow blinkers he did.

Maybe he should have paid more attention to his daughter.

Maybe he shouldn't have gambled.

Maybe he shouldn't have taken those bribes. . . .

Thom Morgan let out a loud, wretched sob. He felt piteously sorry for himself. He didn't deserve this, any of this. He was a good person! They were all picking on him. . . .

The maudlin wash of regret peaked on another chemical dip and turned into anger. Morgan strode back into the bedroom, sat at his antique William and Mary dressing table, and snorted the next of the thick, fat lines he'd chopped out earlier this evening.

Wow! Instant rush.

The indictment, hand-delivered from his lawyers, lay ignored on the bed. Morgan was flying, riding a fresh wave of self-confidence and pride. He looked at himself in the mirror . . . a tall, handsome man in his mid forties, a dusting of powder just under his nose . . . that, he brushed off. Now. The white tie, Washington's most formal style of attire, looked *fabulous* on His Excellency. As ever.

Swap it for prison blues and a mug shot? He thought not.

His Excellency, the Hon. Thomas Morgan, walked over to the Victorian sash windows of his boudoir, threw them open with one arm, and swung his legs over the edge. Fuck them, fuck them all! They'd never catch him. They were no match for him!

Jane's image briefly floated back into his mind. But he didn't want to think of her now. Wasn't the moment. She was *his* daughter. She'd be okay, and besides, her mother was waiting—expecting him. . . .

He tossed himself over the edge, high as a kite. Falling, his arms spread out, as though he were flying, offering himself to the elements.

But he wasn't flying. He was dying. In that long second before the death, Thomas Morgan knew it. His mind threw up a vision of Jane—all grown up—she was happy, he thought.

He blew her a kiss as the ground swallowed him up.

~

"So, how did it go?"

Ali helped his daughter into the car. He had to admit she looked marvelous—modestly gowned, but at the same time, splendidly beautiful. He was pleased—young Ahmed would be a most amenable bridegroom.

Aisha's cousins and their son had arrived, exhausted, a couple of hours earlier and were sleeping soundly in the guest bedrooms. Ahmed was reserved, handsome, silent. Ali had not found him particularly enthusiastic, but he had not seen Helen yet. Ahmed would do his duty and, Ali was determined, so would his own child.

"It was *so* great." Helen sighed with contentment. In all her young life, she had never had such an evening.

The spectacle of it—that was something else. The camel rides and free manicures, the fabulous food and sneaky drinks from the hidden beer keg—not that *she'd* indulged—the fortune-tellers and fireworks! Too much fun.

And then, herself. The girls had all adored her outfit, and she'd felt simply beautiful—not different, for once, just the center of attention. The solid friendship of Sally and Jane had buoyed her. And if young men had asked her to dance, asked for her number—well, she didn't have to say yes—that was nice, too.

"Excellent. I trusted you," he reminded her.

"I know, Baba." Helen gave him a reassuring hug. "It was all fine."

"Tomorrow morning you will meet Ahmed. . . ."

She sighed, but a bargain was a bargain. "I'll be nice to him, I promise you that."

"If you won't sign the nikkah with him, Helen, we must make it up to the family."

Helen stiffened. "How can I do that? I told you I'm not ready to be married, Baba."

"The Egyptians have their customs. We'll hold a friendship ceremony, and you and Ahmed will sign the pledge of friendship between our branches of the family, as the younger generation. I did the same with my cousin twenty years ago," Ali lied blithely.

He kept his eyes on the road, but allowed his gaze to slip toward Helen in the passenger seat. Yes . . . she had relaxed and slumped tiredly against the headrest.

"Sure, Baba," she said. "That's no problem. I like the traditional stuff."

"Good girl." Her father kissed his tired daughter gently on the forehead, and reminded himself that what he was doing was for her own good.

⁓

The sun was streaming through the window of her bedroom when Jane woke up. It was a glorious winter's day in L.A., sunny but not too hot. The ocean was crashing against their private beach in Malibu, and as Jane tossed in bed, she smelled the welcoming aroma of Consuela's bacon and tomatoes, sizzling in the pan. The rented house the embassy provided for the ambassador's daughter was small, but lovely, on a high cliff overlooking the sea, with large windows, modern designer furniture, and of course her latest live-in nanny.

Consuela and Jane got on well enough, which was to say, neither bothered the other.

Jane pushed a hand through her tousled hair and smiled.

For the first time in a long time—maybe forever—she woke up happy.

Last night had been truly wonderful. She looked so good—shockingly good. She'd been asked to dance by no less than three film stars, one soap actor, and a rock star—and asked for her number by countless hot-looking boys. And the girls had fluttered about her, offering compliments, gazing wonderingly at her hair—wow—it felt fantastic!

The tribute paid to beauty. Mothlike Jane had never known it. She was overwhelmed with gratitude to Sally. She'd never look down on that again. Call it superficial all you want—as bookworm supreme, Jane certainly had—but being pretty made *all* the difference. She felt confident, feminine—like the missing puzzle piece had been added to her life. Maybe she'd never have Sally's brazen, starry glow, but Jane Morgan felt good about herself.

She swung her slim legs out of bed and padded over to the mirror. Jane slept in a pair of her dad's boxers and one of his T-shirts, which swamped her small frame. But even without makeup, the beauty was still there; the great hair, ruffled by sleep; her pretty face, without the glasses; a little mascara on her lashes that hadn't come off with the cursory wipe she'd given her face last night.

Jane Morgan was sixteen, carefree, and single.

It was to be the last day of her life she would ever feel that way.

She wandered into the shower and was washing her hair, reveling in the sensation of the powerful jets, when Consuela hammered on the door.

"Mees Morgan—phone—for you."

"Take a message," Jane yelled. "I'll call them back."

"They say ees important. Ees Washington."

"I'll get dressed, call them right back," Jane snapped. Damn! Couldn't she at least put her clothes on?

Still, it wasn't like Daddy to call her and insist on talking. Reluctantly, she hurried through her routine, pummeled out the conditioner, and stepped out of the shower. Jane dried off fast and selected black jeans and a matching T-shirt, then went to find Consuela.

Her nanny put a plate of food in front of her. "Here."

"*Gracias.*" Jane minded her manners. "That number?"

Consuela passed her a scrap of paper and Jane dialed.

"British Embassy."

"This is Jane Morgan," she said, confidently. "I believe my father called me?"

There was a long pause at the end of the line.

"Hold please, Miss Morgan."

A couple of beeps, and Jane found herself talking to Cyril—Sir Cyril Clark, her father's senior attaché.

"Jane?" he said.

She knew instantly, from his tone. Something was wrong—very wrong. Automatically, Jane pushed the plate of bacon and tomatoes away, untouched.

"Cyril, it's me." She could hear the anxiety in her own voice. "What is it? Let me speak to my father, please."

Another leaden pause.

"Now listen, Jane," he said heavily, and her stomach curled into a knot. "You're going to have to be very brave."

⁓

"And this is my daughter Helen."

Baba was speaking in Arabic; Helen's was rusty; she was ashamed of that. Tired after not enough sleep, she had worn a long dress—to please her parents—instead of her normal jeans and a button-down shirt from the Gap.

"*Wa-es salaam,*" she said politely.

He nodded back and said something too fast for Helen to understand. Ahmed was a young man of reasonable height, with glasses and a pleasant-enough, unremarkable face. He looked about as enthusiastic over the whole exercise as she was. Helen smiled at him—he, too, probably had his parents to placate. They'd get through this together.

"Ahmed's parents are also visiting town. They'll be at the ceremony this afternoon. They are still resting after the flight from Cairo."

"What ceremony is that?" Helen asked.

"The friendship ceremony." Ali spoke in English, and Ahmed looked on uncomprehendingly. "The one we spoke of last night. You will go through it, yes, Helen?"

" 'Course I will." She nodded. Fair's fair—they'd let her go to the party, the greatest night of her life. At the very least, she could appear willing. "It will be good to meet your mother and father," she added to Ahmed, haltingly, in Arabic.

"Thank you." He added, "I am very happy."

He didn't look it.

"And I have a surprise for you," Ali added. "Tonight we are all going on a trip—to Cairo, where your mother can visit all her cousins. Afterward we'll go back to Amman." He looked at his daughter.

"Tonight? But it's so soon!"

"You can just pack one case. Your mother and I decided that we should all go on a family holiday, and with Rashid and Firyal here it seemed like the perfect time. After your big Western party." He smiled at her. "It was our surprise for you, Helen. We didn't want you to get *too* sucked into your friends and their life-style. You do want to go back for a visit, right?"

"Of course!" Helen said. Back to Jordan? She hadn't seen her childhood home for years. She thought of all her friends, Fatima, Sayeeda, little Rahma . . . wondered how they'd grown up. "We're really flying out there? *Tonight?* You mean it?"

"I do." He grinned. "I know you always wanted to go back there." And Baba put on his solemn face. "Maybe once you re-mind yourself what our life was like in Jordan, you will wish to get married. . . ."

Helen shook her head. "I want to go back to Jordan, Baba, but that's about all."

Ali reached up to the mantelpiece and patted the envelope that sat there. "I have the tickets and the passports," he said. "First class. You know, Helen, one thing that matters in this life is stay-ing close to your roots."

"I totally agree," she said. Did that mean he was going to give up the whisky?

But she didn't say that. It was a nice moment—no need to spoil it.

"Will you excuse me?" she asked Ahmed. "I want to go and see my friend Sally. I'll be back this afternoon, for the ceremony."

"No later than noon—your mother has a special dress for you to wear," Ali told her.

Helen kissed him on the cheek. "I promise."

⁓

The cab dropped her out front. Green Gables was already immaculately clean—Helen could hardly believe it. An army of servants had descended on the place in the night—even after a few hours, you'd never know there had been a party there at all—apart from a few hoofprints on the grass where they'd had the camel rides. And Helen suspected they would soon be gone, too.

Wow. It was astounding what money could do.

She rang the bell, eager to see Sally. Maybe they could get a ride in one of Sally's father's cars over to Malibu, see Jane. She had a teenager's eagerness to relive her night of triumph. And just wait till they were back at Miss Milton's on Monday morning! The gang of three would become a gang of *twenty*-three—at least.

Helen finally felt like she fit in.

A moment later and the door swung open—Richard, the second butler, opened it.

"Good morning, Miss Yanna." All the staff here knew Helen by name. "Please come in—Miss Lassiter is in her bedroom."

"Thanks, Richard." Helen half ran up the stairs, feeling as light as thistledown. She knew the way, third on the left at the top of the sweeping marble stairs. She hammered on the door. "Sally! You sleeping? It's Helen. Let me in!"

"Just a moment."

Helen blinked; she could hear that Sally was crying.

Why? Last night had been perfect. Some drama with a boy after Helen had left?

"What's up?"

Sally opened the door, red-eyed, tear tracks streaked down her face, and all Helen's thoughts of reliving the party, flying off to Cairo, all evaporated.

"What's wrong?" she asked. "Sal? Are you okay?"

"It's Jane. There's been . . . an accident."

Helen's stomach turned over. "What kind of an accident . . . is she *dead*?"

"Not her. Her father. He fell out of a top-floor window in his house in Washington. . . ."

"Oh, my God."

"The British secret service came . . . took her away. Took her to Washington. She called me before she left."

Sally shuddered as she spoke. She would never forget the bleakness, the desolation in Jane's voice.

"Does she have family there?" Helen, always practical, tried to process the information. "Maybe an uncle . . . a grandmother?"

"Nobody. Her father never got along with them."

"Then who's going to look after Jane?"

Helen wandered in and both girls flopped down onto Sally's huge California king bed with its silken Pratesi sheets.

"I guess I am," Sally said, finally. "She's my best friend. I told her she can come live here, like in one of the guest cottages. We can afford it. . . ."

"Her family will take care of the money, I'm sure. Won't she inherit . . ."

"No, that's the thing." Sally Lassiter wasn't book-smart, but she had some of her father's savvy. "It was all government stuff . . . dependent on her dad's job. Now that's gone, so's everything else. She has no house . . . nothing."

"But her maid. Her driver . . ."

"Helen, her dad didn't really fall. It was suicide." Sally dabbed at her red eyes. "He was embezzling . . . taking bribes. They said he passed info to the Chinese . . . who the ambassadors were meeting and when. Even what they said. He had a gambling habit. The Brits had him under surveillance . . . they told him last week they were going to let the U.S. try him. He'd have gone away for life. Maybe more."

"More?"

"Treason. Spying carries the death penalty over here."

"Oh, God!" Helen cried out. "Poor Jane . . ."

"Everything he *did* own will be forfeit to the Brits."

"But they'll have to look after her. She's still a legal child."

"I guess." Sally mulled that over. "She didn't sound like she wanted anything to do with them."

Helen bit her lip. "We'll have to stay with her at school—all day."

Even with the party and Jane's newfound beauty, Julie and the other bullies would see their chance now. No way could Helen let them snigger over her father's death.

"She's not coming back to Miss Milton's." Sally rubbed her eyes; the thought of losing Jane, whom she felt like she'd known forever, the closest thing to a sister, was dreadful. "She says she never wants to see that school again. And you know what? I think she means it."

"Well, whatever she decides, we'll be here." Helen knew it sounded lame. "Maybe I could get a transfer to her new school . . . wherever the Brits decide to send her."

"Maybe." Sally was anxious. She didn't think Jane Morgan would want to go to any new school. "They might try to send her home. . . ."

"This is her home," Helen said stoutly. "L.A." She looked at Sally, anxious. "My father . . . he booked a surprise vacation for the family. First-class tickets, to Cairo." She blushed at even mentioning cost to Sally Lassiter. "For us that's a lot of money. We are . . . going to visit some relatives and then going back to Jordan. I could ask Baba to cancel but I don't think he'd go for it." She shivered. "Will Jane be okay?"

"Absolutely. She'll be in Washington for a little while anyway. We'll come by when y'all get back." Sally was stout. "I can take care of Jane, don't you worry." She hugged her friend. "When are you coming home?"

"Not sure. About a week, I guess."

"Okay. Y'all hurry back, you hear?"

Sally smiled, but they were both on the verge of tears. There was no joy in vacations now, no joy in rehashing a fabulous party. Their dear Jane was hurting, and both the girls felt the wound with her.

~~~

On the way back home, Helen thought of nothing but her friend. She was worried—extremely. What if Jane went off the rails? There was a strange streak to that girl. What if she wanted revenge . . . on the embassy . . . was that so crazy? Surely she wouldn't think of killing herself. No. That was not Jane's way. But Helen couldn't blame her for not wanting to deal with the shame. School would be appalling. Who could handle Julie and her crowd's torments at a time like this?

As the cab sped under the palm trees, waving gently in a perfect L.A. sky, baby blue with a couple of fluffy clouds, Helen was ashamed for worrying about herself, too.

Jane had been the glue between herself and Sally. The older friend, but clever, able to bridge the gap between them. She could discuss politics with Jane, or history, or anything. With Sally it was all movie star gossip and the latest trends. And rock bands . . .

Helen loved all those things, of course. But Sally and she were just so *different*. She was frightened now. Maybe with just the two of them it wouldn't work out.

Sally and Jane had history. Not Sally and her.

"Eighteen fifty."

"Thanks." Helen gave the cabbie twenty-five, absentmindedly.

"Thanks, hon. Have a great day," he said before speeding off down Third Street with a screech of tires.

There were ribbons tied to her gate, and balloons. Oh, man. Baba was having a party for Ahmed. Helen made an instant decision: it was fine, she was going to go along with everything. Jane's father was dead—the last thing Helen needed was more drama right now.

Aisha hurried out of the kitchen door.

"Come with me, upstairs. I have your betrothal dress."

Helen allowed herself to be pushed upstairs. "What do you mean, betrothal?"

"No, for the ceremony, the friendship ceremony," her mother said hurriedly. "Now here, put these robes on! Where have you been? They are all waiting. With the contract . . ."

Helen quickly got changed; her mother had got her a beautiful Jordanian robe, traditional and, she thought, antique. She admired her reflection as Aisha fastened a flowing headscarf of cream silk around her hair.

"Can I keep this? It's beautiful."

"Of course you can. Now run downstairs, Baba is waiting for you. Firyal and I will come down in a minute."

"Mama—you know I'm not actually going to marry Ahmed."

"Friendship will satisfy family honor, Helen. Just do this for your father," Aisha said vaguely. "Hurry! His father, Rashid, is there waiting for you, too."

Helen sighed and walked downstairs; her father was waiting with an ornate-looking document. Ahmed was there, looking as embarrassed as she was, in traditional Islamic trousers and hat; he didn't meet her eyes as both their fathers embraced.

Baba put Helen's hand into his. Feeling every sympathy for him, she gave him a surreptitious wink. Ahmed looked at her for the first time; his eyes widened, and he gave her a very small smile.

The things we do for our parents! Helen thought.

Baba was speaking in Arabic now. She didn't follow what he was saying. He told her he would lead her, and she should repeat after him.

Helen willingly agreed. She wanted to please her father, to ease the tension for poor Ahmed, and to forget today's troubles.

By the time Helen returned from Egypt and Jordan, Jane would have worked out what she wanted to do. *Insh'Allah,* she would be back at school, with Helen and Sally protecting her. Like always.

They were best friends and they would stick together. An unbreakable trio. An absence of a few days, a couple of weeks even, would not hurt that.

Her father was placing a golden pen in her hand.

"Sign here," he said. "Darling. My little daughter."

He kissed her on the forehead and Helen pressed her head against his. She adored her parents. They were always looking out for her. Poor Jane had lost her father, and Helen thanked God she still had hers.

That night there was a short meal—Ahmed said very little— and then the families packed into two cars. There was much shouting and chattering in Arabic; Helen didn't follow any of it, didn't much care. She had promised to be good, and she was. She had packed her suitcase as quickly as she could. Mama told her not to bother with much; Jasmine and she were taking only hand luggage, it was an adventure, they would buy clothes when they got into town.

Helen had never known her parents so carefree. They were clearly enjoying the company of their cousins. She liked the idea of an adventure, suddenly wanted to get out of town. Her father showed her the tickets: one for Ahmed, and one for each of her family. He said Rashid and Firyal had their own. Jasmine, starry-eyed, chattered about Amman, and about seeing the pyramids in Egypt.

"I don't have to drive with Ahmed, do I?" Helen pleaded to her mother. Now that she'd gone through the ceremony, she wasn't too keen on the actual friendship. He was sullen and quiet and hardly spoke any English.

"How about a compromise?" Her mother's gaze scouted around busily as she made a great show of fetching her passport. "Ahmed will drive with his parents but you will sit together on the plane."

Helen sighed. "There's no point trying to play matchmaker, Mama. I'm sure he's very nice, but . . ."

"Helen," Aisha said warningly, "your father spent a lot of money to make this a wonderful trip. Show the family in a good light. If you are to say no to the marriage, you can at least fly with him! Don't make Baba look foolish in front of our cousins."

Helen surrendered. "Okay, Mama, okay. Where will the rest of you sit?"

"A little way behind you. We're on the same plane so it is all quite proper. You will be chaperoned."

"All right." Helen shrugged. What did it matter, really, if she were bored on the flight? Once they got to Cairo, all this would be over, and her family would soon be heading to Jordan. "I will travel with him."

❧

At the airport there were crowds of people. It was chaotic; Helen followed her parents, blindly, as Ahmed and his family checked in right behind them. Hers and Ahmed's were the only suitcases, so it didn't take much time. They went through passport control and into the duty-free lounge; Baba made a big production of buying a silk tie, which she knew he'd never wear.

Then they called the flight. The family went to the gate, but among the crowd of people, Baba and Mama held back, grabbing on to Jasmine's shoulders.

"You go ahead." Baba gestured at Ahmed, who was kissing his father on the cheek near the gate. "You two will board first. You are sitting together, remember? Be nice to him now, Helen; you promised."

"I will," she said dutifully, distracted. She wondered where Jane was at this moment, prayed someone was looking after her. "See you guys later." And she walked over to join Ahmed.

As Helen approached, his parents gave him a significant look, then smiled at Helen and melted away. Oh, man, she thought, everyone wants to play Cupid.

But she could put up with it for one flight.

"I guess we're sitting together for this one, huh?" she asked him, in English.

Ahmed smiled blankly at her.
Gonna be a long flight.

⌒

"Do you like it? We'll sit here."
Ahmed nodded at her—his English as halting as her Arabic
was rusty.
"They're great seats." Helen thawed a little; she loved flying
first class. She wasn't Sally Lassiter—it took a chunk of her parents' money to send her to Miss Milton's. For her this was a real
kick. The air hostesses were hovering, so she hurried to take her
seat. Baba and Mama must be settling in somewhere behind her.
Helen looked around, but the cabin was full of people, sliding
into their seats, buckling up. Hostesses walked up and down the
aisles, efficiently tucking away bags, and she gave up trying to
find them.
"Ladies and gentlemen, we are about to depart. Please ensure
your seat belt is securely fastened around your waist, and that
your seat-back and tray table are in the upright position. Cabin
crew to cross-check, please, cabin crew to cross-check."
The stewards fastened the doors.
Helen spun around in her seat again, craning her neck in the
first-class cabin. She couldn't see her parents or Jasmine anywhere. Where were they? And Ahmed's father and mother? This
was a family trip—were the rest of them sitting in coach?
She shifted uneasily on her seat. Manners was one thing, but
she did not want her mother in economy while she flew up
here.
The plane groaned, shuddered, and started to accelerate as the
pilot eased it onto the runway.
"Ahmed," Helen said urgently, summoning her Arabic as best
she could, "where are Mama and Baba? Where are your parents . . .
are they all sitting by themselves back there?"
"I do not understand," he said heavily, dark eyes fixed on her.
"What are you asking me?"
Helen tried again. "Where are our parents?"

He blinked. "In America. The airport, they said good-bye. Why are you asking me this?"

The plane heaved again and then pushed up into the sky, the retraction of the wheels shaking the undercarriage.

She felt sick. "Ahmed . . . I don't understand. Are my parents on this plane? Where are your parents? Isn't this a family trip to Cairo?"

"Of course," he said, and for a second her stomach unknotted. "It is a family trip—a honeymoon trip. Yours and mine."

Helen repeated dully "Honeymoon?"

Ahmed showed the first signs of impatience. "We are married, are we not? You and I. Married. *Mash'Allah,*" he added, but, Helen felt, with a sense of duty. Thanks be to God.

"Married?" she repeated, almost hysterical. "Who told you that? Who said we were married?"

Ahmed stared at her anxiously. Helen could almost see him wondering about her mental health. Reflexively, she gripped the armrests of her seat.

"Helen," he said slowly and, she noticed, gently, as one addressing a frightened child. "What of this afternoon? You and I signed the nikkah, did we not? We are married now, in the sight of the Most Compassionate." He offered her a tentative smile. "We have done our duty, you and I, to our parents—as is pleasing to Him—and we will make the best of it. You also believe that, do you not?"

Stunned, she was silent.

"I promise you, I am a gentle man." He reached across her seat and took her hand, and stroked it. "I did not want this, either. But if we surrender our selfish desires, we will find true peace, *insh'Allah.* You also believe this, I think?"

The puzzle pieces fell into place, with slow, terrible clarity for Helen.

That "friendship ceremony" had been no such thing. It was her nikkah. The binding engagement ceremony between Muslims—in the eyes of God, she was already married.

And her parents had *tricked* her into getting on this plane. Even to the point of buying useless tickets. When she and Ahmed had filed down the walkway into the aircraft, Baba and Mama had just gone home. Explaining things to a wailing Jasmine, no doubt. *No wonder they'd only had hand luggage.* No suitcases—the plane could depart without them.

Helen's head spun as she ran through the afternoon. Yes, Mama *had* said it—"betrothal dress." Helen just had not pushed it. Was she being willfully deaf? When Baba read from the sacred Qur'an. God forgive her, she had not been paying attention. But she had happily gone through with it. Ahmed had no idea she was not consenting to be his wife.

"Our parents thought it would be best," he said artlessly. "In truth, I had already lost my one true love. I could have lived forever by myself. But they decided otherwise. And you and I can be friends, I think? Is it not so?"

Helen understood, in a second. She had underestimated her father, her mother, too. And even though she was furious, she understood. They just didn't see things as she did. Her father and mother had schemed a little, and arranged a marriage for her after the old ways. And she, a believing Muslim, had to admit she had gone through the nikkah of her own free will, after being advised what it was. . . .

An imam would likely tell her it was invalid. But Helen looked at Ahmed, older than her, his own face drawn from duty to his parents and, indeed, to God.

He was, she knew instinctively, a good man. She could not find it within herself to humiliate him. None of this was his doing. And Helen was mature enough to believe that what her parents had done had been from sheer love of her. As she knew, they were in an arranged marriage themselves—and as she knew, they had been extremely happy.

This young man had his hand in hers.

Maybe there would be a divorce, but, Helen knew, she had no wish to disgrace or humiliate him. After all, her American passport was in her pocket. Whatever her parents' well-intentioned schemes, she was a free woman.

But she would not hurt this man. Or her parents. There could be a divorce—after a decent interval, of course.

"Of course. We can be very good friends," she agreed, with a generous smile.

"That is well." He beamed at her.

"And friends should be honest," Helen plowed on. "So tell me—why didn't *you* want to go through with the nikkah?"

Ahmed blew out his cheeks and sighed.

"I don't want to offend you."

"You won't."

"Her name was Badiya," he said eventually. "I thought ... well. I thought we were destined for each other. She was not from a good family, but I saw her, in the mosque, each day. I found her outside one time and started to talk to her. She was an exceptional woman. She had a job working for the Department of Antiquities. Badiya was beautiful, modest, and brilliant," he said with fervor.

Helen was strangely moved. There had been nobody in *her* life—nobody she had loved like that.

"But your parents disapproved?"

"I would not have cared for that," Ahmed said firmly. "I loved her." He looked across at Helen. "She died," he added simply. "A car accident. Cairo traffic. So mundane."

"And you did not want to marry again?"

"I was never betrothed to her." He fell silent, and stared out of the tiny window at the cloudless sky below them.

"I'm sorry ... ," she murmured, unheard.

And you're not really betrothed to me. Helen picked up her headphones and plugged them into the jack. She would stay in Ahmed's house for only a short time, then, once the divorce was concluded, come home. Her father meant well, but this was not for her. She would arrange her own marriage—to a man who actually *wanted* to be her husband.

⌒

Two days later, back in L.A., Sally's phone rang.

"Sally. It's Jane."

Sally gripped the receiver. "How are you? Where are you?"

"At LAX," Jane said. Her voice sounded tense and miserable, and Sally's heart sank hearing it. "Can you come and pick me up?"

"On my way. Hang tight."

Sally bounded down the stairs. Jonathan, one of their butlers, was examining a statue in the hallway.

"Any of the cars ready?"

"The Aston Martin is around, Miss Lassiter. It's Jake's day off, but Mike could drive you. . . ."

"That's just fine, thank you. I'll do it myself. After all, I got my license yesterday!"

She snatched the keys from the rail, checked she had the right set—Daddy had so many cars—and made to rush out the door. Paulie waddled out of his study and almost crashed into her.

"Hey, hey, princess. Where's my princess going?"

"I got to pick Jane up at the airport. She's back early, Dad. You don't mind, right? Helen's on vacation."

"No, honey, you go ahead. It's good she came back from Washington. Good. Poor kid."

Sally stopped for a second; her dad was all red-faced.

"You should go easy on that bacon at breakfast, Dad," she said.

"You're as bad as your mom. I drink OJ, I'll live for a thousand years." Paulie patted his rotund stomach. "You'll never get rid of me."

Sally flung her arms round him and gave him a hug; poor, poor Jane, not to have a dad. Especially one like hers.

"I might not be back till late. I'm gonna drive to pick up Jane, then we might spend some time together."

"That's fine." Her dad looked distracted, a little anxious. "Something came up at the office. I'll be late, too."

"Mom'll be stuck with *Jeopardy!* and a TV dinner," Sally joked. She knew she ought to have asked Daddy what the matter was, but she was more worried about Jane right now. Didn't want to keep her waiting. "See you later, Pop." She kissed him lightly on the cheek and ran out the door.

"See you later," Paulie said to her departing back.

Jane was standing with her suitcases, right on the curb, and Sally felt a stab of anxiety upon seeing her. Her friend was still beautiful, but all that new self-confidence had evaporated. She cut a bedraggled, forlorn little figure on the sidewalk, shoulders slumped, the picture of misery.

Sally screeched to a halt, then jumped out and crushed Jane in a big bear hug.

"Helen's not here because she went on vacation, with the family. They planned a surprise trip for her. She wanted to cancel it for you. I told her to go, but I thought you'd be in Washington a while longer, I guess." She looked guilty. "She said it'd only be a week. . . ."

"Hey, it's fine. I'm glad she went," Jane said. "I can look after myself."

Sally put Jane's bags in the car and they climbed in. "Tell me everything," she said.

"Nothing to tell." Jane laid her head back against the headrest as Sally pulled smoothly out into traffic. "We read the will and they told me what my options were."

"So . . . it wasn't good?"

Jane shook her head. " 'Fraid not."

Sally glanced across at her.

"He left you nothing, hon?"

"Some personal effects. I can't bear to keep them, so I asked they be donated to charity." Jane's voice had a clear, cold determination to it that tore at Sally's heart; she had seen her friend throw up walls like this before, a crab scuttling back under her shell. "He was in debt up to the eyeballs, but the embassy got a lawyer who made sure they won't attach to me, as I'm a minor."

"Which means they have to look after you. . . ."

"They refuse to pay for Miss Milton's."

There it was. Sally's worst nightmare. Split from Jane forever. Their threesome broken up.

"That's bull," she exclaimed. "If they won't pay for you, we will. Daddy will, I promise you that."

Jane reached over and squeezed her hand.

"Sally, I love you for that." Tears started to prickle in both girls' eyes. "But I can't go back there, don't you see? There's no money coming in. Without Daddy's salary, how am I going to pay for college? I can't go to Oxford or Cambridge—I'd need money to support myself. And once I hit eighteen, they wash their hands of me."

"Oh, Jane."

"They offered me a small place in Washington in a not-great area and the last year at a local private school. I said no way. Murder capital of America."

"So what are you going to do?"

"Stay right where I am. Consuela will be with me till her wages run out. And then, I guess I'll go get a job. And an apartment."

"But you're not a legal adult. And without a degree what kind of job can you get?"

"I'll work something out."

Jane sounded definite about that. But Sally could hear the tears lurking just under the bravado.

"Y'all can come and live with us," Sally suggested. "The maid and you. We'll pay her wages . . . you can have a guest bungalow. It's what they're there for. Daddy won't mind. . . ."

"Thanks, honey." Jane smiled at her gratefully. "But I want to see if I can figure something out for myself. I want to rely on myself. Does that make sense?"

"You always were ornery," Sally said, but she did understand. Jane had always had that fierce pride, as long as she'd known her. Her father's final abandonment meant she would need to try to stand up for herself. "Come on. We'll go get a nice long lunch somewhere."

"Sounds good," Jane said.

~~~

Eventually, Sally dropped Jane off at her place in Malibu. Consuela was not there; not expecting Jane back this fast, she had bunked off to her brother's house in the Valley. Jane did not mind in the least. She let herself in, switched off the alarm, and went to run a bath.

It would take her a week, just for the basics. Finding out how to get her things from Miss Milton's, without setting foot in that hellish place ever again. She did not want to see the sneering faces of her enemies, or worse, have to hear their fake sympathy. She wanted to research what it would take to get her declared an adult, better yet, a naturalized U.S. citizen. Some of her father's colleagues could help with that one. Jane was selfishly glad Helen was away for a little while. She was shell-shocked, and although she wanted to make a fresh start, sort out her life, for a few days she needed to recover. She wasn't sleeping, and her appetite had gone.

You need some R & R, she told herself, then smiled grimly at the American turn of phrase. Sally was there for her, and she loved her all the more now, but Jane wasn't sure she could take staying with Sal, enduring her bubbly, preppy optimism, seeing her with her own loving family. It would hurt far too much. No, Jane wanted to be out here, near the beach, to pull on her sneakers and run till she felt like throwing up, to walk by the sea, try to stay sane, numb out the pain.

Thomas Morgan had never loved her. He had abandoned her to nannies, and then to school far away in Los Angeles. But Jane had never stopped trying to impress him. And she'd hoped, maybe when she was an adult, so near, so near, she could have gone to Washington, been an academic in a think tank, even a diplomat. . . .

If only she'd had time.

I could have made Daddy love me, Jane thought, desperately.

But there was no time. And he had abandoned her again, this time for good.

Exhausted, she put her head on her knees and wept.

⁓

Sal went over to Jane's house every day that week to check on her. Her friend scared her; Jane was withdrawing deeply: sitting on the beach for hours, staring out to sea, or keeping herself frantically busy researching citizenship and her emancipation. Gossip didn't interest her, clothes didn't interest her. She flatly refused to go to a club or a rock concert, or even a ball game.

But Sally kept trying. She wanted to help Jane, and besides, it was pretty tense at Green Gables. Daddy was having some kind of business trouble, and he hung round the house with a face as red as a tomato, sweating and cussing as he went through his papers. He was drinking too much, and worked later and later hours. It made Sal uncomfortable. She'd rather be in Malibu, working on helping Jane.

"It's Friday," Sally said, finally, with a sense of relief. "Helen's coming home."

"She's not there yet. I left a message."

Sally had, too.

"Let's go see. Maybe they just got back." Anything to get Jane to take a ride; sitting in Malibu stewing in her grief was not good for her.

"Okay," Jane agreed, looking at Sally with bloodshot eyes. She did want to see Helen again. And she was intelligent enough to see what her friend was trying to get her to do. "Let's go."

They pulled up outside the Yannas' compact little house; Sally looked at it with interest, never having been there before. There was a car parked in the driveway. They smiled at each other—Helen was back.

Jane looked forward to seeing her friend. She was reassured by the modesty of the house; Helen Yanna's parents must be reaching to send her to Miss Milton's, just as her father had. Who knew? Maybe Helen's dad could do with a bookkeeper.

"You stay here," Jane suggested tactfully. "I'll ring the bell."

Sally was wearing one of her typical short skirts, just off the knee, with a sexy pleated kick to it, and an outrageous tight white T-shirt that played up her glorious breasts and golden skin.

Somehow Jane assumed that her own plain black trouser suit would be more reassuring to their friend's parents.

She climbed out and pressed the buzzer; there was the sound of footsteps, and a young girl wrenched the door open. She was pretty and slight, not more than ten, Jane guessed.

"Are you Jasmine?"

The little girl nodded, eyes wide.

Jane offered a hand. "I'm Jane Morgan, Helen's friend from school. Is she in?"

"Helen's never coming back," Jasmine said, and her eyes brimmed with tears.

CHAPTER 5

"Excuse me?" Jane asked, bewildered, but an adult figure filled the door, a stocky, bearded man, and he was gazing at her very coolly.

"Mr. Yanna—I was just telling Jasmine that I'm Jane, Helen's schoolfriend. Is she about?"

"No."

Jane tried again. Maybe his English wasn't too hot.

"It's just that she hasn't been answering her phone, and we wanted to—"

"My daughter is not here anymore. She has gotten married."

He obviously wasn't joking.

"I—I don't quite understand. We went to a party last week together. We thought she was on holiday. . . ."

"No holiday. Honeymoon. She decided to get married to her second cousin Ahmed and they have gone back to Cairo to set up house," Helen's father replied flatly. "She may not be back here for many years."

"But she didn't say anything to us."

"A wedding is a private family matter," Ali Yanna said. "If she wishes to call you, she can."

Jane digested this.

"If she speaks to you, will you tell her Sally and I would like to talk to her?" Jane asked.

He shrugged. "Good-bye, then."

The door closed.

Sally wound down the car window and poked out her head. "What happened?"

Jane got back in the car, her face troubled, and motioned for Sally to drive off.

"He said she left the country. Got married to some distant relation and left for Cairo."

"You're messin' with me. She was going on vacation."

"Apparently while she was out there, she decided to get hitched. I don't think her father approves of us, Sal. He didn't seem to want to talk."

Sally's face was a picture of dismay.

"That *can't* be true. She never said a damned thing to us."

"Mr. Yanna told me it was a private family matter." Jane chewed on her lip. "I know Helen. . . . Still waters run deep, but I don't think she would do that."

"She's been hanging out with us long enough to get her some street smarts," Sally said. "She knows our numbers. Guess we'll just have to wait for her to call."

"I guess so."

"Oh, man," Sally breathed. "It just hit me. I'll be all alone at school now. No you and no Helen. I don't want to go back."

They both contemplated Julie Manners and Maureen Smith.

Don't," Jane said, boldly. "Sal, just don't. Get your dad to pay for a private tutor, or go to a different school. You don't have to take that. I wouldn't."

"Maybe you're right," Sally said wearily. "I should think about it. But that's about all the change I can handle for one day." She grinned at Jane. "We still got each other. Let's go get some coffee."

❧

"So." Paulie Lassiter shook his head. He was getting worked up. Here in the Century City offices of his extremely high-priced corporate lawyers, he was surrounded by suits, and not one of them was coming up with any damn solutions!

"What do we do? We gotta fix this." His stare said, *You* gotta fix this.

"I don't know, Paulie. These accounts . . . they're fiction."

"Fiction!" he snorted. "Three accounting firms signed 'em."

"Yeah, but your CFO was cooking the books."

"I told you, I fired the sonofabitch."

"That won't do it." Lionel Javits, head of the lawyers, pushed his horn-rimmed spectacles up on his nose. "You have to notify the feds . . . the SEC . . . the regulatory authorities. The stock is going to go through the floor. Jack Lessing is going to jail."

"Damn right he is," Paulie snorted, as the lawyers exchanged looks. "My concern now is to save the stock. Nobody's selling, not while this is going on."

Ugh. He hated delegating. A month away to look at a new field, some possible strikes in northern Canada, and what happens? His asshole executives cook the books. Paulie Lassiter was an *oilman,* not a damned accountant. Billion-dollar company and he was having to do every little thing himself. He mopped his brow, struggling with his breath. Anger was not his usual emotion.

"Paulie, they already did. Most of your board, even the non-execs. They've been quietly dumping stock for the last eighteen months. It's your workers who are going to be ruined." Javits paused. "And if you haven't been selling, then it doesn't look good for you either."

"But at least it proves you're honest," a junior suit piped up brightly. "*You* won't be going to jail!"

Javits glared at him.

Paulie glanced outside at the bright blue sky. It seemed such a normal day in L.A. How could everything look normal when his world was coming apart?

"That *can't* be right," he explained patiently. "We're not some paper company, not some pyramid scheme of a crooked trader on Wall Street. We got *assets.* Oilfields. Six in Texas, one in Ghada, maybe a new one in Canada . . ."

"Doesn't cover the expansion into natural gas . . . the pipeline in Kazakhstan that was smashed by terrorists. Your corporate policy was breached."

"Not enough security."

"And four of the Texas fields have dried up."

"Lassiter Oil's been trading pretty much on its reputation. And some fancy footwork."

"Your executives have been living pretty high on the hog, Paulie."

Well, he knew *that*.

"But the money was there," he said weakly. His heart started thumping. A picture of his wife, doing the breakfast cooking herself, chattering about Sally's party, floated into his vision. How the hell would he explain this to her? He'd never disappointed Mona.

"No, it wasn't, Paulie," Lionel Javits said gently.

"'It was a fraud by the finance division."

The junior suit was piping up again. Eager to explain in mostly words of one syllable. "Bad accounting. Debt off the books. It created a false market in our shares."

"Fraud?" Paulie ignored Javits's death stare at his employee. That was something he *did* understand. "We hid debt? You mean my workers . . . the pension fund . . ."

"It's bankrupt, Paulie. In fact it's looking to me like the entire company is going belly up. We'll need to show you are an innocent party. You didn't sign off on the accounts personally. Don't speak to anyone. I'll contact the authorities myself . . . you say, 'On the advice of counsel I assert my fifth amendment rights not to incriminate myself . . .'"

Paulie Lassiter felt needles in his left arm, then a huge stabbing pain in his chest. He couldn't breathe.

"Ugggh," he groaned, and struggled to his feet. A glass-topped coffee table crashed to the ground.

"Paulie!" Lionel Javits shrieked. "My God! He's having a heart attack!"

"Call 911!"

"Aspirin—it's in the cupboard—*get* it," the lawyer screamed.

But it was too late. Paulie, clutching ineffectually at his chest, gasped and tumbled forward, the blocked blood rushing to his face. Two lawyers dived on him and attempted to roll him over, start CPR.

"Leave it," Javits said. He found he had tears in his eyes. That was a massive coronary—you didn't need to be a doc to see it.

Paulie Lassiter was very dead.

And Lionel Javits knew what was coming—for Lassiter Corporation and for Paulie's family. Ruin—lawsuits—total humiliation—ostracism.

He liked Paulie. Paulie was dead now. And Javits thought he was better off that way.

~~~

Paulie Lassiter's heart attack was big news.

But the bigger news was the collapse of the company.

Jane watched, horrified, on her TV, as the squad cars proceeded to Green Gables; as a black-clad, half-fainting Mona was taken into police custody, accompanied by her lawyer; as Sally, a blanket thrown over her head to protect her from the paparazzi, joined her.

She'd called—of course. But the phone had been disconnected. Sally eventually called Jane, too distraught to speak much; her bubbly vivacity, her lightness, her optimism—everything Jane loved about her—was extinguished, just gone.

Jane almost envied her her agony. Sally was mourning a beloved, kind, attentive father—her grief, welling up from the depths of her soul, reflected real love. Real family. And at least Sally still had a mother.

But there was no doubt her best friend was facing trouble. Very serious trouble.

"The feds are taking everything," Sally confessed to her, once she'd stopped sobbing.

"What do you mean, everything?"

"We're bankrupt. They froze Dad's accounts . . . it all belongs to the creditors."

"But what are they leaving you to live on?"

"The auditors gave us a payment of twelve thousand dollars for the year."

Jane gasped. "A thousand a month?"

Damn—that wouldn't even cover rent on a one-bed in their old neighborhood.

"And they took the cars, the artwork—everything. Mom's still under investigation, but they think she'll likely get off with innocent spouse defense."

"You sound angry."

"Innocent spouse? Makes my dad seem guilty. And he wasn't a crook." Sally sobbed. "Do you know what Julie Manners said to me today?"

A tear rolled down Jane's own cheek, and she fiercely brushed it away. "Don't . . . just don't. You can't go back there. . . ."

"Without you and Helen . . . no way."

And without the cash that had always protected her.

There was a pause. Then Sally said timidly, "Jane, Mom wants to leave town. But I wanted to know if you'd be okay."

Jane made an instantaneous decision, as she heard Sally grieve, and shoved her own mourning aside.

"Sal, I'll be absolutely fine. I decided to move to Washington after all," Jane said. It wasn't true, but she didn't want Sally to worry about her. And she had to figure out her future. Now Sally wouldn't be able to help, Jane had to deal with this. On her own.

"Yeah." Sally sounded so dull, so depressed. "We have to leave, too. Mom's friends—her *so-called* friends—they've all vanished. Ever notice that in this town they treat failure like a disease? One that might be catching?"

A grim smile. "Yes, I have."

"Lucille Wasserman and Kimberley DuPont won't even return Momma's calls, Jane. They're supposed to be her best friends. I told her she needs to get out of Dodge. We got family in Texas we can go to."

"You'll like Texas, right? That's home." Jane desperately tried to put a positive spin on things.

"Was once." Sally sighed. "I think it's better, away from the press. They live in a small town. I'll write you with our new address, okay?"

"Okay," Jane agreed.

"I'll send it care of the embassy."

"Sure. That works."

There was a long, wretched pause. Neither of them wanted to leave the other. But they both knew they had to. Sally needed to take care of her mother, and Jane had to find a future.

"Take care of yourself, hon."

"And you, Sally." Jane was unused to the emotion that washed through her now. First Helen, now Sally. She was losing everything. "Be kind to yourself," she said. Her voice cracked a little, and she hurriedly replaced the receiver.

"Who is it?"

Jane had the door on the chain.

"Repo!"

The man's voice was gruff. She put her head to the fish-eye lens in the door. Yeah—they were repossession guys, uniforms, van, everything.

Jane swallowed hard and opened the door.

"Hi, there!" She gave them a bright smile. "Come on in. You guys want coffee?"

The guy entered with three other men.

"No, thanks." He couldn't meet her eye. "Which way is the living room?"

"Right in there. I unplugged everything. It was mostly too big to move by myself, though, I'm sorry."

"That's fine." Now he looked at her. "You work here . . . you the maid?"

Well, you could hardly call it living here. "Sort of," Jane agreed.

"Let's start with the TV."

The men moved into her living room and got to work. They moved fast—probably used to doing it while under attack. The big-screen TV, the stereo system, the furniture, the statues and antiques—just like house movers, they took everything. Efficient as ants at a picnic.

Jane withdrew into the kitchen and put the kettle on; they had already removed the cappuccino machine.

"Sure you won't take that coffee?"

"No, thanks. We got to get to West Hollywood." The leader sighed and wiped away some sweat. "At least they didn't have the family here; that's the worst. Crying and begging, you know? Like, have a little dignity. Not *my* fault you fucked your life up."

"Right," Jane agreed. "That's so pathetic."

"The bed . . ." He looked back into her room. "That's not on my sheet—the inflatable bed."

"Yeah, I think that belongs to the daughter. She picked it up after the dad bought the farm." Jane smiled. "Maybe she knew you guys were coming!"

"Cool—we can leave that, I guess. And you can keep that kettle!" He grinned generously at her. "They won't notice a sixteen-buck kettle in my office."

"Thanks. You guys have a great day."

Jane saw them to the door. She shut it, stood quietly with her head against the wood, and listened as the truck's doors slammed and it drove away.

Finally, she was sure she was alone. She glanced around her empty house—not hers, anymore; the embassy had made it clear that the lease was up, end of the month. It was bare, stripped of everything down to the last framed print. There was nothing but the cheap single bed and the white goods in the kitchen.

Oh, and her coffee mug.

She went over to the bed and flopped down on it. And finally, she allowed the tears to come.

⌒

When she was done, she went and took a shower—at least the hot water was still on, and she had a towel and clothes in a suitcase. Sure, the embassy wanted to "look after" her—on *its* terms.

Jane was not into that. Stuck in some hideous Washington two-bit school, where everybody would know who she was? Laugh at her? Humiliate her?

Hell, no. School was a brutal exercise in social Darwinism. Jane Morgan had no room in her heart for further bruising. And what would she get out of it, with her grades disturbed and her college plans disrupted?

She stepped out of the shower, carefully brushed her teeth, and got dressed. Then she let herself out the back door with the key Consuela had left for her when she was fired.

"You'll be okay," her former nanny had told her. "I never saw anybody like you."

Jane had bit her lip, to stop it from trembling; a rare moment of weakness. They'd never been close, but at least Consuela was familiar. And now she was gone, too.

Jane glanced at the driveway: empty now, like the house. She was so young . . . but . . . everything in her world had fallen apart.

Her father—useless, unloving, selfish. But *hers*. Deep down, she had hoped that one day they could forge a relationship. When he was retired, and she was grown up.

That chance had gone. Forever.

And her lifestyle. At least that had been great: independent, stylish, and rich. Her driver, her maid, her nanny, the beach house, the security guards . . .

Miss Milton's, for heaven's sake. Who'd have ever thought she'd appreciate her lousy, unacademic school?

But the money—she felt she could have done without that. In other circumstances. Because, at least, for some time now, there had been the girls.

Her best friends—no, her *family*.

And, like her father, like Consuela, like the money, her friends had gone. Just like that. One blink, and they'd evaporated. . . .

Helen. Vanished the day after the party. And now, gone back to Egypt to get married. To a distant cousin.

To get *married*! She'd never spoken of the guy to them. Not a word. Nor of the fact she was thinking of leaving the country for good. The three girls were inseparable; how could Helen not tell them? She hadn't left an address, a phone number—nothing. Just vanished.

Helen Yanna had left Jane's life the same way she'd arrived—quietly; definitely.

And Sally—her older friend? Far different, and far worse. She ached to see Helen, to cry on her shoulder, but at least Jane knew Helen was happy—was doing okay, getting married. For Sally, life had exploded, in almost the same way it had done for her.

Now Jane sat in her still-neat garden, on the iron bench they hadn't bothered to remove, and looked at the sea. The ocean was clear, blue, and immense. It crashed, and crashed, eternally, on the beach below her; mindless, soothing noise.

She had come out here to think.

The disasters, one of top of the other. No friends now. No money. No contacts. At the end of this month, no house.

She was entirely on her own.

Getting a lawyer would be the right start. Emancipation—Jane read about that in the library. A teen petitioning to be designated a legal adult. Usually due to marriage—she'd stay well away from that. If you got too close to anybody, you exposed yourself. They left—and your heart shattered.

Once she had the important pieces of paper, she'd be two things: an adult and an American. She could go anywhere she liked in the country, do whatever she wanted.

Her first change—no more bookworm.

Jane had learned a hard lesson, and learned it fast. Money counted in this world. When she'd had privileged access to it, Jane had despised money. She'd only sought prestige, position as a tenured professor somewhere.

Now, she wanted revenge. And that meant cash. The kind that Paulie Lassiter used to have—but legitimate, all hers. The kind that protected schoolgirls from taunts, that enabled people to fulfill their every whim. The kind that could help get her own back on Julie, and all those snobby bitches at school. That could help Sally deal with the rich friends who'd seen fit to dump a devastated and grieving widow.

Money was protection. Money was control.

Money was something *women* didn't have.

Yes . . .

Jane watched the ocean and let that thought sink in. Plenty of rich girls in her orbit . . . except they weren't, were they? It was always somebody else's money. Sally had nothing of her own—it was all in Daddy's accounts. When they were cut off, so was she.

Helen Yanna—daughter of a wealthy middle-class man—now married, apparently, to another wealthy middle-class man. Passing from one comfortable lifestyle to the next, but not under her own steam. Jane worried about her. What happened if she fell out with her husband? What happened if her father cut her off? Helen, at school, had been bright, quiet, God-fearing, and shy. Yes, there was a core of determination—but still. The world didn't prepare people like Helen—or Sally—for the moment the Jericho walls crashed into rubble.

What would Sally do now? Regroup . . . heal . . . then marry somebody? She still had those blonde Barbie looks, and right now it seemed she'd be reduced to trading on them.

Jane didn't want that for herself. No way. She didn't want to depend on some university board, either. She was here—by the ocean, in L.A. And she still had assets. Brains—thank God, for everything stemmed from that. Beauty—not like Sally's, but she would never go back to her dowdy self.

Sally had once told her glamour was a weapon. It got you through the front door. After that, your brains had to take over.

It was time to grow up.

Jane saw things much more clearly now. She went inside, picked up the phone book now lying on the dusty floor of the living room, and called the DMV.

"Hi. I'd like to make an appointment for a driving test."

⌇

"Then there's the matter of my fee."

The lawyer looked at Jane down his nose, expectantly.

She sighed. The office was filthy; there was a fat bluebottle buzzing lazily and hopelessly against the glass; the windows were dusty; and he had papers all across his desk.

"Two hundred," she said, hopefully.

"Two hundred!" He snorted. "*Fifteen* hundred, *and* that's a discount because you're a minor." He leaned across his desk and leered at Jane. "In *one* sense. In another, of course, you're legal. . . ."

She knew exactly what he meant.

"Maybe we could work something out." His gaze traveled slowly up her legs.

"Look, Mr. Richards." Jane stood up, wanting to get away from the stare, but he just transferred it to her breasts, so she took a walk to the window. "Can I speak frankly to you?"

"You can be as frank as you want to, honey." Josh Richards regularly screwed desperate women who couldn't pay him any other way. Mexicans mostly. And seeing as how he had bad breath, wonky teeth, and a widow's peak at only thirty-one, it was the only way he got any play.

None of those *mamacitas* were as hot as this limey, though. Damn! She was fine, with her delicately styled hair and peaches-and-cream skin. He dug the accent, too, all cold and haughty. She'd look great bent over his desk with that—

"You're a loser," Jane said.

That brought him up short. He blinked, not sure he'd heard her right.

"Excuse me?" He was outraged.

"You're a loser," Jane repeated flatly. "Going nowhere fast. It's why I picked you to handle my case. I can't afford a decent lawyer, and you desperately need some work."

"Two hundred ain't work."

"I mean real work. Cases. You need your name in the papers. Nobody's going to hire you for so much as a quickie divorce if you slob around like this." Disdainfully, she lifted one of last week's papers, the sports section, lying on the edge of his desk. "You've got to get yourself a secretary—not somebody who's going to sue you for sexual harassment, either. A neat office, a decent suit, and some real clients."

Richards wanted to tell the schoolgirl to take a hike. What a ballbuster! That twitch between his legs had vanished like she was pouring cold water on it.

But it was true . . . he did need work. He was already behind on the rent here.

"All that takes cash. And I got clients like you who don't want to pay it."

"I bring more than cash. I bring you a *chance*. Represent me, and you'll get publicity. You'll have a major client. I can guarantee you press coverage. In fact, forget the two hundred. You'll do it pro bono—much better PR that way. And once it's taken care of, I'll give you a fabulous quote."

"A quote?"

"Yes. Let me see." Jane composed herself and looked at him; her eyes were suddenly brimming.

" 'After my father died the Brits abandoned me,' " she said, her voice breaking. " 'Nobody cared—nobody would help me. Except Josh Richards . . . I know what they say about lawyers but he's one who *really cares*. You can trust Josh Richards. I owe this all to him.' "

She brushed away the tears and snapped back into business mode.

"Wow," he said, impressed. "You should be an actress."

With Jane's looks, she heard that ten times a day.

"No, thanks. Five thousand chicks chasing twelve low-paying jobs."

She had no intention of getting into that; a totally ephemeral business, where success often depended on pure chance.

"How about it?" She snapped her fingers. "Focus, Josh, focus!"

He blinked. He had the uncomfortable feeling he was being railroaded. By a *schoolgirl*.

On the other hand, she did sound like she knew exactly what she was doing.

"I take you on—for free. And you organize some publicity?"

"Hey, you read the papers. Even if you start at the back."

He defended himself against Jane's contempt. "I like baseball. . . ."

"My father was a high-ranking British diplomat who stole lots of money and sold lots of secrets. They had the goods on him. He likely would have got the death penalty."

As she recounted this tale, Jane Morgan seemed almost totally devoid of emotion. Josh flinched—the chick was a robot.

"Anyway, he cheated them—flung himself out of a top-floor window. In full evening dress."

"So where's your mom?"

"Dead." Jane shrugged. "I never knew her. And before you ask, there are no aunts or other sundry relatives. My father was estranged from his only brother. I'm orphaned and on my own."

"I'm sorry," he said, awkwardly.

"It's been that way for a while. Point is, I don't inherit a dime. And I need to get to work. The 'minor' thing is getting in the way. The embassy doesn't want any more bad publicity; they're trying to force me into a lousy Washington school and a cramped little apartment."

"What's wrong with that? At least it's a place to stay, right?"

Jane didn't bother to answer. Maybe he was the sort of person that accepted "at least." She wasn't.

"I want to be a legal adult. And I want U.S. citizenship. I've been here almost all my childhood. I'm naturalized. You take care of the emancipation and get me a pass from the INS. I'll get you great PR for your pro bono work for the traitor's orphaned daughter. Deal?"

She strode back to the desk and offered him her manicured hand.

"Deal." He couldn't suppress his curiosity. "Where are you staying right now? Do you need someplace? I have a couch."

"They're still paying the rent on my house here. I'm fine."

"Whatever you say."

"I'm serious about this," Jane told him as she turned to leave. "I want emancipation. Legal adult status. I need that to work. No time-wasting—you file those papers this morning. Or else I'll walk down the street and find myself another hungry lawyer."

"Don't do that," Richards said hastily. "I'm on it—I'll file this afternoon."

"Good." She walked out, closing the door behind her.

Damn! He pushed a hand through his thinning hair. Why was he worried about getting fired from a job he was doing for free?

But Richards knew the girl was one hundred percent right. It could be a publicity bonanza for him. A lifeline.

When she came in through the door, he'd only seen two things: a fee or a screw.

But Jane Morgan had her eyes on the bigger picture. And he suddenly knew that this was his one shot. Working for a seventeen-year-old schoolgirl who wanted to grow up fast.

He didn't want to blow it. He turned his computer on and got to work.

⁓

"So what do you think?"

Think? She thought the place was a dump.

Studio apartment, above a dive of a record store on Sunset Strip. Winos and crackheads outside the door. Tiny, filthy bathroom, with cracked shower tiles, mildew, and a stain in the loo.

"It has a separate kitchen." The fat landlady puffed her cheeks out. "Y'can see if ya like."

Kitchen! What a joke. A tiny alcove, one cupboard, and an electric socket.

"Fridge is broke," the landlady said succinctly. "Y'can buy a microwave to cook with. They go for cheap outside Farmers Market, got a wetback store selling secondhand electrics."

Jane watched as a fat black cockroach scuttled up the kitchen wall. She shuddered.

"Five hundred a month and same as deposit, minimum one-year lease."

"Forget it. Two hundred and no deposit."

"You forget it." She was outraged. "Get out, you're wasting my time."

Jane stood firm. "Think about it, lady. You won't get anyone in here but addicts. And they'll just trash the property. Now what *I* am is an English lady down on her luck. You rent to me, and I'll clean up this shit-hole. No more roaches—it'll smell good and it'll look good. I'll make it bohemian and funky, and when I'm gone you can rent to a student at a thousand. Or, you could sell it—having a human being live here will add fifty grand to the price at least. I don't do drugs and I'm not a hooker. Plus, I pay cash—no contracts—meaning no taxes for *you*. And you get to kick me out whenever you feel like it."

"I dunno." The fat woman hummed and hawed. "Two hundred ain't enough."

"It's all I got, so it'll have to do." Jane reached into her purse and pulled out two hundred-dollar bills. She waved the portraits of Benjamin Franklin temptingly in front of the owner. "By rights, you ought to be paying *me*. What I'm going to do for this place is like a month of Molly Maid *and* a free contractor. Come on, you haven't been able to move this apartment, you told me yourself it's been on the market eighteen months—even the welfare types don't want it. Two hundred, I'll only be here three months, and there'll be something rentable when I've gone."

"What's gonna happen after three months?"

Jane tossed her head. "By then, I'll have a real job."

"Ha! That's what they all say." But she snatched up the money. "Three months, girlie, then the price goes up to five hundred. Call me if you want to do porno; I got a cousin who's always looking."

"Thanks," Jane said wryly. "I'll bear that in mind."

"You get free electric—no heat. Here's the keys." She fished out a couple of grimy copper Yales and threw them at Jane, who caught them in one hand.

"Enjoy," the woman said, bustling out.

Jane exhaled. She stood by the window, watching until the landlady drove away. Then she turned round and went through her handbag.

Let's see . . . a grand total of . . . three hundred and twenty-two dollars.

All she had in the world.

Carefully Jane hid the money under a squeaking floorboard,

after she had extracted thirty bucks. There was a Shop Smart within walking distance—great, since she didn't have a car. They sold the cheapest of everything. And Jane needed to invest in some sponges, some serious disinfectant, and the cheapest new bedding she could find.

She stripped the bed, emptied the stinking fridge and the garbage pail, nearly gagging, and hauled the black bin-liner downstairs. Then she came back up, threw the window open, and locked the door.

For a second, despair overcame her, but only for a second. No—this wasn't bottoming out. This was independence, she told herself. The start of a brand-new life. And she, Jane, was going to make a go of it.

⁓

That night, she worked her tail off. Mopping, scrubbing, even painting her windowsill. Jane pulled the dusty net curtains from their slide and washed them in the sink, with a capful of bleach. While the drunks and hookers fought and screamed below her, and her floor shook with the dull thud-thud of the booming bass from rap tracks on the stereo, Jane cleaned. She wore out three scrubbers and got her hands raw from rubbing alcohol. The stinking refrigerator she emptied of bugs and droppings, and closed it tight. There'd be no way to get rid of roaches other than keeping zero food in the house.

When the place was done, she unpacked her other purchases. Amazing what you could get for a dollar or two in the bargain bins. A shade for the bare lightbulb that hung from her ceiling; it transformed the bleak glare into a pretty, peach-colored light. Fresh sheets on the air mattress—not exactly matching, but all basically white or cream; a pillow; and a comforter. Gave it a tone-on-tone look that was perfectly acceptable. A snap-up wardrobe made of fabric and plastic, with a zipper, and hangers for her clothes. A cheap Mexican rug, for a splash of color. A shower curtain, discontinued, clear plastic and decorated with little white suns and moons.

Finally, Jane had blown a whole two dollars and fifty cents on a cheerful yellow plastic vase and a bunch of carnations.

She hung up her curtains, closed the window, and put water into the vase; the flowers sat on top of a white cloth on her chest of drawers. No TV, but she didn't want to see the news anyway.

She had about as much reality as she could handle.

Carefully she undressed, folded away her clothes, and showered again, this time using a tiny amount of cheap coconut bubble bath. It felt so good to be clean.

On her kitchen table lay an application form. Shop Smart—always looking for helpers—"greeters," they called them. Paid minimum wage. That was fine by Jane. All she was asking for was someplace to start. She had a driver's license—tomorrow she would be legal. Jane knew quite a bit about Shop Smart—a large company with lots of potential. She had no qualms about getting in on the ground floor.

Jane didn't plan to stay there long.

⁓

"Jane! Jane!"

"Babe! Over here!"

She emerged from the courthouse to find a small knot of reporters and two local TV cameras. Dressed in her best suit and carefully made up, Jane walked out onto the courthouse steps, her head high, one arm threaded through her lawyer's.

Richard was wearing a suit, too. He beamed—he looked almost presentable.

"Can we get a comment?"

"Do you blame the Brits?"

"Jane!"

She held up a hand. "Thank you, ladies and gentlemen. No, I don't blame anybody. I have a very good lawyer, who worked on this case for free. And I'm grateful to be recognized as both an adult and an American."

"How does it feel to lose all that cash?"

"I never expected to have anything handed to me." She smiled dead at the camera. "Tomorrow I'll be going for a job at Shop Smart. I want to work my way up, and that's an all-American company."

They snapped and took pictures, and eventually drifted away. Josh Richards was ecstatic.

"Hey, thanks, babe. I think one of those guys was from the *Times.*"

"I don't doubt it."

"You want to get lunch?" he asked hopefully. Hell, she *was* an adult now—totally legal in every way. "I'm buying. . . ."

"No, thank you. I have work to do."

"Thought you didn't have a job," he sulked.

"That's the work—finding one."

He had a brainwave. "Hey, I'll give you a job. Come be my assistant. I bet you could clean the office up real nice—you'd look great in reception. Clients would love you."

"No, thanks. I don't need all the staring. And I don't want to be anybody's assistant."

"In Shop Smart you get minimum wage—*if* they take you on. I heard the Sunset store is full. It's menial work. And no lunch break."

"Yes, but they have a management program," Jane said. "Goodbye, Josh. Maybe we'll meet again."

She strode away from him, toward the bus stop. Living in L.A., no car, no cash—still as confident as all hell.

"Maybe," he muttered. But somehow, he doubted it.

That girl was made for bigger things than him.

~⌒⌒

Mrs. Watson saw Jane coming, and smiled despite herself.

"Good morning. I was wondering if any vacancies had opened up?"

The English girl was well dressed and groomed. Good accent, too—the customers would love her classy tone.

"Saw you on TV. You said nice things about Shop Smart. My boss said if you came back to give you a job."

"That's great!" Jane felt a wash of relief surge through her. "If you've got a uniform, I can get changed right away."

"You need to fill out a form first."

Jane opened her purse, took out the neatly completed form, and handed it to the recruiter. Disbelievingly, the woman scanned it.

"Damn, girl. You in a hurry?"

Jane didn't reply.

"There are uniforms in back. Put one on and clock in. You're going to be a greeter. Seven-day trial, be here at seven a.m. tomorrow. If you're late, you're fired. Got it?"

"Yes, ma'am," Jane said. She hurried away into the back, before her new boss could change her mind.

⌒

"Good morning! Welcome to Shop Smart. I hope you have a lovely day."

Janice Esposito, junior manager, sourly watched the new girl at the front door. She was standing behind a video rack—Jane Morgan couldn't see her. Ticking off performance stats. Looking for a fault.

Because Janice couldn't believe the new girl really *wanted* a shitty job like this. She'd read the papers—an ambassador's daughter? celebrity orphan? Right, like she was really poor. Why the hell would she want a minimum-wage job that was strictly for the unqualified? The hours were easier at McDonald's.

Janice instantly disliked Jane Morgan. But she had a job to do, as well. And it involved ticking off little boxes. Plus, sometimes they checked up on their own human resource people, so you couldn't fake it—not to mention there were cameras at the entrances.

Jane Morgan had learned something. Sell the sizzle, not the steak.

Bosses already loved her. She'd brought them free PR. They wanted her to succeed—the new citizen, the American dream.

Friendliness—check.

Neatness—check—not a hair out of place; looked like she'd been wearing that uniform for years.

Smile—check. Crocodiles had smaller smiles than this chick.

Enthusiasm—check.

Janice's pen hovered as she watched Jane Morgan quickly glance at her watch. Finally, a no-no—she was *supposed* to be looking out for new customers, one hundred percent of the time.

"Good *afternoon!*" Jane Morgan beamed. "Welcome to Shop Smart!"

"Well, would ya look at that, Dick," the portly matron said to her husband as they waddled in past Janice and her clipboard. "Bang on twelve noon and she switches to 'afternoon.' Ain't that a kick!"

"Yeah, real impressive," her husband said. He glanced behind him at the check-in girl's *impressive* figure.

Janice sighed. Unfortunately, in a job where there was no such thing as taking the initiative, this girl had just found a way to do it.

There was a box at the base of her form. "Consider for promotion?"

Reluctantly, she ticked it.

⌁

Eileen Watson looked at Janice Esposito.

"So, the management program." They were both nursing giant cups of coffee. Janice, despite this chemical assistance, was looking lethargic and depressed. "We're supposed to hunt talent from the shop floor."

"Mick Martin's ready. He does a lot of good work in layout."

"Okay." Eileen ticked another box. "Any more this month?"

The question hung in the air. They both knew. Neither wanted to say.

"Not really." Janice was defiant.

"Jane Morgan?" Eileen asked, gently.

"I think she's a little smug." Janice had scoured her sheets for something more substantial on Jane, but had come up empty. She was blocking this promotion on sheer personal dislike. "I recommend you wait another month. And if she's absolutely clean then, promote her."

Eileen didn't hate Jane like Janice did, but she also was not too keen on seeing chirpy young foreign girls advancing.

"Sure," she said coolly. "Let Jane keep it clean for one more month."

⁓

Jane didn't do a lot of crying. Mostly, she was too tired. The check at the end of the week was unbelievably tiny; man, she resented those taxes and social security payments—yet she still had to save from it. She needed a deposit on a car. Never mind how much of a wreck—she had to have *something*.

The minutiae of grown-up life was unbelievable. So much to do—forms to fill out, stuff to organize. Now that her citizenship had come through, she had to get herself a social security number . . . a driver's license . . . a checking account. Credit was the worst; America trapped you—if you didn't have any, it was hard to get any.

She managed it somehow: a starter card at an exorbitant rate. Yet your score only rose if you used it. Daylight robbery, but Jane started an account, and used it whenever she could—but carefully—and always made her payments on time.

All through Jane Morgan's childhood, she'd been living large. Now she was living lean. It was amazing what you could get for free if you were persistent. Most every day, Jane ate in the staff cafeteria, where food was plentiful and cheap. It was hard to keep healthy—with the disgusting, calorie-laden stodge they served the workers—but she managed it, always opting for the fresh fruit and salad, taking just a little of the protein-based dish and leaving the glutinous baked desserts. There was no private gym in her life—but she still had her clothes, and they included a pair of Nikes and a comfortable jogging suit. Jane ran daily, every morning at six a.m.; a golden hour, when the junkies had finally crawled home to bed and the regular joes hadn't yet surfaced. She ran up and down the Sunset Strip, ignoring the detritus of needles and beer bottles, keeping her eyes fixed on the sun rising over the horizon.

And when she got back to the apartment, Jane forced herself to do forty push-ups before her stretch routine.

Punishing. But energetic. When she got in to work there were free bagels and orange juice—a daily shot of C—and she had the energy she needed to push her through the day.

Because on minimum wage, you needed all the hours they'd give you.

When she finished greeting, smile never wavering, there was lunch—ten minutes flat—and a bathroom break. Next, Jane swapped uniforms and went to the checkout till, where she worked two shifts. She got home nights at nine p.m., showered, and tumbled into bed.

It was a disciplined routine. After a while, it became automatic. And with the free stuff she got from the store—spoiled items, unwanted bottles of shampoo, frayed T-shirts you could sleep in—Jane spent next to nothing. Rent and utilities—that was it. She worked seven days, and actually watched her savings start to mount.

One day blended into another. It was mindless. And that suited her fine. One day soon, according to all Shop Smart's procedures and guidelines, she would be recommended for the management program—and all this drudgery would be over.

Jane Morgan didn't want to do too much thinking. She was ready to go with the flow.

❦

"Let's go see her." Julie Manners stretched out on her air mattress in the pool.

"What do you mean? She's gone." Emma Lightfoot laughed meanly. "Ain't that a bitch?"

The girls extended their legs and applied a little oil. Got to love those private beaches! There were some fine-looking preppy boys across the way checking them out.

"Did I tell you guys? My parents got me a birthday present," said Maureen Smith, tossing her silky black hair.

"We know. A yellow Maserati. You told us already," Emma complained.

"Not that one, another one. Season tickets to the Dodgers. A *box*."

"Oooh," Julie said, instantly seeing the possibilities. "Great for invites; let's have a party there."

What guy could resist tickets to the Dodgers?

"There are some UCLA guys coming. . . . I heard the governor's son was going to be there."

"Boooring."

"And Pete Easterman, you know, from the new Arnold flick?"

"That's more like it!" Julie patted her acolyte's arm. "Definitely a little party. I could like baseball."

"Get the guys to teach it to you," Emma said, seeing herself playing dumb—men *loved* the pouty, little-girl-lost look.

"Right. And we'll drive some of them in your Maserati. And my Jeep. It'll be way cool."

Not exactly Sally Lassiter–style cool, but what the hell? Sally was gone. All three witches were gone.

Julie returned to her theme.

"It'll be even cooler if we go to Shop Smart to pick up the party gear . . . invitations and stuff."

"Shop Smart?" Emma looked at Julie like she was mad. "My mom knows this great woman on La Cienega who will do invites, like, with calligraphy and pressed flowers and shit like that."

"Yes, but *Jane Morgan* doesn't work for her." Julie gave her friends a silky smile. "You girls heard the news, right? Hoity-toity Miss Jane is a *greeter* on minimum wage! Right on Sunset!" Julie snickered at the delicious thought. "We should go see her," she repeated, cruelly. "It'll be fun, let's have her wrap our purchases! Call us 'ma'am' . . . bow and scrape like a little shopgirl. Which she is. And if she acts up, we can report her to her bosses. The customer is always right, you know," Julie cackled.

"Oooh." Maureen's eyes widened. "You are *evil*."

"Come on, you know she deserves it. Don't you remember how *mean* she was to all of us? She stopped you getting invited to that damn party."

"Yeah, it's true," Melissa said angrily. That still burned. "Let's go there and show her who's boss!"

The girls laughed.

"I have the new car parked outside," Maureen said, eager to curry favor.

Julie rewarded her with a smile. "I like it—let's have her walk our groceries to your Maserati, and if she does a *real* good job, maybe she'll get a tip."

"Yeah—like two dollars!" Emma said, and laughed.

~

Jane was exhausted. The night before, Will Fox, the student, had canceled his checkout shift and her boss had asked her to stay—till eleven. She made it a practice never to say no, but she couldn't cope with only six hours' sleep. Not on her schedule.

But she'd done her running, just like always, and here she was—trying to smile, trying to be effusive.

One thing about Shop Smart—they *always* watched you.

It was why she'd chosen them.

But Jane couldn't afford an off day.

~

Rhodri Evans looked over his store carefully. Hollywood—an important location. They were expanding from the Midwest, moving into the cities. He wanted to keep the prices rock-bottom, but soften the image, away from vast concrete warehouses in the middle of nowhere.

This store had been open for two years, and he wanted it to succeed.

Good—so far it seemed busy.

He walked through the front doors.

"Good morning, welcome to Shop Smart." A young African-American college kid shook his hand with a perfunctory smile.

Evans was not impressed, but it was a perennial problem. They didn't pay enough to attract the best staff.

"Good morning! Welcome to Shop Smart. Great to see you!"

He turned his head, distracted. A young woman with a foreign accent, beautiful enough to be a model, was standing at the opposite door. She was smiling as if she'd just won the lottery, and her uniform looked like it had come from the dry cleaner's.

"Who *is* that?" he asked the greeter.

"Jane. Y'all can't have her number, though," the kid said wearily.

"Do lots of people ask?"

"Lots of *men*," he said with contempt. "She's all about work, though. Wants to get noticed. What the hell she's doing here I don't know. She could have got work lots of places."

"Okay. Thanks."

Morgan walked into the store and pretended to browse. He never began an evaluation without actually doing some shopping. You could read all the management consultant reports in the world, and it wouldn't help you.

Jane . . . Jane who?

He stood in front of a rack of VHS players, looking confused, rubbing his chin. Nobody came to help him. One black mark.

The beautiful girl was still there, smiling and shaking hands as though the customers were long-lost relatives.

Evans was fascinated. He edged back to the front of the store and pretended to be interested in a pile of discount khaki pants, made in Taiwan from one hundred percent polyester.

"Good morning! Welcome."

"It's great to have you at Shop Smart today!"

"Welcome, what a beautiful day for shopping!"

Wow! She was always beaming, always performing. He was impressed.

"Well, well, well, look who it is."

There was a pause. He looked up from the polyester pants to see a small knot of beautifully dressed teenagers—girls who were far too rich to be shopping in *this* store. A slim girl wearing Prada, another in a Chanel jacket twinned with designer jeans . . .

"Good morning, Jane," said the lead girl cattily. The others sniggered. "Hey, great place. Nice to see you've landed on your feet."

Abandoning his pretense, Rhodri Evans stepped back from the table and folded his arms, watching.

"Good morning, Julie," Jane said stiffly. "Do you need help with something?"

"Actually yes," said Maureen Smith, smirking. "We're having a little party. My mom and dad bought me box seats at Dodger Stadium. Some of the boys from Fulbrook High are coming along."

"We want napkins and party items."

"They're in aisle three." Jane gritted her teeth, but her face was flushing from the humiliation. "I'll get somebody to help you."

"Noooo," Julie purred. "*You* help us. Then you can carry it all out to Maureen's brand-new Maserati. What are you driving these days, Janey? Or do you take the bus?"

"The name's Jane, and I'm afraid I can't leave my post."

As Evans watched, a pudgy woman, a store manager, bustled over to see what the fuss was about. What was her name? Oh, yeah—Eileen something. Watson. And a personnel woman. Janice Esposito. She had an unpleasant look on her face.

"Hello, ladies," cried Mrs. Watson heartily. "Are you getting good service here today?"

"I'm afraid this young woman was saying she was too busy to help us," Julie pouted. "Which is a shame because we were going to spend a *lot* of money in this store. Oh, well—guess you don't want our business."

"Jane, is that true?" snapped Janice.

Evans didn't like the way this was going. He moved toward the knot of women. Other customers had started to stare.

"You know," the girl called Maureen said nastily to Jane, "if you had been willing to help we'd have given you a tip. On *your* wages I'm sure you could have used it."

"Of *course* she could have, ma'am—I'm so sorry you've had this trouble today," Janice said triumphantly.

"That wasn't the case," Jane said calmly. She struggled to keep her voice under control. "I told these young ladies where their goods were located and I was going to fetch an assistant to help them, since I'm a greeter this morning. . . ."

"We don't *argue* with the customers!" Janice snapped. "Get back into the staff room immediately, Ms. Morgan!"

"That's right," Julie triumphed with a little snicker. Her eyes danced over Jane with total contempt. "Get back inside immediately, *Jane,* so I can be sure you're fired from your crappy little job. Go on, get!"

Jane stood there, and Evans watched her tense shoulders slump, and painful tears of humiliation fill her eyes. He understood at once.

This was a black, bleak moment in this young girl's life.

How could the other girls be so foul? And why weren't his staff standing up for their young colleague? He'd heard staff morale was at rock bottom in L.A.

Perhaps this was why.

"Didn't you hear me? You move," spat Janice Esposito, her own face suffusing with pleasurable outrage. "What do you think you're doing?"

That was it. He strode toward them and addressed his personnel manager.

"What do you think *you're* doing?"

Rhodri Evans stood in front of the group, angry. He glanced at his young greeter—tears were spilling from her eyes now, but she was standing her ground, even as they all glared at her. The ugly looks of satisfaction on the faces of the rich girls annoyed him intensely.

"You did not observe the situation," he said coldly to Janice Esposito, "and you are making a scene in front of the customers."

"Who the hell are you? Security!" said Janice, flushing scarlet and snapping her fingers.

Two security guards, who'd been watching the altercation idly, wandered over.

"This guy's *leaving,*" snapped Janice.

"No." Evans withdrew his wallet and handed the guard his business card. "My name is Rhodri Evans, I'm senior vice president of marketing, western region. And you're fired," he said to Janice. "Human Resources will be in touch to return your personal effects."

"You can't do that," she hissed. "I *am* Human Resources."

"Not anymore." He nodded, and the guard took her elbow.

Janice went bright red. "I'll sue you!"

"Try it." Evans shrugged. "Don't you know the whole thing's on camera? And these young *women*"—his tone was deliberately insulting—"are also leaving," he said the second security guard. "They attempted to harass a member of our staff. They aren't welcome here."

"Fuck you!" Julie Manners went bright pink in the face. "My father will—"

"Save it. There's a video. The contents of which I very much doubt any of your fathers would wish released to the press. You know, bullying is very unattractive."

"You have no idea who I am," Maureen Smith hissed.

"Sure I do—you're somebody who's just been banned."

He turned to Mrs. Watson as security hustled the shamefaced girls away.

"Who is this young lady?" he asked gently.

"Her name's Jane Morgan, Mr. Evans," she said eagerly. "I hired her myself, and she's always been one of our best workers. I fully supported you just then, Jane, I was just about to step in. . . ."

Sure you were.

Evans turned to Jane. "You handled that well."

"Thank you," she said. He realized her voice had thickened from the tears.

"Mrs. Watson, find another greeter." To Jane he said, "You come with me. I want a word—privately."

Jane fought her tears all the way to the office. It was hard—so hard. Somehow it was easier to be strong when she was being attacked. No damn way she'd let those girls see her crumble. But when this man, this stranger, defended her . . .

The emotional walls she'd erected tumbled down. The hard work, the exhaustion, the low pay—and then, pure humiliation. Jane felt naïve; why hadn't she assumed they'd come looking for her?

Maybe she was being dumb. Maybe she should apply for something in the comfort zone—librarian's assistant, or public school teacher's aid. It would pay higher out of the gate—enough for a real apartment, a secondhand car. But it would be a dead end after that—no career prospects—no advancement.

She had come here with a purpose.

For the first time in her life, Jane Morgan was gambling.

Was she about to win—or lose?

This manager—he'd stood up for her, yeah. But he *was* a guy. She had become adept at brushing aside advances. From customers, from staffers, from other worker bees at the base of the food chain. Funny, what being beautiful did for you. Until Sally made her over, looks weren't a problem Jane Morgan had had to deal with.

Did Rhodri Evans have an ulterior motive? If so, this could be the end. Because she *wasn't* going to sleep with anybody. This guy was major league. He could end her career.

"Right in here." He opened the door. "Take a seat."

"Thanks," she muttered.

Jane drew her legs together and tried to tug down the hem of her Shop Smart uniform's skirt.

"Don't worry." Evans was looking at her sympathetically. "I'm not going to hit on you; I'm gay."

"Oh." She smiled weakly. "That's great! I mean . . ."

"I know what you mean." He studied a file on his desk. "You're seventeen?"

"A legal adult," she said quickly.

"There's a note in your file of how you came to us."

Jane didn't say anything; she waited for him to speak. Evans smiled; that was clever.

"You must have known Shop Smart would take advantage of the free publicity and hire you."

"Yes, I did." She started to feel more confident. "Publicity has value. I traded it for free legal advice, and then this job."

Evans decided he was enjoying himself hugely. When did moments like this ever happen, in his tightly wrapped corporate life? She was a most unusual girl, indeed. Seventeen years old, and, simply from the way she spoke, obviously keenly intelligent. He suspected far more so than himself.

"Alright." Rhodri pushed his chair back and adopted a light frown. "Why were you looking at Shop Smart? We pay low wages . . ."

"Minimum wage."

"And require low skills—we are always oversubscribed for jobs. With your qualifications . . ."

"Firstly, I have no qualifications. I even had to leave high school before I finished."

"You could have been a nanny. There are many rich families in this city who would pay highly for a girl with an English accent, from a good school."

"Nannies aren't senior vice presidents, western region."

"Ah." He grinned. "So that's what it is? You wanted to get into the management program?"

"I wanted to get into *management*," she corrected him. "Get noticed—and promoted."

"You always knew this day would come?" Evans teased her.

But her reply was deadly serious.

"Yes. Because if you do something brilliantly, you'll get noticed. And promoted. If it hadn't been you, it would have been someone else. Eventually."

"And you think you were brilliant, at the door?"

"I know I was," she said confidently.

"So I should make you a manager, huh? Give you a department. Just like that."

"I've worked in this building seven days a week for three months. There's nothing I don't know about this store—and nothing your management program can teach me."

"What do you know about business?"

"Try me. I read the *Economist*."

He arched an eyebrow.

"I do," Jane insisted. "I take a bus to the library every Saturday morning—it's my break from exercise. And I read. Magazines, and the *Wall Street Journal*."

"Amazing," he breathed. He believed her. "Okay, rookie," Evans said. "You're up. Tell me. I put you in charge of women's merchandising. What happens next?"

"I say I want a bigger job."

"What?"

"It's part of the problem. Managers for every section of the store, all fighting for their patch. It's one store. It needs integration, not turf wars."

"Example."

"Electronics are in aisle six. But telephones are in aisle two. You need to store like goods together. Food needs dedicated checkout lines. The layout needs to be thought through—customers shouldn't be able to walk right out. You need tempting, quick-purchase items by the tills, not the same old medley of magazines . . ."

Jane went on, sketching a vision for the store. He listened attentively. The girl made a lot of sense.

"You realize this would mean slashing jobs."

"Slashing a wasted layer of management jobs. For a company so concerned about wages, you waste a ton of money on pencil pushers who don't do anything."

"And how do you know that?"

"I've *watched* them," she said simply. "With the savings, you announce an incentive scheme. Bonuses to staff who get special commendations. And an invitation to study for the management program once they reach a level of excellence. You really need to improve morale. Get some family picnics going, events. Better food—the cafeteria can do a lot better on the same budget."

"How would you improve morale?"

"Shop Smart needs to be an excellent store—that means running it smoothly. When I'm manager, I will actually watch staff.

All the staff, including the backroom operators, the caterers, the security guards. Rewards and employee excellence certificates for those that do best. Nobody will put the extra effort into it if they think they'll get nothing back."

He nodded. "I'm not going to make you a manager."

Jane sighed, disappointed.

"It's too much of a risk. I take a seventeen-year-old-girl—plucked from the greeters—and put her in charge of a multimillion-dollar store? If you fail, I become a laughingstock. And get fired."

"I see." She did.

"So what I'm going to do is test you. I'm promoting you to junior manager in charge of staff."

"Reporting to Mrs. Watson?" Jane's tone showed her disdain.

"Only technically. She will be instructed to let you have your head, but on paper you will report to her. It covers my back."

She grinned back at him.

"Your task is to get this lackluster bunch of employees into a team that could be Disney World cast members. You talk a good game—I expect you to deliver. I better see something outstanding. You have six months."

Jane flushed with pleasure. "Yes, sir."

"And that's not all. I want you to continue your observations of the store. Logistics, and cost-cutting. Write daily reports, collate them into a monthly assessment, and send it to me at central office. When you have six months of cost-based analysis, maybe I can see about a promotion. What is your current weekly salary?"

"I do about seventy-five hours a week. Sometimes more. On minimum wage, so that's two hundred fifty a week."

"From now on your salary is forty thousand dollars a year basic. There will be incentives—I'll send you a contract. The signing bonus is five thousand dollars—you can pick that check up today—and you'll get use of a company car. Junior management gets a Ford. Any color as long as it's black."

Jane sat quietly. "Thank you, Mr. Evans," she said eventually. "Thank you very much."

"You didn't tell me you can't believe it," he observed.

"But I can believe it," she said coolly. "I believed it from the start. It's why I came here."

He stood up, indicating the meeting was over, and offered her his hand.

"Then your plan is working out."

She allowed herself a brief smile. "Yes—it is."

⁓

"I don't see why you gots to go." The landlady was sulking. "You wanted the place pretty bad first time I talked to you."

"And I kept my word." Jane looked at her calmly. "You ran a filthy squat, now it's a student apartment. If you're smart, you'll sell it. Otherwise it'll just get wrecked again, and that's money out of your pocket."

"You got a big mouth, lady." The woman glanced round her apartment. It was bright, clean, repainted a gleaming white, with pretty curtains and furniture. It smelled good and she could see no bugs. Shheee-it! A contractor would have charged her plenty to get it looking this nice. She had to admit, that two hundred in rent had come with some sweet added value. "Pick yourself up a fancy new boyfriend?" she sneered.

"No. The three months is up, and I got a real job, and a car. Just like I told you."

The landlady admitted defeat. "Well, you did good. The place looks nice. Thanks," she said, grudgingly.

Jane inclined her head.

"You gonna rent someplace fancy now? One o' those swish apartments over at Park La Brea?"

"Rent?" Jane was dismissive. "I'll never rent again. I'm going to buy my own house."

CHAPTER 6

"So here we are," Ahmed said. *"Mash'Allah."*

He stopped to pray before they entered the courtyard. It was a crowded Cairo street, and Helen was tired, and hot. It had been a long flight, and the city seemed strange to her, even after L.A. The flood of traffic, the constantly honking horns, workers on bicycles, a choking sense of dust, it was all completely overpowering.

She felt out of her depth. Lost—and she was slightly ashamed. Helen had been foreign in L.A.—too dusky, too Arab, only protected by her girlfriends. And now, she felt foreign here. Her native tongue had atrophied; she thought in English, she groped about for Arabic words. The garish billboards with their smiling photos embarrassed her; she could not read the Arabic inscriptions.

Helen felt herself between two cultures—and not fitting in with either one.

"Mash'Allah," she repeated, bowing her head.

Whatever happened, she was determined to use this time. How long would it take to arrange a divorce? Let them bathe, and eat, get some sleep, and she would discuss it openly with Ahmed in the morning.

"This is our house." For the first time, he smiled warmly at her. "I worked on it—many years. The garden, especially. I hope you like it—since that is your name."

She nodded. Helen Yanna—al-Yanna, the garden. She'd always liked that part of her name.

She glanced around, drinking it in.

"Do you approve?" He was hopeful. It touched her that Ahmed desired her approval.

"I do." Helen nodded. "This is beautiful."

The doorway was hidden—almost secret—a gray-painted nothing of a door, set anonymously into a wall of the city street. While Helen waited with their suitcases, Ahmed reached into his wallet and pulled out a small brass key, old, she thought, with intricate casing. He inserted it into the lock; she heard the clicks and tumbles, like a puzzle solving, and the little door, heavy, swung open on its hinges. She had to stoop to enter, and then they were inside.

Now she looked around. The effect was magical. When the small door closed, the sounds of the street disappeared. She was standing in a high, ancient courtyard, where the walls were many feet thick, strong enough to drown out the traffic. The height offered a pool of natural shade. The garden was green; shady palms, as many as seven, were placed strategically around gravel paths. Tiny bricks, painted blue, fenced off flower beds dotted with azaleas, blossoming cacti, and thick beds of lilies. In the four corners of the garden, low-level fountains bubbled with water; it spilled, burbling, into square pools, giving the air a moist feel, a sense of a true oasis. There were birds in the trees, singing; she saw Ahmed had discreetly placed feeders and boxes for them. Butterflies darted around the flowers.

The garden was set in a Roman peristyle. There was a covered walkway around the outside, with flagstones like a European church underfoot, and the pillared arches covered in mosaics, in the Moroccan style; tiny squares of glass, blue and green. Islamic art and architecture, and she felt her soul thrill with unexpected pleasure.

"Wow," she said, in English, as it sank in.

Delighted, he looked at her and chuckled.

"It isn't rich—not a big house," he said, apologetically. "My business is not as good as it should be, not yet. But you will like it, I hope so."

"We can try in Arabic," Helen said, switching, awkwardly. "You've forgotten?"

Ahmed spoke softly, and looked into her eyes with a new confidence. As though he were assessing her.

"I will remind you," he said. "I will teach you."

To Helen's amazement, her stomach started to churn. She blushed and lowered her eyes. A tendril of something . . . desire, she realized . . . was trawling over her belly.

To cover her confusion, she said "I would like to bathe. . . ."

"Of course. How tired are you? Can you manage dinner?"

She was rocky with exhaustion, but she nodded, still blushing.

"And then . . . bed."

Helen's head snapped up. He was still looking at her in that way. As she opened her mouth, wondering what to say, Ahmed lifted his hand and traced a fingertip across her mouth, softly and possessively.

"You are afraid—like a mare, before saddling. No, not tonight. I do not want you tired. I want you fully awake."

"The bathroom . . . ," she said dry-mouthed. "Please . . . ?"

He grinned and extended his arm, opening the house to her. And as Helen walked inside, she was aware of Ahmed watching her. Wanting her.

She didn't know what she was feeling.

The house was not as spectacular as the little garden; it had some tile work, some old woods; she thought it was beautiful, modest, and comfortable. Three large bedrooms, a master suite with a bathroom and two dressing rooms, a kitchen, some servants' quarters, a living room, a dining room, and a small ornate room set aside for prayer, with the mats and a window facing Mecca.

But the decoration! Every room carpeted with a priceless antique: exquisite scrollwork, Persian silks, rough kilims, each gorgeous, lining the house with beauty. And there were artworks: mosaics, brass lamps that cast intricate shadows, scrollwork on the walls, glass vases, sculpture. Small pieces, but carefully collected. The house was like a museum, she thought, but lived-in, warm; the servants who bustled through it, wearing baggy linen trousers and shirts, or traditional robes, greeted her kindly and seemed genuinely happy that Ahmed was home. He introduced Helen, and she was polite.

Now that moment had passed, she was getting a grip; getting her control back.

"I will bathe, also." Ahmed stood back from the master bedroom. "When you are ready, come downstairs; they have made us a little supper."

"Okay. Thank you." She turned aside, toward the large copper tub with the modern, rainlike shower attachment . . .

. . . and then his hand was on her shoulder, firmly turning her toward him, and a strong arm lowered her down into the crook of his shoulder, and his lips pressed onto her mouth, teasingly, lightly brushing over hers, his tongue flickering against hers, probing, owning her.

Helen shuddered, taken utterly by surprise, and feeling his strength; she had never been kissed, and he knew what he was doing. She was light, nothing in his arms; she could feel the strength, the hardness of his muscles under his shirt. . . .

And then, as she was in turmoil, he let her go. And stunned, Helen, seventeen, stood there, her thumb on her mouth, her lips half-open, staring at him. . . .

"Later," he said. His dark eyes swept across her again. And then he suddenly turned and went down the stairs.

Helen went into the bathroom and shut the door; mechanically, she turned on the taps. She didn't know whether that word, 'later,' was a promise or a threat.

She chose, deliberately, a Western dress for dinner; a long-skirted, fitted, navy blue dress from Armani that Sally Lassiter had treated her to. It was modest, with long sleeves and a square neckline, but chic and simple. Helen teamed it with the tiny diamond studs Baba had given her for her sixteenth birthday.

Very important to keep that connection to home. She vowed not to be angry about the fast one her parents had pulled. They had only her best interests at heart; but Helen was determined, she would be the judge of that.

The kitchen was full; servants, cooks, had materialized out of nowhere. Helen greeted them shyly, and went through to the dining room.

It was transformed.

Ahmed had hung up red silks, gloriously embroidered, on the walls. Antique glass and brass lamps were lit, casting detailed shadows across the walls. Perfumed candles, scented with attar of roses, were dotted about floating in water in the powder blue ceramic bowls he had laid out, their flames adding a cheerful light to the ambience.

In one corner of the room, a musician, his head studiously lowered, played a tune on the sitar.

"Will you start with a drink?"

"Thank you," she murmured.

Ahmed had changed, too. He was now in traditional dress. Long black trousers and an open-necked shirt revealed to her that he was slim, but strong. It was his own house, and he was sprawled comfortably against the ornate cushions piled on the divan. Master of his own domain.

"Good evening," he said.

"Hello." Helen blushed. After that kiss, she did not know how to look him in the eyes.

"They have spent a month deciding on the menu," he told her, lowering his voice. "So I hope you eat something."

There was coconut-scented rice, and small roasted birds; tabbouleh salad and some delicious local pastries served in a dish of sweetmeats. Helen, not really hungry, picked a little at everything; it was all good, delicious, she was sure, if she had her appetite back. For dessert, Ahmed's servants laid out chilled fruits: lychees, dates, and pomegranate seeds, carefully scooped out and laid in a crushed bed of freezing ice crystals.

For drinks, they offered freshly squeezed orange juice, pure, icy water, or hot mint tea, heavily sugared and served in frosted glasses.

Slowly, she began to relax. After all, he had said he wouldn't come to her tonight. So why worry?

"This is wonderful. Thank you."

"You don't need to thank me," Ahmed said, dark eyes on her, carefully watching. "You are not a guest here. This is your house."

Helen bit her lip. Should she tell him?

But no, they were both zoning out, exhausted from the flight. Tomorrow would be soon enough.

She made polite conversation instead.

"How long have you lived here?"

"Four years. Since I found the market in America, and my business has done well. It is also four years since Badiya died," he added, unembarrassed. "Had she lived, we would have married and settled in her father's house. He owned land in Qatar—she was in Egypt to pursue her studies."

"And you loved her?" Helen was curious.

"Infinitely."

The answer overcame her reserve; she was conscious of an unwanted, new feeling, a stab of jealousy.

"Then why agree to this? We never met, before that day at my parents." Why would you want to marry me?"

"Because," he said. "Because your mother and mine are related, and I knew you were a Muslim girl, of good family. Because I heard tell that you were a believer. Because I loved Badiya so much that I thought never to be in love again, as long as I lived, with anyone."

Helen noted how he put that in the past tense.

"Because I want to have the joy of a family, and of children, insh'Allah. And what better for that than a young girl, intelligent, a believer of good family? I saw it as my duty. What was the point of looking for love?"

"And now?" she demanded. Her pride, stung. It was she, Helen, who was doing her duty here. Ahmed should be desperate to marry her. Inflamed for her. Who was this Badiya? And she chilled to the unpleasant idea of competing with a ghost.

"And now, I find you interest me," he said. "You seem . . . on the brink. Like a ripe plum, not yet fallen. You stir me . . . you are different. I want to train you."

His eyes bored into hers.

"I am not an animal," Helen managed.

"You are. We both are. Human animals." Ahmed smiled, confident and suddenly attractive. "Tomorrow . . . in our marriage bed . . . I will show you, little American."

"I need to talk to you."

"Talk all you want." He grinned, not allowing her to drop her eyes. "You are a virgin . . . untouched, and terrified. After tomorrow, you will be mine."

"You're very sure of yourself," Helen said.

He smiled. "That's right. I am."

～⁀৲

She had no idea how she made it to bed. Ahmed, soon afterward, had clicked his finger for the *aya*, and the woman came and helped Helen away from the table and through the house to the master bedroom. "Here," she said, opening the bathroom cupboard. There were new toothbrushes, in their packaging, cosmetics, and flannels.

"Thank you. *Shokram*." Helen bowed, and eventually the woman went away.

Drained, she brushed her teeth and passed the flannel over her face. It made her feel clean, good; combine it with the bath, and she no longer sensed dust and grime clinging to her every pore. Air travel . . . such a nasty, unhealthy way to go.

She did not have any energy left to hunt around for a nightdress. As soon as her ablutions were done, Helen flopped onto the bed, and she was asleep almost before she had closed her eyes.

～⁀৲

"What time is it?"

Helen rolled over, onto her side, to find Ahmed lying next to her, dressed in white, his eyes closed. Groggily, she rubbed her eyes.

"Ah." He sat up. "I thought you would never surface. I was about to call the doctors."

"It can't be that late. . . ."

"Try three p.m. You've been asleep for almost eighteen hours."

Helen groaned. "It'll take me days to get over the jet lag."

"I would not worry. You have years." Ahmed smiled down at her. "I have taken a nap myself, after lunch; very civilized, the Spanish siesta. So I will be full of energy tonight, also."

Helen sat up. She was thirsty.

As though reading her thoughts, Ahmed clapped his hands, and a woman materialized, bearing a pitcher of freshly squeezed orange juice and two enormous glasses.

"Better than water," he said. "It will also replenish your body salts."

She didn't need telling twice. Helen thirstily gulped down two enormous glasses of the golden nectar, and it tasted beyond delicious; the oranges themselves even richer and sweeter than those harvested a touch too early in the California sun.

"Excuse me," Helen said, after she was finished. Ahmed nodded to his servant, who melted away as quietly as she had come, and Helen, self-conscious, fled to the bathroom to do her teeth and take a bath.

Once she was finished, wrapped securely in her big toweling dressing gown, glad to have escaped him, she went back into the bedroom.

But Ahmed was there. Sitting on her bed. Their bed.

"Talk," he said, in English.

"Excuse me?"

"Talk. I have now sent the staff home. We will not be disturbed. Whatever you have to say, whatever request you want to make—now is the time." He grinned. "And then I am going to begin training you, Haya."

She was outraged. "What did you call me?"

"Haya," Ahmed said. "It is your name. What you were given at birth. It means 'modesty,' and it suits you. I asked your father. He put 'Helen' on you when you went to the United States, so that you would fit in with all the other girls. But you are not Greek; you are Arab. And your name is special, as you are. Ordained and written in the book of life. You are my Haya. I will never call you by that fake name again."

His speech stopped her anger dead. But she felt obliged to add, "And you can't train me, Ahmed. I told you that last night."

"Let us see if you are telling me the same thing three hours from now."

"I won't be telling you anything," she said, feeling out the name "Haya" in her mind. It was, in truth, very beautiful—much better than boring 'Helen' . . . maybe now she understood why she had never liked her name. "I'm not yours, Ahmed. I'm mine."

"What is the contradiction?" he asked, dark eyes on her. Not backing down.

"I . . . didn't understand what I was doing. When I signed the nikkah," she said.

For the first time, he registered shock. Amazement, then scandal.

"What?" he said. "Do you not understand the purpose of the nikkah?"

"I do," she said. "Of course . . . but I did not realize I was signing a nikkah. They spoke so fast . . . my Arabic is poor." She blushed. "As you know. And my father told me it was a friend-ship ceremony."

He considered this for a second. She had expected to him to curse, to stand, perhaps to be abjectly apologetic. But he was none of these things.

Instead, he looked at her calmly, with that same assessing stare that had disturbed her yesterday.

"Then tell me, Haya," Ahmed said, "were they wrong when they informed me you were intelligent, and a believer?"

She flushed. "No. Of course not."

"Then you know the Faith. And what 'friendship ceremony' did you think this was . . . exactly?"

She had no answer.

"And was marriage never mentioned to you?"

"It was," she admitted. "But I said that I would choose my own husband."

"Yet you met me and, of your own free will, went through this ceremony. Is it not so?"

She blushed.

"Yes."

"So on some level, you knew what was going on. You are not stupid, Haya."

It was true. She knew it in the depth of her soul.

"I have the right to choose my own husband!" she said.

"That is so. I will not force you." He leaned across the bed, and his face was inches from hers; a young man, but older than her, confident, and on his home turf. "In fact, my Haya, I would want you to declare yourself again, now, before I would let you touch me."

Her eyes widened.

"You are so arrogant!"

Ahmed inclined his head.

"And you want me. Do you not think I know my own?"

"How could you tell I am your own?"

"I tasted your lips," he said to her. "And you will yield to me." Ahmed stood up, and gave her a little bow. "Good night," he said, and withdrew.

⌒

She woke up in the middle of the night, sweating, unsure where she was. The hum of traffic and the splashing of the fountains seemed wrong, strange and wrong; as she came to, Helen longed for the reassuring quiet of their house on Third Street, her compact, American bedroom . . . her parents.

She shoved the covers off her and walked to the window, shivering as the night air hit her. The moon was half-hidden behind the clouds; it looked different here, somehow. Her nightdress was thin around her legs. Helen cringed; she felt so alone, so vulnerable, unprotected, no family, no friends. . . .

Briefly her mind flashed back to the two girls. What would Sally say? Some crude joke about Ahmed and their wedding night? She wasn't sure if Sally was a virgin; that was an indelicate question, not one she'd want to ask. Jane was . . . she was sure of that. Jane had only been made beautiful recently, and had never been seen with a boy.

Ahmed, in America, had been very different. Lost—confused. Polite. Here, in Egypt, he was on his home turf. Transformed. Predatory.

Helen twisted her dark hands, confusion springing up in her. He terrified her. Ahmed had all the power in this situation, all the money, all the knowledge. He spoke the language . . . she was his, in his house.

And it scared her even more that she was starting to feel for him. A dark, violent attraction in the pit of her stomach. A longing, in the belly of her, when he was close; wanting him to go away, but wanting, at the same time, for him to reach out, to touch her cheek, her neck, to kiss her, even. . . .

She was disturbed. She hated her own powerlessness. Helen's fingers tightened on the windowsill, and she bit down in anger on her soft lips. She had herself to blame for this, for her modest obedience to her parents, for always wanting an easy life, always wishing to avoid confrontation. Yes, she still loved them. But how, how, had she given the impression that this would be acceptable . . . that they could ship her off to Egypt, and choose the man to whom she would belong?

The traditional ways? While her father drank alcohol whenever he felt like it, and her mother neglected prayers often enough and sometimes snuck food during Ramadan? Helen had seen her do it. Why was it one rule for them and another for her?

No, she thought. No. She would not bow to this. She would not submit to Ahmed's rule of her body. She wanted to go the hell home, right now.

~~~

A night breeze came in through the arched window, fluttering the thin cotton of her dress. Helen shuddered and ran to her suitcase. Frantically she tugged on her underwear, her socks, a pair of jeans, and a shirt. She had no sweaters or coat—who knew it could get so cold here at night? It was a desert country; too late she remembered that. Well, it would have to do. Frightened, she worked quietly, grabbing whatever she could. A few American dollars—not many, she had about thirty bucks; she'd assumed Baba would bring the cash for the holiday. No airline ticket, but she had a credit card. She tried to remember exactly what was left in that account, from her allowance. Four hundred, maybe less. Not enough for a last-minute ticket to the States. Then she would go to Europe, she thought, go to England. Get somewhere safe. And her passport, *mash'Allah,* she thought with a fervent rush of gratitude and relief. Her passport was still here. . . .

She put on her sneakers and quietly opened her bedroom door. It was oiled, and didn't squeak. Helen's heart thumped wildly in her chest, crashing against her rib cage. What if he heard her? Would he be angry, feel betrayed? Hit her . . . beat her? Worse, drag her back to her room and rape her? She did not know this man at all. What if he regarded her as his possession, as a disobedient chattel out to humiliate him?

Carefully, delicately, she tiptoed down the stone stairs, their ancient surfaces pocked and pitted. Helen cast her eyes around, in the gloom, watching for any door to open—he had enough servants, a cook, a night watchman. . . .

But nobody came. They were all asleep. She looked at the clock in the hallway: it said half past midnight. She reached the door to the kitchen, then the door to the garden. Outside, it was very chilly, and she shivered again. The water looked eerie, bubbling in the dark; Helen ran across the courtyard, quietly in her soft sneakers, unlatched the gate, and made it, out into the street. She didn't know Cairo; she had no idea where she was. She picked up her heels and ran, blindly, fast, toward the sound of traffic.

It was dark. Helen, terrified, thudded through the streets, her sneakers pounding the pavement. There were few lights; she thought she must be off the center, somewhere. The storefronts were all shuttered. A man rode by on a donkey, pulling a cart full of trash; he scowled at her. She turned left into a major street, her breath ragged, and slowed to a walk.

Okay. Okay. *Don't panic.* The street signs were in Arabic; she had forgotten how to read it. No English subtitles. She looked around, hoping for a taxi, a bus—did they run at night? Anything. A way to get to the center.

A group of men walked past her and laughed raucously. She heard them say something; it didn't sound pleasant. She thought they called her a whore. Helen hesitated, desperate to ask for directions, but one of the group, a thin man with a scarred face, whistled at her and started to move in her direction. Hurriedly, she crossed the street, starting to feel that this was a mistake. She looked like a tourist, and judging from the broken windows, the tin cans in the gutter, this was a rough part of town. . . .

Helen felt the fear rise in her throat. The gaggle of men were conferring, looking over in her direction. Would they follow her? Rape her? She didn't wait to find out; she raced off down a narrow alleyway, and heard them cursing. Oh, God! She prayed desperately, her mind racing. What could she do? She was totally lost, it was pitch black, cold, no place for an American girl in a thin blouse. . . .

She needed a landmark. Clutching her wallet in her jeans pocket, Haya forced herself to breathe more slowly. She was panting from exertion and fright. Look for a crescent, she told herself, look for a crescent rising above the modern apartment blocks and ancient tumbledown houses. She would find a mosque . . . it would have directions near it, and she would be safer . . . who would hurt a girl in the shadow of the minaret? Helen steadied herself against a wall and peered into the gloom. There—it looked far away, but there it was, a crescent glinting against a street lamp. She walked toward it, down another alley, and then into an open street. More men, staring at her. Not a single woman to be seen anywhere. Helen picked up the pace. She'd keep moving. . . .

There was a squeal of tires and a beat-up red Ford Fiesta screeched to a halt beside her. The window wound down; the driver stared at her, calmly.

"How much?"

That, she understood. And realized with a shock of nausea he thought she was a prostitute.

"Leave me alone," she said, in English. He flashed her a sick grin, displaying yellowing teeth.

"Taxi," he said. "Pretty lady want taxi to airport?"

"Go away," Helen hissed. She started to pick up speed, but he pressed his foot on the gas.

"What you doing out here at night? Ladies don't come here. Give me money, I take you hotel. Airport." He cackled. "Pyramids!"

Helen squealed; he thrust his arm out of the window and took a swipe at her handbag, cursing at her as she flinched. But his arm was strong, and as she screamed for help, he wrenched the bag away, ripping at her shoulder. Helen grabbed, but it was too late, and now his scrawny hand had closed around her wrist.

"You get in car," he said. "Now!"

In her blind terror, Helen remembered a self-defense move from kickboxing class. She bent her hand backward, naturally breaking his grip. He shouted in rage and slammed on the accelerator. Helen pivoted and ran the other way, leaving him to execute a sharp turn in the street. . . .

And then she blinked, her hand thrust in front of her eyes, as headlights, full-on, dazzled her and lit up the whole street. A new car had turned into the road, at speed, a shiny Mercedes, its horn blaring, and rammed the Fiesta, hard, then pulled back and rammed it again. . . .

She stood, frozen to the spot, her fists crammed in her mouth. The red car lurched and skidded from the impact, but the thief slammed his foot down and it lurched off, fast, down an alley. . . .

The silver car was now sideways across the street, blocking her exit, blocking off the entrance to the alley from which Helen had come. She breathed in, shuddering, scared, looking around her wildly for any escape. Oh, God! It was one of the other men, one of the drunks from before. He had tailed her. She had no passport now—and she was going to be raped. . . .

The door was opening. A man was getting out. Helen struggled against the scream that rose choking, in her throat. . . .

"Wait!" he said, in English. "Don't be afraid, Helen. I won't hurt you. . . ."

She stared. It was Ahmed.

He rushed across to her, his eyes searching her body, her lips bluish with cold, her blouse torn where her attacker had ripped off the buttons.

"I heard you leave . . . when I got up you had gone." His words tumbled out. "I followed, I asked men on the street where you were headed. In the end—I found you. Did he hurt you?"

Numbly, she shook her head.

"He tried." Her teeth were chattering; she could barely speak.

Ahmed looked her over. "You didn't have to run. You were always free to go . . . it's your decision."

"If it was my decision I wouldn't be here," she said, wildly. "Stuck in this hellhole."

And then she burst into tears.

⁓

He got her into the car. That was an easy choice; it was obviously safer. As she buckled up, Helen thanked God for the small things: the soft leather, the clean seats, the warmth coming from the heater.

"I went too fast with you. You are too young for marriage." Ahmed shrugged. "I would never force any woman. Do not worry; I will drive you to a hotel."

Helen's eyes swam. "I only have thirty dollars."

"I'll pay," he said, easily. "All you will need is your passport. And I'll arrange for a one-way ticket back to Los Angeles. You can call your parents to come and collect you." A cold smile. "Chalk it up to experience."

She shook her head, plunged back into misery even as her body started to thaw.

"He stole my passport," she wailed. "It was in my bag."

He was silent, turning the wheel of the car, easily negotiating the narrow streets of the old quarter, on his way back to the house.

"Hotels here will not register a foreign guest without one." He sighed. "It would appear you are stuck in my house, at least for a day or so. I promise you, I will not bother you. I will not come to your room, or even your part of the house. A woman servant, my cook, will take you to the embassy tomorrow so you can start on the paperwork." He glanced across at her, hunched and shaking in the passenger seat. "At least do me the justice of understanding that *I* never forced you. I was tricked, as you were. My family and yours are related . . . distantly, perhaps, but the bond is still there. I would not attack any woman. Still less one who is mostly a girl."

She nodded, feeling a little embarrassed.

"It was scary, to be alone in your house."

"A lot worse, out here. Which is why I followed you."

Helen stared at her lap; she noticed the ripped-off buttons and the gape in her shirt and miserably pulled it tighter.

"I . . . thank you," she whispered. "I owe you."

He shrugged. "I think of you as a guest in my house, one under my protection. We will get you safely back to your family, and you can forget all about Egypt."

"I'm sorry," Helen whispered. "I just didn't ask to be here."

Ahmed drove her back in silence to the house. They were not too far away; he parked, and allowed her to get out of the car herself, averting his eyes as he walked into the kitchen. Helen heard him shouting, and the cook, rubbing her eyes, emerged in a night coat with a cloak that she flung around Helen's shoulders, warm, black wool, covering her properly. The older woman clucked and fussed as she led Helen up the stairs, back into her bedroom. The fountains were still splashing, gently, in the courtyard, but she was no longer menaced by the sound; Helen felt stupid, but safe.

She undressed, put her nightgown back on—it had remained, crumpled, on the terra-cotta tiles underfoot—and crawled into her bed.

Within seconds, she found herself drifting off. Emotionally exhausted, jet-lagged, and fatigued, she could not keep her lids from closing. And as she slipped into sleep, she thought of Ahmed, his dark eyes ranging over her body.

When Helen came down to breakfast he had already gone. There was a short note on the table, and a pile of Egyptian pounds. Ahmed wrote that the cook had only a few words of English, but she would drive Helen to the American Embassy, wait with her, and bring her back. He included a list of telephone numbers just in case she got lost. There was a small tourist guide to Cairo next to the note; Ahmed had placed a bookmark next to a city center map.

It was very thoughtful; but very brisk. An efficient little package from a benign stranger. Helen read the note, and felt a pang of loss. Of course, it was insane to suppose they could marry. She was miles too young. But . . . under other circumstances . . .

She figured it would have been good to get to know him better, the handsome merchant with the probing eyes. They might have dated. . . .

But her world was an ocean away. There was no point in pining over him now. Last night she'd been afraid he might rape her. No wonder he was keeping his distance.

The cook bustled in, pointed at the note, smiled, and talked to her in rapid-fire Arabic.

Helen shook her head; the woman repeated herself, slower.

Still no dice. She felt ashamed she had lost her own language.

"Eat," the cook said then, pointing at the breakfast. "You will like it."

"Thank you." Well, at least she still had the simple words. And the food did look delicious: a chilled pitcher of freshly squeezed orange juice, a plate of dates, some hard-boiled eggs in a warm sauce of tomatoes and onions, a bowl of *ful mudammas,* bean dip with pita bread, and a samovar of mint tea. . . .

Helen found she was starving. She ate, and the cook, who said her name was Fahdah, watched approvingly.

"Master Ahmed ordered it," she said. "He says you must eat."

⁓

At the embassy, it was hot and crowded, and it took Helen forty minutes to get through the gatehouse without I.D. She stood in line for over two hours, and finally explained her plight to a bored young man with a Boston accent who hardly looked at her.

"We got a backlog." He barely looked up from his paperwork. "We'll take your prints and details, but likely you won't get a passport for two weeks."

"But it's an emergency," Helen spluttered. "I'm a citizen. Can't you help me?"

He looked up. "Are you in physical danger, miss?"

She shook her head.

"Do you have a place you can safely stay in the country while your papers are processed?"

"Yes, but—"

"Leave a number. We'll call when your passport becomes available. You are a semipriority after cases with no funds and no accommodation."

"Look . . ."

"Miss, there's a long line. We'll be in touch. Next," he called, beckoning a fat woman in a *niqab* up to the counter.

⁓

Helen rode home dejected, trying to pick out a word here and there as Fahdah gave her a running commentary. How humiliating . . . she would have to explain, and then presume on Ahmed's hospitality. For two whole weeks . . . her clothes would need to be laundered here, she would eat his food, walk in the safety of his garden. . . .

That is, if he let her stay. But somehow, that was one thing she did not doubt.

～

The cook left her alone in her room. Helen waited for Ahmed to come home, but lunchtime bled into afternoon, and he still did not come. She sat in her room, then walked outside to sit by the fountains, not daring to venture beyond the walled garden, bored out of her mind. She had nothing to read but a copy of *Vogue* she'd brought on the airplane. And that had been worn to shreds ages ago. . . .

Helen washed her hair, carefully blow-dried it, and plucked her eyebrows. And then, for want of anything better to do, she made herself up, beautifully and carefully, just neutral, natural shades, the way Sally had taught her, and picked out her prettiest *shalwar kameez,* something she had packed for the sun, a delicate white and yellow chiffon layered thing, shot through with gold. She tried on her various sandals, picking a white pair with a curved heel and lacy blue detailing, and regarded herself in the mirror, as though she were dressing a doll.

She was playing with an armful of thin bronze bangles when the knock on her door finally came.

"The master is here," Fahdah said, smiling. "He's waiting in the kitchen."

Helen jumped up. "Thank you."

"Very nice," the older woman commented, nodding at Helen's outfit. And then she slipped into broken English—"You pretty—make good wife."

Helen blushed.

～

"She explained what happened. I'm sorry you have been put out."

Ahmed was standing in the kitchen, reading some papers. He looked at her, just once, and Helen saw his eyes flash with interest. But then he turned away, back to his paperwork, and did not make further eye contact.

"You are welcome to stay here. Under the same rules as before. I can also make some calls, see if I have any contacts among the workers hired by the Americans. Perhaps we can speed matters up."

Helen flushed. "You're very kind." She wanted him to look at her, wanted him to compliment her; maybe that was wrong, but he was handsome.

"Or of course, you can call your parents, and they can arrange for a hotel."

Helen thought about that. She really, really didn't want to speak to them right now. Her anger with Baba had grown white-hot. When she got home, she would confront them.

"I'd rather not do that. I have some issues with my parents."

"Some issues? How very American of you. Then your friends, perhaps. Did you not tell me you had rich friends?"

"Well—one." Jane didn't have two cents of her own; Helen knew she was better off than the English girl. "To be honest with you, Ahmed, I—I don't want her to know." She cringed at the thought of Sally's incredulous stare when she found out what her parents had done. "I feel so foolish. I just want to get home, and get a job and my own apartment. I know it's a lot to ask and it's presuming on your good graces . . ."

"I don't understand that. What are good graces?"

"Kindness."

He nodded dryly, still refusing to look at her. "You are Arab, you should learn Arabic properly."

She blushed again, this time with shame.

"If I can stay with you for this time, I will send you some money when I get home and get a job. . . ."

Ahmed's head snapped up, and the dark eyes bored into hers. Angry. She shrank back; his strong body was coiled, like a predator's.

"You insult me," he said. "Did I not tell you you are a guest in my house? Did I not come to find you, and protect you, when you ran from me? Did I not say we are distant cousins? You have been made welcome here and offered every comfort. And now you think to offer me money, as though I were running some kind of boardinghouse? Even now, you do not think me an honorable man."

"No! I—it's just—it's such an imposition. . . ." Her voice trailed off, and under his unflinching stare she quailed and dropped her gaze. He was right, of course he was right. She was offering him a dire insult, and he had been nothing but good to her.

"Forgive me," Helen said, speaking in Arabic the best she could. "You have been a good friend and cousin. I would like to stay under . . . under your generous roof. If you will permit it."

He was silent, and when she looked up he was still glowering.

"Please . . . I'm sorry. I meant no offense, Ahmed. . . . I want to stay with you, if you will have me."

"And you will regard me as your host; trust me not to force myself upon you; nor speak again of money?"

"No. As my host." Helen bit her lip. "My kind host," she said.

She half wanted to stay, half to run. Feeling him so near was disturbing. And his anger at her dishonoring him made him all the more attractive to her.

"Very well, then. It is settled. I'll call the embassy tomorrow. Will you eat supper?"

Helen had been bored out of her brain; she jumped at the chance.

"Yes, please. And you can tell me all about your work."

Ahmed's eyebrow lifted. "I was going to arrange that your meal be sent to your room."

Helen started. "Oh, no, please don't. I want to talk to you, to spend time with you. It's been so dull without anything to read, and I don't dare go outside and get lost. . . ."

Now he looked at her with a flicker of amusement, and the dark eyes ran assessingly across her pretty outfit.

"But we are not staying married. Do you think it is proper?"

Helen had the strong feeling he was teasing her, toying with her. She felt a rush of desire across her skin, her knees weakening.

"I am your guest. And we are relatives," she reminded him. "So I think . . . it's okay."

"Very well, then; we'll eat."

He clapped his hands, and one of the serving men ran in.

"Bring us some supper," he said. "My cousin and I will eat."

Helen lifted her face and smiled radiantly at Ahmed. She was so grateful. And she was longing for his company.

⌒

He chatted lightly and pleasantly enough, as the waiter bustled about them, bringing *fattah, kaltah,* spiced kebabs with tomato paste and cumin, a dish of tomatoes and herbs, vine leaves wrapped around goat's cheese, figs and honey, and wine. Everything was home-cooked, and there was a pitcher of iced mineral water and another of pomegranate juice; the flavors of the Middle East blended against her tongue, everything natural, nothing processed. Ahmed ate lying sideways, lounging against his silk divan, and Helen, nervously at first, imitated him, picking at a date or a grape and then the meat and rice dishes.

It was so good to have conversation; she had no idea how isolating it would be not to speak the language. Her *own* language.

She could hardly look straight at him. Helen felt so grateful, and so indebted. Without Ahmed, she would be confronting her parents right now.

And Ahmed was so confident; so tough, upright, uncompromising. The thought of how he had driven through the night, sought her, saved her, danced in Helen's head. His proud distance from her, afterward. His eyes, just now and again, sweeping across her, and finding her beautiful.

And she found she desperately wanted him to find her beautiful.

When he was angry, she wanted to please him. To placate him. His dominance lit up something fundamental in her, and the female animal in her responded, setting her blood racing, making her long for his arms, his deep, owning kiss.

Of course, Helen didn't have Sally's dazzling style or blonde halo of hair. And she didn't have Jane's strength and grace, or her newly discovered pale English good looks.

But there was something about Ahmed that assured her he would not glance twice in either girl's direction. He liked Helen; she was not "foreign" to him, except insofar as she had lost her culture. He would—you could argue, did—marry her.

As he talked, politely and inconsequentially, about his business, about the embassy, the Cairo traffic, Helen stared at him.

And she realized, she wanted him.

<hr />

The evening stretched on, and Helen ate slowly, trying to draw it out. When he finally washed his fingertips in a small bowl of rosewater, she followed him, then scrambled lightly to her feet and walked around the table to be closer to him.

"We could have some coffee in the garden," she suggested. "Talk some more."

Ahmed grinned. "Dinner is over . . . *cousin*. And I am sure you know you are far too delectable for me to linger over with coffee and sweetmeats. Already you tempt me. You should go to bed. We can dine together tomorrow."

She sighed. "I will miss you." Helen blushed. "I like to be with you."

His eyes darkened. "Don't play with me, little beauty. I am not the sort of man to be teased. You have signed the nikkah, but you say you want to leave. And yet now you want to be with me. Which is it?"

She stepped back; the longing to kiss him raged in her. Or rather, to be kissed; to have Ahmed reach out and pull her to him.

But he wouldn't make it that easy. He would force her to be explicit. To choose him. Helen could not do that, she told herself.

Ahmed stood, and his dark eyes glittered.

"Good night," he said, "cousin."

"Good night."

And she reluctantly turned from the vaulted dining room to her room.

⌐⌐⌐

The next morning, when she woke, Ahmed was not there. Helen showered and dressed, telling herself to snap out of these schoolgirl fantasies. She was *not* going into an arranged marriage. She *was* going home. It was easier, when Ahmed was not right in front of her.

Sternly, she dressed herself in her best American Levi's, with her Nike sneakers and a crisp navy silk shirt, perching her sunglasses on her head. That looked good, too. Rather defiantly, she stomped down the stairs into the kitchen and lifted her head at Ahmed's staff. But nobody said a word, and she suddenly remembered her cousin had plenty of Western suits.

"Breakfast?" The housekeeper fussed about her, offering meats, fresh juices. Once she had poured Helen's mint tea into a bright red glass, glittering with gold patterns, she came forward with a neat envelope, presented on a silver tray. "The master left it for you." The woman made no attempt to speak English. Helen ripped it open.

> *Dear Helen,*
>
> *I go to the gym most mornings, then on to work. You are free to do as you wish. I have instructed Fahdah to accompany you around the city, with her brother Mahmoud. Mahmoud is my driver. He has served in the army and can act as a bodyguard for your safety. There are many tourist attractions in Cairo.*

Helen's face flushed as she read this. Attractions! He saw her as some kind of holidaymaker.

> *If you prefer, you can return to the embassy and try again. Or there are plenty of mosques, restaurants, coffeehouses, and the like.*

Fahdah knows them all. There are also boutiques. I have left a credit card with Fahdah for your use, should you wish to go shopping. I hope you will have a pleasant day.

The note was all stiff politeness. She hated it. How could she go to a mosque to pray with two minders watching her? Impossible. Eat in a restaurant on her own? Spend Ahmed's money buying souvenirs?

The situation grated. He knew she was a fish out of water here, but she shouldn't be, she just shouldn't.

Carefully Helen sipped at her fresh orange juice. There was no point in going to the embassy again. And besides, she felt an overwhelming desire to prove Ahmed wrong. She was not some mere Western tourist, she was Jordanian–American. And Helen desperately wanted to prove that to her cousin. To impress him.

She looked around for Fahdah.

"Yes, madam?"

"Fahdah, I would like to improve my Arabic," Helen said. "Could you and your brother kindly accompany me to a public library?"

Fahdah gave a toothy smile. "Yes, madam!"

When Ahmed returned that night, Helen stopped herself from racing downstairs to meet him. She was in her room, reading poetry, very slowly, using a dictionary. But after she heard his bedroom door bang, and the sound of his feet padding down the stairs, Helen emerged. Her heart was thudding in anticipation. She tried telling herself not to be so ridiculous.

"Hello, Helen," Ahmed said, in English. "Did you have a good day?"

Helen took a deep breath. "Yes, thank you, cousin." She spoke Egyptian Arabic. "I went to the library, and afterward read in the park. It is a wonderful city."

He raised a brow and smiled slightly. Fahdah rushed forward, jabbering at him a million miles an hour—Helen still couldn't follow it—and pointing at Helen.

"You are trying to recall your Arabic?" He turned and smiled, slowly, and Helen's heart flipped over. "What a wonderful thing to do, cousin."

Helen smiled back. She was proud. And more to the point, she was thrilled that he was pleased. She had surprised him.

"Tomorrow is Saturday," Ahmed said. "If your passport has not arrived, shall we take a cruise on the river?"

"Thank you." She sighed. "That would be wonderful."

⌒

The next week, Helen got intermittent updates from the U.S. Embassy. Her passport was progressing. She thought of calling Sally, or Jane, but the idea of letting them into this whole affair was insupportable. When I am safe home, Helen thought, I will see them both. Jane was mourning, and should not be troubled by Helen's problems with her parents. She had no thought of calling Mama and Baba. They would hear from Helen only face-to-face.

But besides all that, her life in L.A. could wait. Helen relished each day she spent in Cairo. Her Arabic was slow, but Ahmed was patient. He worked, but came home frequently to see to her comfort. They went to restaurants, they took a boat on the Nile, he brought her to the great museum and let her marvel at the treasures. One afternoon he took her on a drive in the country. Always with the smirking Fahdah sitting patiently in the back of the car. Ahmed was punctilious about chaperones and Helen's honor.

Sometimes she wished, just privately, he wouldn't be.

They laughed and joked together. She had never met any man quite so comfortable in his own skin. At first, Helen was merely filled with dread at the thought of her passport arriving, of going back to her neat, modern little house on Third Street. After a day or two, though, she knew she was kidding herself. It wasn't leaving Cairo she dreaded. It was leaving Ahmed.

She was falling in love. And it didn't matter at all how much she tried to fight it. He was attractive, confident, learned. And sometimes, when he looked at her, it was with that predatory intent that made her skin prickle, her body flush.

The call came the next Monday. Eight thirty a.m., prompt.

"It is for you." Fahdah handed Helen the receiver, and her heart was already thumping in her mouth.

"Hi, is that Ms. Helen Yanna?"

She would recognize that Boston accent anywhere.

"Yes."

"Your passport is ready for collection at the embassy, ma'am. Come in any time and pick it up. I have a case number for you. . . ."

Helen wrote down the details and hung up carefully. Her eyes were prickling red. She looked up to find Ahmed staring at her.

"Congratulations," he said, stiffly. "It has been a pleasure having you at my house—cousin. Go with God."

"I will be here when you get back," she said hastily. "I have to pick it up, and then book a flight. Nothing will be settled until tomorrow."

"I must get to work," Ahmed replied distantly, and he turned on his heel and left.

That night, supper was miserable. Helen had cried most of the day. She had tried to sort herself out before Ahmed returned, but repeated washing of her face and application of concealer could not disguise her red eyes and tear-stained cheeks. And Ahmed was visibly cold.

"I hope . . . ," Helen began. She was trying to make small talk, but her voice cracked. Dying of shame, she swallowed hard, and lowered her head.

Ahmed shrugged. "You should rejoice, not weep. You are going home." He gave a minute smile. "Free and unmolested."

Helen could not joke. A tear brimmed under her lashes and splashed onto the table.

"What is the matter?"

She saw him gesture, very slightly, with one hand, and heard the immediate sounds of the servants all withdrawing, melting away from them, the soft pad of slippers as they left that part of the house.

"You know the matter," she said weakly. "I—I don't want to go."

He smiled, a conqueror's smile of pure triumph, and Helen, excited, gasped, but also shrank a little; Ahmed was not a man who would accept half measures.

He reached out and put one rough fingertip under her chin, tilting her face toward him.

"You have been here a while, girl. It is time. You must make a decision. You know you are free to leave tomorrow," he said. "Go back to the West, go and find some gum-chewing surfer who will call you Helen, or some boring lawyer who will ask you to dye your hair blonde. You can call your parents anytime you choose. The international code for the United States is double zero one."

She watched in dismay as he walked toward his own bedroom; but then he halted at the door.

"I will be sleeping on the second floor," Ahmed said, once again, answering her unspoken question. "If you want me, come to me. But come as *Haya*. And come prepared to be my wife. In all things."

Her heart pounded, and her palms broke out in a sweat. Pure adrenaline.

"Ahmed . . . ," she began. But he had turned, and left her.

In turmoil she rose and went to the window. He was still arrogant—son of a bitch, he was arrogant! But a good man, all the same. There was nobody here to police him. Yet there had never been any hint of force, no question he would make her do anything against her will. She could see Ahmed was a believer . . . that he knew her rights, knew his faith, would not attempt to deprive her of her natural liberty.

And yet, if she chose, freely, to go to him, it would be on his terms.

The heat of the afternoon was just starting to fade away. Helen turned from the window and ran down the stairs, toward the courtyard.

"Come as Haya," he had said.

The fountains were dancing; the birds sang. It was quiet, and cool. Helen—no, Haya—she felt the name out again in her mind, and it felt right upon her. Her birth name, her Islamic name. Haya. That Ahmed had given it again to her, that she was here, in Egypt, learning her native tongue, with him; it felt now as if she were crossing into another, ancient, more fitting world.

The name was right. He had put it back upon her, and she settled into it, feeling the Arabic sink into her mind. The first battle he had won. And already she sensed it would not be the last.

Haya sat on the edge of one of the flower beds, and tried to think.

The studious, shy young man she had met in her parents' dining room was no more. Here, Ahmed was an entrepreneur; in charge, successful, a man who had arranged his house, and his life, in his own way.

And a man who loved another woman.

A dead woman. A ghost.

Haya probed herself. Yes, she wanted Ahmed. Her body was in turmoil now. Was it because he was the first, the only one to have kissed her, to have made her squirm? She didn't think so—the boys she'd seen in America, at Sally's party, on the street—none of them had ever made her feel that way. The bland, handsome movie stars and rock singers had left her cold.

Ahmed was different. His dominant, masculine side—you could call it arrogance . . . Haya knew it aroused her. And Ahmed was good—there was that to admire; none of her father's heavy-handedness, combined with hypocrisy; Ahmed drank little, and he didn't attempt to trick her.

If Haya went home, what then? The rage of her parents.

School politics at Miss Milton's. Wanting to be as pretty as Sally, or as clever as Jane . . .

Of course she would see her friends again. But what was to stop her doing that as a married woman?

A little while here, in her own land, and Haya already felt her childhood slipping off her like a snakeskin. She was grown; she had passed into womanhood. And the thought of Miss Milton's and schoolyard politics was ridiculous.

She had left that behind her when she landed in Egypt, by herself.

Haya al-Yanna was a woman now. And she knew that she would one day marry.

If *not* Ahmed, then whom?

True, Haya hadn't chosen him—yet. But Ahmed was demanding she do so, before he touched her.

What was there for her back in L.A.? Somebody more 'suitable'? More Anglo? Richer?

Haya put her fingers to her lip, tracing where his mouth had crushed hers. She felt weak with desire. Ahmed made her stomach churn, excited her in a way she'd never known before.

Right now, at this moment, Haya realized she had no desire to go home.

She knew that if she did, she would never see Ahmed again.

Then what was her choice? To affirm the nikkah. To do it all over again . . . to go in to him, and let Ahmed touch her . . .

Her lip trembled. She was afraid.

For ten minutes she sat there, paralyzed, staring at the water that cascaded into the pond.

Then finally, Haya rose and went back into the house. She turned left under the peristyle, and climbed the stairs to the guest bedroom suite.

Ahmed was sitting in a carved wooden chair, piled with cushions, facing a western window, watching the sun set over the roofs of Cairo. A book lay open, facedown, on the mantelpiece.

"You have come to me, Haya?" he asked, without looking round.

"I don't know," she said, and her voice wobbled.

Ahmed stood up, came over to her, and enfolded her in his arms, gently this time. Haya started to cry. She didn't know why, not exactly. But she was here, in Egypt, and it was strange, and her parents had sent her here. And she wasn't sure if she had fallen in love.

"Come on," Ahmed said, when she had finished. He kissed her lightly on the top of the head. "Do you want to be a tourist, now, at last?"

"What?" she said, dabbing at her eyes.

"Let's go out to the pyramids," he said. "Go and see the son et lumière. It's . . . what do you Americans say . . ."

"Cheesy?"

"Exactly. But it's fun." He stood up and reached for a lambswool cloak, very fine, a soft pure gray, reminiscent of the one she had worn to Sally's party. "The desert gets cold at night."

"Thank you," she said. "And . . . I like that you call me Haya."

He was right; the desert was freezing. She was amazed at how bitter it was. Ahmed got them chairs at the back, and they sat together, the cloak thrown over them, watching the eerie green light over the pyramids, the booming voice of the announcer.

The head of the Sphinx reared, massive, in the spotlight. Haya gasped.

"Do you like it?"

"Like—that's not the word. I mean, I've seen pictures. But they are so inadequate."

"This is your heritage," he said. "Not a sports car, or a hamburger."

"Amazing," she said.

"Tomorrow we will go and see it, in the day. And maybe next week, we can go south. You must see the Valley of the Kings. But I won't overwhelm you . . . the tourists try to see all Egypt in seven days, and as a result, see nothing. It blurs into one."

"We'll take our time," Haya said. She looked up at him; his

profile was strong, his jaw set against the red and green lights on the sand. He was handsome; he cared for her. And she did not want to go home.

Already, home seemed distant, and a little tawdry.

"*We* will?" Ahmed turned his face to her, his dark eyes above hers. And Haya wanted, longed for him to bend down and kiss her. Her lips moistened, parted. . . .

"No," he said, softly. "You did not sign the nikkah."

"I did," she said. "I did. . . ."

He lowered his mouth, close to her, not touching her. Teasing her cruelly.

"Then who are you?"

"Haya," she said, and now her voice was thick with desire. "Haya . . . your wife . . ."

Still, he did not kiss her. And desire curled like smoke across her breasts and belly.

"Please, Ahmed," she whispered.

He laughed softly, and pressed his lips on hers; his arm around her back, supporting her, he kissed her, hard this time, no teasing, his mouth almost crushing hers, his teeth on her lips, the hard muscles of his chest against her breasts.

Haya gasped; she felt lust flood through her.

Silently he rose and offered her his hand; Haya stumbled to her feet, blushing; it felt like everybody could see her wanting him. Ahmed flung the cloak around her shoulders and led her to the car, while the ghostly lights of the show danced over the ancient monuments behind them.

His home—their home, now, she supposed—was still, silent apart from the sounds of the birds and the fountains. Without the servants, it seemed very empty; and Haya felt Ahmed, his body, his strength, his nearness, now, exciting her and scaring her.

He turned to her in the garden. She opened her mouth to speak, but he put one finger across her lips, then scooped her up into his arms, as though she were light as silk, and carried her into the house, and up the stairs, and laid her down on the divan bed in their room, where the intricate shadows from the Moroccan lamp played across the walls.

"Ahmed." Haya attempted a smile. "Carrying me across the threshold?"

He did not smile back. The look he was giving her bored into her eyes. He reached down and started to unbutton her dress, with one practiced hand.

"Be gentle," she said, gasping as his fingers stroked the soft flesh at the top of her breasts.

Ahmed lowered his mouth and kissed her again, hard.

"At first," he replied. "Only at first."

~~~

"Tisbah ala-kheir," he said quietly to her, when the moon was starting its descent over the palm trees in the garden, and Haya lay drained, and sore, and deeply in love, in his arms. They were both sweaty, but she loved the scent of him, and did not want to let him go. "Good night."

"Good night," she said, copying his Arabic. "My darling."

~~~

The next day, when she awoke after a deep sleep, Ahmed had ordered that breakfast be brought up to their room. He handed her an iced glass of juice, and watched her as she drank it, blushing, remembering what he'd done to her.

"Look at me," he said.

Haya could hardly hold his eyes.

"Will you come home early?" she murmured, staring at the floor.

He put a callused finger under her soft chin and tilted up her head, forcing her to stare into his eyes.

"I said, look at me."

Haya flushed; her breathing seemed to be coming raggedly. Ahmed put a hand to his wife, and she gasped.

"So eager," he said, with a grin. "I'm not going to work today. It's our honeymoon. And I want to show you what pleasure means."

⁓

He led her into the shower later, and bathed with her, washing her, until she was so stimulated she had to reach for him again. Haya found her husband was exactingly patient, deliberate as a lover; he insisted on knowing every inch of her, and discovering what brought her to the boil.

Haya realized her world had been black and white. She could hardly cope with the feelings Ahmed induced. At times he was rough, and dominant; at other times gentle, erotic, slow with her. The day ticked by wonderfully slowly, and she lost herself to her body, and his body, and the ferocity of her newly awakened love.

⁓

Their first month together passed in a daze. Haya was beside herself; her emotions ran at fever pitch; love of Ahmed, and desire for him, consumed her, so much that she could scarcely concentrate. And yet there was anger, which started slowly and had simmered into rage, against her father. As happy as she was now, Haya had grown furious that this major change had been done *to* her—that she never had the chance to decide for herself. Baba had tricked her, and now she was in Egypt.

Every time she could not make herself understood in the marketplace, or one of the servants turned against her, pretending her accent was too strange, Haya felt out of her depth. As though only Ahmed could protect her. And that, she hated.

She could hardly stay away from her husband. Ahmed was a dominant lover, not gentle, not soft, and he excited her, made her ready and hot in a way the dull American boys never had. Her passion excited him; her naked desire, visible to him even when she was fully robed, made Ahmed want her more; he was on her, all the time, taking her by surprise in the shower, locking the doors of their study, coming home from work at lunchtime, burning for his wife, and wanting to have her again.

Haya was unused to the sensations that rocked through her at his touch. She had never thought of herself as particularly sexual; never mooned over posters of the latest hot actors, like the other girls at school; never really considered men. And now she was addicted. The more he came to her, the more she wanted him.

Desire made her sick, almost. Haya was so feverish for Ahmed that she could not concentrate, could not get herself together. Her days and nights centered around wanting him. The depths of her responsiveness scared her.

But as Haya stayed in the house, barely improving her Arabic, she got restless.

~~~

"I need to do something," Haya said, after they had finished a sticky session of lovemaking one afternoon. "Ahmed, I'm going stir-crazy here. I was not made to sit still in a house ... even a beautiful one ... and I have no friends, nobody but you." She missed her girlfriends, dreadfully. "Maybe we should go back ... the two of us, to America. Visit my parents. Have it out with Baba," she added, grimly.

"I can't." He leaned over and kissed her on her naked stomach; she drove him crazy, lean and young and hungry for him. "I can't take time off work—I've already spent too much time away as it is. And you can't go."

"I can do whatever I want."

"No way. I'm not letting you out of my sight. I want you far too much for that."

She softened, smiled.

"But you are going crazy. Even the birds in the garden fly elsewhere over the city." He thought about it. "Why don't you come with me? Into work."

"Your work?"

"Yes, why not? Come and see what I do. Do you object to wearing the *hijab*?"

"Not at all."

"The women in our workshops are very traditional. It would save some questions. . . ." He grinned. "And anyway, your hair is so beautiful . . . I want it all to myself."

"Fine by me." Haya groaned and pushed his hand away. "Don't . . . Ahmed."

"And why not?"

"We just did . . ."

"I remember." But he was ready again. "Come here."

She rolled to him, eagerly.

Maybe it was better he take Haya to work, Ahmed thought. Since when she wasn't there, he spent every waking moment looking for excuses to get out of the office. And he loved her, and did not want her to get bored, or restless. Until the children came along, *insh'Allah,* could it hurt? Why not? She was still a teenager, after all, even if she carried herself like a young woman.

Business would be a fascinating diversion. And it wouldn't last too long. Once his wife got pregnant, that was it.

⟡

"And this is the workshop." Ahmed bowed, greeted the women who were sitting there, weaving; they smiled and nodded at Haya. "They make some carpets here. Mostly, I deal with importers . . . or find goods myself. It is all in the eye. Come upstairs."

She smiled at his workers and followed him up the wooden stairs; every inch of the place was hung with beautiful carpets, and the storeroom smelled a little fusty.

"Mothballs," he said, in answer to her question. "Nothing works better . . . no technology, even today. Mothballs to keep the carpets from being eaten alive. And here we are . . . this is the showroom."

"Amazing."

It was. A long room, full of windows, but they had muslin drapes across them all. She understood: daylight would bleach out the precious fibers. Instead, even in the day, the room was gently lit with candles. Piles of gorgeous silk and woollen rugs lay on the floor; they hung from the walls; they were suspended from the ceiling. To counter the mothballs, he had placed scented oil burners in strategic places; there was a strong smell of frankincense.

"Do you want some tea . . . pastries?"

Haya was hungry; she nodded.

Pleased to be showing off his work, her husband nodded to an employee; the man disappeared into a side room, and returned with a silver tray containing a teapot, glasses, and a delicate selection of tiny cakes, placed on a lace napkin.

"We keep a kettle boiling for customers," Ahmed explained. "I serve them mint tea. . . . It is a way of enticing them to stay, to take time, and then the beauty of the goods . . ." He shrugged. "They sell themselves."

As though to underline his point, there was a commotion downstairs; Haya recognized the guttural accents of German, stabbing at English.

"Would you like to watch?"

She nodded.

Ahmed bent down and kissed her on the cheek. It was a modest gesture, but he allowed the tip of his tongue to graze her cheek; he licked her, just a little, where the others couldn't see.

Desire rushed through her, electric, insistent. Haya struggled not to gasp; she forced a smile, and withdrew to the side of the room. She wanted to watch her husband in action; and she couldn't let anybody else know she was turned on. . . .

There was a cushioned bench toward the back. Haya took away her tray, and busied herself pouring out the mint tea.

"Welcome. Come in." Ahmed was smiling at his customers, but it was a smile without warmth. "Would you care for some tea?"

"Thank you," said the wife. She was rather fat and kept her sunglasses on, even in the darkened room. Haya instantly disliked her.

Ahmed signaled to another employee; more cakes and tea were brought.

"Are you looking for anything in particular?"

"We're not going to pay over the value," the husband said, rudely.

"Of course not." He glanced back at Haya and winked at her, quickly. "You will find we offer excellent value. What size of carpet or rug are you looking for . . . ?"

"Something medium. That one." The husband jabbed at a large red Persian silk carpet. "Or something like that," he added, pointing to a completely different Afghan kilim in bright blues and yellows.

"Ah, yes," Ahmed said, with a sigh. "Two of the finest pieces in my collection. But you knew that, of course. Are you a dealer? We do special prices to the trade."

"*Nein* . . . no . . ." The little man puffed out his cheeks, and his wife smirked. "But I know quality when I see it."

"Those rugs are very expensive. Can I show you something a little more moderate?" Ahmed nodded, and two workers swiftly ran forward and unfolded a large, extraordinarily fine Persian rug in creams and blues. Haya's eyes widened; she was no expert, but she saw it was antique, and worth many thousands . . . maybe ten thousand. Or possibly more. She'd seen one in a Fifth Avenue gallery just like it.

"No, thank you." The clipped tones were full of disdain. "Don't try to fob me off with that cheap stuff. It's clearly inferior. How much for that one there—the yellow one?"

Ahmed shook his head, sadly. "That one is over eight thousand Marks."

"Two thousand," he barked. "Not a pfennig more."

Haya grinned, and ate a pastry. Fat fool! Her husband was going to fleece this idiot. And he'd been so rude and aggressive . . . he deserved it.

She hated that sense of moral superiority they came in here with. As though they were instantly going to be cheated. Well, their insults had created that fact. And she was glad.

If she had watched Ahmed bow, and scrape, and allow himself to be talked down to . . . it would have changed them, her and him, forever. How could she feel as owned, as possessed by him as she did ... surrender herself to him ... if he had been weak with other people?

Instead, he was expertly slicing these obnoxious tourists up. Not boorishly, but deftly. And it was not theft ... they were paying only what they wanted to.

She listened carefully. He did not lie, or tell them the kilim was a work of art. Instead he praised its general qualities. And why not? It was a perfectly workmanlike rug.

But it was nothing like what they were paying for.

What fools, she thought. Demeaning another people, a great people, just because they saw them as poorer. It was an instructive lesson in manners.

As they went through the motions, paying with a credit card, filling out customs forms, Haya drank her tea, and drank in her surroundings. Beautiful carpets ... impressive. And that Ahmed had a good business, she could see. Large offices, a staff, a comfortable house, prosperity, and servants.

But she thought about herself. Now she was his wife ... they were a team; they could be more.

She was here, and married, very happily. Against the odds. She had never thought it could happen. Her parents' choice ... far more importantly, her own.

But she had tasted fun and independence in America, as well as romance in Egypt. Why give that up? Why put all those dollars spent on her education to waste?

Haya didn't see why Ahmed should stay here, comfortable, prosperous, a man trading well within his limits. She admired him. And even if Haya was Ahmed's, in his arms, outside them, she was her own woman. His wife. Couldn't he be more?

Better, couldn't *they* be more?

The fat Germans left, talking loudly in their own language; Haya didn't know the words, but she recognized the tone ... the same sneering contempt they had walked in with. Probably laughing at how they had ripped off the poor little carpet merchant. . . .

She was surprised to find a sudden surge of anger, almost violent loathing, ripping through her. She wanted to kill them. No ... she wanted to *show* them.

"So what did you think?"

Ahmed, slipping back into Arabic, came over to his wife, grinning. "Happy customers, no? And so generous. Five thousand, in the end, for that 500-mark kilim."

"You are a wonderful businessman." She leaned across, put her lips up to his, and kissed him. "And your carpets are magnificent."

"Thank you, darling."

Haya ran her hand possessively over his sleeve.

"Do you think I could be involved?"

"Involved?"

"Help you. With the business. I have better English . . . I know America. My father could get some contacts. Maybe you could export."

Ahmed, surprised, smiled back at her.

"That would be good. I'd like you to take an interest." He slid his hands up and down her waist, resting his fingertips on the underside of her breasts, stroking lightly.

Haya shuddered with pleasure, but pulled away, glancing downstairs in case one of the workers came up.

"That way you could be with me all day." He released her breasts, but laid a hand casually against the flat of her stomach, letting her know he could feel the warm blood pooling there, hot under the skin, her belly tense with desire. Ahmed bent down and placed his mouth against her ear, and Haya pressed herself against his hand, her knees buckling.

"Please," she murmured, "take me home. . . ."

"I should make you wait," he whispered.

"Please, Ahmed . . ."

He straightened, and called to his staff that they were going home for lunch.

"Working together. An excellent plan." He grinned.

❦

He left her at three, bemoaning his lack of self-control. But Ahmed was so slow, so patient, a master at heating her and reheating her. He could awake desire when Haya thought she was drained. The Lord only knew when, exactly, they would do *business* . . .

Haya was excited at the prospect. The last of her doubts had lifted with it. Now she would go to America, too, see her family and her old friends. A wave of guilt ran through her at her immolation here, lost in Ahmed to the exclusion of all else. But since he was the first, the only man in her life, the other girls would understand, wouldn't they? It had only been a few months. Extended honeymoon, if you like.

Haya dialed Jane's number, squaring her shoulders, preparing to get a blast for being out of touch for so long. She knew she deserved it!

"The number you have called is not in service," said a tinny American voice. "Please check the number and dial again."

She did. Same message. Damn it, Haya thought. Jane had changed her phone number? Was it the holidays—had it transferred back to the embassy in Washington?

Never mind, Sally would know. She rang Green Gables. This time the phone did ring.

"Waterford residence. May I help you?"

"I'm sorry; I must have the wrong number. I was looking for the Lassiter residence."

There was a pause.

"They don't have this number any longer, ma'am."

Haya blinked. "Okay—sorry—"

But the caller had hung up.

She felt bad. Just a few months and both her friends had changed numbers? It was Haya's own fault for not staying in touch . . . okay, first she'd been embarrassed, but once she'd fallen in love with Ahmed, decided to stay married . . .

Haya thought for a moment, then dialed the British Embassy in Washington.

"I'm looking for Jane Morgan . . . daughter of Ambassador Thomas Morgan . . . I'm a friend of hers."

"We have no information on her whereabouts."

Haya tried again. This was fruitless.

"Look—I went to school with her at Miss Milton's in Los Angeles. I've been out of touch . . . I got married. I'm in Egypt. She's not at her house they rent in Malibu. I called our friend Sally Lassiter. . . ."

"Just a second please."

Haya waited. There was a click, and another voice came on the line; cool, modulated English tones.

"This is Emmeline Berkley. I was Ambassador Morgan's private secretary. Can I help you?"

Haya explained.

"Yes . . . I remember Miss Morgan mentioning you. And you left the country . . ."

"Three months ago."

There was a sigh.

"I regret to have to tell you," Ms. Berkley said, not unkindly, "that Ambassador Morgan committed suicide. Miss Morgan had herself legally emancipated as an adult, and after that the embassy lost track of her, since at that point we had no responsibility for her. I believe she is somewhere in Los Angeles still, but I have no contact information. I'm sorry."

"Oh. I see. Poor Jane," Haya gasped. Now she really did feel low. "I have to find her . . . I'll contact Sally . . ."

"Sally Lassiter? That was Miss Morgan's close friend?"

"Yes," Haya said anxiously, not liking her tone.

"Then you might not have heard . . . Mr. Lassiter's oil company collapsed, and I'm afraid he had a heart attack. The government confiscated the assets; it was rather a big scandal."

Haya's knuckles tightened around the phone. Sally had been close to her father, very close.

"And where are Mrs. Lassiter and Sally?"

"The press reports said they went to Texas." There was a touch of real sympathy in the firm tones now. "I'm sorry, that's all I know."

"Thanks for your help," Haya said, hanging up.

Well—there was nothing she could do now. Nothing she

could do from Egypt, anyway. Haya was wracked with guilt. Both her friends had lost a parent . . . not that Jane's had been much use. And Sally, glorious confident Sally, how on earth would she cope? Life without money . . . Haya couldn't imagine it. Sally had her own personal limo and chauffeur, did she even know how to drive?

She gave herself a little shake. No point in beating herself up, she had to get on with it now, travel back to the States and find them. She could set up some contacts for Ahmed while she was about it. Haya was convinced of her husband's eye, his drive and talent. He needed to swim in a bigger pond. And she needed to find her friends.

~

Haya took it slowly at first. A week or two meeting the staff, getting to know Ahmed's stock, his prices, how he found his carpets. Brushing up on her written Arabic, learning how he kept his books: the old-fashioned way, in leather-bound volumes. Her husband was a visionary, and in love with the beauty of the things he sold. Haya's first move was to buy a computer, enter all his data onto spreadsheets, and start filing on his customer base. Ahmed didn't like it much, but she ignored him, and kept plugging away. And within a few days he was staring, amazed, at the simple, easy system she had set up, and then trying to use it himself.

Haya called her father. They had a long, stilted conversation. She decided to avoid talking about the marriage. What was the use? He would only act defensive. Instead, Haya demanded her father's assistance.

That was the price of forgiveness. She didn't say it openly, but they both understood it just the same.

Baba, chastened by her tone, promised he would help. He could set up some meetings, talk to some people who knew people, that sort of thing. There were exhibitions—trade fairs. Retailers, although many of them already had suppliers . . .

"We will undercut their suppliers," Haya said, ruthlessly. "Tell them that."

Ahmed, overhearing, grinned. "And once they're hooked, the price goes up."

He kissed his wife on the forehead. She was intelligent, and now she was a true help to him. No more long nights grappling with his books in the fading light. No more riffling through his papers to find the right number. She had even helped him with his taxes.

He liked it. Last week, Ahmed had gone on an acquisition trip to Fez and, without rushing things the way he was used to, had picked up better stock at lower prices.

And it turned him on to see his intelligent, dark-haired wife, the scarf draped modestly over her hair, concentrating on the figures, her fingers flashing over the keyboard. She was not one to stay at home, or spend her days gossiping with friends. She engaged with the world, and her spirit was fiery, the same fire that clawed at him and writhed under him in their marriage bed. . . .

It was his business, of course; he was in charge. But Haya argued her case, and Ahmed listened to her.

⟍⟋

"I have some ideas," Haya said one evening after a fine sale. Ahmed had won an order from an Egyptian hotel chain in Sharm el-Sheik, a large order for its lobbies and conference rooms; he had supplied pieces worth forty thousand dollars. They were flush with cash. He had been half expecting her to pounce on it.

"What do you mean?"

"Business ideas. I think you should change."

"Change?" Ahmed blinked. "Change what? This works, my love. I've been doing it since I was younger than you."

"Not the goods . . . well, maybe. Maybe we could diversify." Ahmed frowned at that, so she hurried on. "But I think you should find a new way to sell. Don't deal with these little people. They are not worth your time, my sweetheart." She kissed his arm through the fabric of his shirt. "You need to do it differently . . . to sell these beautiful carpets the way they are meant to be sold. Each individually. Displayed like a jewel. We need to find

more customers like the hotels, and fewer like Begum Sistani."
The rich, fat widow of the interior minister, who always came
back to them when she bought a new villa or Parisian apartment,
probably with ill-gotten gains from the taxpayer.

Ahmed was listening, she saw. Emboldened, she plowed on.
"And given space in windows . . . and each one selling for many,
many thousands. Why should you not be like the owner of a
gallery?" Her Arabic was rough, but she continued. "They give
stories to their artwork. Provenance . . . catalogues. You can sell
your carpets that way. They are all unique. Why should arrogant
tourists from Europe, with no appreciation of them, buy them
and place them in their homes?"

He smiled, intrigued.

"And how would you propose to do this?"

"We must export," she said, confidently. "To America. To the
quality stores. Perhaps first to a gallery. Somewhere very expensive." Haya switched to English. "You know that American expression? 'Sell the sizzle, not the steak.' My friend Sally taught
me that."

He chuckled. "I like that."

"I can help," she insisted. "I speak perfect English. I also know
them . . . the richest Americans; what they want, what sells to
them. Let me be your export director. Let me work for you."

Ahmed's arm stole around her waist. "You *do* work for me."

"That's not work."

"And I told you, I don't want you leaving me for the States.
Even for a week."

"Then come with me," she said persuasively. "Come with me.
I can teach you better English. The same way you teach me Arabic . . . and I know people. I've spoken to my father. . . ."

He thought about it. "You really think I could sell these
better?"

"No question," she said confidently.

Ahmed leaned down and kissed her, hard, on the lips. "Then
let us try it," he said.

He believed in his wife. She was young, but she was brilliant.
There was that core in her that a man could rely on.

They could be partners in business, as well as in life. Let her give him that start, and he would take over. Soon, anyway, she would be preoccupied in the nursery.

"Can I call home again?" Haya said, beaming.

He was mildly offended. "I've never stopped you."

"Then you have no objection. I can tell Baba we're coming?"

Ahmed leaned in to her. "Since almost the first night, I believed in you, Haya. Let's try it."

CHAPTER 7

I t was amazing how fast the whole thing happened.

Her father's death. Leaked, by somebody in that scum-sucking nest of lawyers. On the radio. It hit the TV before anybody placed a call to Green Gables. Mona had been in the beauty parlor . . . her chauffeur had hustled her out, and as they drove home, her sobbing mother was chased by the paparazzi.

Sally herself refused to believe it. She'd rushed out of school—nobody daring to tease her, not even Julie, not that day, at least—demanding loudly to talk to the police, then calling them liars as they tried to pass on the news.

As long as she lived, Sally would never forget that day. The howling rage of her loss, the sick feeling in the pit of her stomach. The photographers, like locusts, camped outside the brass gates of her house; news helicopters chopping loudly overhead, their intrusive spotlights beaming down into their lawns. Rushing in to hug her wailing, disintegrating mother, turning off the TV that showed her father's ample body being loaded onto a gurney, wrapped up in a blue tarpaulin.

"They shouted at me," Mona choked out. "They called me 'the merry widow.'"

Even in her grief, Sally had felt the rage, rising, blocking the air from her throat so she could hardly breathe. Bastards! Some wiseass had yelled her way, when her white car was entering the gates, "Hey, baby! Are you the richest heiress in America!"

What the hell did he know, she thought, tears brimming up and helplessly tumbling down her cheeks. Didn't he understand she didn't give a damn about money? That she'd trade every red cent for one more minute with her daddy's arms around her?

For the first time in her golden, charmed life, Sally Lassiter's devastation overwhelmed her. Every moment, thinking how that was it, she'd never speak to her father again. Not in this world. Not for all the days of her life. He'd never walk her down the aisle, never hold her children. . . .

It was bad. The pain was a hurricane, battering at the hatches of her heart and dignity.

And it was all about to get much, much worse.

~

The next months were a haze of pain and fear. First the funeral—long-lost relatives, people Sally never saw from one end of the year to another, crawling out of the woodwork; charities, colleges, lobbyists, all calling with their palms out, grubbing for cash. Sally, throwing dirt and a rose onto Daddy's coffin. Walking away from that gravesite. Trying to support her mother, who was starting to fall apart.

And after that grim event, worse to come. The lawyers—first her own, then the government's. And the companies. The executors, and the insurers . . .

Her father, she discovered, was accused. Fraud and embezzlement on a massive scale. Thousands of workers who had lost their pensions, ordinary families bankrupt. Her mother—who could hardly sleep, and at times barely dress herself, who had stopped washing, or brushing her teeth, or combing her hair—Sally took care of her as though she were a child. Her mother offered nothing but a blank, Valium-induced stare.

And so the police and the investigators talked to Sally. And roamed through her house. Rifled everywhere, like burglars, looking for documents. Took away every computer. Impounded her parents' cars.

She dropped out of school, and hired her own lawyer. Not for long, though; the federal government froze their bank accounts. And the worst thing was that, as she forced herself to watch the news, long after Mona had crawled into bed, Sally couldn't blame them.

Sick with dismay, she was forced to confront the idea that her father might have been a crook . . . that the luxury they lived in might have been built on the suffering of others. Her father's lawyer, Lionel Javits, promised her privately it was not that way, and Sally clung to that.

"He died right in front of me. You could say of shock."

"Shock," Sally repeated.

The lawyer spoke compassionately, but slowly, as though she were stupid; he does think I'm dumb, Sally's brain told her. Dumb blonde. The old classic.

"There were thieves in that company, miss, but your dad wasn't one of 'em."

"And this house?"

He flinched away from her cool gaze and stared at his hands.

"Please tell me the truth, Mr. Javits," Sally said, her soft Texan tones demanding his respect. "My mother's having a hard time with this. The police and FBI come around here every day. The staff already quit because I can't pay their wages. Tell me what's going on, and I can make a plan to deal with it."

That impressed him—his own children, his teenage boys with their Metallica jackets and studs in the ears, they would never be able to cope, never be as strong as this young woman with the weight of the world dropped on her slender shoulders.

"It's not something you can make a plan for. Your father didn't realize, but the oil profits that paid for this estate were built on paper. What my office is hearing is that the government is about to repossess."

"Can we fight that?"

"Not in my judgment. They've seized all the liquid assets of the estate. This is next. No lawyer can make a case that this . . ." He waved a hand inadequately around the vastness of their kitchen. "That this is necessary as a dwelling."

Sally drew herself up. "I see." She paused, mulling it over, the dreadful news in all its bitterness. "And what will they leave us with?"

"Nigel Farrar is the prosecutor. He's oily, looks slick on TV, wants to run for Congress . . ."

"Wants to look tough on criminals?"

Javits nodded. "I'm very sorry, but he gets good press if you and your mother are left with nothing." He sighed. "Like all the other Lassiter Oil families."

"Nothing? No settlement?"

"He has an excellent case. The longer you drag it out, the better he likes it. Your mother can try innocent spouse relief, but they'll never let you keep above a token amount. . . ."

Sally stood up. "When are they going to do this to us?"

"Maybe next week. Is there somewhere else you can go?"

"You mean that Daddy didn't own this? Not really?"

"Believe me, Sally, Nigel Farrar wants a circus. I think you should do your best to get out of here. Go stay with friends."

Ouch. That cut. Friends. Where were they?

Helen had run off to get married, and Jane—Jane was dealing with her own troubles. Sally felt the abandonment almost physically.

"I tell you what," she said, slowly. "Can you negotiate with them for me? My mom's got some jewelry. . . ."

"Anything Mr. Lassiter gave her is forfeit."

"No. Her own. She was a society belle back home. Brought some into the marriage." Sally almost choked on it. "I have a diamond brooch I can give you for a fee. You go to the prosecutor and get us free and clear on my mother's personal savings account—that was frozen, too. It was a dowry, she never touched it. There's fifty thousand dollars in there."

Fifty thousand—that used to be the wages of their live-in chef. All of a sudden, it looked like it was all she had left in the world.

"I can do that." Javits thought about offering to represent her pro bono, but he was not a strong man, and it wouldn't have looked good. He didn't want to damage his reputation.

"Thank you," the glorious blonde creature said, with a calm smile that made him feel four feet tall.

"Where will you go?" he asked, wretchedly.

"My father's niece is in Texas. We'll go live near her. It's a small town, very quiet." Cheap too, Sally didn't say. "I'll go get that diamond pin for you, Mr. Javits, and you get that account unlocked."

Javits worked fast. And so did Sally. Once her mind was made up, there was nothing more to do. She called Jane, asked her to hire a car and come round and help her pack.

"I'm so sorry." Jane stood by, feeling useless, as Sally packed up her suitcases with a brisk efficiency that Jane had never known.

"Wasn't your fault." Red-eyed, her friend bent down and zipped up the last of the cases. "And I'm so sorry for what happened to your father, too."

"Yeah, well," Jane said, her throat dry. "I never had much of a dad to start with."

"My daddy was perfect." Sally bit down hard on her lip, and Jane turned away so she could compose herself. After a moment's struggle, she straightened herself, and surveyed her room; all mind-blowing luxury, a Barbie palace, with designer dresses, pink silk walls, a four-poster bed, enough sweetness to give you a toothache. The ultimate girlie paradise.

"You're strong," Sally said. "Give me a hand to load up these cases, hon?"

Jane hesitated. "But we're not done packing."

"Yes, we are."

"We need another case—your toys, your bear. . . ." She held up the much-loved fluffy brown teddy with the lopsided eye. "You can't leave Mr. Snuffles, Sal. Come on!"

Her friend shook her head and lifted the largest suitcase.

"Yes, I can." She nodded for Jane to do the same. "I don't need him anymore. My childhood is over. It's time to grow up."

The girls lugged the heavy cases down the long stairs, one by one, and loaded them into the back of the rented van.

"Long drive," Jane observed. "Sure you won't fly?"

"I don't want to face them at the airport." They both knew she was talking about reporters. "By the time we get to Texas, this story will be done. Something else will have happened. I don't need to expose Momma to a plane full of angry people."

In truth, Sally didn't want to expose her mother to people, period. Mona was losing it, and she couldn't bear for her to be seen in public.

"So what about you?" Anything to change the subject. She dragged her thoughts away from her disintegrating mother, and fixed her pretty blue eyes on Jane. "The embassy made you an offer. . . ."

"I'm still a teen."

"Right." Sally hopped from foot to foot. She wanted to get the hell in the car, get in and drive, go and wake her mother from the drunken stupor she was doubtless sunk into.

But that would be so final. Texas. She might as well be in outer space.

"Hey." Jane read her thoughts. "We're best friends. We'll find each other."

"And Helen?"

"When she finishes her honeymoon she'll be in touch. You bet."

"Friends forever," Sally said. She tried for brave, but her voice quivered.

"Forever," Jane repeated. She enveloped Sally in a big bear hug, and, so unlike her, gave her a little kiss on the cheek.

"I'll go get my mom. I better scoot. I hate good-byes."

"This isn't good-bye," Jane insisted. "It's 'see you later.'"

Sally nodded, not trusting herself to say anything else, and ran back into Green Gables to find her mother.

When she was out of sight, Jane quietly crept in behind her. She walked up to Sally's room, retrieved the teddy bear, and came back to the van, slipping it into the largest case.

She wanted Sal to have a friend. Because right now, she thought she'd never see her again.

"Well, now." Emily Harris glanced from Sally to Mona, and Sally squirmed inwardly. She'd done her best to clean her mother up this morning, before they checked out of the final hotel; forcing her to brush her teeth and swig with mouthwash, although she suspected Mona was swallowing the minty stuff just to get the alcohol; eight percent, as good as beer. Washing her hair was a no-go—Sally wasn't strong enough to physically wrestle her mother, so she had to make do with scarfing a brush through it, tying it into a ponytail, and dousing it with hairspray. At least that should take care of some of the dirty, sweaty smell. Mona had agreed to get in the shower; a small mercy, though Sally looked and saw she wasn't washing, just standing there, slumped against a wall, as the water sluiced over her.

In truth, Sally was frightened. Her mother's depression had turned her into another person. A helpless, sick person, listless and lifeless. If her mom had her way, she'd never even get out of bed.

The speed and shock of loss was too much for her mother to deal with. The loss of the only man she'd ever loved had devastated Mona, but then came everything else on top, and it finished her. The scandal, the shame . . . TV headlines . . . and all her fairweather friends melting away like New York slush in April.

As the money vanished, so did Mona's support network. Half of them dropped her before the funeral, afraid to be pictured on the news at the graveside of a world-class crook. The other half vanished one by one as the lawyers and federal government closed down their accounts. Besides her supposed best friends, Lucille and Kimberley, Susan Ermine, wife of a senator, suddenly discovered she had to be in Washington. Milly Fawcett and her husband disappeared on a 'round the world' cruise. Lola Montez actually called Mona, said the family had deceived them and they were no longer friends. Her mother had cried then, shocked for a second out of her apathy. But Sally was fiercely grateful to Lola. At least that one had some guts. At least she'd told them the truth.

The Lassiters, once the billionaire kings of Beverly Hills, were pariahs. And Sally could see the same wary, disgusted look in the eyes of her cousin Emily. Dad's niece had married exceptionally well—into an old Carolina family—and disapproved of Mona, the brash, working-class barmaid that Paulie Lassiter had plucked out of the gutter twenty years ago.

"Well," she repeated, and her smile was bright and cold, "it certainly is a surprise to see y'all here. What can I do for you?"

"We've left L.A. for good," Sally said, taking the lead. "We're going to settle back home. In Texas. Near family."

Family, right. What a joke. The only family Sally had was sitting next to her, staring into space.

"I don't know if that's such a good idea," Cousin Emily said, smiling all the brighter. "Surely you have friends back in L.A. You're hardly Texans anymore."

"I was born here," Sally countered. "Spent my childhood here. I'm as Texan as you are. And of course, you're one of our nearest relations."

There it was. She waited to see what her cousin would say. Emily was a mighty rich woman, not oil rich, but plantation rich; her dead husband had left her plenty of land and some big condo developments. She was in a position to turn their lives around, if she chose to. A grace and favor apartment. A nice car. An office job, something undemanding, to occupy Mona's time.

"I think we better get some things straight," the older woman responded. "When Uncle Paulie left for California . . . well, some of us thought that was best. There was distance, you understand. We were never very close. Y'all never visited me here, and I never came to you. . . . We're not really family in that sense. And I have to tell you, Mona," she turned and addressed her remarks, coldly, to the glassy-eyed woman propped against a corner of her couch, "that I'm really highly disappointed in you and my uncle. You stole from hard-working families—"

Sally jumped up. "Daddy did no such thing!"

A long sigh. "That's not what the federal government says. And now y'all turn up here, poor as church mice, disgraced. . . . I declare, Mona, if I don't smell liquor on your breath at ten o'clock in the morning . . . well, I think it's just too bad."

"I see. Thank you for your hospitality." Sally tossed her golden hair defiantly. "Come on, Momma. We're leaving."

"I'm sorry, but I think it's better to get these things straight. I have a position in society . . ."

"Yes." Sally gave a mighty heave and hauled her mother to her feet. "It's better to know where we stand. You're certainly not family. And yes—you are sorry. A sorry excuse for a Christian woman."

The tears were threatening now. She was tired—exhausted. Her back hurt from days of driving, she had nowhere to go, and her last hope was looking at her with total contempt.

"Please leave," said Emily Harris, flushing with anger.

"Don't worry. We won't bother you again." Sally thrust up her chin, her slim shoulders set firm. "And I won't forget this, either."

"That's as may be," said her cousin, following closely behind as Sally dragged Mona, stumbling, to the door. "But I'm certainly going to forget you. Your family has embarrassed us all."

Sally pushed her mother out across the sweeping, gracious porch, which had looked so welcoming when they first arrived, all whitewashed wood, cane sofas and heaped cushions; an old-fashioned southern veranda.

"Don't come back here," Emily shouted, as Sally opened up the van and helped her mother inside. "We have security."

And she slammed the door.

"Now what?" Mona asked, as Sally, brushing away the tears, angrily spun the van around. "Where do we go? My head hurts."

"Don't worry, Momma." Sally refused to give in; mingling with her embarrassment and fear was a sense of white-hot anger, and she used that anger to keep her strong. "We'll be okay. We have some money, enough to rent a place. Look." She turned left, into Hartford, the nearest signposted town, and slowed as they reached Main Street. "This place has everything." Sally gestured as they rode by. "Look, a drugstore . . . banks . . . a post office . . . rail station." It was small, and the houses were not all that big— a place for the working middle classes, Sally assessed instantly. Which was just what they were, as of now.

Hartford. An anonymous American town. It even had a high school. Perfect.

"Let's pull over, get a local paper," Sally decided. "I'll have a house legally rented by the end of the day. This is home." She glanced at her mother, who was watching the dashboard, betraying no interest.

"We'll be happy here," Sally insisted, bravely. But even she didn't believe it.

~

She worked hard. First, finding a place. That afternoon, Sally trooped round apartments—mostly run-down, with the paint peeling off the walls—and houses, some with leaking roofs or mold. In the end, forced to raise her price, she found a two-bedroom tract home, on the edge of a main road, near a drugstore and a garage. Poor location, but all the basics; neat, clean, with no more than a square patio to look after in the back. Sally put down three months' rent to avoid a credit check, and breathed a sigh of relief. The utilities were connected. There were no roaches. It was poor, yes, but respectable. And she could afford to rent there for a couple of years, at least.

Mona was making noises about going to the local bar, so although Sally hated herself, she went out with Momma and bought liquor, cheap gut-rot vodka, in the forlorn hope it would turn her mother's stomach. And not at the liquor store, either, but not because she was worried about getting carded at either place—she could always make herself pass for twenty-one—but because she could just imagine what gossip would do in a one-horse joint like this . . . they'd go crazy over the new arrivals, a mom and daughter whose first stop was to pick up alcohol in a brown paper bag! Instead, they went to the grocery store, passed the time of day with the clerk, and Sally shopped, for almost the first time in her life, awkwardly putting groceries into the trolley, trying to learn the prices of different brands. Sally picked up milk, eggs, cheese, and fruit; meat was expensive, so she bought spaghetti and mince for Bolognese. Simple; she'd liked to cook, at times, as a hobby, and that would be cheaper than prepared sauces.

And she also bought bread, and a few little luxuries. The

exhaustion had not dissipated, but Sally was discovering the fire she had in her belly. Damn it all, she was going to survive. One step at a time. Get a little money, rent a normal house, fill the refrigerator. And they were not going to live like slobs. For only a couple dollars, she picked up pretty scented soaps and some potpourri. Candles could come later . . . Sally didn't trust her mother not to knock them over and accidentally set the place on fire.

In the discount racks, Sally found other things. A couple of framed samplers. Cheesy, perhaps, but this way they would have art on the walls, not just bare white space.

～

They came home. Momma took the vodka and drank till she passed out on the couch. That was a relief. Sally quietly unpacked, and took a long, hot, relaxing shower. Then she stashed away the suitcases and left a note on the table. She drove out of town to a Shop Smart they'd passed on the way in. That place was paradise for shoppers down on their luck. For an hour or so Sally forgot her troubles; she scoured the aisles, looking for bargains, looking for bright, stylish touches: a five-dollar rug, some artificial silk roses, a white wicker wastebasket, fluffy towels for the bathroom, oversized and underpriced.

When she got back, Mona was still snoring. Her limbs drained, Sally nonetheless managed to unpack, hammer, and hang; to make the beds, fluff the cushions, lay out the towels, put the toothbrushes in the holder.

By the time she was done it was late at night. Sally walked around the house, with the blinds down, a grim little smile on her face. On less than seventy dollars, she'd made the place look normal; it was cheerful and clean, a respectable, basic house.

Quite an achievement. She thought of her mother, staggering around motel rooms, knocking over full ashtrays the maids hadn't bothered to clean. When she woke, hung over, it would be in a proper house for a family to live in. Not what they were used to—but miles away from Skid Row.

She undressed, carefully slipped on her pajamas, and tumbled into bed, enjoying the feel of the brand-new sheets. Tomorrow there was lots to do. Return the rental car . . . buy a new one . . . register for school . . . contact the lawyer . . .

Sally knew her father would be proud of her. Misery probed at her, but she was too tired to dwell on the past. Tomorrow was the start of a new, tough life, but she knew she could handle it. She slipped into a deep sleep.

⌒

"Mom . . ." She hated the way her voice sounded, all whining and pleading. "You don't need that."

"Hey." Mona gripped the vodka bottle, all the way to the sink. She swayed on her slippers. "Don't lecture me, missy. I can't stand it when you get all uppity."

"You've already had too much."

A fat tear of self-pity rolled down her mother's cheek.

"Why can' you leave me alone?" she slurred. "Can' I have a lil bit of pleasure left in this world? . . . He's gone . . . he's gone."

"I know." Sally fought back her own tears. "He's gone, Mom. And he'd hate to see you like this."

She reached out to grab the sink to steady herself, missed, and fell over; the vodka bottle slipped from her grasp and smashed on the floor. Mona burst into loud, drunken tears.

"We gotta go out," she whined. "Gotta go out and get some more. . . . I don't have more here."

Thank God, thought Sally.

She went over to her mother, carefully picking her way through the broken glass.

"Never mind, Momma. I'll clear that up. You come with me. Just take a little lie-down.."

"Yeah . . . a lie-down."

"This way." Sally was slightly built, but she was strong, and getting stronger. Hauling Mona's dead weight around was something she did a lot of lately.

"I don' feel so good. . . ."

Mona was turning a nasty shade of green. Hastily, Sally shoved her into the bathroom. Thank God it was downstairs.

"Go ahead, you'll feel better. . . ."

But Mona had already slipped to her knees and was puking violently.

Sally leaned back against the wall and tried to count her blessings. This was gross, but at least her momma was getting it out now. She was frightened that one day Mona would fall asleep and choke on her own vomit, like a seventies rock star, but without the glamour. Or just die of alcohol poisoning.

She'd drawn down the blinds. Their house was now permanently shuttered, and they lived in a darkened, gloomy atmosphere, like a Spielberg movie just before the aliens come. But Sally had learned to cope with just the cracks of sunlight that beamed through the dusty windows. No way did she want any of the neighbors to see her mom looking like this. Worse still, the press. . . .

They had come crawling around here, those damn vultures. Sally had learned to manage them. When they doorstepped her on her way to her new public school, Sally would just smile and say that she was settling in, and her mother was still in mourning. That it was a beautiful neighborhood. That her daddy always taught her to take the lemons of life and make her some lemonade.

And then she would politely remind the snapper that she was still a minor, on her way to school. Could they please back off?

That always worked. Whether it was from fear of legal action or shame, they left her alone.

The tabloid articles were out there. With their pictures in. "Brave Sally, starting over." "Sally Lassiter, staying strong for Mom." It was human interest, and at least it was better than the alternative—nasty realms of print, castigating her and her mother for living off the backs of the poor.

There was some of that too, of course; the shrieking phone calls, late at night, the hate mail, notes from people swearing her mother was a greedy bitch, that they had money stashed away in Switzerland or the Caymans. Sally tried to remember that these folks had lost everything. Lassiter Oil had collapsed, the pensions of the workers had evaporated, and her dad's old buddies at the top were mostly in jail.

Good—she'd rather have seen them dead. They were murderers—they'd killed her father.

And the aftermath was killing her mother.

Sally dealt with grief. She had to. There was only room for one invalid in the family, and Momma had taken that slot. While Sally tried to piece things together, just the most basic stuff—talking to law enforcement, swearing out depositions, arguing with the bankruptcy courts—Mona had dived into the clear, numbing depths of her vodka bottle, and Sally had the feeling she wasn't coming out of it anytime soon.

Sally knew she wasn't brilliant, like Jane, or even smart, like Helen; Helen, so graceful and diplomatic, aristocratically femi-nine; Jane, the librarian limey, both girls far more sophisticated than the pretty Texas rose who'd had life handed to her on a silver platter.

But Sally had something. Something more than long blonde hair, flawless limbs, and a tan. Sally had street smarts. She knew how to sell herself, and how to sell situations. A parting gift from her dad, perhaps.

Despite it all, she had managed—still was managing—to change the story from "embezzler's widow" to "brave survivors." She had negotiated a settlement with the IRS that left them without any more creditors, at least. And she learned how to shop on a budget. Sally took care of school enrollment, and sign-ing Mom up for benefits and Medicaid.

Sally wasn't embarrassed to go on welfare; she couldn't afford to be.

The most important thing was to look after Momma. Sally didn't mind the press stalking her; but she couldn't bear them to see the wreck of her mom, a slovenly drunk, hell-bent on killing herself and oblivious to shame.

As Mona retched and heaved, Sally glanced around their home. This was getting to be a routine. Put Momma to bed, force her to drink a glass of water and choke down two aspirins, then clean the place while her mother snored in a drunken stupor.

She was getting to like cleaning. It gave her a very small sense of control. At least their home would not be a disgrace.

Mona gave one more dry heave and collapsed.

Sally quietly went to the sink, moistened a washcloth, and cleaned her mother's face. She flushed the toilet, and heaved her mom back into the living room. Mona had already passed out— no way to get her up the stairs.

Carefully Sally laid her mother on her side, in case she was sick again, and put a blanket over her. No water—she was unconscious.

Then she went upstairs, to her own room. To think.

~~~~~

Upstairs, Sally's room was a little haven. A tiny box, sure; her dressing room at home had been twice as big. But she had decorated as best she could with cheap touches from Shop Smart, little pink cushions and swatches of gauze; it had fresh flowers on the windowsill; her clothes hung neatly in the wardrobe; and she had used candles to give the place a soft glow at night. It smelled good and looked fresh, and Sally hung a framed photo of Laguna Beach, California, right over her desk.

There was a calendar underneath that picture, and she noticed the next day was ringed—oh. Right. Her birthday.

Yeah, she thought, morosely. Happy birthday. To me.

A year out here. A year of suffering. Of being ogled by the boys and teased by the girls at a little hick school, where pupils were content to make low grades and scrape by. A school with no Helen or Jane. And, knowing she was friendless, the boys hit on her. One even offered her money.

Sally opened her window, to let in a cool winter draft. It was chillier than usual, to match her mood.

She needed a change. Desperately.

But what could she do?

And then it dawned on her. Seventeen—she was seventeen. She could *leave* school. Why not? It didn't offer her anything. Mediocre SATs, and no money for a university. Community college—that was worthless.

Sally had no doubts. She wasn't clever enough, or qualified enough, to go work for somebody else in some office. That way lay grunt wages and a dull life. The most she could hope for was an eventual slot in middle management, perhaps a tract home in Dallas. . . .

Hell no. If anything was going to happen, she had to make it happen.

She felt like pacing her room, only there was no space. Sally smiled at the irony and checked herself out in the mirror. So what *did* she have? What had she got that other people couldn't offer?

Well, beauty, of course. But Texas had lots of pretty girls. Still, there was something else. She was dressed in a sharp jacket, seamed stockings, and a pleated, swinging little skirt—about the only nice clothes at the discount store, but they fit her perfectly. Even after she'd driven to Dallas to sell all her designer outfits to an upmarket secondhand store, Sally realized with a thrill of pleasure, she'd still managed to look good. For all the "Barbie" taunts they threw at her, girls in the playground copied her style. . . .

Style. That's what Sally Lassiter had. That's what kept those photographers at bay. That's what kept their heads above water, even now, when the bottom had fallen out of their world.

And if there was one thing Hartford needed, it was style. Style had kept her sane, kept her strong against the press and, later, the nasty kids at school. Style had helped her fight her mother's descent into the pit, and if she could only slow it, at least Sally had done that. She made sure that, like it or not, Mona was washed and dressed every day. Once a week, even as her mother gazed blankly at the TV, Sally insisted on giving her a manicure.

She was fiercely determined they would be decent. And Sally Lassiter never left the house without her eyebrows styled, mascara, and a slick of lipstick—at the very least.

The kids were starting to accept her. One of her male tor-mentors had even asked her out the other week, this time for real. And when she'd laughingly turned him down, he hadn't been able to shield the look of disappointment in his eyes.

What did style mean to her? Bravery and beauty. Glamour, as a weapon . . .

That thought made her wince. Just a little. A reminder of past history. When she, and Jane, and Helen, had come walking down those stairs . . .

~~~

Sally wondered if her friends ever tried to find her. Of course, she had intentionally disappeared. Put that down to style, too, if you like . . . the shame, the deep shame, that lurked around the edges of the brave face Sally put on things. She just could not bear for Jane to know how small her life was, or for Helen, kind, gentle Helen, to pity her. . . .

And she hadn't reached out for them. Survival, for herself and her mom, was her first priority. Of course, Sally had told herself that one day in the future, they'd be back. All of them rich. All of them on top . . . like it used to be . . . only better.

Why did I give that up? she wondered. Why did I stop think-ing about it?

The fact was that small-town Texas life, with an alcoholic mom and a dwindling stack of cash, was hard. And Sal hadn't had time for her own dreams. Or her memories. In fact, she had blocked out thoughts of Jane and Helen very deliberately.

Her friends were part of a happier time. And thinking about that hurt. *Damn. I can do better than this,* Sally thought, swallowing hard to push back the tears that were threatening. *Daddy would be proud of me for keeping it together, but survival ain't enough. I've got to have more.*

And style was Sally's way out.

She had it. Hartford needed it.

Sally came to a decision. It was time for Sally Lassiter to get a job.

～

When Sally came downstairs the next morning, Mona was already lying in front of the TV, with the talk shows on.

"Momma? Did you wash your face?" Sally called brightly, fixing herself an orange juice.

"Yes. And I did my teeth," Mona said, like a little girl.

"Shower?"

"I'll do that later."

"Okay." Normally Sally would have argued, but today she didn't have time. At least her mother had worked out that basic hygiene was the path of least resistance. Mona didn't want to look after herself, but even less did she want Sally to poke around her in the bathroom. So these days, Mona was brushing her own teeth and taking care of the basics.

Sally checked; her mother was in her favorite large pair of elasticized jeans and big floppy shirt, with her house clogs on. That was fine; not the height of fashion, but at least she was dressed.

Sally ate a slice of dry toast—always watching her weight—and scurried back upstairs. This was going to take some time. First, Sally washed and blow-dried her hair—no cheating today, no ponytails—then she selected her outfit.

It had to look sexy, but demure. She knew just the thing. A dark blue pair of boot-cut jeans, spray-on tight, to show the dangerous curves rising above her slender legs. Next, a crisp white shirt, three-quarter-length sleeves, to emphasize her hand-span waist and rich, golden tan. A cute silver cuff, to show off her delicate hands and carefully manicured French nails. Next, towering high-heeled cowboy boots. PVC, because she couldn't afford real leather.

Mmm. She smiled at her reflection. That looked fine.

Next, makeup. That was easy; she was going for healthy and young. Mascara, good and thick, on curled lashes that opened up her eyes. A sexy smudged black liner, to give her that bed-head style. A good rust-colored blush, half blusher, half bronzer—real "rose of Texas" stuff. Gold eyeshadow. Natural lip gloss, sheer with just a touch of pink, no liner. A spritz of perfume, and she was done.

Sally didn't normally go to this much trouble but today she had pulled out all the stops. She pirouetted in the mirror, loving what she saw. Yeah. She looked like a model, or a cheerleader for the Dallas Cowboys; every boy would want to be with her, and every girl would want to be her.

Sally glanced at her usual school outfits, hanging neatly in the closet. She had no use for them anymore.

" 'Bye, Mom," she called, running down the stairs. "See you later."

"Be good in school," Mona called back.

Sally grinned. Well, yes. She would.

⌒⌒

The gates of Hartford High were open—she was normally in here half an hour earlier, but that was as a pupil, on the bus. Today she had walked.

Lucy Drew, the hall monitor, was lounging about at the door. Her eyes widened.

"I have to give you a demerit for being late. Two—it's half an hour. And what happened to your regular clothes?"

Lucy was a nice enough girl—average face, brown hair, average body. She'd been kind to Sally when she first appeared, sometimes eating lunch with her if one of her own friends was sick.

"I'm quitting." There, that was a juicy piece of gossip. "You can feel free to tell the girls."

"Quitting school? Why, can't y'all afford the meals?"

Sally flinched; Lucy thought she and her mom were dirt poor. Well, the sorry truth was, with only sixteen thousand left in the bank, they were getting there.

"We're doing fine," she lied. "I'm just fed up with this place. Say, you know where Leo Fisk is next period?"

Lucy blushed; like every other girl in school, she was sweet on Leo. He played football, his daddy owned a chain of garages, and he drove a Porsche already. Plus, he had classic Texas good looks; clean shaven, strong jawed, slim and fit.

"Not sure," Lucy lied, but then admitted, "but I think it might be math."

"Cool. Thanks."

Sally sauntered past her on her way to the principal's office, head held high.

"But I don't understand." Mr. Rogers, the principal, looked dismayed. "You were doing very well in your studies, Sally."

This was truly shocking news. Rogers liked and admired the young blonde girl, and his teachers thought of her as a ray of sunshine, determined and fierce. He personally knew folks who had lost their life savings in the Lassiter Oil collapse, and he had been almost determined to loathe the billionaire princess who had turned up out of nowhere once he realized who she was.

But it had soon become clear that there were no billions left. Whatever else the Lassiters were doing, they weren't living high off the hog. The government had done a pretty good job wringing every last cent out of Paul Lassiter's estate. And in Hartford, gossips soon discovered the mom had serious problems.

Sally had tussled with the press when they first found her, and then with the sneers and jibes in school. He never saw her flirt or sleep around, although clearly she wasn't prudish—she was just too busy keeping her world together.

Prudish . . . definitely not. He was almost glad to be shocked by her news, because it was hard not to stare at the sensational young woman busting out of that shirt and jeans. Hell, she would tempt a statue. John Rogers kept his eyes determinedly above her collarbone.

"I was doing okay," Sally corrected him. "So-so SATs."

"You could make college."

"I want more than a basic college education and a job as a bank clerk," Sally replied, with a frankness that took him aback. "I have other talents. I want to go get a job, and then maybe start my own business. Doing what I'm good at."

"And what's that?"

Sally flashed a dazzling smile that made it somewhat hard to breathe.

"Glamour," she said. "Style."

He had no comeback. Undeniably, there, Sally Lassiter was a born expert.

"And where are you going to get a job?"

"At Fisk's Beauty Parlor."

Her principal blinked. Well, it made sense, if you considered that Elaine Fisk's little store was the only beauty place in town. But he thought that Sally Lassiter got on badly with young Leo Fisk; she'd refused his advances, and he amused himself making sexual cracks about her, loudly, and laughing with his buddies, whenever she came into earshot.

"I wish you the best of luck, young lady." Sally had made up her mind, and he got the sense there was no point in arguing. "And if it doesn't work out, come back to me. There are plenty of jobs around the school. . . ."

But not, he thought, in his office. He'd been married for fifteen years, and he'd like to stay that way!

"Thanks. Same to you, Mr. Rogers." She shook his hand, and was gone, leaving nothing behind but the faint scent of jasmine.

⁓

"We-e-ell," Leo said, giving a long, low whistle. His eyes flickered hungrily up and down Sally Lassiter's knockout body. "Damn, baby. You look about as pretty as a peach like that. What's up?"

Leo wasn't too smart. A meat-and-potatoes guy, he'd hated being humiliated by the leggy blonde from California—she was supposed to be as grateful for his attentions as all the other chicks. And he'd made sure to punish her when she didn't play ball. Rich girl on hard times? She should have been dying to lose her cherry to him.

But at least she'd come to him now. And how. Man. Sally could make just a pair of jeans like it should come with a triple-X certificate.

His buddies stood behind him, book bags over their shoulders, murmuring and ogling. Leo was pleased. The hottest chick in school had never looked hotter. There would be a special pleasure in laying her now they'd all seen what a grade-A piece of ass she was.

"Leo," Sally said, straightening her back, "I'm fixin' to leave school and get a job. And I'm hoping you'll be a gentleman and won't stand in my way."

"Stand in your way? Why would I want to do that?"

"Wanna earn some money, baby, I can think of an easy way to go," one of his jackass friends piped up. Leo turned and scowled at him.

"Shut it, Duane."

"We haven't always seen eye to eye. You know that."

Her voice was soft as melted butter, and there was something strong and beautiful about how she carried herself. He started to think he had been dumb, that maybe she'd make a good date, as well as a good lay.

"I'd love to let bygones be bygones," he said, his gaze traveling the entire length of her tall, delicious body. Imagine what that would be like in a see-through teddy from Victoria's Secret. . . .

He felt himself stirring, not good in a school corridor.

"That's mighty good of you, Leo. Because I'd like to go work in Mrs. Fisk's beauty parlor."

He couldn't stop a broad grin from spreading across his face. Perfect! The sassy little minx would be in Mom's little shop every day, and she'd be real beholden to him. He could have her fired anytime he liked.

"You go right ahead," he said. "I'll put in a good word for you, too. How's that?"

"That'd be real nice of you."

"And maybe you'd consider stepping out with me Friday night. That new shoot-'em-up movie's out. . . ."

"Why, that's a very sweet offer," Sally said, smiling at him. "But I never mix business with pleasure."

He flushed with anger and opened his mouth for a sharp retort, but then thought better of it. As a matter of fact, he just couldn't do it. The girl was too blindingly hot. Better to just put his time in. So she wanted to make him crawl . . . it'd be all the sweeter when she tumbled into his bed.

"I understand that," he said slowly. "So I'll call Mom for you. Maybe see you around."

"Sure thing. And thank you again," Sally said, and this time gave him a real smile, one that reached all the way to those clear blue eyes.

She knew the shop well, passed it every day. Fisk, the only beauty place in town. Really, it was drab and underused—mostly, Elaine Fisk just used it as a gossip shop. All her prosperous friends came in for manicures; Elaine employed two bored twenty-somethings to do manicures and blow-drys, with the occasional hair trim. It seemed to be well stocked but with old cosmetics, since nobody actually used the store. The ladies of Hartford preferred to drive over to Catfield, closer to Dallas and with a bunch of Korean-run manicure places.

But Sally never liked to leave Mona that long. So once a month, she had gone into Fisk's and had her eyebrows plucked. Five bucks, but worth it. She liked that sense she was treating herself. But she'd never go there for anything else. Not worth it; Mrs. Elaine Fisk, a fat woman into velour pantsuits and diamonds at all times, really knew as much about style as she did about advanced calculus.

Which was why this was such an attractive prospect. Far better than a Korean place, where the canny owners knew their business, or a fancy store with up-to-date magazines and tinted-glass windows. Fisk was perfect, Sally had decided. A central spot, and a blank canvas.

"My son speaks highly of you," Elaine Fisk said. "Says you are a very proper young lady."

Her stern eye danced over Sally's breathtaking outfit. Elaine couldn't work out quite what was so sexy about it. The jeans weren't too low waisted, nor the shirt unbuttoned. . . .

But just looking at Sally made Mrs. Fisk uncomfortable; she wished she hadn't eaten that second muffin for breakfast.

"Leo's been so kind to me," Sally said sweetly. "He's a credit to you and Mr. Fisk, ma'am. Y'all have raised a real gentleman. Everybody says so."

That did it; Elaine liked nothing better than to hear Sally Lassiter talk that way about her Pookie, her little baby. And maybe Sally could shake things up, she thought, vaguely. Not that Elaine cared about making money, nothing so vulgar! But her friend Sheila Gunn had recently abandoned her place, not even coming for coffee anymore—she said Betsy-Lou had messed up her trim and taken off two extra inches!

"Well, I could certainly use somebody to sweep the floor, maybe get me a couple of cushions, wash hair in the basins," Elaine conceded.

"Actually, I want to be your beauty therapist." Sally stood firm. If she didn't get it right now she'd never get another chance. "What I'd like to do is work with you on a new vision for Fisk's. Your beauty parlor will be *the* place in town, Mrs. Fisk. You'll have the ladies fighting each other to book a slot. You may have to change your phone number, because all your friends will be *begging* for appointments. . . ."

Elaine looked skeptical. "And how are we going to do that? What do I use to attract all this attention?"

"Me," Sally said, proudly.

"Honey, you don't have two cents to rub together. What could you know about fancy cosmetics?"

Sally didn't flinch. "You remember all the stories? A couple of years ago I used to know everything about them. And you know, Mrs. Finch, I was in L.A., and we mixed with the top Hollywood celebrities . . . I can tell you all the style secrets."

"Hollywood Dazzle!" Elaine cried. "That's the new name for the store!"

Sally bit back a smile. Hell, at least the woman was getting enthusiastic.

"We should stick to what we're known for. Nobody'll buy that down here. At least, not yet," she added, diplomatically. "This is your place so it should reflect *you,* Mrs. Fisk. How about this—Rodeo Girl."

"Rodeo Girl!"

"It's down-home, it's sassy, it's pretty, it's us."

"I like it," Elaine said excitedly. "And so I'll start doing the treatments. More treatments! We can offer makeovers . . ."

"We'll need a little money. Just a little. Some paint, some new lights . . . letters for the storefront . . ."

"My husband will give me that." Elaine waved her fingers dismissively, lost in the dream. Her store, her place, the hottest thing in town. But then her eyes narrowed, and she looked back at Sally. "But just because *you've* got style, how can I tell if you'll be good in the store? You would look good in a potato sack. We don't make a lot of money here . . . I don't think I can give you more than minimum wage; we are taking losses. . . ."

"I want a thousand dollars a month."

Elaine Fisk's eyes widened, and she laughed.

"Young lady, you are plumb crazy talking like that. We don't even take a thousand dollars in a month. Not even half. . . ."

"But we will. Much more than. Look, Mrs. Fisk. You're a beautiful lady yourself," Sally lied. "But when was the last time you had a real romantic date with Mr. Fisk? Tell you what. Why don't you let me style you? I'll show you just how good I am. You'll look ten years younger. He'll think he's romancing your little sister!"

"He better not," Elaine Fisk said darkly. But it was a tempting pitch. "Okay, I'll try it."

Well. This would be a challenge. But Sally gritted her teeth. She could certainly make Elaine look if not good, at least better.

"We'll start with hair and makeup," she said. "No cutting—just styling. And then we'll go shopping for a new outfit. I'll do your nails and brows. The whole bit. Why don't you come on over here, and we'll start with washing your hair."

Elaine hesitated.

"And I give a fabulous head and shoulder massage," Sally tempted.

"Alright. I'll try it." Elaine waddled over to the washbasin and sat down. "Although I've no idea why I'm agreeing to this. You certainly are a sweet-talker. . . ."

Sally hastily ran the warm water into the basin and wet down her new boss's hair. She didn't want to give Elaine the chance to change her mind.

⁓

"My stars," Elaine Fisk murmured. "Oh, my goodness."

She put one hand to her mouth, then lowered it again. She gaped at her reflection.

"I can't believe it. It doesn't even look like me."

Although she was twenty years younger, Sally stood back, beaming like a proud parent. Of course Elaine wasn't about to win any prizes in the Miss Texas pageant, but still. . . .

Her heavily sprayed, stiffly backcombed hair was softly washed, blow-dried, and styled into a long bob around her face. The layers of thick mascara that only a young woman could get away with had gone; Sally allowed her one coat of brown mascara to pick up the blue in her eyes. Similarly, the ugly rouge on Elaine's cheeks, and the face powder that caked in every wrinkle, were replaced with a sheer antiaging formula that tightened up her skin a little, and a neutral blush which Sally cleverly used to design cheekbones that really weren't there.

The vile pantsuit had been replaced by an expensive, well-cut dress in a heavy fabric, which made Elaine look stately rather than fat. The flashy diamonds Sally had swapped for some luminous, cheap freshwater pearls, and she'd picked out a lace shawl to complete the effect; and finally, the masterstroke, a pair of sturdy, stacked heels, which forced Elaine to stand differently and stretch as she carried herself.

She looked younger—thinner—*better*.

Elaine couldn't contain her delight.

"Mark is going to go wild," she said. "Oh, Sally, you're a genius. . . ."

"Just wait until you send your friends out looking like that,"

Sally prompted. "I want to offer makeovers, hairdressing, and a styling service if they pay enough—for the elite customers, two hundred dollars a session. I'll go shopping with them and show them what to get."

"Oh, yes—yes certainly," Elaine said, dreamily staring at her reflection.

"Ask Mark for a budget to renovate the store. And I want to throw an open day on Saturday. Free makeovers. Believe me, that'll get them talking." Sally was almost dizzy with her success, high on her plans and dreams. She *could* make it happen. "If they want me to make them up they have to give us their mailing address and sign a consent form to receive special offers. . . ."

Her new boss wasn't listening; she was turning around in front of the mirror, absorbed in herself.

"You know, this dress looks like what Oprah wore on the Grammys. Except for I'm a white lady . . . but it's so *sexy,*" Elaine hissed, lowering her voice. She blushed. "Do you think you could come shopping with me for lingerie?" she whispered.

"Sure. You'd look great in . . . a teddy. Or baby-doll nightdress," Sally managed. "But first, you should hire me. I wrote up a contract. A thousand dollars a month plus basic health-care benefits . . ."

Sally produced a neatly folded, typed document from her handbag. Elaine signed it without even a murmur, then went to her desk, took out her checkbook, and scribbled in it.

"Delighted, dear," she said. "Say, could you look after the store for me this afternoon? I want to go and surprise Mark."

"Of course. Just give me five minutes while I call Mom," Sally said.

She ran out the front door, an annoying little bell tinkling, and went straight across the street to the bank. Not that she didn't trust Elaine, but a thousand dollars seemed like a small fortune. She wanted to bank it right away.

She returned shortly and told her new boss, "You go on home, Mrs. Fisk. I'm in charge here."

Elaine drifted out, dousing herself in perfume as she went; Sally had put her on to Chanel No. 19, a lighter fragrance, since she knew perfectly well Elaine was addicted to the nozzle.

She looked around the store. Dingy, drab, and underused. Well, she could change all that. Sally moved to the back to grab a broom. In the morning the two hairdressers would come in, and she'd start to teach them how to do a real blow-dry.

I'm in charge now, Sally thought, and it was the first bit of real optimism she'd felt in ages.

And things changed. Not overnight; Mark Fisk, stunned though he was at his wife's appearance, moaned over the fifty thousand dollars she wanted for the renovations—Elaine's place had never been more than a drag on his finances. The two current employees were jealous of Sally, and tried to rebel, until Elaine laid down the law. The builders and decorators were lazy, and it was a constant struggle—and the grand opening was mocked and jeered by women in the street.

But Sally persevered. She had to. She had a job now, and a purpose. Even if everybody else was lazy, she worked like a demon: painting, decorating, sourcing cool artwork and fancy mirrors and bronze letters three feet high, designing and rede-signing the ad for the local paper. And if the renovations took three months, well, that was plenty of time for Hartford to get good and curious.

When the grand opening happened, all Elaine's friends were there, as well as several curious teens from the high school. Sally had trained the other two girls in beauty basics, properly, and left them doing pedicures and neck massages while she flitted from chair to chair, flash-styling the small-town girls in ten minutes each; plucking eyebrows that hadn't been touched for decades; wiping away bright, ugly makeup and replacing it with neutrals; blow-drying out previously gelled-up hair; showing housewives addicted to plaits and buns what natural styling looked like.

The oohs and aahs from the mirrors didn't put any cash in the coffers, but Sally had faith. There was no business as sound as beauty. If you could show women you made a difference . . .

And the store, after all that hard work, was amazing. Rodeo

Girl looked like it belonged on Rodeo Drive. Gone were all the yellowing magazines and peeling paint and the old-style radio blaring out traffic and weather updates. Sally had installed tinted windows, sleek new graphics, a sexy logo of a rodeo chick in heeled boots and a tie-under shirt. Banks of televisions were tuned to CMT, the country-and-western version of MTV, with buff unshaven cowboys and modern western divas slickly belting out their hits.

It celebrated Texas—and it celebrated style. Hartford had never seen anything like it. The older ladies booked the place up almost immediately, and their daughters scrambled for appointments. Sally was busy, nine to five, every day, and sometimes on weekends as well. It was exhausting, but it was a rush. And her salary enabled them to afford little luxuries.

After a month or so, she began to get sizable tips. Instead of wasting the cash, Sally banked it. She didn't know exactly where she was going yet, but she was sure of one thing. She was not going to stay here.

Elaine Fisk basked in all the glory and took all the credit. Sally didn't mind, as long as she kept getting paid. And Elaine allowed her to keep all the tip money, which almost doubled her basic salary. As long as Sally's first priority was to keep Elaine looking good, the owner didn't complain. Her husband was actually getting money back after the third month, so he was happy. And, watching Sally work her magic on the small-town women of Hartford, Elaine discovered a vestige of pride in herself. She confided in Sal that she wanted to lose weight, and Sally put her on a walking regimen, something she could do quietly, without her catty friends noticing. Sally told her where to pick up good, ready-made salads. After a while, Elaine dropped a dress size, then two. . . .

For the first six months Sally's life moved into a routine: working, banking her salary, learning on her feet. She spent her spare time at home, looking after Mona as best she could. Sally felt guilty, at times, that she couldn't turn her mom around the way she was shaping up Elaine Fisk. But fighting Mona's depression and alcoholism would require Sally to be there full-time, and she had to make choices. Right now, Rodeo Girl was letting her save some cash and giving her a better education than a third-rate college could ever provide.

Sally tried not to think too much. She let her days fill up, her savings account slowly increase. It was easier to cope that way.

⌒

"Look at her," Leo Fisk said.

His Porsche was parked across the street, with three of his buddies riding along. The top was down, and they stared at Sally as she sauntered out of the front door, kissing Lucy Drew on the cheek.

"Dude, which one? Lucy's hot now," his friend Barry replied.

"Come on." Leo was scornful. Certainly he wouldn't say no to Lucy Drew, with that cute new haircut and the figure-hugging clothes and dramatic, pouty lips Sally had given her. But Sally Lassiter was a whole other league.

He'd been watching her coming in and going out of his mom's store for months now. The original plan was to drop by, hang around, watch her doing menial tasks like sweeping the floor . . . he vaguely thought that would be sexy . . . and have Sally flirting with Leo, begging him to notice her. After all, without his say-so, Mom wouldn't have hired her.

Only it hadn't worked out that way. Since day one, Sally was surrounded, first by workmen, then by customers. And obviously she was key to Rodeo Girl, whatever his mother told people. Leo had no power over her anymore.

Today she was wearing a short skirt, kitten heels, and a cream silk blouse. Her smooth, tanned legs seemed to run on forever. Her flaxen hair was caught back in a smooth ponytail, worn low at the neck, and her mouth showed wide teeth when she laughed.

All the eager, desperate schoolgirls he'd fumbled with or taken to bed paled into nothingness compared with Sally. And the further away he got from her, the more he wanted her.

"Yeah, she's fine," Barry agreed.

"Pity you didn't bang her when you had the chance," Simon Bernardillo said.

"He never *had* the chance. Remember? Chick turned him down flat," piped up Keith Brand, from the back.

"That's right," Barry said, and laughed.

Simon started to hum "Dream, dream, dream" from the Everly Brothers song, and his annoying friends fell about laughing.

"Can it," Leo said, shortly. "She's just another piece of tail, fellas. Let's go play ball."

Aggravated, he put the Porsche into gear and slammed his foot down. The car screeched off; in the side mirror he saw Sally Lassiter glance in his direction, idly, then, unconcerned, go back into the shop.

It burned him. She'd tricked him, that minx. She'd come up to him, sweet as pie, and teased him, knowing she was never going out with him. He resented it. Sally should have been grateful, and pliant. Submissively asking him to be pleased with her. Now, she had a job, she was effectively an adult, and he still went to high school! Okay, he was a senior, but it was still totally humiliating. The working woman and the schoolboy ...

Leo was a peacock. He hated it when his friends laughed at him. Unacceptable. He was going to have to teach that girl some manners. She damn well *would* go out with him, and in public. Or else.

~

He left after practice, so as not to be obvious about it, and went over to his dad's garage on Fifth Street, where they had a liquor concession and nobody asked questions. Leo took a little supply, some crates of beer and a pint of vodka. He liked that best because it didn't leave a smell on your breath. And it was hard liquor. A man's drink, something to get riled up on before he confronted Sally. She had a snappy, cool way about her when she put you down, and Leo wasn't taking any chances. He wanted to stand up to her. He packed the beer into the trunk, then unscrewed the vodka and took a good, fiery swig before stashing it in the glove compartment. His throat burned, and he felt himself gearing up. Carefully, not wanting to attract the cops, he turned the car south, heading back to Main Street and the way Sally walked home. It was a long walk to the tract on the outside of town, and she never got the bus; she liked the exercise. Perfect for him. He raised his headlights, and started to scour the side of the road.

~

Sally was tired, but glowing. Saturday night, and a particularly great week for tips. Mrs. Ellis, the wife of the local realtor, had been so thrilled with her personal shopping session—Sally guided her to a whole new wardrobe in one afternoon—that she'd pressed five hundred-dollar bills into her hands. And there had been over four hundred from the rest of the clientele, which meant she'd gotten almost a month's worth in just a single week. There was now some real money in their bank account. They lived on a thousand a month, and with what was left over from L.A., and all her work this year, Sally now had thirty-two thousand saved, with the promise of more to come. . . .

It would be almost a year soon, and then she'd ask for a raise. A big raise. Rodeo Girl was a huge success. Three thousand a month, just for starters, and Sally thought she might walk Elaine through share structure and get her to give Sally a slice. Once they'd done that, she could hire staff, maybe start a new store, maybe even one in Dallas . . . she didn't have to be working here for twenty, twenty-five thou a year. . . .

Maybe, Sally suddenly thought, maybe she could even go home. . . .

A car honked; she jumped out of her skin, spun around, her hand flung up against the dazzling light.

"What the . . . oh, hey. Leo." She dropped her hand and drew aside as his Porsche slowed down. "You startled me."

"Hey, what's up?" Leo Fisk was smiling at her, with that familiar, lascivious look in his eyes. "You're far too cute to be tramping home in the mud, Sally. Let me give you a lift."

"It ain't muddy," she replied. "I like the exercise. . . ."

"I know, but take a load off. You should relax once in a while. Go home early."

Well . . . it was unseasonably chilly. And she didn't want to be rude to Leo; he was Elaine's son, after all.

"Okay, why not." She opened the door and climbed in. "Thanks."

"So," he said, pulling out into the road again, "Sally, you never did give me that date. I reckon that call I put in for you with Mom came out pretty good, huh? You owe me a dinner, at least."

Sally sighed. Not that she hadn't been expecting this moment to come. She was only surprised it had taken him this long to get around to it.

"Leo, look. You're a real good-looking boy"—hell, he hated that, he wasn't a goddamn boy—"and I know all the girls are wild to go out with you, but I'm just not ready for a romantic relationship right now."

"What are you talking about? You're eighteen, baby. Legal in every state. I can't believe you've never had a boyfriend."

Well, she sort of had—dates, back when she was fourteen, fifteen. Boys she met from church or sports, or sons of her father's business partners. The odd movie, a kiss in a parking lot. Fumbles. But nothing more.

"I've dated," she said evasively. "But really I'm just focusing on work right now. I want to save up and get a place of my own. . . ."

"All work and no play makes Sally a dull girl," Leo said. He slurred the *s*'s, and she realized with a shock that he was more than a little drunk.

"Make a left right here, Leo," she said. But he missed the turning and shot past the intersection.

"Oh—you missed our street. Never mind. . . ." She didn't particularly want him to turn back, in the traffic. "Just pull over and I'll walk."

He didn't look at her; his eyes were fixed straight ahead, and he pressed his foot down on the gas.

"Just pull over," Sally repeated, uneasily. "And thanks for the lift."

Leo drove on.

"I don't think you're being fair, Sally," he said, and there was a silky tone to his voice she didn't like. "I think you tricked me. Day you came to see me in school. All dressed up in them tight jeans. Made me think you'd go out with me. If you weren't coming on to me, what was all that makeup for?"

They were going fast now, very fast. Too fast. The dial was on ninety, and the car was wobbling. The lights of Hartford disappeared in the distance.

"Please stop," she begged.

"Answer the question," he said.

"I wanted to impress your mother with how stylish I could be. . . ."

"Yeah, well. You impressed *me*, honey. Made a *real* impression."

The car pulled to a halt.

"What the hell are you doing?" Sally cried.

"You wanted me to pull over."

She glanced wildly around. They were in the middle of nowhere, a cornfield to the left. Quiet road—no traffic.

"Leo, you're drunk. I'm walking back and we're gonna forget this ever happened," Sally said. She tried for confident, but her voice cracked with fear.

He reached for her, one hand brushing against her breasts.

"Come on baby, you'll like it. All the girls do."

"Get away from me!" Sally shouted.

"No, I've had it. Enough teasing. You're gonna get just what you asked for."

She tried desperately to twist away, but he was strong. Slight, for a man, skinny, not the type of body she liked. But a man is far stronger than a woman, even a weak man. Sally knew that instinctively, and she was frightened.

"Leo, you're better than this . . . what would your mom think? Don't, don't touch me!"

Angrily, he backhanded her across the face. Sally gasped in pain and shock. That would leave a welt. She kicked back and tried to clamber out of the door.

"You're trying to ruin it," he hissed, grunting. "Bringing my mom into it ... that ain't sexy ... you're just an uppity bitch."

"You're a bully and a coward," Sally sobbed. "I'll scream. . . ."

The light in his eyes was manic. She couldn't believe it. She knew this boy, had seen him at school and in town for years.

"You do, and I'll kill you," he snarled. "And dump you right in that damn cornfield and you can rot away in the fall."

She didn't know if he meant it or not. Sheer terror froze her to her seat.

"Now," he said, fumbling at her shirt, "let's get this off of you. Yeah ... yeah, you sure are well built, baby, and I'm gonna be your first, just like I told them boys. . . ."

His hand was on her. She was tight, dry as a bone. He didn't care. Sally sobbed and leaned her head back. She didn't want to die, so she said nothing.

And Leo Fisk raped her.

⁓

He dropped her home afterward; she said nothing. Leo was full of good cheer. Told her she was sexy, she was hot.

"Don't worry, I'll see you again," he said. "Take you out to the movies tomorrow. How's that? It'll be better next time. You'll get the hang of it, baby, you're too hot-looking, you got it in you."

She climbed out of the car, and he was gone, tires spinning down the road.

Sally had seen true-crime shows about rape victims. How they would get in the shower and scrub themselves till they bled. Or went to the police, and pressed charges.

Sally did neither of those things.

Instead, she ignored the prone figure of her mother, snoring upstairs on the bed, and went to grab her suitcases. Sally furiously started to pack.

The police would not believe her. There were no witnesses. The Fisks were popular. She knew that, sick as it was, deep down in her bones. And she didn't want the publicity ... vultures crawling over her, all that prurient interest in the rape of a teenage blonde. They'd find Mona, too, drunk and depressed, still eking out the days in her personal hell.

Forget this shit-hole of a town. Sally was gone. Earlier than she'd expected, or wanted. But she had thirty thousand in the bank. They could rent, back in L.A. And she could start her own store. Buy a lease—get it done. Screw working for Elaine. She was angry, angry in the very depths of her soul. She was going to go the hell home, make some money, show all of them. The bastards who'd dropped them when her dad died. The snooty friends who never called. All the bullies, all those snooping vultures in the press.

Sally needed money. If she had money again, she'd have some protection. If she wasn't poor, Leo could never have got away with raping her, treating her just like a chattel.

Never again. She knew how to make it. She was a real Steel Magnolia. First, she was going to change their lives, again. Next, she was going to cure her momma and get rich. And last, she was going to take revenge.

Not just on Leo Fisk. On the whole damn world.

CHAPTER 8

"You can't fire me."

He was young, but still, older than her. Thirty at least, in his fancy Armani suit, with a Princeton degree and an arrogant air she disliked. Plus, he was looking her over, checking her out, with a degree of impertinence Jane objected to. Violently.

"I can and I am. You know our policy, Michael. Up or out. The San Diego store is failing to attract customers and growth."

"A rise of nine percent. Read the report," he replied with contempt.

"That is insufficient. The Sunset Boulevard store is making between twelve and fifteen percent growth per year."

"That's a special case," he said.

"Of course it is." She smiled thinly. "I run it. And now staff have been trained to follow my principles. Which is why I'm sitting here in head office, and you're being sacked."

He stared. "My God, you're every bit a bitch as they say you are."

"And I hear that you've sexually harassed every new immigrant worker San Diego took on."

"Bullshit. Prove it."

"I don't have to." Jane shrugged. "I have your lack of performance. There's a severance package on the table, but there won't be one for long."

"What the hell do you know?" He jumped to his feet, puce with rage. "You're just a kid—no college degree, no MBA. A couple of *fluke* years in L.A. and all of a sudden you think you're Jack Welch."

"Grow up," Jane said dismissively. "And get out. I'm busy—I don't have time for this."

"I'm leaving." He turned at the door and stared at her, eyes angry. "Everybody knows why you're here, *Miz* Morgan. You're the best little whore in the company. Fucking half the board of directors, no doubt. And I bet you're *real* good at it."

"Security can be up here in thirty seconds. And they really are good at it," Jane replied, coolly. "So if you value your rib cage, I suggest you leave. And by the way—the severance package just evaporated."

He snarled at her, cheeks mottled with rage, but he left.

She stood up and walked to the window. It was her favorite part of this job; below her, the office building sloped down and to the right, a curved arc of polished marble. The Manhattan skyscrapers jabbed into the hazy blue of the sky, smudged today with autumn clouds; the traffic crawled, in miniature, on the junctions at ground level, little yellow cabs crawling along like beetles, the sunlight flashing off the windscreens in diamond bursts of brilliance.

Her office. Vice president in charge of personnel. And she deserved it, damn it.

She tried to brush off what Michael Tiersky had said as the rantings of a failure. But it bothered her; it certainly did. She heard it far too often, in this job. From any man, and half the women, she canned.

"Sex toy."

"Hooker."

"Bimbo."

Sometimes they threw out names. Who, exactly, was she sleeping with? Rhodri Evans? Carmine Gallo? Richie Benson?

That she might deserve it—be here on her merits—impossible. She was too young. Twenty years old.

And, Jane was starting to understand, too beautiful.

It aggravated her. Rhodri, her first and still best mentor, was *gay*—not that she would tell them that, or dignify the sleaze with a response. She'd proven herself out there in L.A. In six months, she had transformed that workforce, and with it, the whole store's productivity.

At first Mrs. Watson had resented it—but as the cash flowed, so did her bonuses. Before long, she was recommending Jane wholeheartedly for promotion. Amazing what a little influx of cash could do.

And Jane was not the monster they made her out to be. Under her regime, merit was rewarded. Yeah, she cut out the deadwood—but more at management level than among the grunts. People soon came to understand that with Jane Morgan watching—and she was always watching—slacking was impossible.

But if you were a worker, Jane made life good. Even for the lowest levels. She ordered the cafeteria redecorated, new coffee machines installed, and the food improved. Sexual harassment was no longer tolerated. For the college kids, she offered daily internships in the management offices, so that the stint packing groceries would look better on their resumes. For the working moms, Jane brought in a crèche. For the families, she negotiated discounts at Universal Studios and the museums. There were reward schemes, employees of the month, bonuses, and a better staff area.

People had incentive. Jane had revolutionized the store.

They promoted her three times, and then the call. Come to New York. A vice-presidency of Shop Smart. Translate your methods across the country.

Jane had thought about it, but not for very long. She put her neat little house in Encino on the market, donated her stuff to charity, and moved into a smart two-bedroom flat on the Upper East Side. Her Ford had long ago become a Lincoln Town Car; in Manhattan, they offered her a driver.

Jane demurred. She'd take the subway. It was cheaper and quicker into Midtown.

Her bosses loved it, and they loved her. Before she knew where she was, Jane was getting her photograph taken in a studio and appearing in the Shop Smart corporate annual report. Along with a note on her tragic story.

She wanted to object, but didn't. It was all an irrelevance. And if the company looked good for having a woman at a senior level, then fine.

But now—now she was getting sick of it.

Not for the obvious reasons.

Not because her brand of human resources focused more on the resource than the human. She did not tolerate deadwood. A manager's salary was fifty grand a year, and if the university grads did not perform, she had a waiting list of hungry training-program workers, direct from the shop floor, ready to take their places.

She had zero time for lazy placeholders. No tears for Michael. Let him get another job. He wasn't her problem.

No, Jane's trouble was that she did this *too well*. Her success on Sunset Boulevard had blinded them. Shop Smart just wanted more of the same. And since her original aim had simply been money and position, she didn't want to turn this down—the complete package was worth almost two hundred grand a year.

But she wasn't a personnel drone. What interested her in Shop Smart was *selling*. It was the store itself. So she could run a team of workers—big wow.

Jane could do other, more important things. More crucial things. She wanted the chance to try.

But the board had other ideas. They told her they liked her where she was. Why mess with success?

Jane stared down at Manhattan, not seeing it. She sensed danger. This was a trap—a very comfortable trap, a middle-class trap, but a trap, all the same. Personnel had its limits. It was female-dominated, and like all female-dominated industries, underpaid. A safe place to stick your so-called high-fliers. Get a nominal woman "senior" executive, but not one in any danger of actually doing anything important.

Jane wanted to run supply lines, oversee buyers, construct new stores, award ad contracts. She had trained herself to be a *businesswoman,* not an overpaid nanny.

Five months in New York, and she was done.

She made up her mind. Go to Rhodri—he deserved the courtesy—and ask him for a transfer. Marketing would be a start.

Buying, even better. She wanted to try her hand at stock and supply. And if he or the board refused, she would quit.

Shop Smart had a formula. A very successful formula, but not one that allowed much creativity.

Jane Morgan was nowhere near where she wanted to be in life. Yes, she was out of the gutter. Yes, she was comfortable. Probably more so than her dad had ever been.

But she wanted so much more. And she was not sure Shop Smart was going to give it to her.

⁓

"I'll take it to them." Evans sighed, and polished his glasses. "Really, Jane, you're just twenty years old."

"My age is irrelevant."

"No, it's not."

"Well, it damn well should be."

"And you're gorgeous—so my straight friends instruct me."

"Again, irrelevant." Jane flashed on Michael Tiersky and his insults. Fancy girl. Slut.

"A gorgeous young girl in the boardroom would ruffle a lot of feathers."

"You should know something," she said. "In terms of boyfriends—" She blushed. "I haven't had any."

"None at all?"

"No."

What chance had she had? Working twelve-, sometimes eighteen-hour days, doing whatever it took to stay on top of the job. Jane sometimes believed a cloistered nun stood a better chance of getting married than she did. "I understand," Evans said. He had faced plenty of prejudice himself, and he sympathized with her; she was a brain, no doubt about that at all. And a young girl, in a hurry to be going places.

He liked Jane Morgan dearly. She was an amazing woman, and Evans admired her.

That said, he remained a Shop Smart employee; and she was most valuable where they'd placed her.

"In Personnel nobody will question you," he suggested.

"Rhodri." Jane spread her hands, and he was again half-amused, half-impressed. An interesting young woman, to be certain. "I am better than that. I came into this company wanting to learn the business, not wanting to be some glorified suit in charge of the parking rota at Shop Smart picnics. I know all about Shop Smart picnics. I invented them."

"You are *so* young, Jane," her friend tried again. "And you have no MBA. Not even a degree. Can't you see people are jealous of you?"

"Of course I can, and I don't see why I should give a damn." Jane jumped to her feet, passionate. "Who produces, who doesn't produce. That's all that counts. The eighties are over. Haven't we learned anything?"

"You're so young, and already a vice president."

Jane leaned across his desk.

"You know what I tell my juniors, Rhodri? Up or out. If they're not promotion material within a certain time they are gone. Now tell me, why should the rules be different for me? You put me in as veep in charge of staff. Okay—I've delivered. The deadwood is gone. The motivation programs are there. . . ."

"So you should see it through."

"Like hell." She stood and ran a hand through her long hair, and he admired her, dispassionately. "I'm not into that. I want a real job, in business. Supply . . . management . . . marketing . . . there are lots of possibilities."

Evans stood firm. "So you're the no-bullshit girl?"

"Damn straight."

"Then take some plain talking from me, Jane. You are a kid. And already you've been promoted five times higher than any kid would ever be. Whatever the numbers say, shareholders, and more importantly analysts, are going to bitch at seeing you promoted to board level."

"Then explain why."

"We did okay for many years before you got here," he said calmly. "And we would do okay after you left."

"But this is so dumb." In frustration, she pushed a hand

through her glossy hair. "You gave me a task, and I more than delivered—"

"And that's what you're trusted on."

"But I could be so much more. Shop Smart—"

"Time for an object lesson," Evans said. "This store is at a peak of performance and sales. No director is going to give a crap if you come or go. You have to settle in to being at-bat, girl. And I can't help you if you won't do that. At twenty years old, you can expect at least—at *minimum*—five years in this slot. And after that it's a distant maybe as to whether they would transfer you. You're good, and relatively cheap—"

"Don't I know it," Jane said, angrily.

"So why change? Especially since any further movement would threaten their jobs."

She stood. "And if I quit?"

Evans rolled his eyes. "At twenty you're on two hundred K. If you quit, you're a moron. In *this* company you have a track record. Anyplace else, you're just another college dropout—because they won't be giving you a glowing reference."

Jane snarled. "Damn it!"

"You're an analyst." He treated her with the same dispassion she treated everyone else with. "You figure it out. The fact you're so beautiful makes a difference."

"You have a boyfriend. I don't," she lashed out.

"Sweetie, if you want, I can fix that in five minutes."

Jane grudgingly offered him a smile. "Thank you, no."

He was a smart cookie, Rhodri Evans, and a good friend. Maybe what he was saying made sense. She just didn't want to hear it.

"Seriously." He stood up, and walked over to her. "I think I know just what you need, Jane. You're frustrated, but maybe that's not because of work. You need a relationship."

"Yeah . . . sure," she said.

Rhodri didn't know why she dismissed the idea. Eighteen-hour days. Constant phone calls. Staring at the computer until you went blind. What was that? No kind of life for a young woman.

"You could date somebody who works on your schedule." Evans thought about it, and ran through his single friends. The strong ones, at least; anyone else, this girl would eat alive. "There's Peter Ralston, an investment banker. Murray Krasnich, he's a politician—but dedicated. And Leroy Anderson, he's a manager at senior level over at Wal-Mart—ahead of you, though."

Jane shook her head. "When it happens, it happens."

"Okay. Your call. I'm always there."

⌖

For once she availed herself of the chauffeur service. Jane felt adrift, unsure as to what to do next. She wanted a new job—and a new man; somebody to silence the critics calling her a whore. She wanted the backing of her allies, but understood she was asking something outrageous. And yet the pure flame of capitalism told her she should already have the job.

On the slow drive up Fifth Avenue, stuck in traffic and wanting to get home, Jane thought about her life; about her past, and her friends. Where was Sally? What was she doing now? And Helen? Did she have children, was she enjoying herself in some Egyptian suburb? Did she ever even think of Jane and Sally?

But those were crazy reminiscences, Jane told herself. Friendships couldn't last forever . . . why had she ever thought otherwise?

Maybe it was nostalgia. But she was determined to find out. The desire to avenge herself, to prove she was more than the pampered daughter of a worthless diplomat, had been slaked. She was exhausted, and one way or another, she was on the way up.

For the last two years she had been a hermit.

So deep in her work she might have been a nun.

All the more funny that they called her a whore—but Jane wasn't laughing.

If she had friends again—that would be something.

It wasn't like she hadn't tried to find them. But the Yannas had remained tight-lipped, and there was no sign of Sally Lassiter anywhere in Texas. Jane came close, one time; she discovered

Sally had been working at a beauty parlor in a small town in the Lone Star State. But then she'd upped sticks and left, and nobody had the first idea where she'd gone. Vanished in the night, her bank account closed, her landlord without a forwarding address.

I have to try again, Jane thought. Although she had no idea where she would start.

◦◦◦

She tipped the driver, smiled briskly at her doorman, and rode the elevator to the twelfth floor. It had to be high—she'd stipulated that to her realtor. Manhattan, and her job, were full of stress. From way above ground, the city looked peaceful; in her office and at home, Jane Morgan wanted to be in the clouds.

Her apartment was laid out along the same lines. Cool shades of white, tone on tone, punctuated with the occasional soft cushion in soft beige or gray, like driftwood and bones on a beach: oyster, pearl, and cream. Jane had opted for calming neutrals. Getting away from her father's leather-bound books and statues, she was sinking into Manhattan style: sparse, Zen-like, a buffer between her and the world.

It was immaculate, too. No longer did she have to scrub out her tub with bleach or starve out the roaches. Her maid, Janet, came three times a week; the building's concierge delivered her daily groceries and fresh flowers—lilies, white tulips, and snowy roses, the petals bright against dark green leaves.

By her low-slung designer bed Jane kept a couple of books: one on architecture and a business biography or two.

She smiled as she picked up a tome on David Geffen, the legendary record business man. Yeah—she was addicted. Her life, her home, even her leisure activities. All about the bottom line.

This was nice, but it wasn't nearly enough.

Next month was her review. If Shop Smart didn't transfer her, she was gone. She glanced around her flat, mentally saying goodbye to it, without regrets. In this life, Jane Morgan had learned to travel light.

There was better waiting for her, elsewhere. And her friends—

she *would* find them. It would be so good to see Sally. No doubt
Sal would need some help, too. Jane had a rush of guilt; she'd
been so focused, she hadn't tried hard enough to find Sally, and
offer her a place to stay, or a good job. Well, she'd put that right;
she'd hire a private investigator, if need be. Sal could be her assistant. And she'd be the one person in the world who wouldn't
have to come up to Jane's exacting standards. She'd get a nice car,
a great salary, and a fat pension just for showing up. And if Helen
wanted to come back to the States, the same applied to her.

Jane grinned. She'd earned the right to one freebie. In any
other circumstance, Jane Morgan would have shuddered at the
idea of hiring a makeweight.

But Sally and Helen were special. They could have whatever
the hell they wanted. Jane would see to that. Either in Shop
Smart, or someplace else.

Jane Morgan needed her friends. But despite what Rhodri
Evans said, she didn't need anything else.

She absolutely was not interested in finding a man.

⟨───⟩

There was a knock on her office door.

"I'm busy," Jane said, not looking up from her screen. It was
Friday, and her reports from the Southwest were due in.

The door swung open and Rhodri Evans put his head around
it.

"You're always busy. Make some time."

She smiled and clicked the spreadsheet shut.

"For you, sure." Jane glanced at her diary. "I have a free
lunch—would you like to go and get something?"

"I've always believed in miracles," the Welshman said. "Come
on, then, I want to have a chat with you."

⟨───⟩

She took him to Le Cirque; if they were going to eat on the
company's dime, Jane figured it should be a good meal. They

weren't paying her well enough as it was. She ordered caviar, smoked oysters, and a rare steak to follow; Rhodri, not used to quite such luxurious surroundings, stuck with a salad and roast duck. Jane insisted he take a glass of champagne. It was a new decade, and sackcloth and ashes were all the fashion; the stores did a roaring trade in lumberjack shirts, as everybody wanted to be Kurt Cobain; the designers were into black and gray aesthetics, monklike chic.

But Jane rebelled. Even though she was twenty, she thought of herself as a true child of the eighties. Luxury, aspiration, pulling yourself up by your bootstraps; all that was in her blood, and it would never die. The movie *Wall Street* had been a huge smash, and it was meant to be negative, a morality tale. But when Jane sat in the cinema and watched Bud Fox walk into that giant office with the enormous glass walls, the camera following him lovingly, and all Manhattan stretching out beyond them, she was thrilled to her bones. That was what she wanted. That was what she worked for.

"And you?" Rhodri wanted to see her relaxing, too.

"Not for a couple of months."

He raised a brow. "Surely you're not telling me you've never had champagne."

"Of course not. Just that I don't want to be asked for I.D. in a restaurant I take business contacts to." Jane smiled coolly. "I have some Krug chilling in my refrigerator. But I never fight a battle I can't win."

"We'll toast you in here on your birthday."

"That's a deal."

She sipped at her freshly squeezed pomegranate juice while her friend enjoyed his champagne.

"So how did it work out with Peter Ralston?"

The M&A specialist from Chase; newly divorced, older than her, considered handsome. Smooth, certainly.

"We had a couple of dates," Jane said. "Went out for sushi . . . I just don't think we clicked."

"Why?" Rhodri was upset. "You never seem to get on with anybody. Are you really making an effort?"

"I'm an orphan. Shouldn't I at least get a pass on nagging about my love life? What, are you going to complain you'll never have grandchildren?"

Jane chuckled, and Rhodri smiled back. It was good to see her laugh. He worried about Jane; sometimes he wondered if he had done the right thing, giving her that first promotion. She was so unnaturally absorbed in business.

"But he was perfect for you."

"Evidently not," Jane said, wryly. In fact, Ralston had said first that he thought they should knock it on the head, and she'd been relieved. He was coming on too strong; obviously expected her to jump right into bed. And she hadn't wanted to. He just didn't excite her. She didn't know what she wanted, exactly, just that Peter Ralston wasn't it.

"Then I have somebody else you should meet." Rhodri nodded, determinedly. "Somebody different from anyone you've seen before."

"I'm not interested. Really, I'm so busy. And I'm young. . . ."

"But this guy . . ."

"Another damn banker or congressman or high-paid lawyer. I don't think I can deal with that. Face it, Rhodri, I'm just not ready to date."

"He's none of those things. A little slice of home, I'm thinking. Maybe that's what you need. He's English. His name is Jude Ferrers."

That brought Jane up short. "English?"

"Yes. From Sussex. His parents own a farm near the sea. Some place called Rye."

"I know Rye," Jane said. She took a large swig of pomegranate juice to cover her confusion. For some reason, she actually *did* want to meet this one. English, like her? Maybe it was fate. But her lack of interest in all men had just evaporated.

"He went to Eton. No title but lots of cash. He's in town buying a place in the Hamptons. Just broke up with a girl, the daughter of some earl or something. I met him at a party last night. And he wants to meet you."

Her response surprised him.

"Yes—that'd be great," Jane said. "Give him my direct line. Do you know if he's free tonight?"

"I don't . . ."

"Because I am. And if not, tomorrow." She beamed at her friend. "Thank you Rhodri, he sounds intruiging."

Cheered, Rhodri tossed down the rest of his champagne. Finally, then, he *had* solved it, cracked the puzzle. What Jane needed was a guy from her own culture. He'd been born in the States, of Welsh parents, but never felt the need to go back to the motherland—Jane, on the other hand, had spent her childhood in the UK. And that's what she was hankering after.

She seemed to come alive at lunch, animated, chatting, telling jokes. What a transformation, he thought. He could not believe it. As soon as she had paid and jumped into a taxi, Rhodri Evans telephoned his new acquaintance to give him the good news.

It put him in a good mood for the rest of the day. The young woman had fascinated him since the day he had met her, so brave and so tearful. He would love to see her find success in love, as well as a balance sheet. Because without that, what good was anything?

~⌐

Jane enjoyed the rest of her day.

The call had been a good start.

"Miss Morgan?" The clipped tones reminded her of her father. It was a joy to hear somebody who sounded like she did. "I hope I'm not being presumptuous, but our mutual friend Rhodri suggested I call . . ."

Classy, Jane thought. A million miles away from the losers she'd been dating recently.

Jude was going to pick her up tonight at eight and take her to a concert. How romantic! Carnegie Hall . . . a candlelit dinner; his voice on the phone had sounded gentlemanly and urbane. It charged her; she was curious, impatient.

Unusually, she had rushed home at the end of the day, leaving her assistant openmouthed. They usually worked till at least half past six. But today Jane had better things to do.

She dressed with exquisite care: her favorite Azzedine Alaïa dress, black and tight, bands of brilliantly cut black silk tapering around her body, ending just over the knee; high Manolo Blahnik heels, with crystal-cut buckles; Wolford tights; Hermès 24, Faubourg as her scent. Jane went to the hairdressser's first, and had her glossy brown mane blown out, smooth and beautiful, around her shoulders; she chose to make up with a daring plum lipstick and charcoal liner, emerald green shadow on her lids. Vamping it up. A bold look, but the mirror told her, without a doubt, she had pulled it off. Among all the drab little minimalists, Jane would look like a flashing butterfly, a glorious Purple Emperor.

She finished the look with a dress watch, a slim gold Cartier set with diamonds; a present to herself from her last bonus.

Jane paced up and down her apartment, trying to contain her excitement. *Come on,* she told herself. *He might be ugly . . . he might be short . . . he might be far too skinny, or fat as a house.*

But it didn't work. Jude had sounded so different, with his modulated voice and easygoing, unpressured tones. So cultured . . . not like the investment bankers, who always gave the impression of wanting to check their phone messages.

Whole parts of herself that had been submerged for years now were starting to wake up, Jane thought, and she liked it. At least she *wanted* to see him. And that made a change. . . .

The doorbell rang and she raced to answer it.

He stood on the doorstep with a large, expensive-looking bunch of roses, dark red, set with berries and twigs and glossy foliage. He was a tall man, light brown hair, hazel eyes, a handsome enough face, and wearing a good suit that looked a bit rumpled.

Jane felt her heart flip over in her stomach as Jude casually gave her the once-over; she suddenly, ardently, wanted to be found pleasing.

"My goodness," he said. "You might just be the prettiest girl I've ever seen."

"That . . . is the right answer," Jane said, and they laughed.

〜⌒

He was absolutely smooth. He ticked every box. He held open car doors for her, walked on the outside of the pavement, offered her his arm as they climbed the stairs in Carnegie Hall to the box he had hired. Jane sat, fascinated, at dinner, almost unable to eat because of the butterflies in her stomach, while he told her all about himself, his parents' interests in land and property, his own desire to do "something in art history." Jude was "finding himself," and didn't want to work. He told her he had no desire to join the rat race. Jane envied him, and thought it amazing he could be so detached.

"But you're buying a place in the Hamptons?"

They cost a fortune; several million bucks for a decent house. She certainly couldn't afford one.

"I have a trust fund." He shrugged. "You know, the idea we all absolutely have to spend our lives working our fingers down to the knuckle is very recent. Did you ever read any Jane Austen?"

"Of course; all of it."

"Well, Darcy never went and toiled in an office, did he? And nor did Elizabeth. So why should I, when I don't have to?"

"I think that's wonderful," Jane said, a little starry-eyed.

Gosh. Wasn't he handsome—and urbane. So charismatic, so confident! He reminded her, she supposed, of her father— something of Thomas Morgan's self-possession. But of course, this was a date. And unlike Thomas, Jude actually seemed interested in her.

Jane wanted to retain a modicum of detachment. She was enjoying Jude's company. More than that, maybe. Being with him was like entering another world, a half-forgotten world. But her job was still there.

Jude wooed her with commendable patience. He took care to dazzle; they ate out three times a week at the best restaurants, went to a couple of the classier nightclubs, a Broadway musical. Jude squired her to the opera, and dined with her in the city's ultraexclusive Metropolitan Club.

He talked to her about his leisure pursuits, his fishing, his bea-
gling, his holidays in Scotland shooting grouse.

"Do you *never* want to work?" Jane asked.

He shook his head. "I'll leave that to you, babe."

Jane wondered a little at that. But Jude was so charming, it
was easy to overlook. Besides, he gave no indication of wanting
to stifle her career.

Jude seemed to enjoy New York. Jane dressed up whenever he
took her out. He clearly enjoyed showing her off to his friends.
She knew they made a handsome couple. And day after day,
Jane let herself go a little more. Her work was challenging, but
pleasing Jude became very important to her. Every time he paid
attention to her, she felt good about herself.

It was a whirlwind schedule of dates, and Jane enjoyed them
all.

⁓

"Tomorrow's Saturday," Jude reminded her. "Maybe you
could come out to the Hamptons with me. I'm going round a
few more places. You could see them, help me choose."

She beamed back at him, and wondered if this was what love
felt like; she basked in him, Jude Ferrers warmed her. Briefly she
thought of Sally, who had disappeared, and never called her again.
That's what Jude made her feel—golden, just like Sally Lassiter.

The next day she went for smart-casual, as English as she
could; tailored corduroy trousers, green Wellington boots, and a
tight, cute cashmere T-shirt; loose hair, neutral makeup for day,
and a necklace of seashells.

"You look delicious," he said, kissing her boldly on the cheek.
And then, when she responded, lightly on the lips.

Jane blushed and smiled; she wanted him to desire her. It had
been building for a while now. And she'd hardly been able to
sleep, waiting for him to turn up today. A completely new experience for the ice maiden.

They took a helicopter ride to the Hamptons, and Jude
showed her around: a modern, glossy house on the seashore; a

cute four-bedroom white clapboard cottage, old by American standards; a redbrick Victorian in the center of town. Jane loved each one; they were two million bucks apiece. She envied him such an effortless progress through life, and wanted that for herself. Jude bought her lunch at a clam shack, where they drank a delicious, rough Italian white and ate deep-fried soft-shell crabs, whole, and red currants with lemon sorbet for pudding, then a shot of espresso with a sour cherry dipped in bittersweet chocolate to finish it off.

Jane could not remember the last time she had enjoyed a meal so much. She sat, absorbed, as Jude told her all about Rye—a glorious medieval town, she remembered now, full of buildings from history, Queen Anne, Tudor, earlier . . . and the flat fields and rolling downs of Sussex. And she started to fantasize about what might happen. If he liked her . . . what if she switched firms? Or started a branch of the company in London? They could date more over there, slowly build a future. . . .

Jane was careful not to eat too much. He told her about his exes, the models he'd dated. Code for "I like skinny girls." About the social-register parties he attended, the London Season, the big events in Paris and New York.

He said he wasn't interested in buying anything on the spot. Jane waxed lyrical about the white clapboard cottage, but Jude's eyes glazed over. After a few minutes he interrupted her.

"There's the Old Shipping Inn in the center of town. They have a suite open—I checked. It's Sunday tomorrow, you don't have to go to work, do you?"

Jane shook her head.

"I thought maybe we could stay over. Steal a night. Like honeymooners."

She nodded her head, briskly, her throat dry, and he whisked her away to the hotel—in fact, despite the name, very modern and sleek—and up to the promised suite, which was nearly as big as Jane's apartment.

"Ever since I saw you in that tight little dress, I wanted to unwrap you, all shiny and new, like a Christmas present."

Well . . . it had been a month, one month and *lots* of dates.

How could Jane object? Jude had been patient, hadn't he? She nodded, half-eager, half-terrified.

"Mmm, baby, you've got fabulous legs," he said. "Long legs, like a colt's. Let's see what you've got up there."

And he deftly undid her jeans while somehow popping open his own shirt, and tugged her, half-naked, onto the bed.

~⌒~

"A virgin."

He smiled afterward, as though he'd won a prize. Propped up on one elbow, gazing down at her proprietorially.

"I can't believe you were actually a virgin."

"Everybody has to start somewhere," Jane joked, although she was afraid it sounded lame.

"But you're twenty years old. I thought virgins that survived their teens were myths. Like unicorns." He ran a hand across her thigh, touching the drying blood that lay there. "You can be my pet unicorn."

"I'll take a shower," Jane said, feeling gauche, embarrassed.

"How was it?" he yawned. "What you expected?"

"Fantastic," she lied. In fact, she'd been dry and tense; he had started too soon. But she blamed herself. She hadn't told him she was a virgin. . . .

"Well, I'll soon have you trained up to be an expert." He rolled over on the bed. "Sex always makes me sleepy . . . I'll take a nap, we can do it again later." As an afterthought, he added, "You better get on the pill, darling, we don't want any complications. I just hate those, don't you?"

"Oh—of course," Jane said.

She went into the shower; he had already closed his eyes.

She washed herself for a long time, covering her body in fragrant gel, scrubbing the embarrassing blood from her legs. It felt as though the world should seem different now, as if the sky should have a different color. But it didn't; everything was normal.

Except, she told herself hopefully, for Jude. The first man she'd ever felt something for. He had taken her virginity, and she was glad. As she dried herself and dressed, Jane snuck a look at him, lying there on the bed. So handsome . . . so charming. Rhodri had said all the women were flinging themselves at him. No wonder, she thought, and I've got him!

It was a brilliant feeling.

⁓

When Jude woke, he suggested they check out anyway.

"Nobody wants to wear the same clothes two days in a row. I'll pick you up tomorrow for brunch."

"Okay," Jane said, happily enough. She had been looking forward to spending the night with him, but tomorrow would do.

He dropped her off at her door with a little pat on her ass, and Jane spun round to kiss him, deeply, romantically. But Jude laughed, and said, "You're a lot of fun."

She didn't like that. Something profound had just happened—okay, they'd only been dating a month, but still—surely he must feel the chemistry, must feel the instant rightness of it all?

She went to sleep in her own bed, alone, and not wholly happy. But she tried to suppress her doubts. After all, Jane knew very well how beautiful she was. Men were always trying, and failing, to impress her. Jude would understand his luck . . . surely?

⁓

He did call. Bright and early, and picked her up at eleven. The brunch spot was crowded and hip, and Jane nervously picked at waffles with strawberries, while Jude polished off bacon and eggs and a mug of cinnamon coffee.

"So after this we'll go back to my hotel," he suggested, throwing down a hundred-dollar bill, carelessly. "Work off the meal. If you want to. And then tonight . . . we could go to that book launch at the Metropolitan, and back afterward for more?"

"Perfect," Jane said, happy, reassured.

He still liked her. He was still interested. It wasn't wham, bam, thank you, ma'am. Yes, there was some reserve there, but she found it all the sexier, all the more exciting. For once, she was the pursuer. And every time he looked at her, every time that English voice complimented her, Jane thrilled with happiness.

The sex still wasn't great, but she didn't care. She went along, easily enough. It was the price of being with someone so charming. And that was what a relationship was. . . .

Over the next week, at work, she floated through her days, her mind only half on her work. Thinking about Jude, waiting for him to call. They met at odd hours now: in the middle of the night, at lunchtime, often, and then she would duck out of meetings at three or four. Nobody complained. Jane was invaluable. They gossiped a little about how starry-eyed she was, and she knew they could see she was in love. So what? Someday, she knew, she'd be announcing an engagement. . . .

And then one day, at the start of September, he rang.

"Baby." That soft, familiar tone at the end of the workday. How she loved to hear it. "You have to come over to the hotel."

Jane glanced at the clock: four forty-five. Good enough.

"On my way," she said, grabbing her bag and hanging up. These days, all Jude had to do was call, and she came running.

"So." He rolled off her, stretched out for a minute, then jumped up from the bed. Jane grabbed the sheet and held it around her shoulders; when Jude walked away from her—he didn't like to cuddle much—she always felt more naked than naked. "I'm going to miss you," he said, grabbing his dressing gown and pulling it on, casually.

Jude wasn't looking at her. Jane was highly intelligent; she felt the tiny hairs prickle on her arms, and jumped out of bed herself, reaching for her clothes.

"Miss me? Are you going somewhere?"

"Well, the summer's over," he said, lightly. "Time to push on home."

"I thought you were staying," Jane said, worriedly. "You're

going back to England? I have a major project, restaffing in Ari-
zona. I can't get leave for a while."

Jude sighed and reached toward the table where a packet of
Marlborough Lights was half-open; his eyes slid away from her,
and he looked out of the window.

"Leave? To come and see me? I don't think that's such a great
idea, darling."

She shivered. "What do you mean?"

"Oh, come on, don't make this difficult." He jumped up and
started to pace around the room, then said, quickly, as though wanting to get the words out, "I'm going home—you're staying here.
This was a holiday romance, great while it lasted, but I don't think
we've got a future. Not long-term. You've got your career. . . ."

Jane was seized with blind panic. He was leaving her . . . abandoning her. . . .

"Is there someone else?" she whispered.

"Yes," Jude said, brutally. "Actually, more than one. I just don't
want to be tied down. You're beautiful, sweetheart, but you're just
too . . . clingy."

Numbly, Jane pulled on her panties and bra, and reached for
her skirt.

"And we don't have an awful lot in common. In fact," he said,
sauntering toward the bathroom, "there's history . . . isn't there?
Your father . . . well, it wouldn't be right. Not in England, anyway. Not after what he did. I'm sure you can see that, Jane. You'll
be better off here, with a Yank—somebody who won't ask too
many awkward questions. . . ."

Her hands trembled as she did up the buttons of her shirt. Jane
fought it, but the shock and loss . . . the embarrassment . . . it was
rejection, it was utter humiliation. . . .

Deliberately not looking at her, he walked into the bathroom,
and she heard him switch on the shower.

Jane dressed as quickly as she could, her heart thumping and
her mind racing. Nothing in common . . . clingy . . . better off
here . . . *your father* . . .

And then, even as the tears were rolling down her cheeks,
Jane suddenly, in a flash of light, understood everything. Why

she'd felt so attracted . . . why she'd jumped on him . . . why she'd
wanted him, desperately, even when the sex was lousy and the
conversation strained. . . .

Her father. Jude was English. In some weird way he'd reminded
her of Thomas . . . *but he had wanted her.* Praised her. Spent time
with her. Lavished attention on her . . .

She had been trying to claw back the love she hadn't received . . . romantic attention from a boyfriend, instead of the
fatherly love Thomas Morgan never gave her.

And the others? The Americans, with whom she was supposed
to click? None of them had stood a chance. None of them could
be a father substitute, none of them could pay back her pain. . . .

She steadied herself, one hand pressed against her heart, looking out over Central Park, the leaves just starting to redden and
brown. It was so clear, so revelatory.

Jude was *nothing.* She had lost her virginity to nothing.

Calm now, Jane reached for her coat. No more; no longer.
That was all over. She would go on, and succeed, and win, despite
what Thomas Morgan had done to her. If love came, it would
come. But Jane Morgan was not about to go looking for it. And
she would not use romance to heal a childhood wound.

Jude's dressing gown, his clothes, and his packed suitcase lay
on the bed. Jane glanced out of the window; below them was a
terrace. Casually, Jane tossed everything Jude owned out of the
window—the suitcase was heavy, but she made it—and walked
out of his suite, leaving the door wide open.

On the way home, she probed herself, her feelings. Yes—she
felt a little stupid. But also, somehow free. As though now she
could see things clearly. And for that, Jane almost felt grateful to
Jude. A stuck-up trust fund brat with no purpose in life except
sex and snobbery; and he wasn't even good at the sex. But his
careless betrayal had finally ripped the blinders off Jane's eyes.

All in all, she told herself, cheaper than therapy.

She pressed the button and allowed the crisp, cool air to drift
into the cab. It was refreshing, invigorating. The snap of autumn
in New York.

Holiday was over. Time to get to work.

In her apartment, Jane found the answering machine was blinking. She pressed it.

"You goddamn *bitch*!" Jude's voice screeched. He sounded petutlant, womanish, and Jane laughed. "I've got to call damn housekeeping now . . . they might blab . . . this could make the gossip columns . . . I'll be a laughingstock . . ."

She pressed delete, went to her refrigerator, and, ignoring the yellowing celery and Chinese leftovers in their cartons, went straight for the chilled bottle of champagne. Jane poured herself a glass, slowly, and sipped it, thinking hard.

She needed a change. Out of this relationship—that was done. Out of her job, too. It was no longer any fun in human resources. She could be comfortable there, but no more.

Jane wanted ownership. She wanted it to be *her* helicopter, *her* house in the Hamptons. She'd seen a slogan in a dime store once—"It's a strong man who can prevail in the face of comfort."

Too right. She was getting lazy. Middle management was not in her game plan. Let them promote her to the main board, give her a division to run—and stock—and she'd get on a plane, go back to Los Angeles. She was overwhelmed with a desire to recapture some of what she had lost. Find Sally Lassiter, even if Sally had disappeared; find Helen, even if Helen was babied up in a Cairo suburb. They had private investigators these days that were as good as the FBI. This was America; money opened every door.

Yes. As the alcohol cheered and relaxed her, Jane smiled. Time to put her cards on the table. Shop Smart and she would play a game of chicken, and Jane was not going to be the one who blinked.

CHAPTER 9

heir first trip to America was a big success.

Baba and Mama met them at the airport; they hugged and cried, and were obviously so sincerely overjoyed to see Haya, that she could forgive the smug look in her father's eyes. He was triumphing because she was wearing traditional dress and speaking Arabic, and so obviously in love with Ahmed.

"I was right," he kept saying on the drive back from the airport. "You see darling? I was right. We did know best."

Haya wanted to explode, but Ahmed, in the backseat with her, kept pressing her hand, his eyes lit up with amusement. And then he switched to tracing an *A* with his fingers, slowly, in the small of her back. *A* for Ahmed. Telling Haya she was his. It turned her on, and she found her rage was defused.

Ahmed, this time not wary of his arranged bride, looked at L.A. with open eyes. With Haya's eyes. Yes, it was brash, and Western, and vulgar in lots of ways, but it was also exciting, big, and rich. His wife's enthusiasm was infectious. He loved that about her—she made life an adventure.

And his father-in-law had kept his word. There was a meeting at Neiman Marcus, at Saks, and at the Beverly Hills Hotel. And all three places agreed to buy a carpet or two; Ahmed had brought some of his finest examples. Before the month was out, he had a small, interested client base.

"We could be more," Haya suggested. "Sell in department

stores, regularly. Of course, such things take time. . . ." She looked up at Ahmed under her lashes. "And also presence."

"You mean move here?" he said slowly.

"Talal could run the Egyptian store. We could buy a place . . . import some of the stock . . . just for a year or so. See how we like it." Haya grinned. "I'm a U.S. citizen, remember? No problems there."

"I don't know. It's a big step." Ahmed looked down at her, sternly. He had already decided he wanted to do just that, but he enjoyed playing games with his willing, eager little wife.

"We should do it," she said, "Please . . ."

He ran a finger down her cheek. "Persuade me."

In the end it was seamless. Haya trained Talal, his manager, on the computer; they organized insurance, and wages for his staff; a cousin from Aswân came with his wife to stay in the house and pay a peppercorn rent. And Haya took her dowry, paid to Ahmed, and some of the profits from their last year's trading, and purchased a house; Ahmed approved of the third place she showed him, a comfortable, modern villa in mock Spanish style at the foot of the Hollywood Hills, on a quiet street away from the tourist hot spots. The garden was small, but verdant, and they were in the thick of everything; and Ahmed enjoyed the large television, the power showers with multiple jets, the soft mattresses, the air-conditioning. . . .

They moved in, storing a pile of their best carpets in a guest room. Haya helped set up the new American company, and Ahmed made the sales and closed the deals. As easy as the move had been, business was not quite so simple. The famous stores had their suppliers already, and while he moved a carpet a month, the larger orders were slow in coming.

But America was an adventure for Ahmed. He enjoyed going to the beach every day, swimming in the ocean, trying the different foods, and taking trips; San Francisco, with the tall, prehistoric cedars of Muir Woods, the fortress of Alcatraz, and the disturbing cable cars; and Haya blossomed even more, at home, where she was confident. They nestled in the modern house and made love daily, and they flew back to Egypt four times a year, as he pushed and pushed to establish himself.

Slow going, but the orders rose, and rose, and they moved toward prosperity.

Yet he was disturbed by one thing: the months came and went, and still the wife of his heart was not pregnant.

~

Haya leaned on the balcony of the kitchen window; it was low-slung and looked out into their little garden, one of her favorite spots. The sun beamed down on the terrace; she might lounge out there later, under an umbrella, sipping a chilled grapefruit juice with selzer, her latest favorite drink. But despite making lazy plans, her heart was full.

She couldn't find her friends. At first there had been a rush of activity; calling the school, checking the newspaper reports in the public library . . . but nothing, no answers for her. Just a grainy picture of Jane with some young lawyer, outside a courtroom, and Sally Lassiter, her head up, her hand in front of a camera, refusing to talk.

They were gone. And when she'd looked in the phone book, she found there were 407 people with the name Jane Morgan in Los Angeles County alone.

She wanted to hire an investigator. But that took money, and it was slow going, the business here. Ahmed was happy, and so was she, but they had not spread their wings the way Haya had hoped.

She wanted more. When her husband came back that night—he'd made five thousand on the placement of a beautiful Afghan in the beach house of a famous actor—Haya asked him if she could come along.

"Your meeting tomorrow. With Richard Drayson."

The sales director of Broderick Stores. Ahmed was going to try, yet again, to get a department store to place a major ongoing order.

It would be the sixth such pitch meeting he'd had this year. Something was going wrong—they were failing, somehow. Haya wanted to see why.

"If you'd like to," Ahmed said. "Sure. Why not?"

⁓

"We think you have good pieces, Mr. Al-Amin." The buyer's eyes were flat. "And we'll happily take two rugs."

"We were hoping for a proper order," Ahmed said. "The small sales do not cover overhead. We are a reliable supplier and cannot be beaten on price."

Drayson shook his head.

"Your goods are certainly superior, but I can't take the risk."

"What do you mean by that?" Haya protested.

"Our traders deal with thousands of rugs per year. They have shipping systems and a constant supply of product. They get exclusive, or nearly so, presence in the stores because we rely on them. I can't offend them in order to take a chance with somebody who, frankly, is small potatoes. You have good carpets, Mr. Al-Amin, but you're strictly nickel-and-dime."

Ahmed's eyes darkened, and he opened his mouth to speak, but Haya laid a gentle hand softly on his shoulder.

"Thank you very much, Mr. Drayson," she said. He was only being honest.

"So you'll sell us the two carpets. Good."

"No," Ahmed said, suddenly, looking at Haya. "I'm afraid not. We're going to go into business for ourselves, and from now on the line will be exclusive."

She beamed back. Her thought exactly. She was so proud of Ahmed—they were hand in glove. *Mash'Allah,* Haya prayed silently, thank God for my husband.

⁓

That very afternoon, they got to work: found the site— ironically, an old carpet warehouse at a dusty road intersection;

applied for planning permission; and sought out an architect. Baba knew builders—Ahmed was going to make his own gallery.

Haya suggested the name: Sekhmet. The ancient Egyptian goddess of vengeance and war, lioness-headed, beautiful and fierce. How they were going to deal with the competition. She designed the statue that stood outside: striking, playing up their heritage, and of course colossal, like everything in L.A. Ahmed worked with the architect for huge windows, lots of light, UV protection built in.

No more fussy, dusty rooms.

It was their vision, and they worked to make it happen. In the gallery, the carpets were stretched out, displayed like paintings. Each as individual as a jewel. To keep costs low, they went for good light, clean walls, and little else. Baba contacted his network; Ahmed his sales prospects; on opening weekend they sold ten carpets.

Not brilliant, but respectable. Solid.

Haya brought in flowers and Moroccan mint tea. Ahmed placed a small advertisement in the *L.A. Times*. The second week, they sold another twelve carpets.

The gallery was profitable. They were on their way. It was hard work, but Haya enjoyed it, and they continued staying up late together, making love in the bathroom, at home, on the backseat of their car, like teenagers, in a secluded spot. They increased the trips back home, and she got used to dealing with suppliers, visiting the tribal weavers, talking to customs men. Haya's Arabic became perfect, and she was happy; she loved her husband, loved her job, loved her life. They were crafting a future; they became comfortable, and she wanted more. And Ahmed, so dominant in the bedroom, outside of it was her partner and ally. Haya had everything, except her friends. And, *insh'Allah,* a child.

⌒

"It's so good to meet you." Marcus Hardie, the sales director, looked at Haya and gave her a perfunctory smile that didn't reach his eyes. "So often in our business we never get to see the family. Your husband has quite the business model; you must be very proud."

Ahmed's eyes danced as Haya's flashed with annoyance.

"Actually, my wife had a good deal to do with this."

"Of course. We all need the support at home. Couldn't get it done without that."

Support! This whole thing had been *her* idea. Haya stiffened with anger. Now everybody—well, not Ahmed, but everybody else—was trying to take the credit away from her.

Baba insisted it was because of *his* contacts. The press ran stories about the little carpet-seller turned gallery owner. Now the Fayelle Galleria marketing man was ignoring her, too. Even when Ahmed specifically introduced her as his wife *and partner.*

It drove her crazy.

"We think the first consignment should be no more than fifty carpets," she said firmly.

"Per store? We'll want more than that."

"Not per store. For the United States." His chain of luxury goods stores was important, but not vital. "You should have no more than one or two per store, but in Manhattan and Beverly Hills we could go for five."

"That's not going to happen, little lady," Marcus said. He switched his attention back to Ahmed. "What numbers did you have in mind?"

"You heard my wife."

"Our customers want product."

"And they'll get it," Haya said, "eventually. After the carpets become impossible to obtain. When there's a waiting list—like a Kelly bag from Hermès."

"A what?"

"We like to create excitement. These items are works of art. It is an approach that has worked here in the Sekhmet Gallery," Ahmed pointed out.

"Always leave them wanting more. When you have orders in hand for fifty, we ship another ten. It will create a feeding frenzy," Haya said.

Marcus parried. "You can't run a business on hype."

"Actually, you can. But in this case it isn't hype. Our actual goods are exquisite. We merely add to the joy of the purchase." Haya warmed to her theme. "Shopping is like a love affair, Mr. Hardie, if it's done correctly. Prolonging the courtship is no bad thing."

He barely refrained from rolling his eyes.

"I'll think about it." He got to his feet. "Tell you what, Ahmed, come and see me in the office, okay? And you, little lady, nice to meet you. See you again sometime."

Haya exploded once he was out the door.

"Did you hear that? He wants to do business with *you*."

"You can't let it get to you." Ahmed stood up and walked across to her, standing behind her, his hands on her shoulders, tracing a line down them to her rib cage, possessively.

"Not here," Haya whispered, with a smile.

"Why not?" He nuzzled her neck, biting it lightly, and ran his hands across her breasts and belly. "Nobody will come in. Not without knocking. And you're tense." His thumb traced a line at the base of her spine, and Haya gasped.

"We'll go home," she said. "Let's go home, darling."

"You go," he said. "Wait for me. I have to finish up here with Anita; some tax stuff."

"Don't be long." She was trying to get control of her breathing.

"Did you see the doctor?"

That broke the spell; reluctantly Haya calmed down.

"Results this afternoon."

That was it, the one cloud in their happiness. A great business, houses in Egypt and the Hollywood Hills, a foot in both worlds. But no children.

She had not wanted to make the appointment. What she and Ahmed had was so precious, so intense. To lay her womb open to medicine seemed clinical, intrusive. Like slapping nature in the face for the gift they had received: burning love, and a passion as hot now as it was the first night he had taken her. Surely such a love could not be barren. Wouldn't children come in time?

But Ahmed, on this one thing, had insisted. And she had

obeyed him. Children mattered so much to him. It was why he'd agreed to marry her, before he fell in love with her.

Haya had submitted herself to Dr. Felicia Nevins, one of Bel Air's leading ob-gyns. The woman had prodded and poked her briskly, drawn blood, and taken tests. Haya felt like a laboratory animal.

At least there wasn't long to wait now. The results were due at five. And she was nervous about them. What if there *was* something wrong? If, God forbid, she was infertile? Ahmed was hers forever—of that Haya had no doubt. But that would mean the end of this long period of perfect happiness. Their lives would never again be free of sorrow.

"Then hurry home and I'll help you pass the time," Ahmed said. She ran to his arms, and he kissed her, pressing his palms against the soft swell of her breasts.

"*You* hurry," Haya said.

⁓

She paced in their bedroom. Damn it. Where the hell was he? Outside, their little garden was fragrant with bougainvillea and roses. She'd thought about scattering petals across the black silk sheets Ahmed preferred, but then decided against it—too much of a cliché. Haya was still aroused, her body holding the memory of his touch, not wanting to let it go.

This was not like him. Ahmed didn't blow her off for the sake of work meetings. If he said was coming home, he came.

Haya picked up the phone and called their assistant.

"Claire? Haya."

"Hi. What time are you guys getting back in? I have a ton of messages. Marcus Hardie ..."

Stuff Marcus Hardie.

"Getting back in? Did Ahmed leave already?"

"Of course—an hour ago." Claire was confused. "I thought he was going back home for lunch with you, sorry."

"He was." Haya wondered what the hell had happened. "Maybe he stopped off for something. I'll call when he gets here."

An hour later, she called the police. Supremely uninterested, they told her she couldn't report a missing person for twenty-four hours.

An hour after that, she started phoning the hospitals.

⌣

"It can't have happened. No."

"I'm terribly sorry."

"He was with me three hours ago." She felt stupid, just kept repeating it. "He was fine. Can't you put him in a neck brace?"

Ahmed lay there—she could hardly believe it really was him. Bandaged and trussed, with drips and feeders running from his arm. Around her, there was chaos; an overwhelmed A&E, a really bad hospital in Venice.

"Move him," Haya said sharply. "Get him into a private room."

The machines behind her husband's bed beeped. It was a comforting sound. He was still with her, still alive.

"Mrs. Al-Yanna." The doctor, a young woman, Korean-American, was trying to be kind. "We don't have those facilities here, ma'am. . . ."

"Then transfer him! A private clinic. I'll pay whatever it takes," Haya said, tears welling. "I have the money."

"It's not that. There's no point, Mrs. Al-Yanna. It was a very bad accident—the other driver died at the scene. . . ."

What did Haya care? They were just words.

"My husband is still alive," she snapped. "*Mash'Allah*. And I want him to get the best care . . . and I'm staying with him, so I'll be needing a bed, or a cot, or something."

"He is not still alive," the doctor said flatly. "Ma'am, I'm extremely sorry, but you don't understand. Your husband is dead. He experienced total brain death. The stem of his brain is dead."

"People come out of comas," Haya whispered. Tears were rolling down her cheeks.

"He is not in a coma. He is dead."

The woman was a devil! "Then why?" Haya demanded, and

her voice broke on a sob. "Why is that machine sounding? I can hear his heartbeats . . . I can see them!"

"Artificial respiration." The doctor could see that the wife was semihysterical. She had other patients. She had to move on. "We kept him alive in the hope you'd be willing to donate his organs. All that means is his heart is pumping. It's up to you, ma'am." For the millionth time that day, Dr. Kim tried for patience. "But I have a very sick father of two who needs a liver and an indigent lady waiting for a heart with no other options." Haya looked stricken. "She needs it now. I'm sorry there's no time for you to decide. If the answer is no, we unplug him immediately and the medical examiner will take over. I need the bed." She gestured at the wailing, sobbing crowd outside. "I am so sorry. You can see how it is."

At these hurried, harassed words, a strange feeling of immense calm enveloped Haya. He was gone, gone to Paradise, and she was here alone. And Allah is the Most Compassionate, she said to herself.

Ahmed was gone. His tender heart would have reached out to the sick. In saving other lives there was a crumb, just a crumb, of comfort.

"Yes. I'll sign the form. Take what you need," she said. "And then return him to me, this day. He must be buried at once. He is a Muslim, a believer. We cannot delay the burial."

Dr. Kim couldn't believe it. She tried not to smile, but the relief and surprise were too great.

"Thank you—thank you. I'll get you a consent form and a rush on the autopsy, I promise you. Tell me where you want"— her voice trailed off a moment—"*him sent.*"

❧

She went into automatic mode. Calling Egypt, and his parents. Listening to the ululation of his mother. Calling their mosque. Calling Baba and Mama, and forbidding them to come over. Not yet. Ahmed was lying in the funeral home, and she was there, in Hollywood, alone again, a widow at twenty.

Who would marry her now?

It did not matter; she wanted nobody. Ahmed was her life, her love, the sun and moon to Haya. Without him, life seemed utterly pointless.

There was the funeral. She mustered what few mourners she could—her friends, and the Muslims who worked for them at Sekhmet—not many people to stand around his grave, to mourn his shrouded body.

She tried to pray, but felt nothing. Nothing but darkness engulfed her. Without feeling, she stared into space.

The telephone rang. Haya answered automatically.

"Hello? Ms. Yanna?"

"Yes?"

"This is Dr. Nevins."

"Hi."

"I have the results of your tests today. And in fact I have some very good news!"

The American woman spoke with a professional chirpiness that made Haya want to slam the phone down on her.

No, you don't, she thought, *there is no good news anymore.*

"You're not barren. These things just happen sometimes. It takes a little longer than planned. All *your* indicators are normal." The doctor blabbed on. "Maybe your husband had a low sperm count, you should get him in to be looked at . . ."

Rage surged in Haya. "I have to go," she said.

"But it's all academic." The woman responded brightly. "Because, you see, you're in fact pregnant. Congratulations!"

Haya shuddered. "What?"

"You're pregnant. Only about three weeks from conception, but you're definitely pregnant. There's a heartbeat already, which *greatly* increases the chances of a successful first trimester. So lay off the booze," Dr. Nevins wise cracked.

"I don't drink." Haya was swaying on her feet. "I have to go," she repeated, and hung up.

Oh, God! Pregnant!

She ran into her bathroom and started to be sick.

Haya did not tell anybody. She could not deal with that, not
on top of everything else. The fussing and clucking . . . she would
die.

It was enough to have to fly back to Egypt, and be plunged
into a world she could hardly cope with: instructing lawyers, selling the house, enduring the anger of his parents, who blamed her
for Ahmed's death. After all, she had dragged him to America,
that godless, decadent land, and there, he had died.

Then there was everything else. The dismissal of all the staff,
with compensation—generous; Haya arranged six months' wages
for each of them, paid from the sale of the Cairo house; no questions asked.

Yet she could not bear to rid herself of the carpets, the lamps,
the silken cushions, everything he had acquired; the evidence
of that eye for beauty that had assessed Haya herself, and found
her pleasing. The stock, she had shipped to L.A. Everybody told
her she should sell it off, in bulk; there were offers, now their
brand had been established; for the carpets, the gallery space, for
everything.

And in truth, Haya found, she could not keep it going. Even
if she'd had the emotional strength. She had been the inspiration,
the spirit, of Sekhmet, but she had no idea about the details. Line
management, staffing, wages, distribution—all that, Ahmed had
confidently handled.

She was out of her depth. She wound up the company, offering three months to the American workers—their wages were
far more costly—and let the gallery sit vacant. But the stock she
put into storage.

Haya wasn't rich, but there was some money there, now.
Enough for a year or so, for breathing space.

Enough to see her through the birth of her child. His son or
daughter. A small piece of her love, that would come back to
her.

Right now, that was all she cared about.

On the other hand, it wouldn't last. And Haya had no desire

to go back to her father's house. She loved her parents, but she was independent of them. Which meant, one way or another, eventually she was going to have to make a living—more than a living—a success.

She had to give his child all he would have dreamed of. Anything less would be a betrayal.

CHAPTER 10

"We're here. Momma?" Sally reached across the passenger seat and shook her mother, who was snoozing, her mouth open and her neck lolling against the headrest. "Wake up. We're here."

Mona opened her eyes. "We are? Great." She rubbed her lids. "I want a drink," she said groggily. "A little champagne, huh? To celebrate. We're back."

"Let's see what the apartment has for us," Sally suggested. She knew better than to refuse outright. Whatever would get Mona up the stairs. Sally was perfectly prepared to drug her mother, once she'd had a shower and eaten. A few sleeping pills, and she would tumble into bed.

Whatever it took. Anything to get her mom sober for a week, past that first rush of chemical addiction. After that, she'd made the decision for rehab. Betty Ford was out of their budget, but there were other places, if she sacrificed a few months' rent.

It was worth it. And she didn't think Mona would fight that hard. Her mother had surrendered her place in the family, become the child, leaving Sally in charge. And if Sally issued an order, Mona obeyed it.

In her heart, her mother didn't want to be this way. With every day sober, the fog cleared up a little. Plus, they were back in L.A. That gave Sally a chance for some prime emotional blackmail.

"Momma—you don't want to drink the moment we step

inside, do you? You know, people might report us to the papers. You don't want Lucille and Kimberley"—Mona's ex-friends—"to read about you in the society columns, do you?"

Mona shuddered. "Read what?"

"That you were a drunk living in a cheap apartment? Just think—they'd be laughing at you."

Her mom's eyes flashed with a spark of her old spirit.

"Hell, no," she said. "I'll just take a bubble bath."

"There you go," Sally said, relieved. She shepherded her mother inside and up the stairs. The apartment building was painted bubblegum pink, and the paint was chipped; the rails on the stairwells were made of steel, and the flooring was cheap linoleum. But at least the place was clean; there was a strong smell of industrial disinfectant.

Mona clutched at her daughter as Sally fumbled with the keys.

"D'you think they will? D'you think they'll find out we're living here?"

"Listen, Momma, it's a decent place. Better than Hartford. It's got security and underground parking." Sally pushed her mother inside the apartment. "See? Not so bad."

It was plainly furnished with the basic essentials. Couch, bed, table with four chairs, and small seventeen-inch TV set. Functional beige carpets, and all the charm of a roadside motel.

"You take a bath." There was a small tub, the kind where you had to raise your knees. "And I'll go get the groceries." Some hot chocolate with two sleeping pills would do the trick. Sally comfortingly patted her mother's arm. "We won't be here too long, Momma. You'll see."

Brave words. She wondered how she could make them come true.

⁓

Sally got a job the first week. It wasn't hard in L.A., the world capital of glitz and glamour; every other block there was a beauty parlor. Beehive was a cute little place on Sunset with a customer

base of anonymous West Hollywood teens; anonymous and boring. Sally agreed to work on commission in exchange for being
off the books. She didn't want to be found in her own city.

She did makeovers, styled hair, and kept the place clean. Sally
was very good, and very popular. She got to set her own rates and
kept fifty percent plus tips.

One sunny Sunday morning, Sally shook hands with the
owner and told her she was quitting.

The boss pouted. "It's tough, making it on your own."

"I'm used to tough."

"Well, honey, if it don't work out, you always got a job here."

But Sally knew, as she walked out the door, that she would
never return. Tempered by tragedy, poverty, and abuse, Sally Lassiter was ready for the big time.

The next step was the easiest. Sally booked Mona a place in
downtown rehab.

"I don't want to go without you." Momma's latest excuse. "I
can cut down. It's just the stress."

Sally didn't look at her. "Mom, you'll be fine."

"I should be home, looking after you." Mona's teary, drunken
tones turned aggressive. "Stop the car! You can't make me do
rehab! I won't check in . . . I'll look after you, Sally. . . ."

Sally pulled over and looked at her mother, swollen-faced and
drowning in self-pity.

"Do you know why we left Texas, Momma? Because I was
raped. By Leo Fisk. One night while I was walking home after
slaving all day to support us." Her mother's mouth opened in
shock. "And when I came inside, you were passed out drunk.
Again." Sally pressed her foot on the gas. "Which is why we're
here. To make something of this family again."

Her mother started to sob now, in earnest.

"That's how I lost my virginity," Sally said, coldly. "To a rapist.
And I couldn't even tell you, Momma. That's why you're going
to rehab. Because I won't let you lose your life inside a bottle."

Mona relaxed against the leather, surrendering.

"I'll go, baby," she said, dully. "I'll go."

~

"You can't play chicken with me, Ms. Morgan."

Turnbull Scott, the doughy chief executive of Shop Smart, narrowed his piggish eyes at his young vice president.

"Your story is a good one—it reads well in the reports. But you're far too young for this sort of promotion."

"When I evaluate executives, I go by results." Jane felt strangely detatched. A pigeon swooped past, outside the huge window behind Mr. Scott; it made her smile, which infuriated him.

"You've used PR to advance your career. Think what it'll look like if we take a risk on a kid who can't even legally drink the wine we sell."

"My track record proves I'm risk-free."

"Look, get this straight." Nobody ever talked to Scott like that. He loved what the girl had done to his personnel overheads, otherwise she'd be gone. "We are *not* going to put you into a frontline division. You've got an offer on the table." The board had instructed him to keep her—they were terrified a headhunting firm would poach her. "It's a *huge* offer," he insisted, frustrated.

"It is." Jane smiled again. They had begged, and pleaded, and in the end just thrown money at her. The final offer was nearly double her salary. Three hundred fifty thousand dollars. "I don't want it," she explained.

"You'll make *more* than if you ran a sales division."

"I don't care. I want the training."

"Training?" He blinked. "For what?"

"For when I own this company."

Turnbull Scott laughed—Jane didn't.

"I'm serious. Are you going to switch me into a frontline job?"

"No!" he almost shouted.

"Then I quit." Jane reached into her jacket, took out her letter of resignation and her car keys, and laid them on his desk. "It's been nice working with you."

Scott stared incredulously at her. The board was going to yell at him about this.

"You arrogant goddamned *bitch!*" he snarled. But she had already turned on her high heels, and was walking her tight little butt out the door.

⁓

"There's a bit of a slump," Marcy Wilkerson, her real estate agent, told her. "Places have been slow to move. . . ."

Jane turned to her. "You can't snow me. When I was buying, it was all 'Jump on it now, you have to move fast.' I read the property supplements every day."

"The market's changed since you purchased this place."

"No, it hasn't. I want six fifty for this apartment."

Marcy's eyes boggled. "That's a profit of one hundred fifty in eight months."

"It's eminently achievable," Jane said crisply. "Either you do it, within a month, or I'll find a better agent who can. Now excuse me please, I'm busy."

Then she opened the door. Marcy walked out.

Bitch, she thought as Jane Morgan slammed it behind her. Hard as nails. Definitely needed to get laid.

⁓

"I want a ticket to Los Angeles, please."

"Certainly, ma'am." The ticket agent looked curiously at the young girl standing in front of her. So pretty—slim and young, in a neat little designer dress, carrying a small suitcase. She sounded intelligent—probably a student, looking for a last-minute deep discount. "Let me see what comes up for you on the standby tracker. . . ."

"No. First class."

Her eyebrow lifted, but the girl produced a Prada wallet and coolly handed over a gold Amex card.

"And when will you be returning?"

"I won't. One-way."

"That's three thousand dollars," the older woman said tentatively, as if to ask "Are you sure?"

"That's fine. Ring it up, please."

The ticket agent did as she was told, even more curious than before. Who *was* she? Turns up at the airport, flies first class? Why hadn't she booked? And strangest of all, there was no wedding ring. She could see this woman as some investment banker trophy wife, but there was nothing.

"The first-class lounge is upstairs."

"Thank you." She took her ticket and turned to go, cool and collected.

The agent sighed.

That girl definitely had to be someone special.

～⌒⌒

Jane gave a little mental shrug as she walked into the first-class lounge. She felt dozens of eyes on her. Let them stare.

Turnbull Scott thought she was insane. A wild risk-taker. Junking her comfortable corporate life in favor of the wild blue yonder.

But that was only because he didn't understand.

To stay at Shop Smart now was to doom herself to failure. Jane had a clear idea of where her ladder headed, and if the top of it was resting against "well-paid executive," then she wasn't bothering to climb.

She wanted security. What happened to Daddy would never happen to her. She wanted serious rich, Aaron Spelling rich, Paulie Lassiter rich.

And you didn't get that from a paycheck. You got it from ownership.

She felt a little fear as she strode over to the bar and ordered a mineral water, choked with ice. This was new territory. And the business world had her pigeonholed into one box—human resources; stuff that does not count. It was why Shop Smart hadn't given her a shot.

And now somebody else would have to.

"Can I buy you a drink?"

It was a relaxed, confident masculine voice.

"No." She didn't look round.

"That's the right answer. Well done."

Now, she looked at him—annoyed.

"Excuse me?"

He inclined his head. Fifteen years older than her, still young, around thirty-five, she guessed. Dark eyes with thick black lashes. A rather arrogant, cruel mouth; a strong jaw, and a tan.

"I can't *buy* you a drink—because they're free. But we could still have one together."

"I'm already having one. By myself." Jane turned back to it. This game was for losers, and she wasn't playing.

They started out all nice and flirty. And when it became clear she really wasn't interested in being some junior marketing prick's one-night lay, then they called her a dyke and a bitch.

"A great idea." He was unfazed. "I'll have one by myself, too. Right next to you. And then we can both get on our respective planes and we'll never see each other again."

She relented.

"Sorry if I was a little cold."

"Cold? I don't think you need the ice with that drink."

Jane's eyes sparked again. He was *laughing* at her. His eyes were on her, and his body language was completely relaxed, confident and at ease. Another man would have slunk away.

"Does that often work for you?"

"What?"

"Insulting girls."

The bartender girl sauntered up to them and made goo-goo eyes at him. "Mr. Levin. What a *pleasure* to see you again, sir."

Jane's mental Rolodex did a quick check.

"You're not Craig Levin, are you?" Jane asked.

His eyes danced again, with pleasure.

"Yes, ma'am."

"What can I get for you, sir?" the bartender asked. "Your usual?"

"That's fine, and please call me Craig, Iris."

She beamed, obviously thrilled that he remembered her name. "Coming right up," she promised, in a breathy Marilyn Monroe voice.

Craig Levin. Wall Street wonder, except not on Wall Street. Rich enough to import a snow machine to your Los Angeles mansion at Christmas. Rich enough to hire out the city zoo for your kid's sixteenth. A genius investor, Jane had seen him described as "the next Warren Buffett" more times than she cared to count. He had influence enough to swing a stock. Like Buffett, he never split shares in his index fund, and they now traded at eight thousand dollars a share.

Some of his original investors had made hundreds of millions from a tiny initial stake. And Levin had a myth about him. He never gave interviews. No cozy little chats with *Fortune*. No vanity slots on CNBC with Maria Bartiromo, "the Money Honey," beaming on in approval.

Levin was young, independent, and vastly rich.

No wonder he was arrogant.

"Does knowing my name mean you'll be nicer to me?"

Jane was cold with fury; half at him, half at herself. He was still gazing at her with that amused regard.

"It certainly doesn't. I'm not for sale." She couldn't help herself; she nodded toward the bartender, fixing Levin a generous Scotch on the rocks. "Maybe she is, though. You might get lucky after all."

His smile abruptly vanished.

"You're sitting here in the first-class lounge because you've got a first-class ticket. I don't know anything else about you, but I know you're a woman of means. She's a bartender. Probably not getting rich on this job. So you sitting here in that elegant suit and calling her a whore isn't cool."

Jane flushed purple.

"I'm sorry," she said, wrong-footed and ashamed of herself.

But he replied coolly, "Enjoy your drink," and walked away to the other end of the bar, retrieving his whisky from the beaming bartender as he passed her.

Jane winced. She was ashamed of herself. Levin was right; she should have been better than that. And he'd immediately lost interest in her.

Not that she *cared*.

Levin had been bothering her. The pursuit annoyed her. So why was she more annoyed when it stopped?

"Can I get you anything else, ma'am?" the simpering bartender was back, oblivious to anything that had happened.

"No. That's okay. Thank you," Jane added, guiltily.

"That Craig Levin—he's hot. So funny, too. Did you ever hear him joke? He cracks everybody up."

"Is he in here a lot?" Curiosity filled her.

The bartender—Iris, right, that's what he called her, grinned.

"All the time. He has more air miles than Santa Claus. And remembers people's names . . ." She sighed. "And so damn handsome. Don't you think?"

Jane shrugged. "If you like that sort of thing."

"Man! I would in a heartbeat." She sighed. "But the girls I see with him are mostly models. Socialites . . . you know."

"How cliché."

"I guess he can have whatever he wants, and he takes advantage. I never saw the guy be rude to any woman, though. Saw a couple of his girlfriends crying when he left. None of them last very long."

"Rich playboy. It's as old as the hills," Jane said, glad to be able to look down on Levin.

But she still wished he hadn't walked away.

All business, of course. Levin was so rich he could have bought Shop Smart by writing a check. You didn't want to cross a man like that. Maybe it was good that he didn't know her name.

"Flight 961 to LAX is now boarding at Gate 33."

She stood up, half-relieved, half-disappointed. "That's me.

Thanks, Iris." She put down a crisp twenty on the bar as a tip. "Have a nice day."

~

She thought about him all the way through the corridors and walkways of the airport. Jane tried not to, but it didn't work. She had read about Craig Levin—of course. She had built him up in her mind; wanted to meet him—he was one of the giants, one of the people she most admired.

And now he'd asked her for a drink, and she'd told him to go to hell.

She was annoyed with herself. But really, he'd been hitting on her. Hadn't taken no for an answer. And Iris said he had a string of gorgeous girls.

A distraction. Jane tried to wrestle her mind back to the business at hand. Finding Helen and Sally. Starting her own retail chain, her own Shop Smart.

"Good morning . . . second on the left . . ."

The air hostess was repeating her inane instructions; Jane ignored her and walked past. Why the hell did they do that? How tough would it be to find seat 2B? Aisle, on the left. She took her little carry-on and lifted it up to the overhead compartment; a strong pair of hands whisked it away from her and tucked it inside.

"Thank you—"

Jane glanced round. It was him. She gasped in shock.

"We're sitting together." He smiled easily at her. "Hope you don't mind."

"I—no." Her mind raced, and she thought about apologizing for earlier. But the moment had passed, what could she say? "That's fine." Jane slid into her seat, and took refuge in the free magazine provided.

"Yes," Levin said. "That article on the strawberry growers of the Midwest is certainly fascinating stuff. I heard two of their journalists are up for a Pulitzer."

Jane's eyes glittered. "So the billionaire is laughing at the impoverished writers, is he?"

He grinned. "Touché."

Jane felt an unreasonable elation.

"Miss Morgan, can I get you some champagne, or freshly squeezed orange juice?"

"Orange juice. Thank you."

"I'll have the same. One's my limit." He passed Jane her glass. "Are you a teetotaler, Ms. Morgan?"

"For another three months. I'm not yet twenty-one."

"Don't I feel old," he said, with a grin that said he didn't.

"You don't need to worry about me; I'm an adult." She lifted her head defiantly.

"Glad to hear it," he answered, with a soft, predatory intent that sent a tingle down her spine.

Jane chided herself. What the hell was she doing? Months—years—of brushing men off, and she was all but ready to start flirting with Craig Levin just because he was an alpha male?

"So let me see." Levin's eyes focused on a point some way in front of him; it was unnerving. "Morgan—female, twenty, British. That makes you Jane Morgan. Senior vice president of human resources, Shop Smart Corporation."

She blinked. "How the hell did you know that?"

"I have a photographic memory. It's a big help when assessing stocks. So I'm right?"

"All except the last part. I quit Shop Smart yesterday."

"Excuse me a second."

"Of course," Jane said; but she was disappointed. Levin turned from her and swiped a black Amex through his Skyphone, punching in numbers. She had just started to enjoy herself.

"Anna? Craig. Dump Shop Smart. Everything; the whole half-million. Tell the brokers to feed it out slow. See ya, babe." He turned back to Jane. "Tell me the rest of your story."

She struggled with the unexpected wave of desire that rocked through her body. On two words from her, he'd just sold over ten million dollars' worth of Shop Smart stock.

"Why did you do that?" she almost whispered.

"Jane Morgan," he replied, and his eyes flickered across her face, noting the dilated pupils, the flushed skin. It almost made her want to run away from him—except that they were in the air, and there was nowhere to go. "Junior VP. Promoted from the shop floor. In her first year, cut costs in one store by thirty percent and increased productivity by twenty-seven percent, all through personnel changes. Promoted to central management, applied techniques across the United States; immediate savings of fifteen percent on salaries, management redundancies saving another eight percent. Productivity data increase not yet in. You see, in such a low-cost store, staffing costs are about half the overhead. You had something. If they've let you go, they're nuts."

He knew all about her. Jane struggled against her arousal. So what? It was a photographic memory, a trick of the mind.

"I'm not interested in being a VP of personnel. I'm interested in being a CEO. Of my own wholly owned business."

"Why?"

She had not expected that question.

"I don't like being dependent," she said, after a pause.

"I could help you."

"You could buy me Saks and give it to me for a birthday present." She spoke strongly, on more certain ground now. "But I'm not interested in being a kept woman. I want to make it on my own."

His smile deepened. "Impressive."

"And you should know a couple of things, Mr. Levin." Jane spoke up bravely, challenging him. "The first is that I know all about you, and I admire you. Like everybody else working in business, I guess. The second is that I am *not* going to be one of your trophy girls. Your throwaway identikit supermodel arm candy."

"My *what*?"

"Remember Iris the bartender? She and I had a good talk." Jane smiled triumphantly. "And I'm not really interested in taking a number with any man, no matter how rich and . . . powerful." Saying it sent little frissons of electricity across her stomach; Jane ignored them. "So I hope we'll have a pleasant flight, and I'll admit it's been exciting to meet you. But you should know that all this flirtation is just a waste of time. I'm a busy woman, and I'm not interested."

"I understand your feelings."

"My feelings?"

"It's all they are." He smiled unapologetically at her. "You have a perfect right to express all these things, and I have a right not to accept them. But don't worry, Miss Morgan. I'm not going to stalk you. I've never yet tried to force myself on any female. When you come to me—and you will—it'll be entirely of your own volition."

"You're very cocksure."

"I've earned that right."

"Not with women," she said, outraged.

"Certainly with women. Ask any of my ex-girlfriends."

"Ex," she said, with emphasis.

Levin inclined his head. "I'm afraid so. They weren't enough of a challenge."

"You date beauties, and yet you want to be challenged? Give me a break."

"That's about it. I want everything in a woman. Brains—beauty—strength—humor—a certain style." He shrugged. "If we're expected to spend the rest of our lives with only one person, then I think we should be allowed as long a shopping list as we like. I start with beauty, yes."

"Why?"

"It's the only quality than can be instantly assessed," he replied calmly. "To see if someone is intelligent, or spirited, requires dating."

"Has anybody ever told you you're a sexist pig?"

"Am I? So what do you require in a man?" he asked. "How many poor, ugly, underachieving, diffident males have you gone out with recently?"

Jane was silent. She didn't want to tell him there had been nobody except Jude. This was America, where everybody was a shrink. She didn't want to be psychoanalyzed. Especially not by Craig Levin.

Instead, she changed the subject. "So what are you doing in L.A.? Business?"

"Yes, but I can't tell you what."

She understood. The market watched Craig Levin's every move. For her to know what businesses he was looking at would equal insider trading.

"I'm going to start my business there," she told him. "Buy a house. And find some old schoolfriends."

He grinned. "You make that sound easy."

"Why shouldn't it be?" she said. "People overcomplicate life."

⁓

As they touched down, she turned to him and briskly offered her hand.

"It's been nice to meet you, Mr. Levin."

"Craig."

"I don't think we should. We might do business in the future."

"Oh, we never will," he said at once.

"How do you know?"

"I'm attracted to you. And you're attracted to me. That's too many complications for any kind of financial dealings."

The plane halted and shuddered to a stop. Levin was up instantly, retrieving his briefcase and handing her her bag. Jane felt a huge sense of aggravation and loss; the flight was done, he was gone; she had been a pretty distraction, and now she would never see him again.

Her pride would not let her say a word.

"You have no idea whether I'm attracted to you or not," she hissed in a low voice.

He leaned down, in to her, where she was sitting in her seat and he was standing, and placed his mouth to her ear, so none of the businessmen milling around them could hear.

"Of course I do."

Jane bit her lip. She had never come across a man like Levin. God help her, his self-confidence was sexy. She knit her hands in her lap.

"Here." He offered her a business card. "Good-bye, Jane Morgan."

She took the card. Of course, she ought to have shredded it to confetti in front of him. But instead, she slipped it into a jacket pocket.

Levin's hand reached out, and a callused fingertip casually, secretively, traced a line across her neck down to her shoulder.

It was electric. Jane, helplessly, reacted; her body shuddered, and she had to grip the sides of her seat to prevent anybody else from seeing her reaction. She blushed, hot with shame and wanting him, and waited it out.

And in a few seconds he was gone. Front of the line; he left the plane without looking back. Jane had arrived in Los Angeles the way she had left it . . . on her own.

"Momma." Sally knocked on her mother's door. Two weeks back from rehab, and Mona was spending all day in bed. "Momma—what do you think?"

"What? I'm tired."

Yeah, she was always tired.

"I want to show you these new sketches." Sally was determined to have her mother awake, and aware of the wider world. "What do you think?"

She was sure these were the best yet. A short sheath dress in buttercup yellow, with a careful ruched neckline and cinched at the waist. A business suit with sass—tailored jacket and kicky pleated skirt. A little navy dress with cap sleeves, full skirted, fitted at the waist and bodice—something for the girl who could no longer go strapless.

And in addition, Sally had come up with jewelry. Forget minimalist—she was maximalist. Her designs glittered and sparkled with rhinestones and cheap semiprecious jewels.

"Very nice." Mona wasn't even looking.

"Would you like to go for a walk, Momma?"

"Nobody walks in L.A."

"Well, when I get back, I'll drive you to the beach," Sally said firmly. She was determined to get Mona out of the house.

"Where are you going?" Her mother was using that whiny, tearful voice again.

"I told you yesterday, I have an appointment. At DeMarco's."

"Okay, well, good luck. I hope they have some positions. You could be a girl on the makeup counter," Mona said, tiredly, and closed the door.

Sal shook her head and went back into the living room. She gathered up her sketches and the two pieces she'd actually run up herself. The first was her favorite skirt, a wild little thing in blue satin with a scalloped hem, bias-cut and full of motion. The second, a necklace, one she'd crafted very carefully: little round pebbles of semiprecious jewels, with a letter carved into each one; they spelled out LUCKY. She'd strung them on a silver chain, since she hadn't been able to afford a gold one.

They were good, she knew that. Stylish, and hot. Something a little different. She would wear them—any young girl would.

So far, it had been tough—buyers refusing even to see her stuff. But after weeks of badgering, Ollie Foster at DeMarco's had agreed to give her five minutes.

This was gonna be it. Her lucky break!

~

"So you can see the movement." Sally smiled and turned the skirt around, letting the hem flare out in the breeze. "And these stones—they're designed to be sold individually, with a chain. You can make your own message. It's like jewelry as pizza, you pay for each topping. They're like candy, no girl will resist."

"Interesting." Foster steepled his fingers automatically and moistened his lips. She noticed his eyes roaming across her ample breasts and steeled herself not to stiffen. "You got anything else to show me, baby? It's hard to break in to sales in this town—real *hard*."

"I have these sketches. . . ."

"I'm not talking 'bout sketches. Why don't you slip into the changing rooms with me and model that skirt? You know—show me something. Got a cute little ass on you, girl. If you want a deal here, you know what you got to do. . . ."

Sally snatched her necklace back and turned on her heel. Sleazeball! Her eyes filled with tears.

"Where the hell do you think you're going?" he shouted. "I got connections, girl. All the other big stores in this town. You gotta learn to play nice if you want to be in the game. . . ."

But she was already gone.

Sally didn't go home. She couldn't bear to go home and deal with her soporific mother. She was back here on her own turf; she had to make something happen. . . .

Screw it, she thought, with uncharacteristic passion. *Screw them all.* The lechers and the sexists and the ones who just didn't care enough to even give her a chance.

So nobody was going to help her? She'd do it herself.

Wiping the tears away, Sally walked from DeMarco's down Melrose. It was a long walk, hot, but she didn't care. Here was the epicenter of L.A. hip. All little biker bars, leather clothing stores, gothic fashion, witchcraft shops, and palm readers.

She found a place—Fine Fashions, it said—an optimistic name. Run-down and seedy, it was flogging racks of discount T-shirts from Taiwan at five bucks a throw, plastic earrings, and elasticized bracelets.

There was nobody in the store. It was a decent location; half-way up Melrose with an empty parking lot across the street.

For the first time since she'd gotten home, Sally felt a thrill of excitement.

She marched inside. Behind the counter was a little Korean woman, looking bored and reading a magazine.

"Hi," said Sally. "This your place?"

The woman was instantly defensive. "We paid that fine, if you from city hall."

"I'm not. I need a shop. How long is your lease?"

"Six months."

"I'll buy it out. Fifteen hundred a month."

Her eyes narrowed. "You serious, lady?"

"Totally serious. Another three grand for the fixtures and the stock."

"I want five."

"Don't push it," Sally said. "Your place ain't up to much, ma'am; I'm surely saving y'all from foreclosure. This way you keep a good credit rating, you can start over someplace else."

"When you bring money?"

"You call your lawyer, I'll be back here at two with a cashier's check and a contract." Sally had another idea. "You know any seamstresses? I need to hire some ladies who know how to cut and sew patterns."

"Of course. Plenty."

"This afternoon I'll be hiring. I need four women. You could bring them with you."

"Okay." The woman shrugged. "This a rough spot, lady, lots of clothes shops, not enough customers." She waved at Sally's neat little dress and chic platform shoes. "But you rich, you can afford it. Learn the hard way."

Sally smiled, her first real smile in a long time.

"See you at two," she said, and left to find some walk-in lawyer.

⌒

"So this is what we're going to do." Sally smiled at the women; as of now, her employees. "Cut one shoulder off every shirt. Neckline diagonal. And slash the hem like so." She showed them her flame design. "Then sew it back up. You see the pattern? I pay minimum wage plus a dollar. Once this stock is sold out, we'll get health coverage."

An older lady with bags under her eyes spoke up; Sally could see she was used to life in a sweatshop.

"Health?" she asked. "For real?"

"For real. And there's an hour for lunch; I'll get us sandwiches and coffee. We're in this together, ladies." Sally's warm Texas drawl encouraged them. "Do you think you can handle it?"

"Yes," the woman said, smiling weakly.

"Yes, miss," another of them said, looking hopeful. "Here"— and she took a large, square, raspberry T-shirt, applied Sally's pattern, and started to cut.

❧

"*L.A. Citizen.* Editorial."

"Can I speak to Mike Reardon?"

Sally gripped the phone. This was it—she was going all out. But she had no choice. Hiring the staff, buying the lease—their money had almost gone. She had the stock now. Now it was all about sales.

She was about to expose herself. And maybe Momma. But it was do-or-die time.

"Editor's office. Janice speaking. Who's calling?"

"This is Sally Lassiter."

"From what company?" asked the bored assistant.

"I'm the daughter of Paulie Lassiter—you remember, the oilman whose company went bust and he died of a heart attack? Big story. Front-page stuff."

"Okay . . ."

"Mom and I fled to Texas in disgrace." It stung, but she forced herself to say it. Reardon would see her as a human-interest story or not at all. "Now I'm back in L.A. and I want to give an interview. Tell our side of the story." She gave her their number. "Have him call me back on this number if he's interested in doing a feature. Good-bye."

Sally hung up and headed to the kitchen to make coffee, but she didn't have long to wait; she had only opened the jar when the phone rang.

"Is this really Sally Lassiter?"

"It sure is." She tried to sound confident. "I'm prepared to offer you a deal, Mr. Reardon."

"We don't pay for interviews, Ms. Lassiter, company policy."

"Not what I'm looking for. I've started a little store—my designs. I need the publicity. You come and do a feature on me, you include mention of the store and shots of my T-shirts. I'll pose in some of my clothes. I'm not asking for a puff piece—review them however you like." He started to say something, but Sally cut him off. "I'll give you what you're looking for—plenty of emotional stuff about Dad and being poor, public school and taking the bus. All I want in exchange is the PR." She paused. "Well?"

Reardon chuckled. "You've got guts, young lady. I'll take that deal. But beware—we don't puff, either, I leave that to *Vanity Fair*. If your clothes suck, my journalist is gonna say so."

"Fine with me." Sally was elated. "Let's do it."

"When?"

"Now." She gave him the address. "I'll be at the store in twenty minutes."

~~~~~

Sally made them take the photos first. She knew after she'd been speaking to the journalist her eyes would be red. Better get the shots out of the way while she could. She posed, sexy but demure, in her little blue skirt and a white cutoff T-shirt that showed her tan, long blonde hair flowing loose around her waist, nails with a simple French polish, her blue eyes laughing.

The photographer, a woman, sighed with pleasure. "You look amazing, girlfriend."

The interviewer, wearing the skinny black jeans and white buttoned shirt of a fashion maven, was bespectacled and serious. Sally poured her heart out: she sobbed, she railed at Miss Milton's lack of support, she castigated her mother's friends. Explosive stuff; she needed it to be.

This had to make the paper.

"I'm filing it this afternoon." The journalist clicked the off button on her tape recorder, clearly impressed. "And, Sally, I think your T-shirts are hot. *So* sexy. Plus, I adore those beads."

"Here." Sally jumped to her feet, collected a handful, and strung her a necklace. "It says 'Annalise.'" Her name. "That's yours—if you like it, maybe you'll wear it, tell your friends."

"Maybe." She smiled. "This piece runs on Sunday—if I were you I'd stay open that day."

The next morning was Thursday. Sally came to work to find her store already full; Koko, her Algerian counter girl, had opened early.

"There was a crowd outside."

The journalist had brought her friends.

As the chic young women, whom Sally pegged as grad students, lawyers, bankers' wives—nonindustry, civilian Angelenas—shopped, running through her stock like locusts, Sally reflected you could be big in this town if you were hip and you were first. The rich girls wanted a jump on the hoi polloi who'd come here Sunday, when the *Citizen* ran the piece.

At the end of the day she was already showing a month's profit. She gave the girls a tiny bonus: fifty bucks apiece, all she could afford.

"There'll be more later."

They laughed and hugged her, eyes bright with tears. Sally got the feeling her workers didn't often see fifty dollars all at once.

It gave her a thrill. Finally, her own money. Her own style. Her own success.

On Sunday, the piece came out. She didn't read it; no desire to relive that harrowing shit all over again. She just looked at the pictures: herself, golden, laughing, twenty and supremely beautiful, with her kicky little skirt and innate confidence.

Annalise, the journalist, had pegged it. Sally's shop was swarming with visitors. They sold almost every T-shirt, and the jewelry was gone in three hours.

After that, she started taking orders. Payment up front, delivery in two weeks; wait list only.

Sally Lassiter was still small-time. She didn't kid herself. But she was also a success.

Helen stood up, gingerly. She was only five months along, but her feet were still swelling. She walked into her garden, her embroidered slippers flip-flopping carefully.

Her stomach was churning—and it wasn't her baby. That was Sally, her Sally, in the papers. Haya had discovered at long last what had happened to her friends; and she hadn't been there for them; she had been half a world away, sweating out her pleasure in the grip of Ahmed's arms.

They must have felt it as a betrayal. And in a way, she knew, it was. She hadn't tried to find them, even when she got back to America. She had been so lost in her husband, in what he was doing—and after he died, just lost.

And now—here was Sally. And Sally looked so beautiful! Tragedy had burned some determination into her face, made her all-American good looks that little bit deeper.

The clothes looked good on her body. There was fit, elegance, a bit of sassiness that squeezed at Haya's heart—all Sally, big-hearted, optimistic, golden Sally. And she hadn't given up, she was just clawing her way back in. The *Citizen* gave her designs a rave review. The girl was doing well.

Haya's heart beat a little faster, with pure nerves. But she steeled herself. She would go to see Sally. If her old friend was furious, damned her to hell for not being there, Haya would understand. How must it look . . . like Haya had dumped her as soon as she lost her money.

But there were few people, now, Haya liked in this world. Of course she still loved Baba and Mama; but right now, she didn't *like* them very much. And maybe there were others she could have forged a relationship with, but she'd kept her distance. Hadn't wanted to tell anybody yet that she was pregnant.

Sally Lassiter was different. Haya picked up the paper again, and committed the address to her memory. Melrose—right.

⌒〜⌒

"Thank you so much."

"Really—it's fabulous. And I'll take twenty in each color. Just mail them to my billing address."

"I will ma'am, thank you." Sally gave her the patented smile.

"Your stuff is just terrific," the fat lady said, and sailed magnificently out of the room, like a galleon under full sail.

Sally sighed with relief. That was it; the society wife was the last customer. Not that she minded sales, but her heels, dizzy five-inch Manolos, were *killing* her.

With the first little bit of money, Sally had bought herself a killer wardrobe.

That was even more important than a new house, because it was business. They'd all read the *Citizen* article. Half of her customers were rubberneckers—there to see *her*. The golden girl down at the heels. Paulie Lassiter's daughter, starting over.

Fuck it. Sally played the cards she was dealt. If they came to see her, then *she* was the product. Everything she sold reflected her. And that meant being one hundred percent glamorous, at all times.

She added platinum highlights to her butterscotch hair. She deepened her tan with lotions. She wore Manolos on her feet—nothing else. Only her own line of jewelry—her necklace read, SURVIVOR—and her own designer clothes. Sally got her teeth whitened, and wore perfume at all times, even to bed. Glamour, she told herself, was a state of mind.

Beauty and style were like athleticism. They required practice and endless conditioning. If there was one thing Sally Lassiter knew, it was how to be a star.

And the customers drooled over it.

She nodded to Koko to lock up and gratefully slid her stockinged feet out of her narrow-toed shoes.

There was a knock on the door.

"Are you open?"

"Sorry, miss. No. Tomorrow, nine a.m.," Koko said.

"I wanted to see Sally Lassiter."

At the sound of that voice, Sally froze. "Wait—Koko, wait. Helen? Is that you?"

"Yes. . . ."

"My God! Koko, let her in!"

Haya walked in. She was lovely: she wore a long dress, a little shapeless, with gold embroidery stitched across the azure blue cloth; her hair was curled softly just to her shoulders; and her skin was luminous.

"Sally!" she said. She gasped with joy. "Sally! It's you, *mash'Allah*, it's really you! I—I can't believe it!"

Sally squealed, like the girl she once was, then put one manicured hand on the countertop and jumped over it, flinging herself into Haya's arms.

"Helen! You're here, you're actually here!"

She hugged her friend so hard she almost crushed her—Sally never wanted to let Helen go. She might disappear again, might get away to where Sally couldn't find her.

"What *happened* to you?" she demanded, when she finally pulled back "Where did you go? Do you know how long I've been searching . . ."

"Me, too, me, too." Haya was so excited, she felt the years peeling away from her, like she was fifteen again, a carefree teenager piling into the back of Sally's limo. "It's a long story. Wow, you look so amazing, Sal."

"Look who's talking." Sally held her at arm's length, running a practiced eye up and down Haya's long dress. "Fantastic outfit. And you've blossomed, that's for sure. You don't seem shy anymore."

Haya grinned. "It's been a few years since anyone called me shy." She clutched at Sally suddenly. "Jane—are you in touch with Jane?"

A cloud passed over Sally's beaming face, and she shook her head.

"She's gone. I can't find her. The Brits were no good. An actress is living at her place in Malibu now."

"Well." Haya didn't bother to hide her disappointment. "Two out of three ain't bad, like they say over here."

"We'll find her." Sally was instantly optimistic, just like she'd always been. "We'll find her, Helen. Now I've got you, that's all the motivation I need. We'll put our heads together and we *will* track her down."

Haya sighed with happiness, a simple, innocent happiness she hadn't felt since the night of Sally's party.

"I've got so much to tell you, I hardly know where to start."

"Oh, God. Me, too."

"Is there somewhere we can go sit down?"

"Wait a moment. Koko, can you shut up the store and bank the cash for me? I'd like to take my friend to dinner."

"Sure thing."

"Come out the back." She wanted Helen all to herself.

"Nice to meet you," Haya called politely to Koko as she followed Sally out.

"Can you eat dinner?" Sally found herself nervous, hurried. "There's a pretty great Thai place around the corner."

"Sounds great. Thanks."

Sally ushered her out of the back door. The sun was sinking over the hills, the smog settling into a spectacular light show. She felt like she was on a first date. Helen—so stately now; a million miles from the diffident schoolgirl she'd been on the night of their party. Back when Sally used to protect her.

"Table for two."

"Yes, Miss Sally. I seen you in the papers," the hostess gushed. "Everybody said you looked great. Where you want to sit?"

"In the back—somewhere quiet."

"You got it." She ushered them through the packed, noisy restaurant to a dark corner booth, lit dimly by a red lamp. It was a kind light, but Sally could see Helen was beautiful—and that she had a ring on her left hand.

"So. Tell me all about you. You disappeared so fast . . ."

Haya shook her head. "I know I didn't call—I was sorting some things out. I just assumed you'd both be there when I got back."

"Well, I'm here now. And we'll both start the hunt for Jane again."

"Definitely. And Sally—I changed my name. Not just from marriage." Haya sighed. "It's Haya—Haya is my birth name, and my husband preferred it to the American version, so Haya, if you don't mind. . . ."

"Not at all. It's beautiful."

"I don't know where to begin," Haya said honestly. "Well— basic facts—I'm pregnant, and I'm widowed. . . ."

"Oh, Hel—Haya." Sally pressed her hand.

"I was in Egypt." Haya blinked back tears and told her friend the story, as fast as she could. It poured out; it was good, so good, to talk to somebody at last who would understand her. "And you," she said, at the end, as Sally was dabbing away tears. "I had no idea what happened—when we came back here you were gone."

Sally filled her in; it didn't take long; she glossed over her mother, and left out the rape. Not even to Haya, not even to one of her closest friends, could she confess the full truth.

Momma's drinking problem had gone; these days, her secret fear was prescription drugs. What was causing her mother to slob around in the apartment like a bag lady? She shuffled around, a nightmarish shell of her former self.

No; there was enough loss and sorrow with her father, and the poverty, and the sneering, prying media. That explained to Haya how hard it was for Sally to keep her head above the torrent.

"Anyway." She wiped away more tears; it was dark here, after all, and it felt good to let the tears flow, let the emotion out. Sally trusted Haya, in the end. And that was what mattered. "It seems to have paid off. They're here . . . and they're buying. They want a little glamour in their lives."

"I can understand it."

"And the baby? What about that?"

"At least he left me something," Haya said, blankly. "It's what I live for."

⌒

Jane glanced around the bungalow. It was warm, and different from her last place. A view over the ocean at Malibu, if only in the distance. Driftwood and seaweed motifs throughout the house; clean modern lines, all in sands, grays, greens, and whites; a decent little pool in the back.

"Good. I'll take it."

The realtor beamed, and she told him to hold on; her bank would wire the money. It was a savvy purchase, the neighborhood hip but not too expensive, the house tucked away up a sand bank far from the water's edge yet near the coast road. "How much for the furniture?"

"That's not included."

"Give me the number for the sellers," Jane said. "If you negotiate right, everything's included."

L.A. was all about the new and the shiny. She was sure that if she talked them into it, they'd be happy to dump their used sofas and last year's TV for newer models. Jane would get a discount, they'd get a blank slate, and everybody would be happy.

Within fifteen minutes she had her house. Fully furnished, all utilities in Jane's name. She took care of the basics first. It was good to have something to do; that meant she didn't have to face her major problem—how the hell to start.

Also, she didn't think about Craig as much—when she was busy.

She called a cab into Beverly Hills and bought herself a car. Something hot and successful—the right look for the young female entrepreneur on the move. A small silver Porsche, chic and flashy; with her Ray-Ban shades on top of her head, and a bright red leather briefcase by Coach at her side, her look was well on its way.

When all *that* was done she bought a load of groceries and stocked the fridge.

And when that was done—it was time to go clothes shopping. Jane had donated her New York wardrobe to charity. She hadn't wanted to be held up at the airport with cases, and more importantly, the right look mattered. When she was raising finance with banks, she needed to look like she didn't need their help—to suggest that she was already rolling in cash, and that she understood the hip, hot L.A. scene. Subliminally, Jane needed to project that she knew exactly what kind of goods would sell best.

Money—and style.

She had a plan. Mix high-end goods with a fresh Angeleno look. Designer jeans, an eye-poppingly expensive Chanel jacket, and a hot little T-shirt underneath it. Something that said rich *and* trendy. A million miles from New York Jane's muted palette of creams and grays, a look to appeal to Wall Street. Here, she wanted to be something else: a maverick entrepreneur on a mission.

The rich-girl purses, jackets, and coats were easy to pick up. A quick trip to Rodeo and she was done. The stylish, newest T-shirts and jeans were harder. You couldn't use the convenient shorthand that luxury offered. You needed to prove your sense of style. Jane planned her wardrobe like a military attack. It was a key selling tool. If she wanted to pitch herself as a buyer of goods, then she had to buy the right stuff now.

She asked around—not the snooty senior sales assistants in the expensive boutiques, but young girls, stylish Latinas and African-Americans or tanned Anglo surfer girls with tattoos that she saw waiting at the bus stops or on line for a rock gig.

One name kept coming up—Wave, on Melrose. It was the hot new place in town for low-end glamour. Even some celebrities shopped there, they told her, their drivers pulling up outside and waiting while they dashed in and bought tees by the armload.

Jane thanked them and got the address. Perfect. A Wave shirt under a Chanel jacket. That would impress her investors. And she'd also look good in it; something that was starting to matter, despite herself.

~

There it was. Jane parked across the street and slid her sunglasses down her nose, watching the place for a couple of minutes. Damn, it was packed. And she could see why. The storefront stood out in a row of dingy shops; painted bright white, with a pale blue wave design all over it—unmissable. It was brightly lit and the doors were flung open and covered in sea grass matting. A little slice of the beach, right here on the boulevard, a unique look.

And the girls—the women. They were everywhere—almost fighting to get inside. Blondes with bright red nails, curvy little brunettes—Jane noted shoppers from every price bracket, skinny girls and heavy ones. She hated to think what the changing rooms were like. Forget that—she was a size six. She'd just buy up some basics, pieces with the Wave brand easily visible, and get out of the scrum.

Jane wondered about the owners of the store. Definitely had their fingers on the moment. Could she make them an offer? Designers for her? Once she had the financing for a superstore . . . why not?

She locked the Porsche and crossed the street, clutching her new Prada handbag closely to her. It really was crowded in there.

The store was beautiful, though. It was just as bright inside, with mirrors on two walls to take pressure off the changing rooms, and a sand-and-sea motif. The signature T-shirts were brilliantly laid out—instead of racking by style, forcing the shoppers to riffle through them hunting for the right fit, Wave had laid out the racks by size—six through fourteen. Once you found your size, anything you liked on that rack you knew you could wear. Brilliant! Jane was impressed. Even she hadn't thought of that.

She pushed her way up to the size six and took ten T-shirts up to the counter. It was a long line; Jane took a moment to observe the sales staff. They were smiling despite the crowd; mostly immigrant women, she thought, all dressed in a semiformal uniform—pale blue pants and sandy-colored tops of various kinds. They looked good; busy but exhilarated. It was how she wanted her staff to look.

The line moved up a little, giving Jane a sight of the counter. She gasped with shock.

Standing behind it, ringing up purchases, chatting and smiling, was Sally Lassiter.

CHAPTER 11

They met for dinner that night in Jane's backyard. She picked up some dishes from the farmers' market and laid out a spread: roast chicken, ham, strawberries, melons, French bread, wine and juices, a pitcher of sparkling water and crushed ice. It was an arid garden, but somebody had planted it cleverly: rosemary and lavender, palm trees and cacti; drought-resistant roses next to beds of Provençal herbs. Jane lit candles everywhere, soft light amid the gathering L.A. dusk; she remembered leaving this city, a house just like this one, stripped down to nothing, poor and lonely. Her friends gone, her so-called nanny off as fast as her car could take her.

She allowed herself to revel in the moment; she was back, and they were back together.

~

"Do you like it?" Jane asked. She'd finished giving them the tour; it didn't last long, but she could be proud of the house. It was more than she'd ever had under her father.

"Fantastic. You did the best of any of us," Sally said, with a touch of wistfulness.

"If you like, I'll give you a carpet—a housewarming gift," Haya suggested. "I have a silk Kashmiri rug that would go perfectly in your bedroom."

"I couldn't accept something like that."

"I want you to have it. Ahmed would have hated to see his things gathering dust in some warehouse in Laguna Beach."

"You should sell them. . . ."

"I can't. I have no store," Haya said. "And I won't dump them wholesale to some dealer. They are precious and deserve better." She shrugged. "Maybe sometime after the baby's born, I can deal with it. I'd like to find all his things good homes—the way Ahmed wanted them sold. With respect."

"My crowd is only into fashion," Sally said.

"How is that going?" Jane asked, curious.

Sally smiled. "It's wild. I'm hiring new seamstresses every day. Can't keep up with the demand. And doing interviews . . . all the local press wants to talk to me, and I have to say yes to everyone. You know." She blushed. "Give them a little razzmatazz. They love that all-American look. So what about you? Why did you quit that cushy number back East?"

Jane filled them in.

"So now I want to start a store. Tomorrow I'm going to the banks. I have thirteen appointments." She shrugged. "It'll be a tough sell, but I think I could follow the Wal-Mart / Shop Smart model and find some savings. At least I do have a record there. I'd need money to lease out the warehouse and buy the stock lines, computers, staff . . . it's a major amount of cash." She tried to look confident. "Somebody'll spring for it, though."

Haya carefully sliced into a ripe nectarine.

"Why don't you *not* do that?"

"I told you—I'm not interested in taking a salary."

"No—why don't you do it another way? All of us have problems. Sally needs space for her stock and a manufacturer—she can't rely on housewives sewing in back rooms forever. I don't want to run a shop by myself—but I know about the business, and I have stock—beautiful stock. And you have trained in the mechanics of selling."

Sally blinked. "You're suggesting we form a company?"

"A store. Yes. Why not?" Haya warmed to her theme. She looked at her two friends and realized it was the first time in ages she'd gotten excited about a career. "Not just any store. A *great* store. Like Harrods or Saks." She turned to Jane. "I know you were thinking of mass volume and deep discount, but that field is packed. Why not turn it on its head? Designer goods. Low volume, high price. Each one sold like a jewel. The way Ahmed wanted our rugs to be sold. Like art. We had the right idea with the gallery, I think; we just didn't know the mechanics."

Jane shivered with excitement. Man! Why not? Instead of trying to clamber up the mountainside all by herself, why not harness these two? Sally knew glitz like nobody else—she'd seen that. And from what she had seen of Haya, the woman had grown up, grown through her tragedy. She had that serene beauty, the depth, that Sally's sizzle lacked. Why not start a store that sold treasures for the discerning . . . glorious Eastern carpets, objets d'art, hot fashion, the best makeup? There were so many rich women in L.A. And it had worked as a concept all over the world.

The superstore itself as star. In Los Angeles, as Jane well knew, the upmarket stores were just malls—big, soulless malls where you rode escalators and walked down corridors of luxury shops. Do it this way, and Jane could provide those women with a single destination.

She got into the spirit. "And beauty . . . we must have makeup."

"I can design a range of cosmetics," Sally said at once.

"And I can go home—back to Jordan. Source your moisturizers from the Dead Sea. Those muds have properties all the laboratories in Paris can't replicate."

"What about a location?"

"I have the gallery. It's empty now, but it's about ten thousand square feet. And it has a good-size parking lot."

"We'll need a lawyer." Jane wanted to move, immediately; she couldn't hear a perfect idea and sit still. "Form the company. What do you say, ladies, a third each way?"

"Sounds good . . ." Sally was nervous. "Look, you girls both got money. I'm just starting to sell, I don't have any yet."

"The company will loan you what you need." Jane waved that aside. "Sal, you have style we'll never get. That's what we need from you—interior design, fashion purchasing. It has to be talked about. It has to be packed from the word go. Just like your little store on Melrose."

"So that's what we'll call it?" Haya asked. "Wave?"

"No," Sally said. "This is brand new. This is ours. We need a new name. Something that sells what the store is all about."

She thought for a moment, then smiled.

"GLAMOUR," she said.

⁓

"No."

"I'm sorry—not for us."

"I don't think so."

"You have to be kidding me—you chicks are barely legal."

It was the same story wherever they went. Just with varying degrees of rudeness.

Managers shaking their heads. Laughing at them. *Leering* at them.

"I wish Ahmed was here." Haya bit her lip. "He'd have smacked that guy in the face. Did you see how he looked at me?"

"It's your boobs," Sally said, insouciantly. "You have those big pregnancy boobs, Haya—some men go nuts for that, especially since your belly doesn't show."

"My dress isn't low-cut. . . ."

"They can still see."

It was true. Haya was wearing a modest, long cream dress with an empire waist that Sally had selected for her; Jane was in a Chanel suit—no need to go half-funky anymore, she had Sally for that—and Sally wore a signature Wave cutoff, a flippy short skirt, and beads of her own design.

"They wouldn't treat men like this." Haya glowered.

"Well—they wouldn't ogle them, I guess," Sally said wisely. "But they might kick them out. We have some experience, but it's not a lot."

Jane glowered. "You guys go on home—Sally, you get back to Wave, sell some shirts, we need the cash."

"And what are you going to do?" Haya asked.

"I'm going to get us some capital." Jane shrugged. "From . . . another source."

"Hope you're not gambling your house on the Dodgers," Sally said.

"No." Jane grimaced. "Regretfully, this is nothing that sensible."

When the others had gone, Jane got back into her car and shut the door. Her feet ached; she was exhausted. But she was focused on what she had to do.

She took out her heavy cell phone and dialed.

"Levin corporation. Craig Levin's office."

All by herself, Jane blushed. Deeply.

"May I speak to Mr. Levin, please?"

"He's not in the office today, ma'am." The smooth response kicked at Jane's guts; she couldn't believe how disappointed she felt. "May I tell him who called?"

"Certainly. This is Jane Morgan."

"From which company?"

"From GLAMOUR, Incorporated." It was sort of true. "My number is 555-9856."

"I'll pass on the message," the assistant said blandly. "Thank you for calling."

Jane hung up, and gently rested her head on the steering wheel. Why? Why had she done that? He wasn't going to call her back. Craig Levin had bigger fish to fry.

No—she was just going to have to start over. Find some independent banks. Some venture capitalists . . .

Her phone rang. She jumped out of her skin.

"Jane Morgan."

"Craig Levin," he said, and she felt the warmth spread from her face all through her chest and curl its tendrils down into her belly. "I'm disappointed, Jane."

"Why?"

"You didn't call me at home. Or on my cell. Which means you want to talk business, or at least that's what you're telling yourself."

Since he couldn't see her, she smiled.

"You got me."

"Then come see me. At home. Hollywood Hills." He gave her the address. "I'm free right now."

"Do you promise not to hit on me?" Jane demanded, fighting for some control.

She could hear his grin over the phone. "I certainly do not. On the contrary, I promise to hit on you hard. Come see me—at your own risk, baby."

He hung up. Jane immediately started the car and pulled into traffic. What choice did she have? She had to go.

No matter that she wanted to.

~⌒~

"Good afternoon. Miss Morgan?"

"Yes," Jane said, dry-mouthed.

The butler smiled at her. "Please follow me, miss."

Jane's father had taken her into quite a few grand mansions. But never in her life had she seen anything like this.

The house was huge. Even the entrance hall; clad in marble, and full of pillars. Interior designed, with modern art and old masters jostling side by side; internal fountains; and lush greenery. As she followed the servant, Jane was led through peristyles and garden squares, caught a glimpse of a vast library, a home cinema, an internal swimming pool complex. It was a staggering, vulgar display of wealth. Nothing understated; Levin, she saw, was from the Sally Lassiter school of style. He made Sally's dad's estate look like a cottage in Virginia.

"He's sitting in the walled garden, miss."

"Like there are more," Jane joked.

"The house has six separate gardens," said the butler, unsmilingly. "Would you come this way?"

Meekly, she followed him.

~⌒~

"Jane." He was sitting on a lounger by an Olympic-sized pool carved out of the hillside; smooth and glassy, it perched on the edge of the estate, so that you appeared to be swimming into the sky. There were Bali-style carved daybeds, hung with silk, a full poolside bar, and topiary hedges interspersed with frangipani flowers. "Good to see you." He got up and came over, kissing her on both cheeks, as his butler melted away. "I took the liberty of fixing you a Bellini—fresh peach juice."

Jane took the cocktail. It seemed the safest thing to do. That way she could concentrate on sipping the chilled champagne and not have to stare at his body. Levin was working on his tan, in oversized shorts, casual flip-flops, shades—and nothing else. His chest was thickly muscled—this was a guy who lifted weights—and oiled with sunscreen.

She had a visceral reaction to that kind of strength. It did not help that she was here, now, as a suppliant; effectively flinging herself before him to ask for help. It charged the whole thing erotically.

And she was, she realized, already turned on.

"Thank you for seeing me . . ."

"If you say 'Mr. Levin' I'll throw you out."

"Craig." She surrendered.

"You want finance, and the banks won't help."

Jane blinked. "How the hell do you know that?"

"If that weren't the case, you would not be here." He grinned, lazily. "It would have taken you two or three more months to come find me. You wanted to start a discount chain; no commercial lender's gonna fund you. And you could have taken a few more weeks, exhausted all the bankers and venture houses. But I know you. You're impatient. You want the world, yesterday." His eyes fixed upon her, and Jane felt her knees weaken. "So you came to me, because I can give it to you. Correct?"

Her throat was dry. "Correct." She took a sip of her Bellini. It was delicious, the scent of an Italian peach orchard.

"I told you I would not do business with you."

Jane's confusion deepened. "I see." She tried to gather the shreds of her dignity. Maybe this had been crazy. Why would the guy sanction a multimillion-dollar deal on the strength of one plane ride? "Well, thank you for seeing me."

"But I'll give you the money," he said. "A gift. No strings. A million dollars."

She didn't ask if he meant it; that much was obvious.

"You know I can't accept that."

"You're an adult, like you told me. You can do whatever you want."

"I can't—can't be dependent on a man. If you give me a million dollars, I'll be like Marie Antoinette playing at shepherdess." She gripped the stem of her champagne flute. "Mr. Levin—Craig. Give me the million not as a gift—as a commercial loan. You won't be doing business with *me*. You'll be doing it with GLAMOUR—and that's a company. Not just me. There's Sally Lassiter. She's our fashion buyer."

"I know her." He nodded. "Big spread in the *Citizen,* hot shop on Melrose. I was considering making her a finance offer in exchange for a stake."

"And Haya al-Yanna. My friend from school. She married an Egyptian. She has an eye, I've seen her stock. Haya brings us the physical building with a great lot, and some glorious Islamic arts and antique rugs. And she will source other stuff for us too, exclusive cosmetics you can't get in the United States." Jane wanted to be the evangelist; he would give her the money anyway; now she wanted to convince him.

She desperately wanted to impress him. And she didn't examine her motivations too closely.

"Haya wants something special for GLAMOUR. She wants us to be at the forefront of ethical business—and I want to do it because it sells. Like the Body Shop. Like Anita Roddick. Haya will set up a worldwide operation for us sourcing handmade goods from women in Jordan, where she has contacts—Egypt, too—everywhere in the Middle East. Later on, in Africa and Asia, too, once we have the money for scouts." Jane rushed on, aware she was gabbling. "Women will like it; the press will cover it. And Haya is determined. It's the way she is—if you could meet her, you'd know."

"Perhaps I would."

"So. Consider us as an investor. You know something of my

track record with staff and costs. You said you might have approached Sally anyway." Jane was passionate. "And as for Haya, okay, that is my say-so. But you can't deny that she brings us the store and the parking. So our company has physical assets."

Levin inclined his head. "Good pitch. Done."

"No." Jane stood strong. "I want two million. For this store to work we need the best. Staff, uniforms, valet parking, stock. I'm ahead of the game because I have the real estate. But I need it to be *rich*, Craig. We're selling the all-American dream, with a little exotic flavor thrown in. And that has to be good."

"Three million," he said. "And I take ten percent of the company."

"Then four million," she countered.

Levin grinned. "Three, sugar, or I'll walk away, and believe me, I know just how to do that."

"I have to run it by my partners." Jane smiled in the flush of victory. "But I'm pretty sure they'll be okay with it."

"Good." He walked up to her, towering over her, his face above hers, his mouth close, too close. "That's done. Can we move on?"

She struggled; fought with herself; the heat was spreading through her; Jane longed for him to kiss her, so much it made her weak.

"I'm not for sale," she whispered.

Levin's eyes bore down on her; his mouth inched closer to hers; Jane's lips moistened, parted; just before the kiss, he pulled back; she was left aching and frustrated.

"I don't want a girl I can buy." His eyes flickered across her face, assessingly. "I'm going to have those papers signed and the money in your corporate account by tomorrow. Once my lawyers have reviewed the share agreement. After that, you have what you needed from me, and I won't be able to take it back." He reached out and ran a fingertip down the side of her face; unable to stop herself now, Jane shivered at his touch.

"After that . . . I guess we'll see what happens."

She forced herself to take a step back.

"My lawyers will be in touch." She had to add, "Thank you."

"Tomorrow," he said. "See you, Jane Morgan."

She turned on her heel and fled.

⌁

"I don't wanna go," Mona whined.

"You have to." Sally was firm. "Mom—you have to. Here, here are your sneakers. You want me to lace them up for you?"

"I can dress myself," Mona snapped.

Sally was glad to hear it; lately, she'd been wondering. Mona's room did not smell too pretty. Sally had stripped the sweaty sheets from the bed but the stale odor of too much sleep, of dissipation, still permeated the room.

No more. She wasn't going to give up on her momma. The company was formed, they had financing; for the first time in years, Sally believed good things, *really* good things, were about to happen.

"Here. I got you a new tracksuit. Nike—the best. Mine matches." She showed her, a pretty thing in pale pink. "We'll jog along Venice, next to the beach." Because none of Mona's old friends would be there. "After that I'm giving you a makeover, and you can come and see our new store."

"What store?"

"GLAMOUR," Sally said. "You'll love it."

If she could change style in L.A., she could change her mom. Couldn't she?

Mona was an addict. Sally had faced that, as calmly as she could. You couldn't get an addict to just stop the addiction. It had to be replaced by something else. A positive addiction.

Sally decided on fitness. Mom would become a fitness freak. If that meant Sal had to jog an unnecessary three miles a day then so be it. She was going to make her mother wash her hair, get a manicure and a wax, put makeup on daily, and run to the beach. Mona had lost all pride, all self-esteem, but she still had a pretty face, for an older woman. It shouldn't be this way. Crawling into a bottle or a box of pills.

"Good. You ready?" Mona was sitting sullenly in her oversized pink tracksuit, and Sal, her long blonde hair swept back in a neat ponytail, was wearing the same, only half the size. She was painfully aware how pretty she looked and how wrecked her mother was, Mona's once thin thighs and bright complexion dulled by alcohol, ruining her skin and fattening her up.

But Mona could change. Everybody could. Sal had—she was a company director now.

She *believed* in the GLAMOUR philosophy. Beauty was more than skin deep—it was a matter of pride. Not everybody could fit the golden girl ideal like she could, but everybody could look their best. And Momma's best was better than this.

"Come on." She forcibly grabbed her mother by the elbow; she smelled bad, of stale sweat, but Sally stuck with it. "Let's go, Momma. Come with me."

Every morning and evening, for a week, Sally forced Mona to jog. At first it was little more than walking pace, and her mother could only manage a mile. The second day, Mona occasionally broke into a trot before slipping back to walking. Sally didn't care. It was progress.

She tried to make her mom feel proud. Day one was the best—forcing her into a long shower, making her shave her legs, wax her lips, and get her hair washed and styled. Sally cleaned all the bed linen and filled her room with lavender and roses. On day two, after the postjog shower, Sally took time off work to give Mona a makeover. On day three, she took her to the shell of GLAMOUR and helped her pick out a couple of dresses— forgiving, beautifully worked Arab gowns from Ghada and Egypt, flown in the day before from one of Haya's suppliers.

And it was working. Sally could see the glimmer of interest that came back to her mother's face, the basic stirrings of self- esteem; Mona started showering, combing her hair, getting up without being nagged.

At the end of the first week, Sally came back from the store to find her mom had been shopping—all by herself. She'd bought some cushions and candleholders, and she had rearranged the décor in their little apartment.

At the end of the first month Mona fit back into her old jeans. She hadn't touched a drop of alcohol—not even in mouthwash—for a month. She asked Sally if she could go to the dentist and get her teeth whitened. Mona even joined a gym—she added weights to the running, morning and evening. And Sally signed her up to a yoga class, where for the first time since Paulie died, Mona started to make friends.

Sally had tears in her eyes the first day she waved her mom off for coffee with a girlfriend. Fitness had done that—fitness, and self-esteem, and feeling good about life. Sometimes lipstick and a good dress really mattered. It wasn't too much of an exaggeration to say that this had saved her mom.

While Jane did her wheeling and dealing, hiring staff, meeting accountants and bankers, inking deals with suppliers, and planning store layout and infrastructure, Haya took her pregnant body off on weekly flights to the Middle East, sourcing amazing, ethically produced lamps, rugs, mosaics, and jewelry, and Sally instructed her team of designers. She drew sketches, she placed factory orders, she did deals with other unknown talents. Anything to get GLAMOUR hung with the hottest new styles and the simplest classic pieces. Nothing cheap; nothing skimpy. Sally designed flaws away; she didn't want clothes that required a perfect body. All skirts and dresses were made of heavy material, and lined. All tops had at least something on the sleeveline, however slim, so they could be worn with a bra. And she started out with color palettes that could be worn together.

There was a working woman's corner, too. Why sacrifice your femininity at the office? Sally paid for rich fabrics, silks, satins, velvet, and heavy cotton—no linen, it wrinkled—and worked exclusively in black, white, sand, and navy; every piece went with every other piece. Classic cuts but with feminine tailoring. The blouses had cuffs and little shell buttons, but they were tapered at the waist and had a silky effect; the skirts swung to the bias and hovered on the knee, or fishtailed at the floor; the pantsuits had narrower waists but wider thighs, a little help where most women needed it. Add a pair of Sally's own design for slightly stacked heels and you got height, comfort, style—immediate weight loss of five pounds.

But Sally knew GLAMOUR had to be more than that. It needed to be a destination, an experience. Great clothes and cool rugs and pretty mosaics were nice, but Sally understood why women shopped. It was for a sense of Aladdin's Cave, of being surrounded by pretty, gorgeous things. She started work on the smaller stock: independent cosmetic houses, organic cruelty-free cosmetics, the ones that didn't do business with the bigger stores. And she only went for gorgeous. Lipsticks with jewel-studded cases, faked-out rubies and diamonds. Soft makeup brushes, straight from the East, that used real hair. Perfume spritzers in dazzling cut glass. Little charm bracelets with pick-your-own gems to hang off them—you'd scoop them up with a mother-of-pearl spoon, like caviar, and pay per scoop. Delicate necklaces worked in Frisco by an artist she admired, glossy leaves sculpted from copper and gold, that jangled when you walked. Ankle bracelets, with bells on them. Little eyeshadows from a joint in Venice that packed them cleverly into seashells. Essential oils, in droppers, that could give fragrance to a whole room. Candles twisted into slogans—HOTSTUFF was her favorite, with a wick on each letter.

And so, slowly, the stock took shape. A lacy Parisian fan. A pair of tangerine leather strappy heels with cute white roses worked into the straps. Floris bath oils from Europe. Charbonnel and Walker chocolates. Scottish cashmere and Irish linens. Austrian silver coffeepots. It was the ultimate shopping destination, she thought, delighting when she found an original Black Forest craftsman who'd sell her a line of ornate cuckoo clocks, complete with dancing peasants, foxes, and squirrels, and a real Roman gelato maker who would fly the original stuff in to serve in GLAMOUR's café. The store would be like a vacation for rich Americans who didn't feel like grabbing their passports. It was paradise. Little, irresistible, gorgeous things that just called out to your wallet . . .

Sally worked like hell. She worked like an obsessive, like Jane or Haya. All Jane thought about was getting that Levin guy his money back. Haya was into finding a legacy for her kid and helping poorer women who had been dependent on a man; profit meant little to her. Sally, on the other hand, thought about her mom, her dad, style, and pride. She wasn't selfless, not some plaster saint. She wasn't Mother Teresa, forget *that*. Her sense of style had gotten her this far. If she could help other women, then *she* would get rich. She would get her whole life back.

While Mona worked out, sinking herself into her new fitness craze, Sally Lassiter got lost at the office. She dived into fashion, and she loved it.

Sally never thought about anything except her new job and keeping an eye on her mother, making sure she didn't relapse. There was no time for anything else.

Certainly not for men.

⁓

"And here's the ocean, right on the left."

Sally nodded, conserving her breath. Great. Mom was fitter than she was, now. Showing her the new route she was taking, out to the highway and then cutting down to the beach.

"We'll go half a mile and hit the canyons."

"Perfect." Sally didn't want to talk, she was conserving her wind. She was still slim and tanned, but her endurance had gone to hell.

"We'll cut through here, through the woods." Mona was turning left, and Sally saw her legs moving efficiently down the sandy path. Damn, that woman had got some musculature going. . . . "Come on, honey!" her mom urged.

Sally blew out her cheeks. "Coming . . ."

"Aaah!"

Her mother slipped. It was so quick, Sally barely saw it coming. Mona's ankle twisted; she fell and something cracked—Sally heard her groan, heard the nasty thud as she dropped to the ground—and Mona plummeted off the clifftop path, slicing through the scrubby plants and crumbling, sandy earth, her manicured nails futilely scrabbling for a hold, down the side of the rock.

Sally grabbed for her mother's arms and missed. She screamed, and rushed to the side of the rock face. Mona was slipping and tumbling down the almost-sheer hill, crashing and veering; Sally could make out patches of blood on her arms and legs. She shrieked, almost hysterical, calling wildly for help, but they were out here on their own. . . .

Mona groaned and thudded and fell awkwardly onto an outcrop of rock; she didn't move. She was clearly unconscious. Sally felt a wash of dizziness surge through her body; black spots floated in front of her eyes.

"Oh, God! Help me!" she screamed.

"Hey."

Sally jumped—it was the sound of a man, further down the path.

"You need help?"

"Yes! Please come! It's my mom—"

"I'm coming," he shouted. "Hold on."

There was the sound of running feet and he appeared on the path, a tanned, strong-looking man with mirrored shades, a shirt, and a Dodgers baseball cap; an enthusiastic Labrador bounded along at his heels.

"What's the problem?"

She grabbed his arm, babbling. "Oh, thank God. My mom— her ankle gave out. She went over. She's down there. . . ."

He took one look and straightened up. "Stay right there. I have a car phone, I'll call 911."

"Thank you . . ."

He ran back down the path. Sally looked over; her mother did not stir. She wondered wildly if she were dead. The seconds dragged on horribly.

Eventually he came back. "Highway Patrol is sending a cruiser. I argued with them, looks like you need the Coast Guard and a chopper. They said it shouldn't be long. . . ."

There was a shiver in the rocks; some stones, dislodged by Mona's fall, tumbled onto her prostrate body; one of them struck her ankle; without regaining consciousness she shifted, and hung further off the edge of the lip of stone, a dead weight pointing down.

Sally sobbed. "Mom, oh, God, Mom. They won't be here in time. She's gonna fall. She's gonna die."

She clutched at the stranger.

Mona slipped a couple more inches. She was in a bad position. They could both see what gravity was doing.

"Wait there."

"Don't leave me," Sally wept. But he was gone. She inched closer to the edge herself. Her mom—her mom was all she had in this world, really. When you came down to it, what did a career mean? Without Mona, Sally was lost. Had she saved her from addiction just to watch with her own eyes as her mother plunged into the sea?

But she saw no way she could climb down. The edge was too small to support them both. And since Mona was unconscious, Sally knew she couldn't lift her. If she climbed down the rock, they would both die. . . .

"Okay. Watch my dog."

The man was back. He had a length of rope coiled around his waist and a pair of spiked shoes on. He ran up to the nearest tree, an elm a few feet to the right of her mother, looped the rope around, and hastily knotted it; then he tied another loop, and another, around himself.

"What are you doing?" Sally asked, hesitantly.

"No harness. I'm gonna get her."

She bit her lip. This man didn't have the right equipment. He could slip—die.

"Watch Felix," he said again, and slipped a length of rope between his hands.

Sally crammed her knuckles into her mouth. The elm tree did not have a wide trunk. It bent forward, leaning with his weight. He was tall, a strong, heavy guy, lean but bulky with muscle. She could see the strong muscles of his back working as he moved, quickly and with purpose, down the rock face; stones and plants gave way under his footing, but he just shifted his weight.

Mona slipped a little further.

"Hurry, please," Sally shouted. He ignored her, and kept abseiling; lower, lower . . . almost there . . .

There was a loud crack; the small stone ledge shifted, tilted; Mona Lassiter's unconscious form slid inexorably forward. . . .

And his thick, weightlifter's arm reached out and grabbed her by the elbow. . . .

Sally watched in horror as the elm tree buckled and doubled over, the rope fraying. The man gasped and grunted, his feet losing their grip, scrabbling to get it back as he heaved, with brute strength, her mother's unconscious form over his back.

She ran to the tree and put her arms around it, desperately trying to hold it back. But her strength was as nothing—she couldn't stop it bending forward.

Sally looked over the cliff. He was climbing, slowly, agonizingly so, in contrast to the way he'd dropped down, fleet and surefooted. She could hear the grunts of pain; her mother's weight was being supported by a single hand as he used the other one to climb. Oh, God! She was not a religious woman, but she prayed. Please let him be strong. Please let him not drop her. . . .

After an eternity he was at the top, his face puce with effort, sweat pouring down his forehead.

"Take her," he gasped.

Crying and laughing, half-hysterical, Sally tugged and pulled at Mona's arms; her mother slipped off her rescuer's shoulders and flopped forward onto the grass. She was bruised and bleeding, cut in several places, obviously concussed, but still breathing. As Sally examined her breathing, trying to loosen her shirt, wake her, the man hauled himself onto the grass and fell onto his back, panting, struggling to regain his breath.

Sally looked at him with pathetic gratitude and then winced. His palms were raw, cut and bleeding from the rope burns. His barrel of a chest was heaving, trying to get his breath, to recover from the monstrous effort.

"You saved her life," she said. It was obvious, but she had to say it. "Thank you—thank you so much, mister."

He opened his eyes. "Where's my dog?"

Sally's stomach flipped; she'd forgotten about the dog. This guy had asked this one thing of her, and she'd lost his damn dog. She looked around wildly; the dog was sitting calmly behind her, wagging its tail, as though its owner had been engaged in a shopping errand.

"Right here," she mumbled, guiltily.

He closed his eyes again. "You forgot; it's okay. Felix is trained."

There was a wail of a siren in the distance, getting closer. He struggled to sit up.

"Thank God for that." Sally was in tears from the relief. "The police are coming . . . they'll get you both to a hospital . . . you need the paramedics."

He looked at her for the first time. She couldn't see the eyes behind the sunglasses, but she did register how his eyes traveled over her face, flickered over her body. A man who had looked at a lot of women.

Sally felt an answering pang of lust and dropped her gaze. An instinctive reaction, she told herself. The guy had just saved her mom. But all the same, she suddenly, fervently wished she didn't look quite such a mess; hair sweaty from the run, eyes red with tears, no makeup, unwashed morning hair scraped back in a jogger's ponytail.

"I'm not staying." He stood up. "Your mom will be okay, once she's checked out."

"Are you a doctor?" She didn't know why she asked him that; she just wanted him to stay.

"No. But I see a lot of sports injuries." Finally, he took off the shades; and Sally, already red, blushed scarlet.

Along with the muscled body and square jaw, she now saw a pair of light gray eyes, unusually pale, like wolf eyes in the dark skin.

"Now you recognize me," he said, without false modesty.

"I—yes." She tried to cover her confusion. "You—on the cover of that magazine." Why was it coming out so stuttery? She felt like a moronic sports fan.

"*Sports Illustrated.*" He grinned. "You really had no idea, did you?"

"I didn't. You're Chris Nelson. The baseball player."

Sally wasn't a fan, but she knew about Chris Nelson, the shortstop for the Dodgers. Single-handedly turning the team around. An All-Star. A megastar, in this city; even Hollywood types sucked up to him.

"Yeah, well, do me a favor. Don't tell anybody about this. I don't need the publicity; the press will just dog me for weeks."

"I won't."

"I would stay to check on your mom, but I'm sure she'll be fine."

"Thank you, again." Sally bit her lip. She couldn't ask anything more of the guy. To do so now would look like she was just another one of the girls that tried to crash practice wearing the shortest skirts. "We'll be good once the cops get here. And . . . you know, you're a hero." It had to be said; her blush deepened.

"That's cute." He winked at her, and Sally's stomach flipped over. "Long time since I've seen a girl blush."

"Your hands are all messed up."

"Yeah, well. My shoulder's practically dislocated."

"I think your trainer is going to put out a hit on me," Sally joked.

"John Tepes will, if I miss the series against the Yankees," he said. Tepes was their manager. "But don't worry. I'll come around and save you."

The siren sounded closer. He stood up, and Sally was ashamed of herself for feeling such a bitter pang of disappointment while her mom lay feet away, knocked out.

"Your name is Sally Lassiter, right?"

She jumped out of her skin. "How . . . do you know that?"

He smiled. "Papers. My girlfriend showed me a picture. She bought some T-shirts in your store; looked hot on her."

Girlfriend. Right. Of course. Like a hot superstar athlete like him was going to be single.

"Thanks, Mr. Nelson."

"I think it's Chris, after all that. Good-bye, sugar. Felix!"

He whistled, and the dog sprang from its sitting position and followed him, bounding, down the hill.

Sally was still sitting staring into space when the troopers arrived, a couple of burly men with guts that would have done credit to Santa Claus. They would have been zero help.

"She's okay—we'll get her to Malibu Memorial Hospital. What happened here, ma'am? How did you get her back?"

Sally told the story, leaving out Nelson's name. They whistled as they grabbed her mother by the shoulders and ankles and staggered down the path with her.

"Some story," the other one said. "Some guy."

Yeah, Sally thought, regretfully. *Some guy.*

Mona had suffered little more than a concussion, a broken arm, and some bad bruising; it was almost a guilty relief for Sally to have her tucked away in hospital for a few days. She tried to fling herself into her work. The baseball player had disturbed her, profoundly, and she woke in the mornings restless from half-forgotten erotic dreams.

But now she was aware of him, she was reminded of him everywhere: on the news, flicking through the channels, whenever she saw a fan in a Dodgers shirt. An undisclosed "injury" had put him on the disabled list for a month's recuperation. Nelson on the DL was the talk of L.A.

Sally waited fearfully for something to happen, for the story to break; if the cops had traced his cell call or something . . . half the sports fans in L.A. would be picketing their new store.

It didn't happen.

She got on with her job. Designing. Buying. Making GLAMOUR a statement.

She had a vision, and the other two girls let her go with it. GLAMOUR. The name said it all. Every shopping trip would be a vacation. Something to justify their sky-high prices.

Maybe Laetitia Berry would come and shop there.

Laetitia, or Letty, as the press called her. Former Miss Minnesota and now sitcom star. Tall, slim, African-American, with flawless ebony skin, a retroussé nose, and blindingly white teeth. She shopped at only the best stores, drove a Maserati, and, as Sally was finding out, had been dating Chris Nelson for about a year. There was a pregnancy rumor. The gossip rags said they were getting married.

But of course. For Nelson to be unattached would have been fantasy. Sally was truly grateful, and she tried to be happy for Letty. And Chris.

She tried to tell herself there were plenty of other fish, and all that. Now that she was interested in men ... now that she'd saved her mom ... now that she felt she could breathe ... there were plenty of places a pretty young woman could meet men in this town.

That didn't work, either.

Sally was busy. Like it or not, pining or not, the store was rolling toward the grand opening. Now she had a PR campaign to organize. She got the hell on with it. What else could she do?

❧

Haya stepped into the limo with relief.

It was air-conditioned, a blessed change after the baking heat outside. She was an Arab, and she'd thought she could handle this weather, but the further along her pregnancy got, the less she liked it.

"Take me to Bar-al-Yanni, please," she said to the driver.

"Of course, ma'am." He spun the car directly into traffic with practiced ease and Haya struggled to stay awake. Jet lag was bad, but she really wanted to get this trip over with. After that she could go back to the hotel, unplug the phone, hang the little sign on her door, and she'd be done.

It was vital to buy enough. She had to be four times as good on this trip, because her baby was getting too big, too restless in her belly. There would be no more sourcing from the Middle East after this. Haya needed enough goods to last in the stockroom for at least five months; she wasn't getting on a plane until her child was six months old and weaned, and it would take her four months to train another woman to her exacting standards.

At least she knew, now, that she couldn't do it all herself.

Choosing the precious objects had been a big deal for Haya. Sally took care of the Western fashion and the store design, and Haya added the exotic flavor and the ethical dimension. She knew she had to live up to both ideals. Sourcing art, jewelry, cloths, lamps, and rugs from the Islamic world—but not from dealers; from individual women, or from the nascent collectives that had sprung up of widows, unmarried women, women whose meager income from the glorious things they worked was keeping flesh on the bones of their children. Haya had big ambitions there. She wanted those rich Americans to get addicted to this beauty, and pay top dollar. Everybody would win—the buyers would get something unique, not mass-produced, something that would look great in their houses for generations. The women who made these things would finally receive a fair price, even a generous one by local standards. Haya had no doubt it would transform lives. And of course, GLAMOUR would take a hefty slice out of the middle.

It was ethical commerce, not simple charity. Haya had to answer to the demanding Jane Morgan on that. And she wanted to make money, anyway. For her own independence, and her child's—Ahmed's child. Profit and principles. If she could combine them, Haya thought, she could be happy; she could salvage something from her husband's death, make a difference in the world.

Ghada was her last stop on the tour. She had already shipped enough Jordanian mosaics, Moroccan carpets, Egyptian lamps and carvings, and Palestinian cushions to fill the holds of a small ship. This remote kingdom was the final destination; Haya wanted to invest in a line of traditional jewelry from Ghada. The desert tribeswomen in the north crafted elegant necklaces and bracelets dripping with small metal disks, a variant on the coin jewelry in other Arab countries; Haya thought they looked feminine and delicate, good on any woman, and when she had showed Sally

Lassiter a sample Sally had gone wild. The intricate pieces would be the center of the opening GLAMOUR jewelry collection. The traditional metal was silver; Haya wanted to negotiate for a commune of women to work them for her in copper; the Americans didn't like silver, it was too dully familiar. Jangling, luxe bracelets of fiery red-gold would knock the Hollywood ladies out. Haya was sure of that.

"We may have some delays on the road north of the city," her driver said, lapsing into the Egyptian Arabic that was a lingua franca in the Middle East.

Haya sighed. "Why is that?"

She didn't want to be late. They were waiting for her at the small oasis town and she had had some difficulty in securing this meeting; these women did not trust Americans, even Arab-Americans.

"There is a visit there from one of the sheikhas. Sheikha Alia, the daughter of the king's half uncle. They will have security."

"Of course." Haya didn't want to be rude, so she chewed on her lip. The royal family of Ghada, highly wealthy from a combination of oil and booming real estate in the metropolitan cities on the coasts, was large and well funded. There was the king, old and tired, an absolute ruler. His many brothers and sons, daughters and sisters, all princes and princesses. A few degrees removed from that, the royalty had lesser titles like Sheikh and Sheikha. Just in case, Haya reviewed her protocols. Prince, or Emir; Royal Highness . . . Sheikha . . . just Highness.

"Why is she going there—is there some function?"

"The royal women often patronize the markets and bazaars there. They support the traditional crafts."

"Ah." Haya smiled. "Do they indeed?"

Perhaps—who knew. Perhaps she could get something out of this. She thought of the Western love of titles. If they could market the Ghadan necklaces as "worn by royalty" they would sell even better. Would the sheikha agree to be photographed in a necklace? There would be some samples waiting for Haya today. She got excited, she could see the advertising campaign now. Even better, maybe there would be another lady, somebody further up the tree; one of the king's daughters or granddaughters, a true princess.

"If you can get me there half an hour faster I will pay you a bonus," she said, "especially if you take me as close as you can to where this visit is happening."

It was a triumph. First, Haya had the pleasure of seeing the work presented to her by Begum Fahdah al-Ali, the widow of a former chief. She had organized this group, of abandoned or poor women, many of them widows or now-grown street children, who had lived in grinding poverty. They worked the tiny metal disks into the most delicate, exquisite pieces. There would be no problem in selling these as they deserved to be treated, Haya thought, as her husband had planned to do: as works of art. She signed a deal, the women toasted it with mint tea, and she left money behind, just as down payment; the joy with which it was received made her day.

And second, with great determination and a couple of sample necklaces in her hand, Haya had approached a woman in the sheikha's retinue, an efficient-looking matronly sort in a Western suit with a neat scarf tied around her hair, and sunglasses. The lady would not see her now, she was told, but she took a number, and said somebody from the palace would be in touch. Yes, they liked to support the work of traditional craftswomen, and yes, they were looking for trade opportunities with the States. If the sheikha could be sure that the deal the women were getting was fair . . .

Haya had no doubts on that score. She left a card with the protocol officer and took a cab back to the hotel. There she took a long bath, washed her hair, and went to lie down on the bed, wrapped in a soft white toweling robe; her room was air-conditioned, and all she wanted to do was sleep well, then rise and get on the plane.

Job done. Nothing more to do than to wait for the birth of her child . . .

The phone rang. Sighing deeply, she rolled on her side to answer it.

"Hello?"

"May I speak to Haya al-Yanna, please?"

The voice was modulated; Arab with an English accent, she thought, educated abroad; a young man.

"Speaking."

"Ms. Al-Yanna, my name is Jaber ibn Mohammed. I work for the palace and the government of Ghada."

Haya closed her eyes briefly. Damn it, a call she couldn't blow off.

"It's good of you to call," she lied.

"I understand you are to fly back to the States first thing to-morrow. Do you have time for a meeting earlier this evening? I can come to the Radisson."

"Of course, I'd be delighted."

"If we are going to get involved in any project like this, we have to vet it."

"I quite understand," Haya said, mentally relinquishing her night off. "Is six o'clock convenient? We could meet in the lobby, or have dinner."

"Wonderful. See you then."

"Wonderful," Haya echoed, and hung up. Damnation. She set her mobile phone to alarm; at least she'd have half an hour, and anything was better than nothing.

He was waiting in the lobby. Haya was surprised to see he was a young man, maybe a little older than herself, and tall, with an aquiline nose and aristocratic, searching eyes. Olive-skinned, with a tan from the sun, and a beautifully cut suit; a strong body, she thought, not bulky.

"Ms. Al-Yanna. Thank you for seeing me."

"Thank you for coming."

His eyes swept over her, appreciatively, she thought, and then blinked; his glance had come to rest on her belly.

"You're pregnant," he blurted out.

She smiled. "Yes, *mash'Allah*."

"Excuse me—I didn't mean to be rude. I was just surprised. Is your husband with you?"

"I'm a widow," she replied coolly.

He flushed, embarrassed. "I'm sorry."

"How could you know?" she replied graciously.

"Shall we eat?" Initially confident, Haya could see he'd been thoroughly fazed. "Uh, a pregnant woman shouldn't go too long without dinner. They have some good cuisine here, even though it's a chain; some local dishes on the menu."

"That sounds good." Haya was pleased; he was thoughtful, she was hungry, and now he'd be trapped with her for as long as it took to eat a meal—long enough to pitch him on her plan.

"Then come this way." And to her surprise, he offered her his arm.

Beautiful manners, she thought. *And a handsome face.* And then felt instantly disloyal to Ahmed. She was six months pregnant, even if it had not showed too badly on her body, except for the gentle swell of her stomach. What was she doing thinking about another man like that?

~⁓~

They ordered a perfectly reasonable meal, some local specialities, vine leaves wrapped around spiced meats, tiny roasted birds, a Ghadan version of tabbouleh, and a lemony goat cheese in oils and herbs. She discovered Jaber had been educated at Cambridge—St. John's College, he said—and had served a military apprenticeship in the United States, at West Point.

Haya told him some of her story. Just a little, though; she did not want to drag Ahmed too far into it.

"I must ask you about your store," he said eventually, getting down to business.

"It's going to be prestigious and luxurious, and will charge high prices. We have backing from a senior financier—Craig Levin."

"Levin," he responded, clearly impressed.

"I am a full partner; the site is my husband's former gallery. My further role is to source art from the Middle East. We are hoping to engage in ethical commerce, to buy from women, and to pay them fair prices."

"And to make a profit."

Haya was unabashed. "Yes; like the Body Shop, this is a for-profit enterprise. In the end, you know, these women do not need handouts, they need long-term commercial partners. That can only be sustained if the buyers are making a profit."

He smiled slightly. "You sound like a woman who knows her own mind."

"I am." Haya inclined her head. "And we must be perfectly honest with you, since we want the participation of a sheikha or a princess."

"That is true."

"The photograph of that lady in the jewelry will help our cause; it will make our company richer—it will make me richer." Haya blushed a little. "Although I have no doubt these pieces are of sufficient quality to sell without it. But it will also benefit these women who are your citizens and more generally help in my plan to keep trading ethically with the Middle East. Eventually we'll be in other places, too—Europe, Africa, Asia. Wherever there are women with skills that we can help through business." Haya smiled. "So you see, Mr. Ibn Mohammed, I'm trying to be honest; it's a business proposition, though, in the end."

"And a sound one." He paused, his eyes traveling across her. "As long as you can prove you will be paying a fair market price to the Ghadan women who are supplying you."

"As soon as I get home, I will fax the documents to the palace."

"Very good." He smiled, lightly, and his eyes moved, again, across her face; Haya was embarrassed, and looked away. "Then we may be able to do business. I suppose you will not be back here for some time?"

"Not until after the birth of my child."

"I can see Sheikha Alia consenting to the photographs. If you do well with sales, and our women are benefiting, a more senior woman from the royal family might become involved. The king does want that trade."

"That's wonderful news," Haya said, blushing.

"But we would want a bigger shift of your buying to Ghada—including carpets and lamps and so forth."

"I would hope we will open more than one store," Haya replied confidently. "But I wouldn't come back to you unless it happened. And we could order a lot more from Ghada."

"Then I'm sure we can do business." He lifted his glass of mineral water to her in a toast.

"I'm glad to hear it, Mr. Ibn Mohammed."

"Please call me Jaber."

"Then Haya." She smiled.

"And . . ." He hesitated. "It isn't Mister . . . as it happens. I take a close interest in the affairs of Sheikha Alia because she's my mother."

Haya's water went down the wrong way; she spluttered a little, embarrassed.

"You mean . . ." He said nothing. "I'm sorry, Highness," she said, wanting to run off and hide.

"Nothing to be sorry for. I led you to believe otherwise. I should apologize . . . it's just that I hold a government position, and I'd rather be dealt with that way, than as a member of the family."

Haya saw he hadn't said royal—he hadn't had to.

"I understand. Highness," she added, again.

"I'd much prefer Jaber." He signaled for the waiter, and spoke to him in the Ghadan dialect, too fast for Haya to follow. "I should be leaving—I hope you have a pleasant flight, Ms. Al-Yanna—"

"Haya."

"Haya." He grinned. "And we'll be in touch."

She wondered if she should stand and curtsy, but it was too late. He bowed briefly to her, turned, and left.

⁓

"I'd like to check out, please."

"Certainly, madam."

"Room 406." Haya slid across her key and her credit card.

"There were some phone calls to the States, and two bottles of mineral water. . . ."

"It's quite alright, madam; there's no charge."

"Excuse me?"

"Your bill has been settled by the Kingdom of Ghada. Orders of His Highness Sheikh Jaber."

"Dinner, perhaps . . ."

"The entire bill, madam."

"I see." Haya bit back a smile. "How generous of His Highness. Could you possibly arrange for a taxi to take me to the airport?"

"That won't be necessary, ma'am. His Highness has sent a government limo for you. It's been waiting outside for an hour."

∽

All the way home Haya told herself it was just a courtly gesture. She had done some important business, maybe secured a PR coup. That was what mattered.

Jaber was a sheikh, and a government minister. He was probably married already. A man in his position was not going to be interested in a pregnant widow. It was important to keep her feet on the ground.

Even in the first-class section of her Royal Ghadan Airlines flight—since, when she got to the airport, Haya found Sheikh Jaber had ordered her business-class ticket upgraded.

When she got home, she had one of Jane's assistants fax the business details to Jaber's office. She was now starting to grow heavy with her child, and she wanted to leave the grand opening to Jane and Sally. Haya had walked through the store, seen the beautiful displays of the things she had sourced; together with Sally's exuberant fashions, they would be the heart and soul of GLAMOUR.

Right now, though, she had a baby to attend to. It was foolish to hope for romance, and she didn't want her heart broken twice. She made no attempt to contact Ghada other than through the office. She decorated the nursery instead, a nice neutral yellow.

No man was going to want to raise another's child, and even if he did, Haya was not sure whom she'd consider worthy.

Once the baby was born she'd forget about any romantic considerations.

She hoped.

~

"Well?" Sally stood back, and just looked at it. "Are you girls ready?"

She had her arms linked with her two friends. Jane on her right, Haya, almost ready to pop, on her left. They were standing in the parking lot, looking at the store.

It was six thirty, and the sun was sinking over the horizon, streaking the L.A. sky with a spectacular show of golds and reds. The building, gleaming white, was hung with banners of gold and silver silk, and pennants of scarlet and blue flying from every corner; it looked like a ticker-tape parade.

"Tomorrow," Haya said. "I can't wait."

"Nor me." Jane agreed.

Tomorrow they would open. The big day; the climax of months of grindingly hard work, of forcing themselves to act like a team, even when it got annoying. Exquisitely appointed, staffed by experts, and laid out, as Sally said, "like Christmas morning," they thought it was the hottest, richest, most luxurious store in the world.

The full-service beauty parlor. The roving reflexologists, ready to offer manicures and hand massages to tired shoppers. The fabulous goods, the soft lighting and dove gray carpeting, the mood music and attentive staff, the valet parking, the gift-wrap service . . .

It was a dream.

"They're all coming." The other two knew Sally was talking about the press. "The *Times,* the *Observer,* the *Citizen, Variety,* the *Hollywood Reporter*—everybody."

"Tough crowd," Jane observed.

"Let's hope it works," Haya said.

"It will." Sally was determined. "It has to." She looked at her friends, all three of them, in this moment, young, beautiful, and determined. "Get your rest in, ladies. We have to look *good*."

❧

"Jane! What does it feel like for the store to be this mobbed?"

"Sally! Are you taking the offer from Chanel?"

"No," she shouted, trying to be heard.

Behind them, in the store, it was pandemonium! Jane had told them to be calm; her staff were wonderful, they had everything under control.

"Haya! When is the baby due? Boy or a girl?"

The flashbulbs popped around them; reporters shouted questions. As word of the frenzy at the store got out, more and more journalists had showed up. It was beginning to resemble a movie premiere.

"GLAMOUR by name, glamour by nature," Sally whispered, nudging Jane.

Haya squeezed her hand. "I don't feel so good. It's crowded in here."

"I'll get rid of them," Jane whispered back. Her friend looked bad; her face was pale, and her breathing was labored. They'd done more than enough questions; Sally was brilliant with the media.

Whatever happened now, opening day would be a triumph.

Jane stood up. "Ladies and gentlemen—"

"Uuuugh," Haya groaned, to her left, and doubled forward, clutching the table.

"Haya! What is it?" Sally reached across, pushing her chair back.

"My water!" Haya gasped. "It broke. Oh, God! Get me to the hospital, Sal!"

Jane said unceremoniously, "That's it, we're done," and helped Sally to support Haya under the arms; she was writhing and moaning, obviously in serious pain.

"My car's closest!" Sally shouted.

"Right. Come on." The two girls took Haya out, stumbling between them, and a second forest of lightbulbs popped and flashed as they passed.

⌒⌒

"Ms. Al-Yanna, your mother is here," said the midwife. "Shall I send her in?"

Haya screamed.

"Send her in!" Jane said.

"I need Ms. Al-Yanna's permission," the woman fussed.

Jane turned to her with an icy-cold face. "She's a little busy right now. And I heard her say yes."

"So did I," Sally chimed in.

"Send her mother in." Jane's voice brooked no argument, and the woman obeyed.

The baby was close now, very close. Jane could see the head crowning. She gripped Haya's hand, sweaty and hot, to encourage her; Sally was hooking her legs back.

"Here he comes," Haya gasped. The door swung open and her mother bustled in, saying something rapid in Arabic Jane didn't understand. She let go of Haya's hand.

"No!" Haya said. "Stay! All of you stay!"

The older woman grabbed her other hand, leaned over, and whispered something to her daughter; Haya screamed again; and the baby popped out of the womb in a wet, slithery rush, into the waiting arms of the doctor, who took the child, rubbed a towel all over it, and cut the cord.

"Let me see!" Haya cried.

The doctor brought the baby across, wrapped in a striped cotton blanket. She said, "Here, Ms. Al-Yanna, a beautiful daughter."

Haya's mother's face fell.

"A girl," Haya said wonderingly.

Sally cooed, "How precious—she's so tiny."

"She's perfect, absolutely perfect." Haya's face was a picture of joy, and Jane did not need to ask if she was disappointed. She bent down and kissed the baby on the forehead. "Praise be to God," she said. "I love her . . . her name is Noor. Light. Because she's the light of my life."

Mrs. Al-Yanna, with the beginnings of a smile, leaned over and kissed her daughter and granddaughter.

"Congratulations," Sally said, with tears in her eyes.

"She's adorable. We'll see you later," Jane said. But Haya was already lost in her baby.

"Come on, Sal." Jane wiped away a little tear from her own eye; she thought briefly of the mother she barely remembered. "It's been a long day. Let's go get some lunch."

~~~

They sat in the front of Jane's Porsche, the top rolled up, at a discreet distance, eating thin-cut roast beef sandwiches and drinking iced Diet Cokes, watching the parking lot.

There was a constant line to get in and out; women swarmed around the lot like well-dressed ants, weighed down with GLAMOUR's signature glossy navy and gold bags. Every few minutes, male attendants in crisp navy GLAMOUR uniforms appeared carrying rolled-up carpets, more bags, or heavy items of furniture, and transported them to waiting SUVs.

"I guess those articles that came out last week really helped," Sally observed.

Jane licked a spot of mustard off her lower lip. "It's only the first day. We can't get carried away. Lots of PR. We have to see if it's sustained."

"But this is good," Sally insisted. "At Wave, we had something a bit like this. And it stayed that way until I quit for GLAMOUR."

"Yeah." She could not deny it. "It's good." Her brow furrowed a little. "I hope we have enough stock. . . ."

Sally hit her. "Cheer up."

They grinned at each other, companionably.

"I'm going back to the office. Field some more press queries, do a debrief of the staff at the end of the day." Jane sucked up the last of her Diet Coke. "Call our bankers."

"You mean Craig Levin," Sally suggested slyly.

Jane blushed. "Last time I looked, he was our banker."

"You won't be able to hold him off forever," Sally said. "I'm going in to the store. I'm gonna serve behind the counter, like at Wave."

"You'll be mobbed. You know you're getting quite the following. The press seems to love you, Sally. You're turning into a star."

"Girlfriend, please." Sally opened the door of the Porsche and tossed her long, blonde hair. "I have always been a star."

~~~

It was only half a joke. In reality, Sally was starting to think of herself that way. The press had a story—riches to rags to riches—and they adored how she combined all-American good looks with design savvy.

She was it. She was back. She was GLAMOUR.

She glanced back at Jane's gorgeous car as she went inside. By the end of this week, Sally promised herself, she'd have a sports car, too. A better one—a Ferrari. And a home in the Hollywood Hills, like any aspiring star too small, at least for now, for a Beverly Hills mansion.

~~~

"Hi," Sally said, for the fiftieth time.

She had ducked into the staff bathroom, fixed her makeup, brushed her hair out, and whitened her teeth, and now here she was, smiling at the customers. The *fans*, as she was starting to think of them.

"Hi! You're Sally Lassiter. I saw you in the *Citizen*. Oh, I just love your stuff, it's simply too darling."

"Why, thank you, ma'am."

"And those fabulous little moisturizers from the Dead Sea. I tried one on my hand, and it was so soft and luxurious . . . and the gift wrap was great. We bought a rug, too, and they're shipping it."

"Satisfaction guaranteed," Sally said, smiling broadly. "It's been an honor serving you, ma'am."

The fat woman clutched her husband. "Isn't she amazing?"

"Amazing," he said, looking Sally over with a mixture of lust and resignation.

"You know, sir," she said, deftly wrapping the woman's Ghadan disk bracelet, "we have an electronics area on the third floor. It sells gadgets and the TV screens are permanently tuned to sports. We also provide armchairs and couches to sit in, if you'd like to wait while the lady shops. . . ."

"Get out of here," he said, blinking. "Really?"

"Yes, sir. And there are waiters serving pretzels and ice-cold beer."

The wife looked hopefully at her husband.

"Kitty," he said, "you enjoy yourself, honey, charge whatever you like. This is a hell of a store."

He lumbered upstairs and Sally rang up the wife's purchase.

"You see, ma'am," she stage-whispered, "that was my idea. That area—it's like a crèche for husbands."

The fat wife giggled. "Wonderful! Fabulous. What a brilliant idea, I shall tell all my friends."

"Please do. And keep shopping." Sally winked at her, and she went away satisfied.

"So tell me," said a low voice, one she recognized, "do those TV screens also show baseball?"

Chris Nelson was standing in front of her. Today, he wore a nondescript blue shirt and khakis.

"I—yes, sir. They do."

He leaned in a little closer, his eyes moving across her body. Sally felt acutely aware of the extra button that was open at the top of her blouse; her lips moistened, and parted.

"Don't call me sir," he said, his voice low. "Got that, sugar?"

"Yes"—she wanted to say "Mr. Nelson," but dared not give him away—"Chris."

"Better." He gave her a lazy smile. "Pretty busy place you got here."

"It's just the first day." Oh, God! He was so handsome. Sally stiffened her back and lifted her head. She had to fight this. "Maybe you could get Letty to come here and shop. We have some special cosmetic ranges for all skin tones. Or she might like our perfume section, or a handcrafted mosaic from Jordan."

"How's your mom doing?" he asked, ignoring her catty response. Sally blushed.

"Well. Thank you." She lowered her head. "Sorry, that was uncalled-for, I—I know you didn't mean to hit on me or anything."

"Sure I did."

Her head lifted. "What? I don't fool around with other women's men."

"Even me?"

Arrogant bastard! "Yes, even you," she snapped. "But I'll send Ms. Berry an engagement gift to your office, no charge."

"It wouldn't reach her." He looked at her, amused. Toying with her, Sally thought, with a fresh rush of heat. "We're not engaged. So send any gifts to her own office."

She opened her mouth, but he cut her off. "And to clarify, we're not going out, either. We split up."

"Why?"

"That's between me and her," he said, easily enough, but firmly. "She's a wonderful woman."

Not that damn wonderful, Sally thought, annoyed.

"So what time do you get off work?"

"Whenever I want to. I'm the boss."

"Then maybe you can buy me a cup of coffee," he suggested. "Apologize for forgetting my dog."

"You want me to ask you on a date?"

"What's the matter? Not a modern woman?"

Sally tossed her hair. "I don't beg."

"We'll see about that," he said, softly, and she felt her stomach turn inside out and her knees weaken. "But for now . . . coffee?"

Sally's throat went dry. She turned to the sales assistant, a bright Korean woman whose smile never failed. "You can finish up here, right?"

"Yes, Miss Lassiter. Of course."

"Thanks." Sally came out from behind the counter, feeling naked now that she was so close to him. To distract her, she asked, "How come you haven't been mobbed?"

"In here? You got to be kidding, this is estrogen central. Maybe if I went upstairs. To the husbands' holding zone." He grinned. "Now that is a smart idea."

"Where are you parked?"

"Right outside. And I left the dog at home. Come on, I know a great place we can get something."

Sally followed him, meekly, her head down; she didn't want to be stopped either. Not right now. The store, her success, none of it seemed to matter. He was all she could think about. She hoped to hell it didn't show.

As they left the store, he slipped his shades back on, and put one arm possessively round her shoulders; as a couple maybe they'd attract less attention.

"Hey!" a voiced called. They were almost at his car—she recognized it, a large Jeep, top of the range. "Aren't you Chris? Chris Nelson?"

"Not today, pal."

"That's Chris Nelson," somebody else shouted.

"Oh, my God!" a woman squealed. "I love him!"

"What now?" Sally asked, dismayed.

He chuckled. "Run!"

They made it to the car with moments to spare. Chris opened the passenger door, Sally jumped in, and he wound up her tinted window; within seconds they were inside. She watched as he wound down his own window, where a thick little knot of fans was banging on the glass, and smiled broadly.

"Hey, it's good to see you folks." They cheered wildly. "Enjoy shopping at GLAMOUR?"

"We love you!"

"Thanks for all your support." He reached out his hand and brushed at various grasping fingertips. "I better get to practice, we have to whup those Cardinals Monday, right?" They cheered again. "See you guys here again, maybe. It's a great store."

Then he pressed the button, the window wound up, and he

put the Jeep into gear. The crowd scattered, obediently, waving, and he spun the wheel and deftly took the Jeep into the anonymity of the L.A. traffic.

"You're very good at that," she said.

He smiled. "I've had a little bit of practice."

"So where is this place?"

"Malibu. Out on the coast, not too far. It's tucked away and they know me there. Nobody bothers you, plus, they have an open-air terrace overlooking the ocean." He glanced at her. "Don't worry. We won't get too near the edge."

Sally laughed. "Okay, then."

Suddenly he turned the car and pulled into a lay-by.

"You made a wrong turn?"

"No." He looked across at her, light eyes hot. "I just want to introduce myself properly."

Sally blushed, her skin tensing, and Nelson reached across the car, put one large, callused hand behind the soft skin of her neck, and tugged her to him. His mouth crushed hers, his tongue probing deeply across her teeth, the roof of her mouth. His left hand brushed lightly, teasing, across her breasts. Sally felt desire so intense rock through her, she could hardly contain herself; she kissed him back with helpless passion. . . .

And then hated herself for it. Why? Why had she done *that*? What girl didn't melt in the arms of the big superstar? She fought, and reluctantly broke away from him. Thank God her bra was padded, and he couldn't see exactly how turned on she was.

"Why did you do that?"

"I had to," he said simply. "Sally, I've been thinking about you for weeks. Why do you think I broke up with Letty?"

Then, without giving her time to think, he started up the car again, put his shades back on, and concentrated on the road.

Sally was grateful; she turned her head aside and looked out the window. Hoping he could not see her smile. Hoping he could not smell her desire. Oh, God! She had to be careful, now. Going out with somebody like Chris Nelson was fun, but it could never last. Too many girls, everywhere, too much competition.

She had to be careful not to fall in love.

⟡

"Good to see you again, Mr. Nelson. And Miss Lassiter, welcome."

Sally's eyes widened. Sensing her nerves, Chris slipped her hand into his.

"I've got everything ready, sir, just as you ordered. This way, please."

The maître d' conducted them through the expensive-looking restaurant—Sally recognized two movie stars and a senator—out to a terrace at the back, a manicured lawn surrounded by topiary hedges and climbing roses wound over trellises. There was a single table, directly overlooking the ocean, set with a crisp white cloth and beeswax candles in silver holders. A large silver bucket on a stand held a chilled magnum of champagne; from here Sally could see it was vintage Pol Roget. There was a bowl of crushed ice, filled with fruits—nectarines, plums, crisp-looking grapes—a luxurious arrangement of green and white flowers, and a series of small dishes set out across the table.

"Tapas," Sally said, surprised. "I love tapas."

Chris grinned. "I know."

The maître d' showed them to their table, uncorked and served the champagne, and then melted discreetly away.

"Here's to the start of something," he suggested. And she drank, thankfully, in the hope that the wine would make her feel less nervous.

"How did you know I liked tapas? And how does he know my name?"

"After that day I did some research on you." He shrugged. "Read that article again. Asked around. Found your store on Melrose was closed, and had my assistants tell me what you were doing, with those other girls. I thought it was pretty ballsy stuff."

"You researched me?" she asked, outraged.

"That's right," he said, easily. "And I bet you researched me, too. Went and looked up my stats on ESPN. Didn't you?"

Sally blushed scarlet. She had. And more.

"But that waiter?"

"I told him I was coming here with you, as my date. No questions about Letty, we'd broken up."

"You used to bring her here?"

"Of course." He shrugged. "It's my favorite restaurant. Have one of those spiced ham slices and you'll see why."

"But . . ." Sally was trying to process it. It felt like Chris Nelson was three steps ahead of her. Maybe because he was, she thought, and found the idea to be totally erotic. "That means you knew I'd say yes."

"I did know it."

"Isn't that arrogant?"

He gave her a lazy grin. "Sally, I've known a lot of women. And I know how they look at you. You were interested, that day. You didn't say anything, but you didn't have to. I knew once I'd finished with Letty you'd see me."

"Good job you were right, or you'd have lost your girlfriend for nothing," Sally said, acidly.

"It was." He picked up a plate of vine leaves stuffed with rice. "Try one. I ordered them specially for you."

She bit into one; it was delicious, the herbed oils drizzled a little across her lips. She licked it away, and blushed again. Everything she did here seemed to be charged with sex.

"I'm a virgin," she blurted out.

His eyebrows lifted; the first time she had surprised him.

"You're not a teenager anymore, are you?"

Sally shook her head.

"Then don't worry," he said. "We can fix that."

She felt herself almost dizzy with wanting him.

"I'm not—not going to. Not with you."

"And what's wrong with me?" He was leaning forward now, eating, but not concentrating; his eyes never seemed to leave her body.

"You're too much," she said. "You're too good-looking, and strong, and you saved my mom . . ."

"I hope that's not going to be a strike against me."

"You're famous. Like, really famous. And rich. And you date supermodels."

"One. Singular."

"You're so . . ." She flailed, wishing she could be as cool as Jane or Haya, find some fancy words to finesse it, instead of saying what she meant. "You're so damn hot."

"So far, this doesn't sound like a list of crimes of the century."

"Stop playing with me!" Sally said passionately. "You know what I mean. So I sleep with you, you get what you want, you dump me, and I'm left pining after you like some bitch in heat. And you move on to the next chick. Some actress or another model . . ."

Nelson's face softened.

"I'm a virgin and . . ."

"Saving it up for marriage?"

She blushed, defensively. "Somebody special, anyway. Special to me."

He sighed. "Well, I guess nothing's gonna happen tonight. Although you'd have enjoyed it."

She could hardly deny it; he'd had her leaping and squirming in his arms, just from a kiss.

"Maybe tonight, yes. But what about tomorrow? I have to be careful." She lifted her chin defiantly. "I know who you are, Chris Nelson. But I know who I am, too."

"Okay, then," he replied, and gave her a warm smile. "You're something else, Miss Lassiter. No more pushing. But I want to tell you something."

"Go ahead." Sally took her flute of champagne, drained it, and poured herself another; his smile broadened.

"You want to accuse me of having laid a lot of girls. I'll tell you right now, guilty as charged. I started in school as the best batter in the team. Went up the minors. Got drafted in college. All the way through, I got raging hormones and I got the prettiest young girls throwing themselves at me. You do the math."

She nodded, smiling slightly. At least he was honest.

"Only thing I can say is I used a condom, because my elder brother wound up knocking up this girl he quickly grew to hate, marrying her, and getting divorced after eight miserable years.

Rough on the kid. Anyway, same time I hit the bigs, it starts to get old. Can't tell you why—just did. I looked down on them, started to look down on myself. Waking up in a strange room with some random broad who might start crying, or stalking me, gets to be a headache." He paused. "And this may sound dumb but I started thinking about my aunt Esme, who raised me since my mom died when I was two. She's like a mom to me. Anyway, she's been married to Uncle Jake for twenty years and they have three kids apart from me. Didn't used to have much money but they were always happy. I want that."

"They didn't used to have money?"

"I bought them a house and some cars and gave them a bank account. My cousins, too. They're all millionaires now. Anyway, I decided to cut out all the one-night stands, grow up and pick a girl. So I decided she had to be especially beautiful—like you say, there's a lot of temptation. And also strong, because I don't want to be bored. When I met Letty, she seemed like a good fit. Also she was as rich as hell, so I knew she wasn't a gold digger."

"Makes sense," Sally said, hating Letty Berry.

"It was never great, but it was pretty good. We went out for five years, and I never cheated on her."

"So what happened?"

He ate a chicken wing. "Told you, baby. You did. Just—I don't know what. You looked pretty, when your mom was safe. Messed up, but pretty. Brave. Polite. You carried yourself different from most girls, when you knew who I was. Reserved." He shrugged. "Even though I could see you wanted me. Of course I told myself it was only an intense moment, nothing to get worked up about."

Sally smiled; she had thought the same.

"But then I started looking you up. Your guts. Your talent. How you looked after your mother, not just that day at the cliff. You and your friends. They're cute, too—"

Sally frowned.

"I mean, nothing like you, though! And you know, I started to think about you all the time. I used to take a detour and drive past your store and watch the trucks loading in the stock. It was really happening. What kind of a twenty-something girl does that shit? They're all wasting Daddy's money at college, working on their MRS degrees. And one night, I was with Letty and I started thinking about you. Closest I ever came to cheating on her." Sally blushed. "I broke up with her the next day."

"Was she upset?"

"Yes. I don't want to talk about it."

"I'm sorry . . ."

"Are you?"

"Sorry she was hurt."

"If I loved her for real, I wouldn't have been thinking about you." He smiled and reached for his own wine, draining it, then refilling his glass and topping hers up. "Not going to say I love you, I hardly know you. You might be a psychopath. But if you want to wait to find out before you slide into bed with me, that's cool. I can wait." He paused. "As long as it takes."

Sally smiled. "Thank you." She wanted to reach out and take his hand, but he drew away.

"Do you like the food?"

"You're changing the subject."

"Don't tempt me, girl. I'm only human," he growled.

She felt the familiar hot press of wanting him and meekly bit down on a slice of chorizo.

"Yes. It's delicious," she said.

Chris stood up, leaned across the table, and kissed her on the lips, his mouth just brushing hers; a more modest kiss than the first; but Sally was still on fire.

"Try a peach," he said. "They're sweet. They're cold."

She blushed richly.

"Don't worry," Chris said tenderly. "We're gonna put things right for you. I mean it. When you're mine, I want you whole."

⌒

He took things slow enough. Sally half expected her phone to ring the next morning, pestering her for a date. But Chris waited one entire day. Next time, he took her to a discreet restaurant in the city. The third date was on a weekend; he asked her if she wanted to go to the movies, and when Sally said yes, he drove her off to a private screening of the latest blockbuster movie, fresh out of the edit suite, at the home of a studio president. Eventually, Sally was even able to tell him what had happened to her that night in Texas.

Chris didn't mention sex again. But he held her hand, slipped his brawny arm around her shoulders. When they walked together in public, he always twisted his muscular body, like he was physically protecting her.

Sally appreciated that he wasn't pushing her into sex. He was waiting for her. And she started to feel like she hadn't lost everything that night in the back of Leo's car. Her first time had been snatched from her. But there was a second time, and all the times after that, to come.

If she ever wanted to.

And to her astonishment, this brawny, rough, ultramasculine guy was apparently ready and willing to wait.

Six weeks going out, and he had never discussed her rape. But Sally knew it was going to come.

He was cooking dinner for her at his gorgeous little bachelor pad in the Hollywood Hills, all glass walls, leather couches, and cowhide rugs.

"Want some wine? I got a pinot grigio. Goes good with spaghetti and clams."

"Yes, thanks." Sally curled her long legs under her on his gigantic, custom-made La-Z-Boy chair.

"Babe," Chris said. He stirred the pasta and didn't look at her. "If you feel you can, I want you to tell me how the rape happened."

"It's not important," Sally said. "I've moved on."

"It is important." Now he did look at her. "It's important to me. You're important to me."

He poured her a large, chilled glass of wine and handed it over.

Sally nodded. Chris had dated her now for quite a while. He deserved to hear about it, hear about what was holding her back.

She described her life in Texas, leaving her mother's illness out of it. Leaving school. The beauty parlor. Elaine. Leo Fisk.

When she was done, Chris didn't say anything for a few minutes. Then he expertly lifted the steaming pasta out of the pot with his pasta forks and tossed it with the clams, ripping some fresh oregano over it and squeezing lemon; he brought two large bowls over to the table that looked out over his pool deck, the water illuminated at night.

"What you got down there is unfinished business," he said.

Sally stared. "You're not going to do anything, are you?"

He gestured to her plate. "Eat."

Sally did; it was delicious.

"I'm from Mississippi," he said. "We don't let stuff like that pass by. You felt you couldn't prosecute, I understand. But he's gonna get his."

Sally blinked. "What do you mean?"

"I mean I'm going to go down there and kick his ass."

She blinked. "Beat him up?"

"Nothing permanent. I'm gonna break his arm." Chris said it very matter-of-factly.

"It won't solve anything."

"It will. It'll stop him thinking he can rape women and get away with it." Chris looked at her. "Who says you were the only one, baby? No, I'm going to confront the guy. My two cents, you should come, Sally. Put that ghost to rest. And then"—he took her hand—"you and I can move on."

CHAPTER 12

They flew to Dallas the next day, and within an hour, the
limo arrived in Hartford. Sally was wearing a gorgeous
Chanel suit, pale yellow, with a Prada blouse of buttercup
silk, canary diamond studs, and yellow-and-white Jimmy Choo
heels with calf straps. She carried a Gucci purse, and her long
platinum hair fell straight and glossy to her shoulders.

Chris made no attempt to hide his identity. He even wore a
Dodgers shirt with his own name on it.

"Is it like you remember?" he asked, as they pulled up on
Main Street.

Sally looked through the tinted windows. "Yeah. Almost."

The town was as drab and dispirited as when she and Mona
had first rolled in. The liquor store was still doing good business. But when she looked for Rodeo Girl . . . the bright, breezy
storefront had disappeared. In its place, paint peeling, was a new
version of Fisk's Beauty Parlor. Looked like business was bad.

People had gathered around, across the street. A limo! Limos
were not usual in this town. Some of the folks even started snapping pictures with their cameras.

"Come on, baby," Chris said, grimly. He opened the door and
stepped out.

There was a moment's pause. Then some of the men shouted
in recognition, and the girls started squealing.

Chris offered his hand to Sally. She took it, swinging her impossibly long legs out of the leather seats of the limo, her slim hand in his callused one. The crowd oohed and aahed at the girl they assumed was a model.

But then, as their chauffeur was closing the car door behind him, there came another cry of recognition.

"Oh, my good Lord! If it ain't Sally Lassiter."

Sally walked across the street. Chris followed her, and slipped an arm around her shoulders as she talked.

"Lucy? Lucy Drew?"

"You remember!" Lucy had taken Sally's style lessons to heart. She was wearing a simple combo of jeans and a white tee, and she'd lost twenty pounds and looked great. Leo's old asshole pal Simon Bernardillo was standing next to her. He looked at Sally, swallowed nervously. Stared at Chris. Eyes darting from one to the other, like he couldn't believe it.

The entire crowd squeezed tighter. Faces she remembered, lots she didn't. Lucy was about the only one she'd liked. And everybody was hanging on Sally's reply.

"Of course. You look great."

"*I* look great!" Lucy squealed. "What about *you*? Oh, my gosh. Sally Lassiter, you look like a millionaire! And is that really . . ."

Her voice trailed off, and she blushed.

"Yes, it is. Lucy, this is my boyfriend, Chris Nelson." Almost a moan of pleasure went up from the crowd. "Chris, this is Lucy Drew, she was nice to me back when I was at school here."

Chris lifted his baseball cap politely. Several of the girls in the crowd clutched themselves.

"It's an honor to meet you, ma'am."

"And this is my boyfriend Simon, you remember?"

Sure she did. Simon was dating Lucy now, and he had the good grace to look shamefaced. Maybe he'd matured.

"Hi, Sally," he muttered. "Those are mighty nice earrings Mr. Nelson bought you."

"Hey, I didn't buy 'em." Chris rubbed his hand up and down on Sally's shoulder, proudly. He looked at Lucy and smiled. "She's gonna be a millionaire, someday real soon. Sally founded the GLAMOUR store in L.A. So she pretty much buys her own jewels."

There were gasps of envy. Sally saw them now, the kids that had teased her at school. Grown up. Still losers.

"That's fantastic," Lucy said. "That's just incredible. And you're dating a star."

"Can I have your autograph?" Simon burst out, unable to stop himself.

Chris looked at Sally, and she nodded.

That unlocked the floodgates. The men shoved forward, desperate for a signature. Some ran to their houses to fetch baseballs.

"You go ahead," Chris said to Sally. He nodded at Fisk's. "I'll be there in just a minute." And he unhurriedly started to sign, and smile, like the All-Star he was.

⌒

Sally entered Fisk's. The musty smell was back. The little bell, too, that tinkled over the doorway. A new girl was sweeping up hair; she looked like she was from school, on a summer job. Her eyes widened when she saw Sally, in all her finery.

Elaine Fisk was standing over in the corner, dispiritedly polishing a mirror. She saw Sally at first in the reflection; and then slowly spun around.

All the weight was back. The years had taken every ounce of vivacity from her face. Elaine Fisk was a beaten woman.

"It really is you," she said. "And"—her gaze traveled over Sally—"you're rich. I knew you would be."

"Afternoon, Elaine." Sally controlled herself. Elaine Fisk had done nothing to her. "I'm looking for Leo."

"Leo?" Elaine blinked, stupidly. Then she scowled. "You left me, Sally Lassiter, you left me without any word. My goddamn business fell to pieces. Mark lost his shirt. It was you, it all went around you . . ."

"Momma?"

Sally froze. She'd know that voice in the depths of hell.

"Are we all out of Bud Light?"

Leo ambled into the salon. He wasn't shaved, and he was fat.

His shirt had grease stains on it, and it was open at the neck, so you could see a graying vest.

He glanced up. "Holy shit," he said, and his mouth broke into a broad grin, revealing crooked teeth. "Don't you look hot, baby?"

The bell tinkled. Chris Nelson entered. Leo stared, and his jaw dropped open. Sally remembered, Leo loved his sports.

"Shit," he said again.

"Miss." Chris turned to the schoolgirl, who had stopped sweeping and just turned to stare. "Why don't you shut up shop for today?" He reached in his pocket and pulled out a hundred-dollar bill. "My girlfriend needs a moment with Ms. Fisk."

"I—sure. Yes, sir," she whispered, then she snatched the bill and ran out the door.

"I fucking love you," Leo said to Chris Nelson. "You're my hero. You datin' our Sally? For real?"

"Elaine," Sally said, her voice loud and clear, "I'm sorry to have to tell you this. You're a good woman. But I left Hartford for one reason. Because Leo raped me."

There was total silence in the room. Elaine Fisk turned her head, very slowly, and looked at her son.

"Tell me that ain't so," she said quietly.

He flushed and bared his crooked teeth. "It ain't, Momma. She wanted it. She was hot for me."

Sally looked at Elaine. "He picked me up walking home. When I got in the car, he was drunk. He drove through town, out to the cornfields. Threatened to kill me, leave me right in the crop to rot away."

Elaine crammed her fist into her mouth.

"I didn't mean none of that," Leo muttered. He looked at Chris, at Chris's solid, muscle-bound athlete's body, at the eyes like flint. Fear was written bright across his face. "Look, mister, I—I was drunk. Maybe I pushed it too hard, maybe."

"I was a virgin, Elaine. A virgin when he raped me."

Chris moved toward Leo.

"No!" he squealed. "Don't hurt me!"

"Chris!" Sally said.

"I won't kill him." Chris kept advancing, as Leo tried to scuttle away. "I'm just gonna break his arm and his leg. You see, he'll hit me first. At least, the judge won't know different."

"Chris." Sally ran up to him, put her hand on his arm. "Baby, please. Don't you see? He's got his. Already."

"What do you mean?"

She whisked back the curtain, pointed to the empty liquor bottles scattered around the couch, where ESPN was on.

"He's broke. He's living with his momma. He's an alcoholic. And there ain't a lot worse than that. I know."

She pulled him away, gestured to the faded beauty parlor.

"This used to be a moneymaker. Could have been something big. Elaine could have started a chain with me. Now look. Look what happened to this family. Leo did it to them, not me. And for the rest of his days he has to live with it."

"Oh, my God," Elaine said, wretchedly. "I'm sorry."

"Don't be. You didn't do anything."

Chris turned to Leo, cowering in a corner of the room.

"I'm a very rich man," he said. "Sally's turned herself into a successful woman. We'll have people keeping an eye on you. If you lay one hand on another female in anger—even one time—I'll send some guys after you. And they'll be pros. And they won't have any young ladies with them, to call them off. You follow me?"

Leo nodded.

"Can't hear you."

"Yes, sir."

"Apologize to my girlfriend."

Leo said, "I'm sorry for what I did, Sally," and then he started to cry. High-pitched, girlish, drunken sobs, like he was feeling very sorry for himself.

Sally looked at him. The anger she'd kept in her heart melted right away. There was nothing left but contempt.

"Don't blame yourself, Elaine," she said. "You ain't responsible for any of this."

Then she held out her hand to Chris. And for the first time, she truly felt she was in love with him.

"Come on, sugar," she said. "Let's go."

∽

When Chris dropped her off at her apartment block, he kissed her again.

"I'm going to send you tickets to the game tomorrow night. There's a box for the players' wives and girlfriends. Starts at eight, so maybe you'll be done with the store."

"The press will see me . . ."

"Honey, I lay you two to one they already know. You going to be there?"

"You know I am," she said, surrendering to the fact that she was totally, insanely, passionately hot for him.

"Good. It'll help me wear down your resistance," he said and winked at her. Then he rolled up the window and drove off.

∽

"So where have you been?"

Mona was sulking; her arm still in a cast, she was fussing at not having heard from Sally all night.

"Sorry, Mom. I'll call next time. Hey, that thing can come off tomorrow."

"Yes, well, that's good." Mona sniffed. "I can't run for four weeks, but they have an Olympic pool at the gym, so I'm starting swimming."

"Sounds like fun."

"Sally! What man were you with?"

Sally started, guiltily. "How do you know I was with a man?"

"That look on your face."

"Just . . . a nice man. We're going out again tomorrow. He's the man that saved you, Mom."

"Oh—well. I suppose it's okay, if you don't do anything stupid. Remember Daddy is watching over you."

"I will," said Sally, feeling the heat in her evaporate. How did Mom know exactly the right buttons to press? Maybe mothers did that by instinct.

"And some people called. Jane and Haya. Haya said you should come by to see her tomorrow."

"Okay."

"And Jane wanted you to know that the store broke some sort of record this week. She says you have a problem with enough stock and can you bring in anything extra from Wave?"

"Okay!" Sally grinned. There it was, that glow of achievement. Chris Nelson wanted more than a pretty face, and she had no intention of just being that.

"And then lots of journalists called and asked if you were going out with a baseball player. They said you got spotted at the airport together."

She froze. "What did you say?"

"I hung up on them."

"Good job, Mom."

"So are you?"

Sally surrendered. "Yes; the man who saved you plays a little ball, yes."

"He's an All-Star shortstop?" Mona asked, determinedly. "For the Dodgers? Cover of *Sports Illustrated*? Future Hall of Famer?"

"I don't know why you're asking, if you already know," Sally sulked.

"I didn't. The journalists told me." Mona smiled. "If somebody famous was the man who saved me, I reckon he must be a good man. Those celebrities are usually pampered brats. He took a risk."

Sally remembered the welts on his hands.

"He certainly did."

"Just remember, honey, you only have one heart."

Sally went over and kissed her mother on the forehead.

"Believe me, Mom," she said, "I'm trying."

~

Jane Morgan was trying to keep her feet on the ground. It was only seven weeks, not even two months yet. There had been factors; curiosity. Well-managed press. Additional coverage after that, from stuff you could never script: Haya in labor, Sally starting to date some famous athlete—boy, they'd loved that. Even Jane, who tried to stay in the background, was getting well-known.

But you couldn't fool people forever. If the shoppers came back, it would be because of their excellent service, first-rate staff, and the whole experience she was selling.

Maybe she would wait and see if they did come back.

But damn, these numbers.

Out of the park. Like a ball off the end of Sally's new boy-friend's bat. Home-run stuff. Records.

She was now fielding new calls. Not just from newspapers' Style sections. From Wall Street analysts.

She turned off her computer and flopped down onto the bed, exhausted. These last three weeks had been mad. And with Haya gone, and Sally's eyes dazzled by Chris Nelson, all the stock rear-rangement had fallen on Jane, as well as staff evals, billing, and the rest of it.

They needed to hire management, she thought. Vice presi-dents. Who could she steal from Saks? And that wasn't all. At this rate of cash flow—be honest, she knew it wasn't going to drop, in fact it was going to increase. The brand now had critical mass, and their foundations of quality were there. It was an out-of-the-gate success. Well, at this rate, they'd have to expand. Move into the East Coast. New York. Then Chicago. Then D.C., Seattle. She ticked the cities off in order of importance. After that, they'd be looking for major new investment and some places abroad: Paris, London . . . and to be different, perhaps a boutique in Mauritius. GLAMOUR was just that. It had to be open in St. Tropez and Milan. . . .

Jane sensed exhaustion creeping up on her, and she couldn't have that. Burnout was what happened to other people; bond traders. . . . She had to be able to cover Haya for a couple months. Resolutely, she peeled off her clothes, dumped them in the laun-dry hamper, and put on her swimsuit. The pool in the yard would do fine. It was a blisteringly hot day, and she would cool off and work out at the same time.

Tomorrow this house would go on the market. Sally and Haya

were already moving. This place was cute, but far too small, and she could now afford to upgrade, Part of GLAMOUR was the fantasy, anyway; of course the owners had to live well. They were the brand, as Donald Trump had learned.

She plunged into the pool. Man, she loved exercise. It was the one time when she could totally focus on herself. The physical effort forced her to clear her head. Figures, money, deals just melted away. Without exercise, she thought she might crack. Jane swam twenty laps, reveling in the movement of the water against her body, then propelled herself lazily up to the steps in the shallow water and slowly walked out of the pool, reaching for her towel. . . .

"Good evening."

She gave a little shriek. Craig Levin was sitting there, on her sun lounger, dressed in a lightweight summer suit. His gaze ran quickly across her body before she wrapped it in a towel.

"What are you doing here?" Jane snapped.

"I called, I faxed, I e-mailed. No reply." He grinned. "Started to think you were ducking me, Miss Morgan."

She had been. "I was busy," Jane extemporized. "Start-up time . . ."

"I noticed." He inclined his head. "I do have three million dollars in your store. And ten percent of the company. Which I believe makes me the major nonowner shareholder."

"The only one," Jane conceded.

"And it appears I'll be getting a nice return on that ten percent."

He certainly would.

"I'll buy your shares," she said. "Four million dollars, and you make a million profit in six months."

"Now why would I sell something for four that's worth five now and, I strongly suspect, twenty or thirty in a couple of years?" Levin asked coolly. "If you were me, would you sell?"

Jane had to shake her head. "No."

"Then don't ask foolish questions."

She stood there, dripping, water from her soaked hair streaming down her back, her feet naked on the hot tiles. Nothing but a towel between Levin and her nude thighs; her suit was high-cut, with a hole across the belly; she understood clearly that he had an excellent idea of her body, right now, down to the flat of her stomach and the swell of her breasts.

Levin was clothed, wearing a smart pair of shoes and a paisley tie; they looked good on such a young man.

"I have to get dressed," she muttered.

He spread his hands. "Nobody's stopping you. But please don't bother on my account."

Jane fled into her bedroom and whisked the curtains closed.

Five minutes later she was back out there again, wet hair combed through, her feet in stacked mules, wearing the closest thing to hand—a sample of one of Sally's new summer dresses; it had spaghetti straps and a close-fitting bodice, with a light skirt that fluted prettily around her knees.

"Nice," Levin said, making her wish she'd added a shawl. Only it was just too hot.

"Can I get you some iced tea?" Jane was flustered. "I have a jug in the fridge."

"Thank you," he said, to her discomfiture. It meant that he was going to stay. And that she would have to fetch him the tea. A small act, but one he somehow imbued with meaning.

At least she was out of her swimsuit. Jane fetched him, and herself, a large glass of tea choked with ice and a slice of lime in it.

"Delicious," he said. "Unsweetened."

"I'm watching my figure," Jane confessed.

Levin shook his head. "No need. Believe me."

"So what can I do for you?" she asked, as briskly as she could under the circumstances.

"I want daily accounts sent to my office."

"You can't have them."

"I own ten percent. I want a seat on the board."

"Can't have it. Talk to your lawyer."

"If you want my money for expansion, you'll cooperate."

Jane shrugged. "I think the banks will be ready to talk to me, now."

He grinned. "I think so, too. But you won't be able to do the mom-and-pop thing forever, you know. Even Branson went public. And when you do, I'll be there with my checkbook."

"And until that time, I'll send you a monthly summary," Jane said. "And we'll be repaying your loan early."

Levin was still looking at her in that disturbing way.

"You do understand what I could do to the store, right? That I could take anything I wanted from you. I could have city hall ride you on parking or health and safety. I could buy out the contracts with your suppliers. I could hire away your staff by doubling their salaries and sending them on fact-finding missions to Cancun."

His words were tough, but he was smiling at her, softly. She knew his fencing was a game.

Jane squared her shoulders. "We'd sue."

"Whatever resources you have, throwing them at me would be like dropping a pebble into the ocean," he replied matter-of-factly. "I have so much money that consortiums of commercial banks wouldn't take me on."

She gritted her teeth. "I will not let you sit on the board. I'd rather go under."

"Don't worry," he said, smiling at her. "I wouldn't force you. But I want you to know that I can."

"Does that usually work? Puffing out your chest like a pigeon in mating season?"

Levin laughed, delighted. She'd called him on it. Most women wouldn't dare.

"You respect work. And success." He made his case, and his eyes lingered on hers. "Yes, sure—I want to remind you of mine, so you stop fighting me so hard. We're *supposed* to be allies. Last time I saw you, I wrote you the check that allowed this to happen. And what do I get for it? My calls—blanked. My assistant's calls—blanked. My faxes—ignored. I've been treated better by companies that were my takeover targets."

Guilty. She knew it. He knew it.

"So tell me," he said, drawing the sentence out. Clearly enjoying himself. "Do you treat all your benefactors this way?"

She tried to think of a comeback.

"So why me? You know I could have been of greater assistance. More money. Contacts. An advertising budget. You should now have full pages in *Vogue* and *Elle*."

"I apologize," Jane said, blushing. "I should have been more responsive."

"My question is why you weren't."

She tried "I've been so busy . . ."

"Making hundreds of business-related calls. Just not to me."

"I . . ."

"Tell the truth," he said, grinning. "Admit it. You'll feel better."

Oh, man. Jane shook her head. He was too close to her, too strong. Too damn powerful. And so, so good-looking. She was briefly amazed at herself for ever having glanced at Jude Ferrers. She was made for a guy like this.

His questions were unanswerable, except with the truth. Jane surrendered.

"I—I find you attractive."

"Better," he said. "You know, I think that's still legal in all fifty states."

"And it's best not to get involved with a colleague!" she added in a burst of inspiration.

"Now, Jane. You were doing so well. And then you relapsed." His confident, teasing tone was so arousing; Jane could hardly look at him. Coloring, she stared at her sandals. "Shall I help you out? You're a tough woman—and you want to stay that way. You're frightened of me. Frightened of wanting me, frightened of my past girlfriends, frightened of being on a list. Slightly ashamed of yourself for having used my attraction to you to get this deal. Determined that you'll return my money and never see me again. Scared of any romance, any man, maybe. Thinking that one day, perhaps you'll marry a househusband, a nice, unthreatening guy with self-esteem problems, who can give you a baby or two and then run a farm somewhere, while you bring home the bacon; somebody who'll never challenge you . . ."

Jane's eyes flashed. "Cut that out!"

Levin put his face close to hers. "Pretty near the knuckle, am I, baby?"

"I'll tell you this. I'm never going to be used by any man."

"But you used your stunning beauty to get to me, didn't you?"

"No."

"Oh, yes, you did," he said, softly. "Oh, yes, Jane, and you know it."

She ran her tongue over her lips. Wanting to kiss him. Or run.

"You're hard," Levin said. "The hardest woman I've ever met. I have no idea why I'm chasing you like this. And no idea why you're running."

"I just . . ."

"And now I'm going to kiss you," he said, and came forward, and she froze, couldn't move a single muscle, and then his lips were on top of hers, hardly touching them, just brushing lightly against the skin; she could smell the scent of him, feel the strength of his torso right in front of her . . .

Jane was unable to help herself. He was teasing her, not taking her. Daring her to resist. Or ask for more. But her legs under the thin skirt were writhing; she was moist and hot for him; her body, so focused and tensed, melted and warmed and she moaned under her breath and surrendered, her tongue thrusting back into Levin's mouth, her lips pressing against him, pleadingly . . .

He chuckled deep in his throat. Underneath her dress her body was leaping against him as he ran a hand slowly across it. Jane fell into his arms, feeling his jacket, his belt, the buttons of his shirt. Her senses felt unbelievably heightened. She wanted him so much. A voice in her head was telling her not to, to leave him alone. They hadn't even dated. But she would not listen. His strength, his assured touch, all over her, like he owned her . . . she wanted it, at that moment, more than anything.

Levin kissed her again, triumphantly, and swung her into his arms; her weight was nothing to him; Jane buried her hot face in his chest, pressed her breasts against him. As he carried her through the sliding glass doors and into the coolness of her bedroom, Levin was already unbuttoning the top of her dress.

~⟋

She lay naked, drained, against him. It was night now; they were both covered in sweat; Jane's body was relaxed, as though orgasm had unknotted every muscle under her skin. She wondered if she had the energy left to move.

"Craig . . ."

He dropped a slow kiss on the top of her shoulder.

"At least we've got rid of Mr. Levin." He laughed out loud, a deep laugh of pure pleasure. "I was lying when I said I didn't know why I was chasing you. I knew, okay. That you were the most sensational girl I'd ever met. One in a million. And now this, now this." He kissed her. "Man, you are just wonderful, Jane Morgan."

Jane hung her head. "What have I done?"

"I could remind you," he said. "If you have short-term memory problems."

"Stop it," she protested, smiling a little. Was it possible he could have her again? Three times, in rapid succession; he had the vitality of a teenager.

"I'm done," he said, sighing. "At least, I think I am. You're dangerous. It's a good job I keep in shape." He pulled away from her. "Let's shower. Together."

But Jane looked down, knotting her fingers together in the bed linen.

"Am I going to see you again?"

She was miserable now; her body felt good, but her heart was sick. This was it, exactly what she had feared. She'd wanted him, craved him, for months, and as soon as he touched her, she'd fallen into his hand like a ripe peach.

And he had made her body leap, and dance, and finally satisfied her, made her yield herself so completely that she was now helplessly and hopelessly in love with him.

But the chase was over; he'd got what he wanted. Now she was just another conquest.

Yet when she looked up at him, Craig Levin was looking right back at her. Disturbed, even upset.

"Do you think I'm that kind of man?" he asked. "Jane, I respect you. Hell, I think I'm even a little obsessed with you. I wouldn't use you like that."

"I don't know," she said. "That's the point. I hardly know anything about you."

Just that I want you, she did not say. *Just that I have to have you. Just that I think about you all the time.*

"So get in that shower by yourself," Levin said, his eyes flickering across her naked body, dappled by the moonlight, still warm from his touch. "And then get dressed. And come with me."

"What do you mean?" Jane asked, embarrassed to show that she was crying.

"You want to see me again? Because I want to see you, Jane."

She nodded; he knew her intimately, knew the intensity of her response to him; there was no point trying to hide anything now.

"Then why wait? See me again now. Come home with me. Spend the night at my place."

"We didn't even date," Jane said.

"So this will be our first. Dinner. I could eat. Couldn't you? Then breakfast. And I'll pick you up for lunch. That makes three dates in, what, eighteen hours?" He smiled at her. "I know how to play catch-up."

She slid her long legs off the bed. Even now, when she was trying not to hope, not to get overexcited, he was leaving her no choice. Jane tried to come to terms with it; where there were two people, she could not have total control; and she was afraid of how much she liked that.

"Okay," she said. "Okay."

"And you want me again. Like I want you, gorgeous."

Levin came and sat down on the bed, and stretched his hand out; she gasped again, pressed against him.

"You're hotter than hell," he said. "Hotter than I'd ever imagined. And I'd imagined plenty."

Levin gave her his hand. "Come on, Jane. Let me earn your trust."

⁓

It was strange how shy she was. After all that passion, after all her athleticism. Levin wore the marks of her nails raked across his inner thigh, the small of his back; her own skin was covered in small, delicate bruises from his lips and teeth. Yet they were now dressed, and sitting in his dining room—or one of his dining rooms. Over the dinner table. It was a romantic setting: candlelight, Sèvres porcelain dishes, fresh flowers. But Jane felt as nervous as a teenager.

"Come on. Eat something." Levin gestured at the slices of roast partridge, delicately fanned out in front of her, next to buttery parsnips and spinach. "If you don't like that, the chefs can get you something else."

"You've got more than one?" Jane joked.

"I've got five. But they rotate shifts."

Damn. She moistened her lips.

"I'm not hungry."

"After that, you must be." He forked up a floury roast potato, crisp and browned around the edges, and wolfed it. "I chose this because I thought it was British. But they can get you anything you like."

"I'm . . . I'm embarrassed," she murmured, and lowered her head. Levin watched her and, to his amazement, found himself stirring again. What a woman. Why was she like this? So reserved, and so beautiful?

"Because you don't know me? Other than in the biblical sense?"

"And the pages of *Fortune*," Jane admitted.

"Ah, yes. I recall you saying you 'admired' me." He grinned. "I hear that a lot. From you, it was a turn-on, though. Tell you what, I'll make a deal."

"A deal?"

"Eat your food. Drink some water, some juice. A glass of champagne. I don't want you passing out on me later."

"Later?"

"If you're good; no promises." She had to smile at that. "You eat, and I'll talk. The unofficial version of my life. Then you'll know me. Anything to get you to relax."

"Alright," Jane said softly.

Levin was unlike any man she'd ever known; he didn't buckle to her, or crumple in the face of her coldness. He stood firm. But he encouraged her.

She took a bite of the partridge; it was good, after all.

Craig poured himself some champagne, settled back in his chair. Smiled at her, and she felt herself unstiffen, open up to him.

He meant it. He was really going to woo her.

Starting with letting her in on his secrets.

"I don't have a rags-to-riches story. I grew up an only child, and that's about the only bad thing you can say of my early life. Dad worked in the Sanitation Department as an administrator; Mom was a court reporter. We had a little tract house in a decent part of Queens, back in New York, a nice car, took a vacation to the Jersey shore most summers. I had two working parents and a big extended Jewish family; we weren't religious, but there were still plenty of weddings, bar mitzvahs, you know. Most of my friends were Jews, too." He grinned. "I hated it, my life. Does that sound awful? Loved my folks, hated my life. It was so suburban. I felt so trapped. And at school, I was the weeny little Jew. There were bigger kids there who used to kick my ass on a regular basis. Dad wouldn't let me quit, said I had to be tough. Good girl—now drink some wine."

Jane took a sip. Warmth started to spread through her again, and she didn't think it was just the alcohol.

"There had to be more. I knew it. Every time I took a subway into the city—it was the seventies, it was full of crime, and dirty, but it was so exciting. Those skyscrapers—electric. Wall Street. The big theaters, Times Square, Fifth Avenue. Manhattan was life and Queens was nothing. It was like you had your nose permanently pressed up against life's shop window, and they wanted me to get a good union job. At the most, to get into real estate or become a school principal. I was brighter than most kids, they knew. Partly because of my memory; with a photographic memory you ace most multichoice tests. But mainly because I was good at math. Better than good. School bored the hell out of me."

"So what did you do?"

Now she had started eating, she was ravenous; Jane devoured her vegetables and helped herself to a slice of the raspberry cheesecake set on a silver platter in front of her.

"First, I joined the Y and started lifting weights. I waited till I was big enough to kick a little ass myself. They say violence never solved anything. Bullshit."

Jane grinned.

"Next I sat down and figured it out. If I wanted to get into Wall Street other than on the subway, I'd need to be a broker. So I started buying the *Wall Street Journal* with my allowance. Next I started figuring out the numbers, and the charts. Seeing patterns. Looking at stocks. I quit school early and my parents cut me off, but by that time I had a job as a gofer in a brokerage house. I used to give them tips—and they worked. They thought I had insider info." He smiled. "Nothing they couldn't have figured out if they were paying attention. But at eighteen I was a trader. Before I could drink, I owned my own apartment. Sound familiar?"

"So far," Jane said, inclining her head. "But I'll never be as successful as you."

"That's true," he said, cool as you like, and she thrilled to it. "You never will."

"Your parents forgave you?"

"Soon as they knew I'd be okay. I was a senior broker at twenty, VP at twenty-one. Had a nice little brownstone in the Village at twenty-three, drove a Ferrari. At twenty-four I quit. Started to put together a fund. You know most of the rest."

"I heard you were a workaholic."

"I don't see it as work." His eyes lit up, and she responded to his passion. "I love business, I love numbers. I can just . . . I *see* stocks. I don't know how else to explain it. For me, trading is like a computer game. Winning is fun. Money is fun. Five chefs—I always wanted this, I wanted to live like my house was a hotel. Got lots of staff and I pay them outrageous wages. Give lots to charity. My parents are in Florida now, in a mansion with a private beach. I keep my head down, I don't talk to the press, I just play the game. And I win, nineteen times out of twenty."

"And the twentieth?"

"Maybe I sabotage myself sometimes. Just to make it interesting."

"So." She spooned up the last of the cheesecake, meltingly sweet, the tartness of the raspberries a perfect contrast. "Tell me about your personal life."

"I thought I just did. Oh—you mean women?"

"I mean women," Jane said, her eyes narrowing.

Levin smiled. "There have been a few girls. I like beautiful women. I never promised any of them anything serious, unless I meant it. I've had three proper girlfriends—one for six months, one for two years, another for a year. It just didn't work out in those cases."

"Why not?"

"If I knew that, I never would have asked them out," he said, reasonably.

"And me?"

"You're different. Incredibly so."

"Tell me why."

"Let's go to bed."

"Before bed."

"Don't trust yourself, in my arms, to be objective?" Levin grinned. "Very well. You are more intelligent and more independent. I never dated fluff—maybe when I was younger, there were a couple of trophy dates, cheerleaders for the New York Giants, that sort of girl. Later on, models, but always smart ones. One of my long-term girlfriends was a lecturer at Vassar." His eyes flickered across her. "None of them were like you. In business, a self-made woman. One who came back from a tragedy—an orphan. What you did with Shop Smart was amazing. And leaving your job was pretty great, too. Maybe it's vanity; I saw something of myself in you. You didn't want that comfort trap. A house in the suburbs or a vice president's salary, it's all bull if you know you can do better. And of course, there just aren't that many women who do well in business."

"Sexist pig."

"Come on." He defended himself against the accusation. "I respect you too much to bullshit you. It's the truth, and you know it. You and your girlfriends have something here. A good model. Excitement. Achievement. You're more than beautiful, and sexy, with that British accent—"

"English."

"Whatever. You're like me. You're in this game. You're"—he paused, then smiled—"not a civilian."

She smiled back, and stood up from the table.

"Not to mention that you're breathtakingly lovely," Levin added.

Jane held out her hands to him. She sensed she was in great danger, that he already had her heart, and she had surrendered every part of herself. Because she wanted so badly to believe that she was the one, she was the woman who could take him out of this life.

But her body was a traitor; it wanted him. Now.

He came over to her, leaving the rest of his food untouched.

"I thought you just wanted to sleep," he murmured, whispering into her neck, kissing it, his tongue tracing the line of the caress.

"That was then," Jane said. "And at least now we've had the first date."

The next day, he drove her home himself. Then called and asked her to lunch. And dinner.

Craig Levin was perfect. He talked with her, he made her

laugh, he dissected some of his business deals with her, asked her advice.

They relished each other's company. He complimented her all the time. Made Jane feel seven feet tall.

Soon, he became one of her best friends, as well as her lover. And that was fatal. It didn't matter what barriers she tried to keep up. He was great in bed, he made her laugh, and he appreciated everything about her.

Jane Morgan fell more in love as every day passed.

⁓

"You can trust me." Mrs. Wilkins—Emily—was firm. "She'll be fine. Won't you, princess? *Who's* a clever girl?"

Noor waved her little clenched fist and gurgled happily. She gave a gummy smile to her mother and her nanny.

"Do you know about warming the baby food? And don't use those commercial wipes. Just tissues in warm water, or she gets a rash . . ."

"Ma'am, I've brought up four of my own." The Irishwoman shook her head. "Now get in the cab. The sooner you go and do your trading, or whatever it is, the sooner you can come back to her." She gave Haya a shove. "They need you at work, too. Now go."

The limo driver honked his horn, and Noor scrunched up her face. She started to wail, and Haya wanted to, as well.

"Go," Emily Wilkins insisted.

Haya did as she was told, and as the limo door shut behind her, she watched the nanny put her baby comfortingly over her shoulder.

"LAX?"

"Just drive," Haya snapped. She turned her face to the window, so that he would not see the tears splashing out of her lashes.

Being a single mom and a businesswoman could be hard sometimes. Whenever she had to leave Noor, she hated it.

Everybody in L.A. knew who Haya al-Yanna was now. He said a quick "Yes, ma'am," and stepped on it. Suited her fine.

The last year, she had been there for all Noor's important milestones. When she sat up, her fat chin wobbling. When she was weaned. The glorious moment when she crawled. But combining it with buying for the store, then the stores, was exhausting. Haya inspected, ordered, and arranged as best she could from Los Angeles, either from the GLAMOUR headquarters or her home office. And Noor sat and crawled with her.

But the business was expanding so rapidly, Haya knew she'd have to let her nanny take a little bit more of the slack. She wanted to keep her place at the top table, by right. Noor was older now, a confident and happy toddler. And Haya felt the old tug, the challenge, of her career pulling at her.

It was time to step things up. She had to leave her comfort zone for a few days, go to the source of her goods, her commerce. And it was exciting that the first stop was Ghada.

She knew she had no choice. Haya couldn't stay in the States forever. Not with the way GLAMOUR was going. They had lines at the store daily, just to get in. Jane was negotiating with some defunct American chains, trying to buy up real estate, looking for a good lease on Fifth or the Avenue of the Americas, jetting off to Paris and London. Sally, when she took an evening off from the ballpark, was turning into a bona fide star; her days were spent designing, her nights at glittering premieres, jetting off to talk shows, or giving interviews for magazines. They called her "fashion's Martha Stewart" and, more cruelly, "Business Barbie." But Sally rode it all like a pro, and every single item she wore in public was sourced from the GLAMOUR store.

Their next opening was to be New York, and Jane and Sally had personally begged Haya to come back. Ethical business was a money-spinner—the women's magazines loved what they were doing with local craftswomen, and when Sally posed in *Women's Wear Daily* wearing her own new trademark, a floor-length red velvet sheath, with one of the Ghadan necklaces draped around her long neck, orders had just gone wild.

"We have only a few hundred carpets—we're on a waiting list."

"The jewelry sold out weeks ago. We've got empty sections of the store."

"Haya," Jane insisted, "you can't just go on buying trips; what you have to do is find staff—buyers—people you trust. They can purchase the ethical trade in bulk as long as it's up to standard. We can't jeopardize the brand."

"Jane found a spot in Venice, too. We have to have enough for six new stores. By year's end it'll be twelve." Sally grinned. "Say hello to GLAMOUR Tokyo."

"I suppose you're right. There's just no way I can fulfill that number of orders." Haya was excited. "Is it really that busy?"

Sally groaned. "Please come back."

Haya glanced around her nursery, at the infant toys everywhere. Of course she adored Noor, her little sunshine, but . . . it was time to get back to adulthood; Haya had missed her friends, missed her business.

"So, recruit buyers?"

"At least twenty. I can give you a salary structure. Please don't deviate from it," Jane said.

Haya spread her hands. "Staffing is your baby. They have to be the right women, though, people I trust not to buy any old junk, and only to pick the right suppliers. . . ."

"You could hire male buyers. As long as we maintain the policy of sourcing from poor women," Sally said, "our customers want that. It's a little bit of sisterhood in with the designer jeans. Like fair trade chocolate."

"Okay, then." Haya nodded; she would need the help. With a baby, no way could she go back to full-time jet-setting. "I think I'll pick buyers in every country—you know, somebody in Egypt, in Morocco—to look for the different goods."

"It's your turf," Jane said. "Handle it however you want."

Haya agreed. The frazzled faces of her girlfriends had added the coda: *but handle it.*

Fair enough. And so now she was on her way back, to Ghada City. Leaving Noor behind for four whole, brutal days.

It had to be done; but she didn't have to like it.

⟍⟋

"Welcome, Ms. Al-Yanna." The desk clerk was all smiles. "It's good to have you back, ma'am. I hope you enjoy your stay in Ghada."

"Thank you."

"Your meetings have been arranged in the Roosevelt Conference Room for nine a.m. tomorrow, as requested."

"Great. If I could just get my room key . . ."

Haya was very tired; it had been a long day, and she was looking forward to a quick TV supper and then bed.

"Here you are. The presidential suite—take the penthouse elevator, second on the left."

"I didn't book that suite . . . ," Haya said wearily. She hoped that this wouldn't delay her all that long; tomorrow's work started early.

"No, ma'am. It is a complimentary upgrade. And we have a message to deliver to you," the receptionist said with a coy smile, "from His Highness, Sheikh Jaber."

Haya blinked with shock. He remembered her?

They had negotiated with the Ghadan palace through the office, and over the phone; Haya had sent documents via one of Jane's assistants. She had never expected to hear from Jaber again.

"Here." The receptionist handed her over an envelope: thick vellum, with a small gold crest, a stylized palm tree, on the back. "Shall I have a bellhop show you to the suite?"

"No, thank you, I'll manage."

Haya walked into the elevator, barely noticing her surroundings; her case was compact, neatly packed with lightweight, long dresses. She rode up to the presidential suite; it was incredibly luxurious, with tinted windows on four sides looking out over Ghada City. Haya gave it a cursory glance, dumped her suitcase on the bed, and ripped open the note.

Dear Ms. Al-Yanna,

Congratulations on the birth of your daughter. The Office of Protocol has kept me up-to-date with developments with your company; His Majesty's government is quite satisfied with the funds that have flowed in to our citizens thus far. We are willing to consider further involvement of the royal family in exchange for more significant orders worldwide.

I would, however, prefer to discuss such matters with you personally. Could you call the palace and confirm if you are free for lunch on Saturday at one o'clock?

Wa-es salaam,
Jaber

Stop it, Haya told herself. *You're reading way too much into this.* He is a handsome young sharif, not a man to be tempted by a widowed single mother. And anyway, what if he was? She was a partner at GLAMOUR, Inc., and he worked for the government here. They could hardly form a relationship flying back and forth across the Atlantic.

But it was no good; her heart pounded as she dialed the number on the stationery. She should just see it as a business success.

Whatever. It was thrilling. Haya gave herself permission to enjoy that. She thought of Ahmed, her love. He would not mind, if anything was to happen. Before, she had felt guilty; now that she had his Noor to love and cherish, she felt, instead, an overwhelming peace.

Haya looked round the suite, properly. She understood at once why she had been given the best room in the hotel. As hot as GLAMOUR was, there were other rich businessmen here. No, this came from the favor of His Highness. And she took every lavish inch of it as a compliment.

"Good afternoon," said a voice in Arabic.

"Hello. My name is Haya al-Yanna—"

"Oh, yes, thank you for calling, madam. Will you be able to join His Highness for lunch?"

"Yes, I will," Haya said, taken aback that the operator knew so fast.

"That's wonderful news. We will send a government car to your hotel at twenty to one, if convenient. If you could bring your passport for identification."

"Thank you," Haya said. A government car! She couldn't believe it. Why was he laying out the red carpet?

"We'll see you tomorrow, madam, *insh'Allah*. Have a wonderful day."

She hung up and went into the suite's sumptuous bathroom; it had a stand-alone tub made of pure copper that you could almost swim in. Tomorrow morning she had interviews, eighteen candidates for six positions, and they would have to be done by twelve forty.

Haya could manage it. She had learned to trust her instincts. Those with a love of beauty and of Ghada would stand out. The important thing was to get them hired, fast, lose the deadwood, and then come back here. Whether she was right about Jaber's interest or not, she had to look fabulous. If she could get a true princess of this country involved . . . forget it! GLAMOUR's PR and marketing would explode just as Jane was opening the new stores.

Haya had been out of commission for a while. She wanted to contribute, to be as much a part of this as Sally and Jane. Originally, they had been the two friends; Haya had come in late. She did not want to be an outsider, the third wheel, in GLAMOUR.

If she could bring more sizzle than Sally . . . then nobody could accuse her of being some kind of afterthought.

⁓

"Here we are, ma'am. Passport, please."

Haya meekly handed it over. The chauffeur—or was he a soldier, in his Ghadan uniform with the palm trees on his epaulettes?—passed it across to the guard at the gate. Haya leaned forward, out of the window, and looked down the drive to the palace complex.

It was exquisitely beautiful. Vast, and covered with blue and gold tiles, like the decoration on a Pharaoh's headdress. It glittered in the sun like jewelry, and the gardens they had driven through on their way here stretched ahead of her, lush and beautifully stocked. There were fountains playing in the courtyards, and Haya noted the brickwork, old and red. There was something of the Alhambra about this place. She shivered with tension. Did she look good enough? She had selected a traditional Jordanian caftan, red silk, embroidered with gold thread, antique, stretching down to her ankles and flowing beautifully about the body; almost no makeup, just a touch of foundation and some lip gloss and mascara; and a delicate scent, Chanel No. 19, one Haya had always favored, fresher and greener than the more famous brand. Round her neck, she wore a jangling, original Ghadan coin necklace, one from GLAMOUR's own stock; it was disturbingly sensual, she thought, like bells on her when she moved.

"Thank you." Her passport was returned to her, and the limo pulled through the ornate carved gates, covered in Moroccan-style mosaic work. Haya tried not to stare as the driver took her around the left wing of the palace, past marching guards, into a small courtyard, and parked in a spot they were waved to by a saluting guard, who came round to open the door.

"Greetings, madam," he said in thickly accented English.

"Thank you," Haya responded in Arabic. The soldier smiled, and lapsed into his native tongue.

"*Sidi* Jaber is waiting in his office. . . . If you'll come this way." Haya nodded, and was led through marble corridors of unimaginable opulence, set about with wooden panels carved in an intricate Islamic design, to a small, modern room—part of a cleverly designed extension—where Jaber was sitting.

He jumped to his feet.

"Your guest, Highness," the soldier said, bowed slightly, and withdrew.

"Haya." He came forward, and clasped her shoulders warmly, kissing her on both cheeks in the Arab fashion; Haya, feeling awkward, clumsily dropped a low curtsy.

Jaber raised an eyebrow. "You do not have to curtsy to me. Although your manners are as beautiful as your face."

She blushed, deeply; hopefully she was tanned enough that he would not notice.

"I was delighted to get your letter, sir," she began, formally.

"Good. And it's Jaber. I won't have to spend the afternoon calling you Ms. Al-Yanna, will I?"

She shook her head. "Haya."

"Then come." He extended a hand. "I have had them cook for us in my mother's apartments—she is at an Arab children's conference in Dubai."

Haya tried to eat, if only to be polite; she was a guest, it was rude to refuse hospitality. But she was intimidated. Stroppy American businessmen, rude suppliers, government customs officials who enjoyed demonstrating their power; none of them had made her feel like this. She respected Ghada, and Jaber; it was a beautiful country, a rich country, and yet they cared about the nomads, the tribeswomen, the indigent widows she was trying to protect.

And here she was, in a small corner of the center of power. And he was across the table, as deferential servants attended him, and then her; incredibly handsome, charming, and powerful—not so much in the abstract way one describes a banker or a newspaper magnate, as one having influence, but absolutely, in his own right. As a government official, and a member of a ruling family that still ruled.

Jaber took his time. He made small talk with her, about the store, the candidates she had interviewed, the GLAMOUR expansion program.

"And you?" he asked, at length, when she was picking through a delicate pastry of roasted chicken and raisins. "You are taking a full part in this? You look to me as though you were never pregnant at all, although of course I know differently."

"This is my first trip abroad since Noor was born."

"And it will be profitable," he said, with a calm assurance. "I wonder, have you been following events here in Ghada?"

Haya was embarrassed. "I haven't—I have hardly listened to any news since she was born—I was nursing . . . busy in the office." Her voice trailed off. Was that too intimate a detail to have shared with him? Why was she starting to think of Jaber as a friend, rather than who he was? "Anyway," she added hastily, "I think the *New York Times* on the plane on the way over was the first paper I've really read in months. Please excuse my ignorance, High—" She caught a sight of his face. "Jaber."

"Much better," he said. "And don't worry. I find it refreshing. Anyway, His Majesty has decided to honor my mother, his cousin, who is widowed, by raising her to the rank of a princess here, with the title Royal Highness. Under our law, these things are at his absolute discretion."

"That's wonderful," Haya responded automatically, trying to work out what that meant for her company. She already had photos of the sharifa—now princess—in GLAMOUR jewels. Was her work here done, then? They could start a whole new ad campaign on that.

"And me," he said, matter-of-factly. "I have been involved in government, as you know. A little more than protocol; there was a dispute with Dubai over some oil pipelines. We managed to reconcile it. I was directly involved with the king in the matter."

Haya was confused. "And he moved you out of the protocol section?"

"I am now foreign minister," Jaber said. He shrugged. "And my rank has been raised to emir, prince."

Haya digested this. "You are a Royal Highness now?"

"Yes."

"I can't go on just calling you Jaber."

"To do otherwise would be most discourteous," he replied.

The servant arrived with a service of mint tea and sweetmeats to round off the meal; Haya thanked him profusely, glad of any distraction. Jaber waved a hand, dismissively; at once the waiter and the other servants melted away.

"You do not need to court us," he said brusquely. "I, and

my mother, am convinced of your bona fides. My mother will work to promote the Ghadan goods you sell. You can arrange it through my successors in Protocol."

"Thank you." Haya nodded; that would be a real coup. It was what she had come for. But now, should she leave? Her business was concluded.

"I was wondering if you would consider spending the afternoon with me," he said, his words suddenly coming out in a rush, uncharacteristically fast. "Not for business—on a date."

Haya half jumped in her carved chair. He had asked her—he had actually asked.

"I—yes, thank you," she said shyly.

"That's good news." He grinned back, as though tension had been released. "There are some wonderful Persian ruins outside of the city. I thought you might like to go and see them. No chauffeurs—I have my own car."

~

She walked with him around the glorious, crumbling, ancient walls of Shirah, marveling at the winged lions with the heads of bearded men, the carved vulture gods, and cuneiform writing littered around the streets on half-tumbled pillars, now lying amid scrubby desert grass while lizards and butterflies played around them.

"It's truly magnificent."

"We want to promote this as a tourist destination." Jaber smiled at her. "I'm glad you like it. My house is near here."

"You have a villa in the royal complex?"

"I do now."

Haya nodded. He had told her something of his life: father dead at three, his mother fighting to give him as much normalcy as possible; education in Britain, with a stint in the army as an officer in the Desert Rats; trying to find a place for himself in government, wanting to be useful. And he had probed Haya, gently but efficiently, about Ahmed, about her parents, America, Noor, every part of her life. When she told him about Miss Milton's,

Jaber smiled wryly; he, too, had been bullied at school in the West.

She found herself trying for reserve. He was so intelligent, so charming, and yet so sharp; and obviously, there was no future for her with him. *Nice to go on this date,* Haya was telling herself, *but you'd be a moron to get those hopes up.*

"The promotion of your family by the king must have been a great joy."

"I'd be lying if I said my mother wasn't thrilled," Jaber admitted frankly. "Not so much at the rank, although that's nice for her. But over what it meant for me. King Nazir trusts me. And he's old; there's jockeying among his sons over the succession. So for a while, I can do things—change things. We're building schools in every district, establishing a court system. Eventually I'd like the monarchy to be nothing more than decorative, like it is for the Brits. But it will take time. At least now I can make a start."

"And I suppose the king will select a princess for you?" Haya teased.

He stopped and looked deeply into her eyes; surprised, she could not hold his gaze.

"I'm old-fashioned. I don't believe in divorce. I don't want a succession of wives. The woman must be right—she must be perfect. I have made it clear I will not accept an arranged marriage."

"I understand." Haya would not look up at him. She tried to change the subject. "Look at that amphitheater . . . amazing."

Jaber was having none of it.

"Yes, let's sit," he said. "I want to say something to you."

Haya allowed herself to be led to a shady spot; they sat together on the white limestone benches, thousands of years old, with a view of the arena; she wondered if men had died here. It was an old land, beautiful, and full of ghosts.

"I'd like to see you," he said. "A lot. I think you're beautiful. You're modest, and a lady, but you have something else. A steel spine. You started this amazing business, you flew round the world building it up, you found a way to make money and to help others. I admire how you work with your friends from the West. Yet you are a believer. Your daughter has a Muslim name."

Haya smiled. "Her father insisted I change my own. He never liked anglicization."

"And you have guts; you're not afraid to talk of your husband to me. I would not have admired a woman who could abandon his memory."

"I loved him."

"That is clear." Jaber put it to her with that directness she liked. "Tell me now, before I fall too deeply. Could you ever love again?"

"It is possible," Haya said. "I only loved Ahmed when I got to know him. . . . I don't want to rush marriage again, Jaber."

"No. Of course." He was eager. "And you have a child. And an enterprise of your own. I see that you are not about to be mine for the asking, Haya. So I have a proposal. Not of marriage," he added, with a grin, and she smiled. "Yet. Why do you not establish yourself in Ghada for six months? You can have offices here, you can go on short trips, by car, with your child; I will have the palace provide a nanny, or two. You can buy locally and send your deputies further afield, to Europe. We have all the major technologies you would need—phones, fax. Running water." He winked. "In essence, you could establish a department here, a buying division. Which you could head. That would consolidate your position in the stores more than a few one-off purchasing jaunts. Meanwhile, your child can grow here, where she will hear Arabic spoken every day."

"And I can see you?"

"I never said I had no ulterior motives." Jaber shrugged. "Let us see if we like each other, really. Whether or not you do, you will have my protection. In the end, if you can't stand me, what have you lost? Nothing. Your career will be advanced."

She thought about it. She did love Ghada. And she did want to be the equal of Sally, and Jane. It would mean leaving them behind, of course. Haya would be breaking up the trio, for the second time. . . .

But GLAMOUR was big now. Bigger than all of them. It could no longer be run by three friends making it up as they went along. Haya had tasted power, and competence, and she had liked it. Anita Roddick had managed her own global empire in ethical commerce and become a billionaire in her own right. Why not Haya al–Yanna?

"It is a brilliant idea," she said. "Of course, I will have to discuss it with my friends."

"But if they say no?"

She looked at him, and at the beauty of the Persian ruins, with the desert horizon stretching out westward in a shimmering haze of heat.

"I will still come," Haya said. She smiled. "I have got used to making my own decisions."

⁓

They discussed it over dinner, two days after she got back and found Noor thriving and not particularly overwhelmed to see her; the baby was engrossed in loud banging on a tin drum Emily Wilkins had bought her.

Haya grimaced. "What did I ever do to you?"

"Hurrrr," said Noor, happily, smashing her wooden spoon down.

"Ah, let her enjoy herself. I'll be putting her down in a minute." Emily cluck-clucked over the baby, who gurgled and buried her chubby cheeks in Haya's skirt. "You have a bath and go to your meeting. You can see she survived."

"All right," Haya laughed, looking at her daughter. Wondering how she would cope in the desert. And how Haya would cope without her two friends.

⁓

They dressed up for the meal. Nobody suggested it; all three women knew they had to. At this point, they were minor celebrities, and Sally was turning into a major one. Haya chose a sweeping, floor-length gown of Egyptian cotton in bright yellow, embroidered with green thread, a Kate Spade purse, and one of the jangling Ghadan bracelets; her feet were encased in buttercup yellow leather Manolo strappy sandals with sky-high heels. Sally wore her own red dress, with a GLAMOUR necklace of rubies by Montfort Jewels; Jane chose a cream silk suit with pearls, Wolford tights, and Christian Louboutin shoes in dove gray.

They met at the Ivy, and posed for pictures outside; arms around each other, smiling and laughing; all three knew the snap would make the business press the next day, Sally in the middle, the golden girl sheathed in in-your-face scarlet; Haya, ethnic, elegant, and stunning, the creamy yellows bright against her clear olive skin; Jane, English and reserved, the picture of the sexy businesswoman.

"I know what this is about," Sally said glumly as soon as the waiter had departed. "It's Noor, isn't it, Haya? You're quitting, right? You've hired those buyers, and you're quitting. You want to stay home."

Jane looked at her quizzically.

"I'm not quitting." Haya felt the tears well up; it had been such a wonderful ride with them, so rewarding, and thrilling; success on their own terms, and a friendship that had lasted all through their lives. "But I am leaving."

CHAPTER 13

Haya explained her proposition, leaving out the part about Jaber; that was too precious, and too fragile, a thing to talk about, just now.

Jane listened in silence and then looked over at Sally.

"You can't leave!" Sally was saying. "We'll never manage . . ."

"But we will," Jane said. "And actually . . . I think I should go, too."

Sally blinked. "What?"

"To New York."

"I don't get it. Who's gonna train the staff?" Sally demanded. "And what are you talking about? I can't manage the damn store by myself."

"I have VPs there now who can train the staff. Ari Gabriel, he's brilliant. Lillian Kovac. I trust them. You have to delegate. Even you, Sal."

"Salads, ladies!"

The waiter put down their salads with the fried soft-shell crabs, wittered on about the wine list, and mercifully, eventually, vanished.

"We're too big," Jane said, simply. "You guys have to decide what you want. The company can't go on like this, with us in L.A. I need to be in New York. I'll do the banking, the real estate, the distribution deals. Sally—you're the designer and the public face; you *are* GLAMOUR—what every little girl wants to be.

We don't need you stuck in a back office in L.A., we need you out there, on magazine covers. And if you're the face, Haya is the soul. She needs to establish the fair-trade business and get a steady flow of goods and art to stock multiple stores around the world. Which will mean building up a buying division. She can do that properly in the region, not here. She's wasted in L.A. So am I. But it's where you should be—you're the *star*."

Haya told them about Jaber's mother.

"I love it!" Sally momentarily forgot her anger. "Get a princess to a photo shoot? I'll do it with her. That'll make *Elle*. Maybe *Vanity Fair,* if we do it right."

"You're the glitz, Sal; now we have some royal gravitas. That'll help in New York. All they talk about is the American Queen of Jordan." Jane grinned. "My goodness, girls, this is really going to be big."

"And it means we can't stay together?" Sally asked glumly.

"It's not like we won't be friends," Haya replied. "We still will."

"I know it has to happen." Sally sounded heartbroken. "I just . . . I didn't think it would be this soon."

"It's just life," Haya said, and examined Jane. "There's a man, isn't there? Craig Levin. He lives in New York."

"He has a house here," Jane said defensively.

"But he mainly lives there."

She couldn't deny it. "It may have something to do with this, yes."

Sally clapped her hands. "The ice maiden melts?"

Jane blushed. "God help me, I love him," she said; and her girlfriends thought she sounded a little despairing. "But that's why you can stay here, Sally, isn't it? You're practically living with Chris Nelson."

Sally blushed. "Actually, I am living with him. I moved in yesterday."

"What about your mom?"

"She's in a guest cottage at his estate in Malibu, but she's talking about getting her own apartment. There's a luxury block in Century City." Sally smiled. "She likes Chris—doesn't want to scare him off. And she doesn't need me anymore."

"And you?" Sally flicked her fountain of glossy, blonde hair. "Haya . . . you have been very quiet on the subject. But I know these things. There's something in your eyes. Is there a man?"

"Possibly." She wouldn't say any more. "In Ghada . . . but I don't know; we haven't really started going out yet. . . ."

"Well, you'll need to be back here in six months," Sally said firmly. "With or without your date."

"And why is that?"

"We weren't going to announce it, but since you two are skipping town . . ." Sally lowered her voice. "Chris and I are getting married."

~~~

"Sally!"

"Sally Lassiter! Over here!"

"Give us a smile, baby! Let's see that rock!"

Sally turned and waved, and gave them a dazzling smile. "There you go." She extended her finger, to display the princess-cut natural pink diamond, three carats, a million dollars.

"I have to go shopping," she informed the crowd of photographers, blinking her long lashes at them.

"Sal! Gonna get your wedding dress in the store?" somebody shouted.

She practically purred. "Of *course*. What do you think inspired me to open GLAMOUR's bridal boutique? And I'm getting my wedding day scent specially blended for me in GLAMOUR Paris. Chris and I are going there on our honeymoon."

They loved it. The flashbulbs popped again. She was now almost as famous as he was. But Sally was quick on her feet; she turned and dashed into the store, waving to shoppers who were dizzy with excitement, while security guards escorted her to the staff elevator. Make them wait outside; the press always had to be left hungry, wanting more. Sally was shopping at GLAMOUR for the sports wedding of the year. That was what they needed to know.

"Great stuff out there." Maxi, her assistant and PR booker,

rushed to greet her, bearing Sally's usual tall glass of fizzy water and crushed ice with lime.

"You watched?"

"From a window. You work them like you were born to it."

Oh, I was, Sally thought.

"And the *New York Times* called. They want to do a Style section feature on you and GLAMOUR ..."

"Say yes."

"*Access Hollywood* wants to film the wedding ..."

"No, but they can do a short bit at the reception."

"Ma'am, it's Mr. Nelson on line one," said one of the secretaries.

"What are you doing, baby?"

"I'm at the store. Getting the gown. So don't pick me up, it's bad luck."

"At the store?" he grumbled. "Damn, girl, you are such a salesman. Even with our wedding."

"They watch me ... you know that."

"Don't I just," Nelson said darkly.

"Don't be mad. I'm running out the back door, I'll be with you soon." She wanted to tell him about all the new magazine covers, the TV slots, the offer from Hollywood that she was turning down—business was the star, and she, Sally Nelson, *was* GLAMOUR. "I'll make it up to you, baby," she promised.

Sally could hear his grin through the phone. "You certainly will."

"Mark Cohen on two." She punched the line to hang up on Chris and pick up Mark. Wow! This store was a rocket. If she didn't physically leave the building, her phones would never stop ringing. Mark was Jane's latest hire, shipped in from New York to be the general manager of GLAMOUR L.A., their original, flagship store. Jane had insisted they run every store like a first-class hotel.

"We got the extension from the city."

"Fabulous." Haya and Ahmed's place was way too small; they had discovered that months ago. Now she could concentrate on building something glorious. Lots of smoked glass, she thought, and an indoor garden, with fully grown trees, like they had in the lobby of CAA . . .

"And the monthly sales figures have *tripled*. We're selling stock as fast as we can ship it in." Cohen was ecstatic. "Ms. Morgan called and told me to pass on to you that three more consortiums have made offers. She also wants a meeting to consider going public." He paused. "Ms. Lassiter, what with the amazing figures from the opens in New York and London . . . do you understand how rich you are now?"

"Doesn't matter. We've only just started," Sally said coolly. "And tell Ms. Morgan's assistant I'll call her back."

She hung up, told Maxi to deal with her messages, and got ready to sneak out the back door.

She had an important appointment. With a realtor, and her fiancé. *Let's face it,* Sally thought. *Life is pretty damn sweet.*

⌒

Chris whistled a little, as soon as the pushy broker had left them to themselves.

"This is quite a house," he said. "Are you sure we need this much space?"

"Think of the fun we'll have christening every room."

He kissed her, one of those slow, lingering kisses that got her squirming and impatient.

"If you like the place, folks, ask is twenty," said the agent, bustling back in after half a minute. Sally pulled away from her fiancé, annoyed.

"We need much more time to think about it. Please give us some privacy."

"Oh, certainly," the woman said. "But I have another viewing at five o'clock."

"If you don't leave right now, I'll call the owners and tell them you personally cost them a sale."

The agent bolted.

"Tough cookie," Chris said, admiringly, feeling her ass; Sally shifted under her dress, wanting him, right there on the kitchen floor. "But baby . . . twenty mil. I'm not *that* rich. Sorry."

"We'll bid fifteen," Sally said. "They'll take it. I have to have this house."

"There are lots of other good ones. . . ."

"You're not that rich, but I am," she interrupted, kissing him back, stretching up on her toes to do it. "GLAMOUR . . . it's doing well. More than well." She summarized for him.

"Man." He blew out his cheeks. "When I met you, you were living in a scummy walk-up apartment. Is the store really that hot?"

Sally nodded proudly. "Hey, at least I know you're not marrying me for my money!"

Chris gave her a slap on the rear. "Just for that, when I get you home, I'm gonna make you work out naked."

"Promises, promises," Sally teased back; but she was turned on, and he could see it.

Chris took her hand. "Let's go. I want to see you on that exercise bike . . ." He whistled loudly, and the realtor came running back in.

"Fifteen mil. Not a cent over. And they're lucky my fiancée likes the place," he said dismissively. "Call me back only if you have a signed contract. Come on, sweetness. . . ."

And he ushered her out, back to the car.

They hadn't driven more than half a mile before the car phone rang.

"Chris? It's Jemma."

"That's Mr. Nelson," he said sharply. Neither of them liked the woman.

"Yes, sir," she said eagerly. "They've accepted! I'm having a signed contract messengered over to Malibu. Congratulations! I'm sure you'll enjoy Beverly Hills . . ."

"Good. You'll get the money wired by tomorrow." He punched the button and hung up. "Looks like you got it, baby." Nelson shook his head. "Man, that place is so big it's like owning my own country. It's a long way from the Bronx." He casually lifted her skirt with his left hand, and felt her inner thigh. "So why did that place appeal to you so much? There are lots of other mansions. . . ."

"You don't understand," Sally said. "That was my home. My dad's place. The one they threw us out of." Her face was bright with a fierce pride. "And now it's mine again. Mom can live in the guest cottage. Maybe one day I'll give it to her."

He was shocked. "Fifteen million?"

"The way things are going, we'll soon be able to afford six of them," Sally told him.

"Man, what am I doing in practice all day?"

"Getting ready to win the World Series?"

"There is that, I guess." His hand went higher. "You're still gonna be working out naked. Somebody has to keep you under control."

～⌒

"Have you seen the latest consignment?" Haya was angry. "I expect quality control, Muna. You can't assume honesty."

"Nine times out of ten—"

"Ninety-nine out of a hundred," Haya interrupted. "But we serve an amazingly expensive, luxurious chain. I need the quality to be there *one hundred times* out of one hundred. When I made a surprise inspection at the Cairo docks I found four machine-woven carpets. Machine-woven! Do you know the scandal that would cause, if we misrepresented them? Furthermore, do you understand what that means?"

The older woman hung her head. "That the suppliers did not buy them from the artisans?"

"Exactly. So not only are we being cheated, some poor woman who depends on us for her survival is, too. . . ."

"It won't happen again, *Siti* Haya."

"It better not. Or you're fired. And don't call me *Siti*," Haya snapped. They were always doing that—she hated it, all the assumptions, the idea that Jaber would marry her in due course, make her his. . . .

The more she was seen at the palace, the more they said it was a done deal.

When she talked with him, she was free to be herself. He was intelligent, strong, and masculine, and yet respectful of her—interested in her business, and how she was shaping it. Jaber relaxed her, and she knew that however hard she tried not to, she was falling for him. . . .

Yet in the last month, he had withdrawn from her. They had met for dinner only twice, and he was moody and distracted. The only time he seemed like his old self was when he played with Noor, already toddling around.

There was some other woman, Haya was sure of it. And her heart ached at the thought. She loved Ghada now with a passion, but she couldn't stay here; couldn't turn on the TV, read the local papers and see the emir, the favored foreign minister, accompanied by a new princess, his chosen bride; Jaber worked hard for charity; he would attend every benefit, every concert Haya got involved with. And as one of the world's most successful Muslim businesswomen, that would be quite a few. Haya and GLAMOUR were famous in Ghada. Famous across the Middle East. She had insisted on sticking to her principles—ethics *and* profit—and people loved her for it. Haya only talked to the regional press. The company had its strategy; let golden Sally be the face of GLAMOUR in the West.

So she would have to move. And Haya had already decided she would go back to Amman, live in a villa, somewhere secluded and safe for Noor to grow up in; the country her father had left for America; with her, it would come full circle. She would always love the States. But she would live with her heritage.

"I understand," Muna said, chastened. "I'll check them all personally, Ms. Al-Yanna."

There was a hard rap on the door.

"Come in," Haya called.

A soldier opened the door; he wore the epaulets of the royal house and had a gun at his belt. Muna shrank back, toward Haya, who instinctively stepped in front of her employee.

"What do you want?" Haya asked, fighting to stay calm.

"Madam, you must come with me," he said in guttural English. "It is His Royal Highness who orders it."

"I'm not going anywhere."

He looked at her, his eyes expressionless. "I have orders to take you by force if necessary. It is for your own protection." He lifted the gun. "Please come."

Haya was terrified; her palms started to sweat from adrenaline. "What's going on?" she cried. "Where is Noor? *Where is Noor?*"

"There is trouble at the palace. Your baby and her nanny have already been collected—they are at His Highness's compound." He moved forward to grab her, but Haya was already ahead of him.

"Take me to my daughter," she said firmly. "At once. Do you hear me?"

Startled, the soldier gave a small bow.

"Yes, *Siti,*" he said.

This time, she did not object.

∽

"You're here." He walked over to her and kissed her on both cheeks. "*Mash'Allah,* you are safe."

"And Noor?" They were standing in his private apartments, and Haya was still shaking; the ride through the streets, her car, armored, flanked with five riders with guns, had taken fire; screaming, she had dropped to the floor. The center of Ghada City was on fire. People in the streets were running, yelling, throwing rocks. Even inside the royal compound, it was all different: rows of the palace guard, no longer ceremonial, AK-47s at their sides, were dressed for battle.

"She is upstairs. One of my servants will show you to a guest room. We have supplies, baby formula. You are too well known as my companion—they would have come for you."

"What's going on?"

"The sons of the crown prince are impatient; they have prepared a revolt. There are mercenaries here, and they intend to kill the king. I am to fight them. If I fail, take this." He looked behind him and withdrew some papers and money from a cabinet. "Passports in a false name for you and the child, money to take you across the border. My personal bodyguard will see you out of the palace."

Haya wept—she wanted to hold him, to kiss him. But they were not even engaged.

"Be careful," she blurted out. "Come back to me, come back safe. I pray you will come home!"

"It will be quick," he said grimly, and then, to her astonishment, he leaned forward and kissed her lightly on the lips.

"Haya—I love you. Maybe this is not the time or the place, but I have no choice. If we survive this, will you marry me?"

She opened her mouth to consent, but Jaber stopped her.

"I knew this was coming. It is why I did not ask you. But Haya, know this. If you are my wife, you cannot be directly involved in GLAMOUR anymore. You will be a princess. You will have to be merely a partner, and instead of commerce, perform other duties with me." He pressed her hand. "And they *are* duties, Haya, and there is no time off. So you will have to choose."

There was gunfire in the distance—she looked at him; now her heart was on the line, there was no choice. Not really, not when he might die.

"I accept," she said, and kissed his hand. "Go with God!"

He looked back at her, briefly, then picked up his gun, lying on the table, and rushed from the room.

A nursemaid in palace uniform crept into the apartments and gave Haya a small half curtsy.

"I will take you to your daughter," she said.

"Yes—let me see her." Haya's heart was full. Terror and joy and loss, mingled together. Oh, God! She loved him now, loved him so completely.

She had no idea what the night would bring. She clutched the papers to her. Of course, if she had to flee, she would flee. . . . Noor's safety came first. But she didn't want to go. She never wanted to leave Jaber.

The baby was toddling around the bedroom, with a frightened Emily Wilkins manfully trying to play with her; she laughed with delight at seeing Haya; there was another burst of gunfire outside the windows, closer this time.

Haya picked Noor up and covered her with kisses, slinging her over her shoulder.

"What are those?" Mrs. Wilkins asked, looking at Haya's papers.

"Safe conduct to get out. If you want to go, Emily, you can get an armed escort to the border. I'll see to it."

"I've grandchildren of my own." The older woman wrung her hands. "Oh, God! What shall we do?"

"It's absolutely fine if you want to leave, but I believe if there's unrest here, there will be at the airport, too. Prince Jaber has an armed force to protect us. I'm staying here," Haya said. She was cool and, the nanny thought, regal. "You must make your own decisions. There's plenty of money here, and a passport for you."

Mrs. Wilkins looked at her friend and employer, Haya's shoulders squared, the caftan swirling around her feet.

"If you think we should stay, we'll stay," she replied. "You've a smart head on your shoulders for a lass who's not even Irish."

Haya took control. She arranged calls for Emily Wilkins and herself to their worried families on a secure line; she dictated a will, and faxed it off to her father; she tried to distract the anxious staff in the villa by organizing the cooking of a meal on the single working gas ring in Jaber's kitchen. When the violence was close, so close you could hear the shots outside the gardens, less than a mile away, Haya sang nursery rhymes to Noor, loudly, so that the bangs and crashes would not frighten her.

By the time the baby was sleeping soundly—Haya had her cot moved into the center of the villa, into Jaber's own bathroom, as far away from the sounds of violence as possible—the fighting had died down. Into the night there were occasional bursts of gunfire, or a flare arcing overhead. Haya remained awake, with

her papers at her side. Ready to run, at any moment. Her bags for
Noor packed, by her feet.

⁓

At half past three he finally returned; there was blood on his
shirt, and some more that had dried in his beard. Exhausted, he
slumped on a couch in the reception hall; his servants gathered
around, and he muttered a few words in the Ghadan dialect; they
smiled and clapped.

Haya leaned forward anxiously. "It's okay? What happened?"

"They put down the coup attempt. The ringleaders are in
custody. Nobody liked them coming here with a foreign force;
in the end the men of the city took to the streets and destroyed
their vehicles. Then it was over."

"*Mash'Allah*. And you? Are you injured?"

"A knife wound. Don't worry," he bid her as she darted forward. "A doctor has dressed it. There was hand-to-hand fighting
at one point. They came within feet of the king."

"The man who wounded you?"

His eyes darkened. "I killed him." Jaber looked away. "I didn't
want to tell you of this, when I had my suspicions. But I should
have spoken up, warned you. Instead, I was too confident of their
loyalty. I put you in danger."

"You warned me." Haya was too shy to kiss him. "I just didn't
listen."

"Is the baby okay?"

"Fast asleep." She pointed in the direction of his bathroom.

"I have to sleep," he said apologetically. "I'm sorry; I am dropping. But call your parents, have them fly out here, first class on
the first plane, and anybody else you wish to be here. The palace
will reimburse them. We will sign the nikkah the day after tomorrow." He squeezed her hands. "That is, if you still wish it?"

"I do," Haya said, her heart full.

"And you will even give up your enterprise?"

"I will still own it," she said, with a touch of stubbornness.
"But otherwise, yes, I can see it is necessary."

"Good." Jaber sighed. "That will certainly make things a little easier. He'll be pleased that at least I persuaded you to that...."

"He?"

"The king, of course. He did not want me to marry you."

Despite the desperate circumstances, Haya felt a moment of shock and annoyance. "Why not?"

"You are a believer, but you are also an American. That's tricky. And not a virgin—and there is already a child."

Haya frowned. "That's backward thinking, Jaber."

"I know it." He shrugged. "But it is protocol. I have been trying to persuade the king for some months now, my love. It wasn't good to be seen with you."

"And if you had not been able to persuade him?"

"Then we would have left Ghada together." Jaber looked into her eyes. "You are not the only one who can fight for what she wants."

Haya was bold; she leaned forward and kissed him passionately on the lips.

"You sleep," she said, "my love. I will make some calls."

Jane Morgan tossed on her bed. It was Indian summer in New York, blisteringly hot and muggy. Her apartment was a ten-million-dollar penthouse on Fifth, overlooking the museum, a real palace, with eight bedrooms and four bathrooms. All her own. And now the air-conditioning had broken down.

There wouldn't be an engineer available till tomorrow, and who knew what time. She would be taking four cold showers a day just to keep from getting sweaty.

She bet the air-con was working just fine at Craig's place, in the Village.

Her body ached for him. Levin was like an addiction. Big, strong, thick, the perfect antidote to her softness—in body at least. And too much for Jane. She was struggling with her feelings. Trying, and failing, to give him up.

Craig wouldn't marry her.

They had been together now for over a year. Well—if you could call it together. Dating, and sleeping together, minus the sleep. Sex that was smoking hot. His touch was certain, and inexorable. She couldn't fight it, in any way that mattered. Levin turned her inside out. Jane would get aroused now whenever she so much as read his name in the papers. If she saw a clip of him—they were always brief—on TV, she would be useless for business for the next half hour, her unruly, frustrated body crying out for him.

And yet, and yet. He would not marry her. He had not asked. Jane had followed him to New York—but GLAMOUR needed her. Proud, she had purchased her own fabulous apartment, and hired full daily maid service, a concierge, and a gardener for her rooftop oasis; Levin shrugged, and kept his own town house in the Village, four thousand square feet of Victorian brownstone, right next to his fellow billionaire Magnus Soren. He would have this relationship on his own terms. Jane wanted it on hers. Not that she said anything explicit; Levin kept seeing her, she would not beg to be loved.

They both continued with their business. Jane worked like she never had before. Haya was sending excellent articles and generating lots of goodwill; Jane traded on it expertly. Sally Lassiter—now, there was a superstar. Jane rejoiced in seeing Sally's golden prettiness beaming out at her from the cover of *In Style* or *Women's Wear Daily*. Jane herself had a different following: smaller articles, fewer pictures, but ones that mattered to her. Her peers, those who read things other than fashion magazines, knew all about her.

To the girl on the subway, Sally was GLAMOUR. To the broker reading the *Wall Street Journal,* it was she, Jane Morgan. At a ridiculously young age, shaping up to be one of America's most notable businesswomen. There were others ahead of her, but Jane wanted to change all that.

Jane's real competition was Craig Levin.

He played in another league. Fact. Jane didn't want to compete in the girls' division. She wanted the championship. Yes, okay, she admitted to herself, as the sweat drenched her skin. When Craig used to tell her, his hands moving capably across her arching body, that he could buy and sell her ten times over, it was a turn-on. But in the morning, she tried to fight.

All her rage, all her frustration, she poured into her business. Expand. Invest. Supervise. Hire. Repeat. As the GLAMOUR empire spread—her empire, her baby—Jane's plans got bigger. Turn it into the Wal-Mart of luxe. Own the sector. They thought retail was dead until Sam Walton came along. Why not her?

Maybe one day she could compete with Craig, on his own terms. . . .

There were days when she didn't know if she loved him or hated him.

Sally was getting married. And her blithe, bubbly love of Chris Nelson grated on Jane. Whenever she saw Nelson on TV—and as the Dodgers were tied in the Series against the Red Sox, that was quite a bit—she was reminded. Chris was *marrying* Sally. He'd asked, she'd accepted, and it was to be just like the old days—a party at Sally's former house, with eight hundred of their closest friends.

Jane couldn't bear Craig to come with her. Couldn't bear the jokes. "So when is it *your* turn?"

"Gonna catch that bouquet, Jane?"

She was rich, beautiful, aristocratic, and a self-made woman, and yet, here she was, a slave to love. Sick with desire. Shamed to be so much Levin's, and know that he was not hers.

She thought, too often, about that first night, that long, intense night by the pool.

If only he had not come over. If only she had not had sex with him. Those fires, once lit in her belly, apparently could not be put out. And all Jane wanted to do was to cry out why—to ask him why he would not marry her.

But there could only be one answer, one she did not want to hear.

He didn't love her.

That was it. Wasn't it?"

She felt tears, private tears, wetting her cheeks, and let them fall; this was her sanctuary, after all. Nobody could see her here. She was completely alone.

Her cell phone rang.

Jane blinked. It was three in the morning. Who could be calling? Almost nobody had this number. She prayed it was not Craig, but nope; that wasn't him on the caller I.D.

"Jane Morgan."

A brief pause. "I've woken you—I wanted to leave you a message, I'm sorry. I thought the phone would be off."

"Hey, Haya. It's never off. But don't worry about that, I was awake anyway." Jane dashed the tears off her face. She could do with a little business talk—refocus. "What's up?"

"I know it's short notice, but could you get a flight to Ghada City tomorrow?"

Her stomach squeezed. "Are you okay?"

A laugh. "I'm fine. Actually . . . I'm getting married."

Jane blinked. "Huh?"

"Well . . . it's the nikkah ceremony. There will be another formal wedding later, but once the nikkah happens, you are married. Just my parents, you and Craig, and Sally and Chris. If you can come."

"Who is he?"

"Jaber." She could almost hear her friend blushing. "I think I might have mentioned him to you."

"A little." Jane blinked, disbelievingly. "You don't mean *Prince* Jaber, do you?"

"Yes. We've been seeing each other . . . I didn't want to talk about it until I was certain." Haya paused. "There was some political stuff here."

Jane ran the details through her mental processor. "But Prince Jaber is the foreign minister of Ghada. How can you . . . ?"

"Jane, I can't," Haya said, knowing what Jane was about to say. "I can't. I have to retire. But I've trained up some excellent people and the systems are in place. . . . I've got to be a blind partner now. Devote myself to charity works and do-gooding," she said, self-deprecatingly.

Jane's stomach churned so hard she thought she might pass out. Emotions washed through her, one after the other, so strongly she could hardly believe it. Haya! Haya, too. Married . . . *twice*. A damn *princess*. An actual princess with an actual crown. Sally, in her way, American royalty. And she, Jane . . . rejected by the only man she had ever loved. Or ever would love.

"Sally and Chris will be there," Haya went on, oblivious to Jane's torment. "Can you and Craig make it?"

"I—no." Her and Craig? Last time she'd seen him he'd shut the door of his office and bent her over his desk. They weren't a true couple. He was at a meeting in Stockholm; the chances of leaving it for a social trip to the Middle East were nil. And to go by herself? No way. "We can't. I'm sorry, it's too short notice." Her tone was cool, that practiced formality she used against all pain. "I'll come to the real wedding."

"This is the real wedding." Haya was a little distant now herself. "But of course it is hugely short notice . . . we just want to be married."

"I understand." What woman in love didn't? Jane thought for a few moments. "If you are retiring from business, Haya, will you sell me your shares? I'll happily give you market price, or a premium, even." There was silence. "Haya? Are you still there?"

"Yes; no, thank you, Jane, I won't be selling. The business of GLAMOUR is key to Ghada and the region, and I've built it up quite carefully. I'll just be leaving day-to-day management to you and Sally." Her tone now was as crisp as Jane's had been before.

"I see—that's fine," Jane lied. She was angry now, though she couldn't immediately fathom why. But this was out of her control, the whole thing. Her business. Her life. She wondered if Haya would sell to Sally—those two had always been closer. "Congratulations on your wedding, Haya, I'm sure you'll be extremely happy, and I'll come to the next ceremony. Can I send a gift to you?"

"Just donations to the Red Crescent," Haya said.

Donations? How impersonal. Jane felt it as a rebuff. Was her friend already acting like a princess, and not the Haya she'd known, whose legs she'd held up as she squeezed out her daughter?

"I'll be glad to make a donation. A hundred thousand, first thing tomorrow."

"That's very generous, Jane. Thank you. Good night then."

"Good night, Haya," Jane replied, hanging up.

She crawled back into her bed, tears welling up again. When Craig got back from Sweden she would take a good cold shower and dress in her most beautiful outfit. And she would go to see him, and once and for all, she would finish it.

❧

"I can't believe I'm doing this on our day off." Chris was still pissed off; he took care to speak sotto voce, though. "It's as hot as balls out here."

"Ssh," Sally hissed, angrily. "You're here now, make the best of it! You can sleep on the plane on the way home."

"Two days' rest before Boston and I'm spending them thirty thousand feet in the air."

"And how many other royal weddings are you going to get invited to?" Sally whispered back.

He squeezed her arm. "True, but you'll always be my princess."

In front of them, Haya was bending over the scroll; she lowered her head and signed it.

Sally stared at her friend with something close to awe; she felt loss, too; envy; a touch of anger. With that signature, Haya, as she knew her, had gone, and not like the first time; she had vanished forever.

Vanished from the company. Vanished from their friendship. There she stood, robed head to toe in fluttering golden silks, a long caftanlike dress studded with seed pearls and embroidered with crystals; the headdress she wore made her look like a storybook princess from Sally's childhood; it was square, with delicate chiffon scarves of pale gold floating behind it. What a dress! Haya did not look real to Sally. Her husband wore a traditional, embroidered coat; it was white satin, and appeared to be encrusted with diamonds.

He had signed first. The imam said something in Arabic. The assembled guards presented their guns in a salute, pointed them out at an angle and fired.

Chris instinctively moved to cover Sally with his body.

"It's okay. It's ceremonial."

He grinned. "Jumped out of my skin."

But she was already watching her friend. There were women in the same sort of robes, just less ornate—Sally guessed they were maids of honor—and they were coming forward; they removed the square headdress from Haya and the round white cap Jaber wore, and then they led the pair forward to two ornately carved chairs. As they passed the king, Jaber bowed, Haya curtsied; the king, too, said something to them; then they sat down in the chairs.

Two soldiers came forward bearing white silk cushions.

"What's that?" Sally whispered.

Chris leaned forward, blinked, then put his mouth next to her ear.

"Crowns," he said. "Little crowns."

Openmouthed, Sally watched as they placed the glittering golden circlets first on Jaber's head, then on Haya's; her tiara, all gold and icy white diamonds, glittered in the sun.

There was a burst of trumpets from the assembled military guard; then Jaber and Haya stood, he offered her his arm, and they processed back down the red carpet, past the assembled Ghadan court; and Sally watched as everybody curtsied or bowed as Haya walked past them. Her parents' faces were a picture of ecstatic joy; as her daughter walked past, Mrs. Al-Yanna sank into a curtsy so low her knees practically scraped the ground.

The royal couple were approaching them now. Chris stood up straight; he smiled appreciatively at Haya as she walked past; Sally, blushing scarlet, aware she was Haya's only invited friend, dipped into an awkward bob.

It was amazing how much it stung. As she rose, looking now at Haya's extended train, Chris stared at her, amazed.

"You're a damn American," he said. "What the hell did you do that for?"

"We're the only Western guests without some kind of title. I wanted to show respect. Not let her down."

He shrugged. "I don't bend the knee to no man, baby."

"Another reason why I love you," Sally said, honestly. But nonetheless, she was jealous; it couldn't be denied. What all-American little girl didn't grow up wanting to be a princess? And Haya was a real one; nothing metaphorical about it.

The band struck up a Debussy waltz, and the ceremony was over. A uniformed officer from the palace approached them.

"Mr. Nelson, Miss Lassiter?"

"Guilty," Chris said. Sally dug him in the ribs.

"Her Royal Highness, Princess Haya al-Jaber, asks me to conduct you to the top table; may I take you to the emira?"

"Why, certainly," Sally said.

Damn! What a moment. If her mom could see her now. If her *dad* could see her . . .

It struck her that Haya would definitely, absolutely, not be coming back to GLAMOUR. What if she could take her shares? Then maybe she'd have a chance, for once, not to feel like this—inadequate, the dumbest of the three of them. Jane charged ahead, and never took or asked Sally's advice. Haya had been out of touch for months. Yet she, Sally Lassiter, had been the driving force behind the store—who'd launched it, who inspired its fashion, who was on magazine covers the world over?

Haya had won the lottery here. Good for her. Sally wished her joy—and no doubt she was going to get it. GLAMOUR would be little more than a toy to her now. But the store had been Sally's redemption.

"I would love to sit next to the princess," she said, confidently.

⟨~⟩

Haya ran to the back door of the villa to check on Noor, and found Mrs. Wilkins waiting for her.

"She's fine. Just went down for her nap," the older woman said, then smiled and curtsied. "And congratulations to you, Your Royal Highness."

Haya was horrified. "Don't do that!"

"Oh, I have to. People are watching. You might as well get used to it, at least in public—*ma'am*. You can't put Prince Jaber under the microscope. He chose an unconventional wife, don't make him look bad!"

She twisted uncomfortably.

"You're absolutely right. I just feel funny about it."

"There's gossip among the other nannies," Mrs. Wilkins said, lowering her voice. "About your husband's position. They say he's in high favor right now. I wouldn't ruin it. Don't stop anybody from observing the protocol."

"Okay." Haya had heard some of that gossip herself. She blushed. "I'm not good at politics."

"Just be a princess. Remember that you are one. Be as good at it as you were at business. All right—I'm done. And congratulations again, my dear." The old woman kissed her on the cheek. "You'll have a very happy life."

❧

On her way back to the marquee Haya did not run. She walked, slowly and elegantly; cooks and waitresses bowed, curtsied as she passed; soldiers saluted her.

She knew what her nanny meant. Of course she did. There was speculation that Jaber would be raised, made prime minister; second in Ghada only to the king. And if that happened, what an opportunity!

If her husband had the king's ear, what could be done with the vast oil wealth of a country like this? Schools for the poor, cultural festivals, the start of democracy, improved relations with the West, promotion of arts and crafts on a global scale . . . she could actually make a difference, improve the lives of hundreds of thousands.

Jaber had rejected a royal cousin, one born to this, in her favor. She had to prove to the court that he had not made a mistake with the boorish American girl.

A uniformed servant held back the doors of the marquee; the entire crowd dipped down as she walked to the high table.

Haya lifted her head, feeling the coronet upon it, and smiled graciously. As she passed the gold thrones on which the old king and his wife were sitting, she herself sank into a profound curtsy, her wedding robes billowing about her. Jaber smiled at her, and extended a hand to lift her up.

"Your friends are here," he said. "Mr. Nelson and Miss Lassiter."

"Great," Haya murmured. She walked round to Chris and Sally, suddenly feeling the eyes of the entire court, the queen in particular, boring down on her.

"Hello," she said. "It's so wonderful that you could come."

Chris Nelson was wearing a lightweight suit, and looked ill at ease; he shook her hand briskly. "Hey, Haya, it's great to be here," he said.

She suppressed a wince. Haya? Couldn't he suck it up and be just a little formal in public? They'd never once met before. And the guy didn't even have a carnation on.

"Sally, you look beautiful." She turned to her friend. Sally did bob a curtsy, her golden head down, but when she came up her face was flaming. Haya did a quick inventory; Sally was wearing a long evening gown, very pretty, in azure blue velvet, but it had shoulder straps, and was cut to display the tops of her impressive bosom. It would knock them out at any ball in California, but Ghada was a little more conservative. "I'm so glad you're here," she said quickly and urgently.

"Am I next to you? I don't know a soul," Sally whispered.

"My dad's on my other side, but you're right opposite me, how's that?"

"Fine," Sally said, a little disappointed. But hey, it was Haya's dad.

"You must be cold," Haya said, she thought diplomatically. "I'll have somebody bring you a shawl; it gets chilly in the desert at night."

"Congratulations," Sally replied, giving her an awkward hug.

Haya squeezed her friend's hand. "I hope we'll get to talk . . . the guard will show you to your seats."

Sally nodded briefly as they were led away; Haya beckoned a serving woman.

"Get my friend a large shawl and arrange it around her shoulders. Quickly, please."

"Yes, Highness," the woman said, throwing a scandalized glance at Sally's gown.

"So, Haya," Sally said, as soon as they were seated. "You're quitting the company?"

"Day to day, yes. I'll be a silent partner. So, how are your own wedding preparations coming?" Haya tried to change the subject—she didn't want all Jaber's relatives listening to her talk business on the day of her nikkah. His mother, Princess Alia, was already looking her over with a narrowed glance of disapproval. Mentally she tried to signal to Sally. Damn! Why were *her* friends so tone-deaf when it came to culture?

She knew Jaber secretly considered Sally some sort of bimbo, riding on the success of his wife and Jane. Of course she knew better. But why did Sally pick that dress?

"Just fine. Y'all will enjoy it," Sally promised, smiling broadly at Jaber. "It's going to be a lot like this, but different food. Hope you don't mind American!"

"Not in the least," he said, with a broad smile.

"We'll get you cooking on the barbecue," Chris Nelson promised the prince. "I make my own marinade. It's famous in the locker room."

Haya died a thousand deaths.

"So, Haya." Sally came right to the point. "If you're going to do the princess thing full-time, you should let me buy you out."

This was too much, really. On her wedding day. Haya nearly lost it.

"Funny, Jane asked me the same thing. And I'm not selling. Surprised she didn't tell you that, Sally."

Sally recoiled, shocked. *Jane* had asked to buy the shares? Jane

Morgan? Didn't she already have enough, with all her stock deals on the side and her billionaire date? GLAMOUR was Sally's baby, it was all she had.

And—Jane hadn't told her. Was she trying to force Sally out? Take the whole thing?

"But why? You know you don't need that company now."

"Because it's mine," Haya said, shortly.

Sally's eyes flashed. She was being a damn dog in the manger about it. Didn't she *see* that pretty gold crown sitting on top of her head?

"And we won't talk business on my wedding day, if you don't mind." Haya decided hinting was no good. "That's not the custom here."

"Madam . . ."

The servant woman came forward, holding out the shawl, and a little officiously tried to tie it around Sally's shoulders.

Sally was now properly angry; she'd moved heaven and earth to be there, taken Chris away on his two days' rest in the middle of the biggest event of his damn life, the World Series. And Haya—with her fancy title—had suddenly turned into some kind of impersonal megasnob.

Sally untied the shawl and firmly handed it back.

"No. Sorry," she said. "I'm not cold. I don't think I will, thanks."

The woman muttered something in Arabic and nodded at Haya; Sally caught the word "emira"—that one she knew—princess.

"It's all right," Haya said, in both Arabic and English. But her face had flushed red with embarrassment.

Haya hadn't been ashamed of Sally back when Sal was protecting her from the playground bullies. Chris squeezed her hand, sensing her anger; slow to spark, but deadly once it had ignited.

"Wanna split?" he whispered.

She shook her head, biting her lip. Haya, with a frown, had turned aside to speak to her father.

"I need Ghada for the company," she whispered back.

There would be no scene. Sally made small talk with Chris, and sat through the first course of tabbouleh and the second of spiced beef. After that she gave her fiancé the smallest look; he cleared his throat.

"Haya, it's been great. But Sally and I are feeling kind of beat, and we have to get back to the airport—I can't skip practice tomorrow, facing the top of the Red Sox rotation Monday. Jaber—many congratulations. We wish you guys all the best."

He offered his arm to Sally, and she took it, thankful that she had a man who wasn't going to be fased by anyone or anything.

"Haya, congratulations to you both. Hope to see you in the States before too long. It was a wonderful wedding," Sally said, drawing on her reserves of politeness. "Enjoy the rest of your special day."

Haya blinked—they were actually walking out of her wedding, leaving two empty places at the top table, where the whole of the royal family were sitting.

"Have a safe flight," she said, icy cold.

Sally nodded, gave her a brisk smile, and left.

Tears of embarrassment and anger were prickling in the eyes of both women.

Jaber leaned over, kissed his wife on the cheek.

"Not your fault," he said. He turned aside and beckoned sharply, murmuring softly to one of his bodyguards; the man nodded, and within moments a sharif from the protocol office, and his wife, overjoyed at the honor, had been shown to the empty seats.

❧

Chris waited while Sally packed her case—in her current mood, she threw everything in there, and was done in five minutes—and arranged with the hotel for a limo to take them to the airport. He took charge, as Sally fumed; pulled out his credit card, and had them safely ensconced in their first-class seats on Royal Ghadan, winging their way to New York.

He was the first to speak. "Don't let her bother you, doll. She was beyond rude. Princess? I've seen barmaids with better manners. No idea about making guests feel welcome."

"I don't know." Sally shook her blonde head. "Ever since she first went out to Ghada, before Noor was born, even, she's been drifting away from us. She was so serious about her damn carpets and lamps. Made me feel bad about having a little fun."

"But that's not it, is it?"

"No." Sally chewed her lip, the way she always did when seething. "She wouldn't sell me her shares. One. And she told me Jane already asked—two. Jane didn't tell me."

"Did you tell Jane?"

"I only just decided to ask. Anyway . . ." Sally wasn't a hundred percent sure that was true; she glossed over it in her own mind. "The *point* is that neither of them is being fair. Haya's a princess now—she's richer than any of us will ever be. What the hell does she need to hang on to GLAMOUR for? GLAMOUR is my deal."

"And Jane?"

"Same thing. She doesn't care about the store, to her it's just a business deal. She doesn't design anything, she doesn't care about the stock or the shopping experience. To her GLAMOUR could be a baked-bean factory. She just wants the money. Why can't she get it trading shares? I *live* GLAMOUR, Chris. I design all the fashion—I do worldwide press and interviews for it twelve hours a day. I've got *fans*."

"Starting with me," he said.

But Sally was absorbed in her anger.

"When the customers go into the store they aren't going there because Jane Morgan knows how to get a good deal on a fleet of distribution trucks, or because Haya al-Yanna found them some great carpets. They're going there for the *sizzle*. For the *style*. For *me*." Her small fist clenched. "You know, those girls will always be my friends—I hope." She didn't sound certain. "But I have to make sure that GLAMOUR is mine. It matters more to me than anybody. And when we get home I'm gonna find a way to take control."

Jane checked herself out in the mirror. Yes; she looked good. Fresh and rested, for one thing. Maybe it was a good thing she hadn't been able to get a meeting with Craig yesterday; his plane, stuck in a stormbound Scandinavian airport, had saved her from herself.

Yesterday, with no sleep and a broken heart, she'd had a drawn look no concealer could disguise. Bags under her eyes the size of the new Hermès Kelly. Circles so dark you could suck a star into them, Jane thought.

She wanted to look good every time she dated Craig.

For breaking up with him, though, she wanted to look perfect.

She switched on the TV. It was Sunday morning, no need to rush to his place before the morning coffee had brewed.

"Thanks, John. We'll be catching up with the weather every thirty minutes here on *Good Day America*. And now for a little light relief." The coanchor turned her head to the man on the couch, tossing her chestnut brown bob and giving him a glossy smile. "Did you hear this one, Ken?"

"What's that, Molly?"

"America has a new princess!" Jane stared as the TV cut to footage of a sumptuous marquee in the desert; there were uniformed soldiers and ladies in ball gowns, and there in the middle, sitting on a damned throne, next to a handsome man in white, wearing a real crown, was Haya. "That's Haya al-Yanna, better known to America's women as one of the fashionable trio of ladies who run the GLAMOUR superstores. And now she's Her *Royal* Highness, Princess Haya of Ghada! Princess Haya grew up in L.A. and was the daughter of a local businessman."

"Hey, GLAMOUR by name, GLAMOUR by nature, I guess," said the male anchor, turning a bland white style to camera.

"Sally Lassiter, America's sweetheart, the *hottest* designer coast to coast, who founded the stores with the princess, was in attendance with superstar fiancé Chris Nelson."

The screen flashed to a shot of Sally sitting next to Chris; he had her hand in his.

"Definitely the royal wedding of the year. Two amazing couples there. I expect this will bring even more shoppers through the GLAMOUR doors."

Jane waited for them to mention her.

"And now we'd like to welcome our next guest, a celebrated chef who . . ."

Bitter, Jane flicked her remote at the TV. Turn that bloody thing off. It wasn't just the States; everywhere was like that. Part of a couple, glamorous, *then* you got attention, *then* you got credit.

She, Jane, was not as beautiful as her friends. She had no princely crown and no va-va-voom figure.

Hers was the business of business. She was the one whose brain had come up with this store. She had financed it—single-handedly. And as it turned out, at the cost of her heart.

Who had found sites for twenty more stores? Who had managed every aspect of the corporation from staffing to invoicing? Who had bought the ad spaces, featuring Sally Lassiter's pretty face on billboards across America?

Jane Morgan. De facto CEO—but on paper, sharing that title. Multimillionairess, sure, but sharing it with two friends who had ridden to the top on her coattails.

And Haya had blown her off when it came to the shares.

Jane was almost grateful. She didn't begrudge Haya and Sally their fame, their celebrity status. But she wanted the business side of things, her own project, to herself. Had either of them lived in a roach-infested apartment, or worked eighteen-hour days? No. She thought not. Jane had done fine by her friends; she'd given them wealth and position beyond dreaming. It was time to take control for herself.

A blessing. Something to focus on. Something to get her mind off her inner pain.

She went into the kitchen and, mechanically, made herself a pot of coffee and toasted half a bagel. She wasn't hungry, but she didn't want her stomach to rumble, or to get dizzy from lack of blood sugar.

When she was done, she brushed her teeth again to lose the

coffee breath, spritzed on a little scent, and headed for Craig Levin's house.

～⌒

"Jane? That you?"

There were no staff at his place Sunday mornings—Craig gave them the day off. And Jane had the code to his keypad entry gates. Another excellent reason to do this today.

"Take all your clothes off except your jacket," he called from the bedroom, "and your high heels, and come upstairs."

Man. She loved that thick-throated, sexy voice. Craig Levin was as funny and as raunchy as hell. And she loved how he knew she was wearing a jacket.

"I'll be right there," she shouted out, and went to the refrigerator; before leaving last night, the chefs had prepared various things for breakfast. Jane selected the large, ice-cold pitcher of freshly squeezed orange and peach juice, poured out two tumblers, and brought them up with her.

He was lying sprawled under the Pratesi sheets on his designer Swedish sleigh bed; they cut off, very sexily, at the thick line of hair right above the flat of his groin.

Jane wanted him instantly. She took refuge in a long pull on the chilled, delicious juice.

"Here's yours." She handed him the tumbler.

"You're not naked," he observed, taking it. "That's not good, honey."

Slowly—Levin let himself sleep long and solidly on Sundays, and he was still groggy—he raised himself to a sitting position; the silk sheet slipped dangerously, but Jane didn't look.

"Here," she said. She opened her Chanel purse and handed him two sets of keys. "The spares to your place in Hollywood. And the flat in Rome."

"I don't want to know what this is about, do I?"

Jane shook her head; she was already fighting down the tears.

"I'm finishing it."

"You've said that before." He caught her round the waist. "And I remember how I talked you out of it."

"I love you, and you don't love me." She dashed the back of her hand against her eyes and forced a smile. "Not a good position to make a trade."

"I do love you," Levin insisted. The "but" hung in the air.

"Both my friends have got married."

There. She had dared to say it. The *M* word.

"But they're not us. What's right for them is not right for us."

"Says you." Jane sighed. "I never should have slept with you, Craig."

He shook his head, annoyed. "What is that? Are you some kind of Catholic now? No sex before marriage?"

"You tell me," Jane responded wearily. It was over, she didn't have to watch her words anymore. "You have what you want. Sex and friendship, no strings, no commitment. Why should you change that?"

Levin winced, just slightly; perhaps she was too near the knuckle, after all.

"I've never cheated on you, Jane. I gave them all up for you."

"Your trouble is you want a gold medal for doing the right thing." She sighed. "You're an amazing man, Craig. You're brilliant; you're funny; you're driven; you're charming."

"Exactly what you're looking for," he said, quite serious. "Jane, if you make the perfect enemy of the good, just because I'm not ready . . ."

"I told you," she said. "I love you. I can't be with you and give myself to you when you hold yourself apart from me. I always wanted you, from the first conversation we ever had. But since I slept with you, it's like an addiction. There's no reason not to get married, not to have kids. Unless you haven't decided I'm the one for you. On some level, you're keeping your options open."

"I'm just not ready," he repeated. Levin had no wisecrack. Not this time.

"Unfortunately I am. So. This is it. I'm going to take over

GLAMOUR. I want your ten percent. Please give it to me, Craig; I'm asking you, as a favor."

"Jane—"

"Don't. Just don't," she said, crying in earnest now. "I never tried to force you into anything, and I'm not now. I just won't settle, Craig. Not with you. Either you choose me or you choose your freedom."

"I've never felt about anybody the way I feel about you."

She flinched; the soft words hit her heart with a physical stab of loss.

"It isn't enough," Jane said. "Will you sell me your stock?"

"My broker will call tomorrow and sell them to you at market," he said, a touch bitterly.

"Thank you." She paused. "Good-bye, Craig Levin. I love you."

"But Jane—I love you, too—" he responded; but her heels were already clattering down the stairs.

Levin flopped back onto his bed, it was a sunny day, and he could see the leaves of an elm tree, golden in the autumn sunlight, waving gently outside his skylight; but his world had gone dark.

No. He would not marry her. Even though she was young, and beautiful, and intelligent, and feisty, and the hottest damn lay he'd ever had in his life. Not because she was skilled, like some high-class hooker, but because of her intense, shuddering responsiveness.

Was she the kind of woman a man married? Everything that drew him to her shouted no. So hot, so strong, so driven. Passionate and independent. Would she settle with him? Mother his children, look after them?

He could not tell if Jane would ever stop looking, ever stop being hungry.

She said she wanted to be married. Levin thought that would ruin it. What if she did stop? Would he want her, if she was there all the time, available, not having to be chased? Would he want her after a morning of picking out drapes or talking to some boring interior designer?

He loved his freedom. And Jane was freedom.

But he did not want to let her go.

Ruefully he stared at the ceiling. It was so, so like her. To confess her pain and love so matter-of-factly—like he hadn't known, of course he had—and then ask for his shares. At the one time he could not deny her.

She was moving on. Moving up. He thought she was just tremendously impressive. Burying herself in work was exactly what he would do himself.

God, how he loved her; they were partners in crime.

Levin, a man's man, never cried. He tried to ignore the fact that as he rolled over onto his pillow, his eyes were wet.

Top of the eleventh. Sally breathed in, deeply. She couldn't take the tension. If the Dodgers struck out again, she was going in search of some alcohol—the real stuff in the VIP boxes, not that useless beer the vendors carted round the stands. Anyway, they'd run out hours ago.

It was a bitterly cold autumn night in Boston, but nobody felt that. The electricity in this stadium could have powered the national grid.

Game seven. The World Series. Tiebreaker. This was it—win, or go home. Baseball's biggest prize, eternal glory or ignominy, on the cards. Every player on the field had been dreaming of this moment since he was knee-high. For half of them, that lifelong dream was about to turn into a nightmare.

Just to up the pressure, the game was in overtime.

It hadn't been Chris Nelson's finest hour. He'd scored a useless single in the third, got a walk in the seventh, apart from that he was 0 for 8. This from a guy with a postseason average of .376.

Sally didn't need to have a radio with her to imagine what the commentators were telling America.

"He's exhausted."

"What was Nelson thinking, spending two days off in the air?"

"Manager John Tepes should have put his foot down."

"His fiancée dragged him to a fancy Middle Eastern wedding. Hope that slice of cake was good, Chris! Looks like that's the only trophy you'll be picking up *this* season."

The guilt boiled up inside her. They'd all be right, too. What the hell had she been thinking? Lost Chris his dream so that he could get snubbed in the desert, thousands of miles from here.

The World Series, the championship, was more than just one match. It was life. It was the ring you wore forever. It was the Hall of Fame. Lose it, and you might sink into alcoholism or despair. Would that happen to Chris? Would their relationship even survive?

She bit her knuckles. Every inning he failed to connect was a new chance the manager would pull him. In Tepes's place, *she'd* have pulled him!

Leo Olsen—first up. Single. Thank God. Sally clapped wildly. Even if Chris couldn't do it, it wouldn't matter as long as the Dodgers won. His performance thus far would make him man of the series—even with a terrible last game.

Next, Rick Angelo. Swing and a miss. Ball. The crack of the bat, connecting—she could hardly look. No—no good, no good! He popped it up, and the Boston shortstop caught it with ease.

Another Dodger came up to the plate—hit a flyout, just shy of that magic wall that would have added two runs to their total.

That meant Chris was next. Sally shut her eyes tight. Then she opened them. She couldn't miss this, she had to share in his pain. That was her punishment.

And she thanked God she did, because a second later the in-ground cameraman found her and flashed her face up on the jumbotron screen, next to a still shot of Chris's face.

The crowd booed. Sally wanted to shrink in her seat. As far as the fans were concerned, she was public enemy number one.

Then the cameraman found Chris, at the plate. He was listening to them booing Sally. His face, his handsome, square-jawed face, looked monumentally angry. The Dodgers fans shut the hell up. The Red Sox fans cheered even louder.

Holding his hand up to the pitcher, Chris turned round, looked up in Sally's general direction, and blew her a kiss.

The knot in her stomach melted; his protection, his salute, was like a shot of hot buttered rum against the cold.

The umpire shouted something. The pitcher, eyes cold, wound up and swung forth with a deadly fastball—

—and Chris connected, not off pitch like the other two, dead in the middle of the bat. She could hear the crack in the stands. The ball was soaring, higher, deeper; Chris's bat had shattered; he flung it from him and raced to first base; Olsen was already at second. . . .

But the ball wasn't stopping . . . it arced high, long, and into the stands at left field.

Home run!

Sally blinked, hyperventilating. Home run! A two-run hit! And Boston had already replaced most of their hitters, slicing through the roster in a desperate search for firepower. Olsen and Nelson raced around the bases. The Boston fans sat in stunned silence as the Dodger fans went nuts.

The jumbotron had fixed on Sally again. She waved, she smiled—she blew a kiss back down to Chris.

The fight trailed out of Boston. When the Dodgers' closer, Ramiro Sanchez, came up to the plate it was a foregone conclusion. Two strikeouts.

And just to add a little sugar to the cake, Chris unerringly caught the final out; a pop-up direct to the shortstop.

Sally could not stop shrieking. She raced down the stairs, down through the tunnels reserved for the players, and rushed out onto the field, mixing with the other wives, the children, the girlfriends; Chris was just being lowered to the grass by his teammates who had hoisted him around; he caught sight of her, ignored the forest of microphones shoved in his face, put his arms around the small of her back, and bent her into a slow, powerful kiss that had every housewife in America fanning herself.

"Don't you think you should sleep?" Sally asked, as they settled into the small private jet parked on the tarmac at Logan

Airport. They had just come from a riotous postgame dinner, yet Chris had refused more than a single glass of champagne, and had told Sally not to have anything, either. "We have a suite at the Victrix . . . we could just go back, make love all night . . ."

"I don't want you listed as my girlfriend for one more minute." Nelson shook his head. "This has been the most spectacular day of my life and I don't want it to end."

"But going back to L.A. now . . ."

"We're not going to L.A. We're going to Vegas. We're getting married. I have it all arranged."

CHAPTER 14

Sally gasped. "Married?"

Chris bent forward, kissing her lightly on the lips. "I decided that in the seventh-inning stretch, win or lose. Called the owner on my cell; this is his jet. Screw the party, we can do that, too, but I want to elope. Just you and me. No damn guests. No protocol. It's the fairy-tale night, baby. Anything's possible."

"Oh, God!" Sally burst into tears. "I love you, Chris!"

"Glad to hear that," he said. "I love you, too, honey. And it's a good thing, because I have nothing else to do with myself now except make love to you and bring up the rugrats."

She blinked. "Why?"

"I'm quitting baseball. I'm thirty-five; at the top of the game . . ." He grinned. "World champ. Hit the winning homer. Caught the last out. You know what every last athlete does? They hang on, they try to repeat, one more season. They wind up getting less and less dough, watching their stats slip, being booed off the field and playing in the minors or retiring from injury after a losing season with the damn Detroit Tigers." He shook his head. "Not for me. I don't need the cash or the back problems. You be the star now, 'cause I'm looking forward to a long, anonymous retirement, as rich as Midas and getting laid every day."

Sally wiped away the tears and started to laugh.

"You know you're crazy as hell."

"Not gonna try to talk me out of it?"

"Hell, no. I want to be Sally Nelson. And I want you there, not halfway around the country."

She moved closer to him, sensing his warmth, slipping one hand inside his shirt; he was aroused, she could tell just by looking at him.

"No," he growled, batting her away. "Insatiable little minx. If I can wait, so can you."

⁓

He'd done it perfectly: the honeymoon suite, an enormous bed covered with rose petals—white, her favorite; no tacky Elvis chapel, just a black-robed justice of the peace, with an off-duty cop as a witness; fruit juices, bagels, crisped bacon laid out in their suite, so they didn't have to interrupt themselves to get the door for room service. The management, sensing a coup, had somehow managed to obtain some World Series Champion memorabilia, and decorated the suite; the TV was replaying the game when they walked in the room.

After they were legally wed, Chris politely shook hands with the judge and the cop, then half shoved Sally into the nearest elevator. He rode it in silence to their suite, and unlocked the door. Then in one strong motion, he swept her, squealing, into his arms and hoisted her unceremoniously over his shoulder, head down, long hair streaming, and he carried her into the suite and flung her down on the bed.

"Evening, Mrs. Nelson," Chris said, straddling her and pinning her down with a kiss.

Sally moaned; it was four in the morning, but she had never felt so alive. She reached down, fumbling, for the buttons of her shirt.

"No time," he said, yanking down her jeans.

⁓

Eventually, three hours later, sweating in each other's arms, they surrendered to sleep as the sun came up over the desert.

"I've got to call Mom," Sally said, when they woke at noon.

"That can wait. You'll be just as married tomorrow," Chris said. "Come here."

They stayed in the honeymoon suite for three days, ordering room service, leaving only for a dip in the rooftop pool; Sally sent orders via the bellhop, and fresh clothes were delivered to the suite; they had packed nothing. It was pure bliss. Mona, once told, didn't even mind; Chris's parents were mad, but managed to swallow it for the sake of family harmony, especially when he reassured them the big wedding party was still on.

Sally was bruised in the best way; she decided she loved it; Chris couldn't get enough of her. And to hell with protection. If she got pregnant now, all the better.

Finally, even Chris wanted to go home; it was fun being cheered every time he set foot outside his rooms, but even poolside they wanted his autograph.

"That eighty-acre plot in Beverly Hills is starting to look real good."

"Told you," Sally said smugly.

He patted her on the ass. "Watch yourself, Mrs. Nelson."

"And I want to get back to work, as well. Jane Morgan's left several messages on my voice mail. She's flying down for a meeting." Sally looked at him out of the corner of her eyes to check if he was annoyed, but Chris just shrugged.

"Like I said, knock yourself out. I'll be the one taking laps in the pool. And lying on the couch with the remote."

Sally beamed. Haya could eat her heart out; he was the *perfect* man!

The GLAMOUR boardroom was a beautiful thing. Architect-designed in the new extension, it said that the company was owned by women. Sally had been meticulous. A long table and chairs, Scandinavian blond woods. Some of Haya's finest tapestries framed on the walls; a few select magazine covers—Sally on the cover of *Time,* Jane on the cover of *Fortune.* Fresh flowers, daily, just in case. Soft Aubusson carpets. The latest in audiovisual equipment. And a terrific view of the Pacific from the huge windows, tinted against the ferocity of the sun.

Not that they needed all that space. Jane had insisted that nobody be there except Sally and herself. No secretaries. No lawyers.

"But if it's a board meeting, don't we have to notify Haya?" Sally had asked.

"It's not a board meeting. I just want to talk to you."

"Fine."

Sally had hung up, intending to be there. She still liked Jane, but she no longer trusted her.

And now here they were. Adults; beautiful women. Jane would never be as sexy as Sally, but she definitely had something: fiery New York chic. That hard casing, though; it would put men off—all but the toughest. Sally wondered what Jane had to prove. She had a suspicion she was about to find out.

"I want to take the company public," Jane said.

Damn, Sally thought. *No chitchat. No pleasantries.* Jane meant business.

"Why? Financing?"

Jane nodded. "We can go global. And we can still retain enough shares to have a controlling interest."

Sally nodded slowly.

"You asked Haya if you could buy her shares."

Jane flushed. How did Sally know that? She saw the flicker of anger in her partner's spine, and stiffened. Jane had underestimated Sally, perhaps. But it didn't make any difference. What she was doing was just.

"She wouldn't sell them to me."

"But why didn't you tell me?"

Jane's dark eyes narrowed. "Did you ask her the same thing, Sally?"

Sally nodded slowly.

"For the same reason you didn't tell me, I suppose." Jane gave a great sigh; she was glad, cards on the table. "I know both of you have made a huge contribution, and I'd never force you out, and you're both rich. But GLAMOUR is mine. I'm at the stage where I want to control it. I think it would be best for me and the company, and you guys, too. Haya can get on with being a princess, you can be a star. I'll take care of the dollars and cents."

Sally was furious. What blatant contempt!

"Um, excuse me, Jane, but GLAMOUR is mine. *My* designs, *my* image. Being a star, as you put it, is what sells this store. I could get anybody to do the financials, any damn firm in New York. That's backroom stuff."

There was a long pause.

"Don't let's fight over this."

"I think that ship has sailed," Sally responded.

Jane twisted her fingers. "Do you have the other shares, then? Did Haya give them to you?"

"No. And I think she's being a total dog in the manger about it. She doesn't even want to stay involved. At least you and me both live it."

Jane nodded, hugely relieved. There was still a chance, then. "We can force her to go public. You and I, together, can vote for that with two-thirds of the shares. That way things are on the open market. If you can get control, good for you. You know I'm going to try to. I value our friendship, Sally, you know I do. But this is apart from that and it's my life. You've got Chris, Haya's got a whole new life . . ."

"So what's Craig Levin? Chopped liver?"

Jane had to smile at the New York expression. "My ex-boyfriend," she said, simply. "We broke up." She blushed, and admitted, "He sold me his shares."

"God *damn* you!" Sally shouted, jumping to her feet. "You never even told me . . ."

"Less of the histrionics," Jane responded sharply. "Same way you never told me you had decided to elope to Vegas? We both think our way is best. Let's not make this personal."

"It's always been personal. GLAMOUR is me. Not some random brand. Me. In a store. It's what America loves."

"If we go public, you have a chance to compete for those shares. So do I. I want to form my own company now, aimed at taking over GLAMOUR. Morgana, Inc. It'll have financial offices everywhere. And no partners."

Sally sat down again, slowly. "I want to make Nelson a company, too. My own brand of cosmetics, as well as GLAMOUR's Lassiter brand. And I want to mop up whatever's out there. You can do just as well with any stock, Jane; to you it's just money."

Jane swallowed the insult. Tempers were high. If she said what she was thinking, she could lose Sally's friendship for good.

"If we don't go public, it'll be eternal stalemate. You and I on each other's nerves. Both of us resenting Haya. No good for us or the company."

"I agree with that."

"I'll never sell up to you, nor you to me."

"And Haya's sitting tight. No—it's the only way. I see that." Sally nodded. "I'll call our lawyers and vote my stock with yours. So long as we have seats on the board and a controlling stake."

"Of course. You want to tell Haya?"

Sally thought of the wedding, of Haya's haughty attitude, the waitress thrusting a shawl over her carefully chosen dress.

"You better do it.

"You two fallen out?"

"Not fatally. We seem to have drifted apart a little." Sally felt a pang; anger, relief, regret, she wasn't sure. "Same as you and me. Same as all three of us."

Jane was silent then, her dark head bowed.

"I'll make you a very generous offer for your shares, Sal. I can get the money. Then this wouldn't come between us."

Sally stood up. "At the end of the day we are friends, not sisters. Things happen. Life happens. I want GLAMOUR, Jane. I hope you get even richer any which way, but I want this store."

Jane nodded sadly. "I'll call Haya. And I'll be in touch. We

should do it fast. I'm looking to float in six months. In the mean-
time, I can still work with you?"

Sally laughed. "You kidding? I'll be tripling the promo. We
want this to be the biggest launch ever. When GLAMOUR
floats, I want it to be a proper global chain."

Jane reached across the table and offered Sally her hand; after
a second's hesitation, the blonde girl shook it. She gave Jane a
knowing smile.

"I think you Brits might say, 'May the best girl win.' "

～○

"It's beautiful," Haya said. "Thank you."

She gave the little Moroccan girl a hug and a kiss; her parents
looked on, beaming with pride; they called down God's blessings
on Her Royal Highness.

Haya lifted up the little picture, clumsily drawn on paper in
bright felt-tip pen, showing Haya standing beside a GLAMOUR
store that resembled a large bazaar. Appropriate, really, that's what
it was. The girl, Salma, was twelve, but had Down's; the drawing
was garish as a five-year-old's. Salma grinned toothily, pleased
with her hug and kiss.

The special school was a new one in Casablanca. Haya was
making a whistlestop tour of charitable schools in the region;
she'd planned out a full schedule with Jaber, and started on it the
day after their honeymoon.

"But you've got an event every day," Jaber had said, shaking
his head. "Four tours a year, not counting my state visits . . ."

"I can't sit on my hands, you know that," Haya told him. "If
I'm going to do the charity thing I want to *do* it. Full-time. Use
the title, use the position. I've been a company director for years
now, I need that buzz. Noor will come with me. And they're
mostly in Ghada; I'll only be apart from you a couple of weeks
a year, at most."

"And when our children come, *insh' Allah*?"

"Then I'll stick to Ghada. But hey, princesses here travel in
style," Haya teased him. She wondered if she'd ever get used to it:

the enormous limos, the outriders, the crazy jewels and exquisite robes. First-class, air-conditioned comfort wherever she set foot. Being the prince's favored girl had been one thing; this was a whole new ball game. But Haya was determined to earn her keep. She refused to be one of those spoiled women who spent their lives at polo matches or shopping in Dubai.

"I'm proud of you." Jaber ran his hands possessively over her body, tugging her toward the bed. "The people love you. Everybody is noticing. Even the queen is starting to approve."

"After that wedding . . ."

"Never mind that." He brushed his thumbs across her breasts, feeling her shudder, then slipped the robes from her shoulders, gently biting down upon them. "Come here, Princess . . ."

Haya grinned, remembering. She felt guiltily pleased that today was her last day in North Africa and the royal flight would be taking her home tomorrow. She hated to be away from Jaber.

Her equerry, a Miss Salmah al-Akhtam, was giving her that discreet little wave. Haya stood up, gave an enthusiastic little speech about Salma and the wonderful work being done at the school, shook hands with the bowing and curtsying staff, and allowed herself to be escorted out by her bodyguards.

"You have some calls, Highness."

"Thanks, Salmah—give me the mobile."

The diplomat shook her head, emphatically. "No, ma'am. We must get you to a secure place."

"There's trouble?" Haya demanded, instantly alert. She beckoned the new nanny to come over with Noor and cuddled the toddler, who was already half-asleep. Emily Wilkins had long since tired of the heat and gone home to Ireland; Haya still missed her.

"Yes—no—please get into the car, *Siti* Haya."

She obeyed. A face like that was not to be argued with. But as soon as the driver had pulled on to the streets—miraculously cleared by her omnipresent outriders—and they were safely headed to the airport, Haya demanded to know what the problem was.

"His Majesty is gravely ill."

"The king?" Haya shook her head. "Poor man, God spare him! Where is my husband?"

"That is just it, Highness. The prince asks you come home at once. He says things are happening and you must be there. Your appointments for this afternoon have been canceled."

Haya did not like that. "At whose orders? I never canceled them."

"Prince Jaber's," Salmah said firmly.

Haya bit her lip. Her husband outranked her, of course, and could do what he liked. She found it slightly sexy that he was ordering her schedule around. On the other hand, Jaber would never do that unless something was up.

"Is there any danger?"

"No, Highness."

"Then let's get going," Haya said.

"And one more thing—your friend rang from the United States. Miss Morgan. She said it was important."

What now? Haya could tell that this was exactly the wrong time for Jane to be calling her. "That can wait."

Salmah nodded. "She said if you said that, to tell you they are selling the company."

A rush of adrenaline poured through Haya; her palms started to sweat; she felt the soft hairs on the back of her neck start to prickle and rise.

"Get me on that airplane!" she said to her driver.

"Yes, Highness," he replied, and stepped on the gas.

While Noor was settled, eating her lunch of pureed fruit and soft cheese, Haya retreated into her private cabin to call from the Skyphone. They had in-flight TV, and although the national station was censored, she could pick up what was going on; the king, suddenly ill with a stroke, and now recovered, was tinkering with the succession. His eldest son, who had tried to kill him, had long been exiled; the younger brother was a playboy, and was apparently being removed. That meant it was wide open. He had five other boys, a half brother, and a vast array of cousins.

Would the new crown prince favor Jaber?

She wanted to get back there, to be with her husband.

When she got through to him, he was calm. Talked about the king's health and said it was all in God's hands; Haya thought the palace lines might be bugged; if he was anxious, he wouldn't discuss things over the phone.

That left Jane. What the hell? Haya wanted this nonsense out the way, and fast.

She dialed the number Jane had left.

"Morgana, Inc. How may I direct your call?"

"I'm sorry, I was looking for GLAMOUR," Haya said, confused.

"Were you looking for Ms. Morgan, ma'am? This is her new company. Any queries about the stores can go directly to her office. Whom shall I say is calling?"

Haya felt an icy chill. What the *hell*?

"This is Haya al-Yanna," she said, angrily. "Put me through to her at once."

"Yes, certainly, Your Royal Highness." Haya was impressed; typical of Jane to hire the best staff around, right from the get-go, she thought; even the operators were capable of putting two and two together. "One moment, ma'am."

There was a pause, and Jane came on directly. Haya supposed she should be grateful for not being put on hold.

"Haya?"

"I got some crazy message, and believe me, Jane, this isn't the time," Haya said, crisply. "We're not doing anything dramatic with GLAMOUR right now. My husband—"

"Yes, it's on the news. I know you'll want to focus on him, Haya."

"If that's another pitch for my shares . . ."

"Not directly. Look, I've known you too long to soft-soap it, and I can see you have your hands full, so here goes: Sally and I are determined to take GLAMOUR public. We're holding a board meeting on Monday, and this is your notification. You don't need to be there, because we form a quorum without you, and we are going to instruct banks to put the company on the market."

Haya gasped. "You wouldn't."

"It has to be, Haya. It's gotten too big. And we all have different visions." Jane sounded slightly wistful, but she was plowing on. "The fact is both Sally and I want to own the company, and the only way out of the stalemate is to float the shares and compete with the stockholders. We'll be holding back enough of a personal stake to make sure the three of us still sit on the board—that is, if you still want to."

"Damn right I do!" Haya was shouting, and she didn't care who heard her. "Are you two using this crisis to shove me out of the picture? I'm the *soul* of our store, it's *mine*. I provide half the stock and ninety percent of the vision. Without me you wouldn't bother with one ethical sale. . . ."

"When you're a public company, ethical is making money for the pension funds who own your shares. Families have their savings in you."

"But we're not public!"

"We're going to be." Jane was clearly amused by Haya's claim, and that drove her to a white-hot fury. "It seems all three of us think we made the biggest contribution here."

"So much for friendship."

"We could argue that since you are now a bona fide royal with no intention of working again, you would have been a friend to sell your shares to Sally and me. It's a bit Marie Antoinette, Haya."

"I could never trust anybody else with my regional operation. You know how much heart I put into that."

"Haya, face it." Jane was blunt. "You're done. You're finished. Princesses and boardrooms don't mix, at least you got that right. You could at least let your cofounders run with the ball."

"We'll see if I'm finished," Haya shouted. "I don't want to be just somebody's wife. Ahmed had his business and Jaber has his politics, but GLAMOUR was my own. My store, my stock, my damn business model! I'll be there on Monday, Jane Morgan. If you start that meeting without me I'll sue your asses off!"

She slammed down the phone and jumped to her feet, pacing around the cabin, seething with rage.

There was an urgent knock on the door, and Salmah, her face shiny with excitement, poked her head inside.

"Highness!"

"Did I say come in?" Haya was simmering with rage, and her unfortunate lady-in-waiting was in the line of fire.

"Excuse me, Highness!" Salmah said. She bowed her head low, and sunk into a very deep curtsy, which brought Haya up short. Salmah and she had been working together for a while now. Except in public, Salmah never curtsied. "But you must come in here, you must come and see the television!"

Haya hurried out into the main cabin. Everybody was staring at the wall-mounted TV, which was tuned in to CNN via satellite; as she entered, they all turned to look at her.

"Mama!" Noor said, obliviously.

The screen showed her husband, dressed in a dark Western suit, sunglasses on, surrounded by soldiers, exiting from the Queen Fizouleh Hospital in Ghada City; Haya's mouth dropped open as she saw the anchor began to speak.

"And regional sources confirm, I repeat, we have confirmation," the redheaded anchor was saying, "that King Nazir has appointed his prime minister, Prince Jaber ibn Mohammed, as the new Crown Prince of Ghada. Prince Jaber's wife is Princess Haya"—her own face, smiling with Sally and Jane, an old PR shot, flashed up—"an American citizen and a founder of the wildly successful GLAMOUR chain of luxury stores. So we could wind up with two American queens in the Middle East, Jack!"

"Prince Jaber is known for his moderate attitude toward the West and a strong commitment to social justice and democracy," the coanchor said. "But Ghadan officials were keen to stress that the king's health remains good . . ."

Haya paled, and steadied herself against a seat.

"Turn it off," she said quietly.

A soldier leaped to obey her.

"We will all pray for the health of the king," she added. And as they were staring at her, she covered her face and turned toward Mecca.

Oh, God . . . please spare him!

She didn't want to be queen. She hadn't signed up to be a queen!

Haya thought of her daughter, her husband, her new country, her parents. And she thought of the news item she had just seen. If her life was to shift again, in this cataclysmic way, the one thing she was damn sure of was that she was going to save her company.

She hoped Jaber would understand why it mattered. But come hell or high water, Sunday night, she was getting on a plane to L.A.

CHAPTER 15

"Great doing business with you." The broker shook hands briskly with Jane. "It's a great space, I think you'll be very happy. If we can assist you with anything more, do get in touch."

"I will. Thanks." Jane had just got a steal of five thousand square feet on the Lower East Side. And even better, it came fully carpeted and equipped; she wouldn't have to waste time.

She walked around her new offices. Great views of lower Broadway, looking toward the World Trade Center; perfect for a Wall Street newcomer.

Jane would employ fifteen brokers, two analysts, and fifteen assistants. As she expanded she hoped it'd be more.

Maybe she could never be another Craig Levin, but she was sure as hell going to try. Until GLAMOUR was hers, that meant trading in currencies and stocks; Jane intended to take buy-and-hold positions, maybe start a retail hedge fund. Her track record there was golden. Plus, she thought she might dabble in real estate.

She didn't want to be just another woman executive. To persuade stockholders to sell their GLAMOUR shares to her, she needed to be playing in the mixed divisions.

The thought of Haya, shouting and raging, crossed her mind; of Sally, telling her any broker could handle the finances.

And then of Craig . . . her love . . . lying there, not stopping her, not holding her.

Her father; the last time she had seen him, clutching ineffectually at him as he got into his diplomatic car.

Friends. Lovers. Family. In the end, you could trust only yourself.

Let Monday come. When she sat down in that boardroom, her offices would be fully staffed, fully funded, and trading.

She walked out. Time to get her hair and nails done. The press would be there, Monday. Haya was an almost-queen, and Sally was a star. She, the single girl, didn't want to look bad.

Jane thought of Craig, and winced from the sheer physical ache of it. She wanted him so badly. Wanted his body driving into hers, his strong, bearish frame on her slight one, her fingers clutching at his back.

But she wanted so much more than that, too. And he wasn't going to give it to her.

Love—whatever kind of love—was always dangerous, a bad risk. She'd never gotten away with her heart intact. Now she was just playing to win.

But as she locked the office door behind her, there were tears in her eyes.

Jane despised her own weakness.

Sally glanced down at the little stick. She'd had the pregnancy test included in her grocery deliveries; that way it could be anonymous—she got them with a credit card in her assistant's name, to stop the tabloids raking through her trash. Didn't want to read about it in the *Enquirer*.

The little blue flush crept up to the window. Sally held her breath . . .

But no; there was only the one line. She waited. Nothing. Not pregnant.

Sally sighed. Of course, it wasn't gonna happen right away. She was just gonna have to be patient. Oh, yeah—and practice a lot. She smiled.

She was fitter than she'd ever been. Chris loved to play around while working her out. Talk about an incentive! He made her watch while he lifted weights with his shirt off. Got her so worked up, watching his strong muscles slide around under that tanned skin, his biceps straining, that Sally could scarcely keep from jumping on him as soon as he was done.

Before, it had been good. Now they were married, it was perfect. Every time she looked down at the thick round band of white diamonds—there was enough ice on her left hand to satisfy a polar bear—Sally felt a rush of deep, profound pleasure. He was hers—signed, sealed, delivered. She relaxed in bed in a way she hadn't thought possible. All she wanted now was to have his babies. . . .

And to run her company.

Looking down at the single, lonely little line, she consoled herself. Hey, this wasn't a once-for-all thing. They got an infinite number of attempts.

With GLAMOUR, not so much. Sally threw out the stick, washed her hands, and went downstairs to call her lawyers again. She might not be the world's biggest brain, but she was savvy. And there were brains around for hire.

And she was her father's daughter. Let Haya and Jane pit their bookish minds against her street smarts. She was damn sure who was going to win.

⌒

"But aren't you under contract? To GLAMOUR?"

The gray men in suits were sitting behind the table in the Chicago office, trying not to ogle Sally. She knew how she appeared to them—a butterfly among moths; her tight, short dress displaying her perfectly toned figure—Chris was, like, the world's best personal trainer, and she did mean *personal*—her long, blonde hair shimmering with fresh white platinum highlights shot through a buttercup base, like liquid strands of sunshine; her teeth, whitened with porcelain veneers to Hollywood-like perfection; a ruby and diamond necklace, another gift from Chris, lying against the creamy hollows of her throat.

"Yes. The Lassiter brand is theirs. Which is why I'm proposing to start a new one." She dazzled them with a smile.

"But what could be more recognizable than Lassiter?"

"*Sally,*" she said, and winked.

The chemists and marketing executives sighed. *Sally.* Of course. It was perfect. One word. One name. America's sweetheart.

"I'll want the highest quality and on-time delivery; we'd be talking to America's premier outlets, not just GLAMOUR. This would be on sale at Harrods, at Saks Fifth Avenue, at Scruples in L.A. And that means zero mistakes. I'm thinking Crème de la Mer—but bigger. A little less expensive, too. Affordable luxury, like a Chanel lipstick."

They nodded frantically, as similar execs had done in every cosmetic house she'd visited.

"And the marketing?"

"I have it out to five top Madison Avenue firms."

"It's been a very impressive presentation, Mrs. Nelson," said their chairman, standing up and all but rubbing his hands together in glee. "And we'd love to be in business with you. We'll messenger our costings to your people later today."

"Total creative control," Sally repeated firmly. "It's my brand; you'll be supplying the raw materials—that's going to be in the contract."

"Mrs. Nelson, you *are* the brand," he replied, looking surprised. "Why would we go anywhere else?"

Sally shook hands, delighted. Yeah, they got it. If only her two former best friends could see things the way the marketing men of America did!

On the limo ride back to O'Hare Airport she mulled things over. She could get this going by the end of next week. Samples on her desk, packaging included . . .

She'd intended to use it purely as blackmail. But now another idea was forming. Two companies—one public, one her own. Why not? If Jane could branch out, why not Sally? Showing she was competent, showing she could run things—that would sweet-talk the shareholders into selling GLAMOUR back to her.

Yeah. It was a great idea. She took out her mobile and dialed the direct line to her chief lawyer. He was head of a big firm in L.A., and available to her whenever needed.

"Tony? Sal. Listen, I'm going ahead. Can you draw everything up, get it registered in my name? Sally Lassiter Cosmetics. Thanks, doll. Have the papers waiting when I get home."

She listened as he gave her a report. Perfect. Everything was going fine.

❧

Jaber sighed with pleasure and rolled off Haya, panting; drained, he lay on the bed and stared at the mosaics in the ceiling.

She was exhausted, herself. But man, was he good. Patient, exacting, knowledgeable. He knew just how to handle her body. She responded, intensely, unable to help herself.

"I couldn't handle this without you. None of it."

"You couldn't have refused?" Haya asked, timidly.

"Refused?" Jaber propped himself up on his elbows and stared down at her, her glorious dark hair pooled out over the white Egyptian cotton sheets. "You can't refuse your destiny when it calls. That way lies eternal regret."

She turned onto her belly to meet him, and nuzzled kisses into his ear and throat.

"Which is exactly why I have to go."

"Haya." He sighed. "The king could die any minute. While you're out there. You would be the Queen of Ghada, and sitting in some boardroom in Los Angeles! How would it look?"

"Like you aren't a man who compromises his principles," she said. "You took a risk when you married me, Jaber. You know what a woman I am—a businesswoman, a professional. Yes, I set it aside. But not so that they can destroy everything I've built up. Let me save the company. One day. It's all I ask."

He shook his head. "Haya—I cannot deny you. But make it as quick as you can, and be back on the jet the second you get out of there." Jaber sighed. "Women. You'd think as a king I might have it easier."

She hit him on the chest, grinning. "No chance."

"I should have married that distant cousin," Jaber said, darkly. He reached for his wife, yanking her to him; Haya was amazed at his inexhaustible energy.

"Never mind." He kissed her lightly, deliberately. "I'm going to give you a chance to make it up to me."

～～○

"The press is coming," Sally told Jane, bluntly. "They got word of what we're doing—and the fight."

"You told them?"

"No," Sally replied coldly. "There are three sets of lawyers' offices involved now, Jane."

Jane pursed her lips. Damnation.

"Then I suppose the answer is dress well and act civilly. If the analysts think we're at each other's throats, the IPO will be disappointing. They need to understand we remain a team—you and I, at least. Haya's out of the game."

"Agreed. See you Monday," Sally said crisply, and hung up.

Jane was listening to a dial tone. Slowly, she replaced the receiver. She had no doubt that Monday afternoon, Pacific, she would be making the deals with institutions that would give her control. So why did she feel so down?

Her phone rang again—and Jane jumped. But it was only the double tone that meant the concierge was calling.

"Yes, Ortiz?"

"Miz Morgan, we got a delivery here. Boy, do we ever." The fat old man was chuckling. "Flowers, from Mr. Levin."

She shivered. Why would he do this? Hadn't she been clear? She wanted a clean break.

"You can bring them up."

"No ma'am—*I* can't. But the delivery men will."

"What do you mean?"

"He sent you flowers—like, a *truck*load. There has to be about a hundred arrangements. In pots—there's even a flowering orange tree, smells pretty good down here, ma'am."

"Is the truck still there?"

"Unloading now."

"No," Jane said. The pain was as bright and sharp as a diamond now. "Ortiz, refuse delivery, okay? I don't want them. Tell the men to take them back."

There was a pause, but he knew not to argue with her.

"Yes ma'am. Any message?"

She thought about it.

"Yes. Tell him 'All or nothing.'"

She replaced the receiver again and fled into her rooftop garden. Somewhere with no phone, high enough that nobody overlooked her, where she could lie on a recliner, by her Japanese fountain, look at the sky, and have a little peace.

My heart can't take this, Jane thought. I know they all think I'm made of stone. But it hurts to love him, it hurts so deeply.

She decided she would check into a hotel, the Victrix on Central Park. Nice and anonymous—strictly no incoming calls—and stay there until the flight left on Monday.

Craig would get the message. She loved him far too much to act like his personal hooker. And perhaps her rebellious heart would get the message, too. Maybe in its own way grief could help her move on.

⁓

Craig Levin sat in front of his desk and tried to concentrate. Behind him, a sheer wall of glass looked out over Wall Street. It was an office for a master of the universe. His playground, too. He'd had it modeled on Gordon Gekko's pad in the movie; a cautionary tale, but Levin used it as a motivational tool.

Last night he'd dated a model. Very smart girl, Israeli, dark and doe-eyed, a premed student before she quit for the catwalk. Just a date; just dinner. Even though she was obviously willing, and her body had been rounder and lusher than Jane's ever was, he'd stopped at dinner; feeling sick, feeling like he was cheating on Jane.

Ridiculous. They'd broken up.

He spent a poor night thinking of his ex. Angry with her. Make that furious. Why had she taken the hottest thing in his life, the best thing, and messed with it? Stupid, conventional notions of love. He *did* love her—passionately. What the hell difference did a ring make?

Lots of folks had told Levin it was their way or the highway. He'd never failed to take the highway, and it had worked out well enough.

Not this time.

He knew her, though. It was better because she always fought it. She was so damn hot, an ongoing challenge.

He knew every inch of her. Knew just how she was pining for him.

What was he thinking? He had gotten Jane in the first place with a planned campaign, patient months of waiting, letting her longing do the work. Now all he had to do was get her back. He had lifted the phone and called the all-night florist, delivery first thing in the morning.

Just now, his chief assistant had called with the news. And Jane's message.

It was so—so strong. So classy. She was everything the model hadn't been. She fascinated him. Levin felt himself start to weaken, to surrender. For once in their relationship, he thought, she was going to triumph.

He called her building.

"She's gone, Mr. Levin," the doorman told him, with, Craig thought, a touch of pride. "She said to tell you to please stop chasing her. She won't be back until after her meeting, and she doesn't want you to call even then."

"Thanks for telling me, Ortiz."

He hung up as his assistant buzzed him.

"Craig, your nine a.m. from Bank of America's in the outer lobby and the nine twenty from KKR are waiting in reception . . ."

"Emma—apologize to them, cancel all my appointments."

"All of them?" she protested.

"All of them. For the week."

"Are you feeling okay, Craig?"

"No. I'm sick. And I'm going home. Tell Peter to deal with everything." His deputy in the firm. "And don't call me."

"You got it," she said. The light disappeared. Secretaries who argued the toss with him didn't get to keep their jobs very long.

He called one of his personal PAs, back at the house.

"Claudette, send the limo to the office. We're going to JFK. I want to be on the first flight to L.A. Call the people at the Hollywood house and get it ready."

He had no idea what he was going to say to Jane, but he was going to see her. And she couldn't hide forever. She'd be in L.A. Monday morning, going to that meeting at GLAMOUR. And Craig Levin was going to be waiting.

⟳

By Thursday, the story had broken.

And boy, had it broken.

In a suite at the Victrix, in the vast master bedroom in Bel Air, in the palace of the crown prince in Ghada City, the three young women opened their papers, logged on to their computers; nobody liked what they saw.

It was ugly; a bloodbath.

The dry, dull pages of the business press had something juicy, for once. A scandal involving pretty girls, billions of dollars, athletes, financiers, and kings.

The *Wall Street Journal* said it all: the single-word headline was "Catfight."

Haya—in both robes and coronet, and a T-shirt and jeans, figured prominently. The Yank princess. Another Anita Roddick, or an obsessive putting her cash before her country?

Jane—a workaholic boss from hell. Laid off thousands of Shop Smart workers. Loner, antisocial, not a feminine bone in her body. Why should shareholders trust her? A fluky career, too young, no track record . . .

Sally—business Barbie or brainless bimbo? The dull gray suits in the business press had been waiting to tear her down. Daughter of the disgraced Paulie Lassiter. Athlete's wife. Good to design clothes and get her picture taken—hardly the stuff of corporate governance.

Put together, the news hacks reluctantly concluded, these women had something. But it couldn't last. After a burst of explosive growth and more cash than most male CEOs made in a lifetime, they were already at each other's throats. When GLAMOUR went public, it was a great opportunity for some *true* retailers to come swooping in.

On Monday, the shares would be out there for the grabbing. It was time, the consensus said, for the market to clean up the mess.

There was a little speculation as to which shark could mop up most of Jane Morgan's shares the first. Surely she'd be most easily elbowed aside. Her expertise could be replicated. . . .

But what about the princess? Ethical business? What was the point of that? On the other hand, Haya had made, to say the least, a *very* good marriage. As crown prince, Jaber had sixteen palaces! What if he used his personal fortune to hoover up the shares before U.S. brokers could get to him? Nobody could compete with that kind of firepower. . . .

And Sally? Well, that was different. America just loved her. She was the homecoming queen, all grown up and sitting pretty at the boardroom table. Wife of the champ. Brand gold. The male writers agreed she'd have to be placated. The new corporate owners should pay her a very handsome premium, give her some placatory title, a nonexec directorship, anything to keep her there. . . .

Whatever; it would be interesting. The shares were to go on sale right after the meeting; ten a.m., Pacific time. Of course, they'd all be rich: but one, or all, of these women would find her dream had been ruined.

⟡

"The embassy is on the phone, Your Royal Highness."

Jaber frowned. He did not need to ask which embassy. This was the third call this morning.

His Excellency began with the usual formalities, then got right down to business.

"The princess cannot come, sir."

"Haven't we had this conversation, Ambassador Rashman?"

"Yes, but Your Royal Highness has not seen the press ..."

"Indeed I have," he said heavily. He did not want Haya there, either. The king was sinking. The whole thing was disastrous.

"I mean the physical press. It's only Saturday, and they are already gathering near the store. It might as well be the Oscars. They are staking out positions. You must forbid this scandal, sir, you must—"

Jaber cut him off. He did not like Haya's plans, but she was her own woman. And he would not be dictated to by anybody.

"*Must* is an interesting word to use to your crown prince ... *Excellency*."

A long pause. "Sir, forgive me—your wife—"

"Her Royal Highness has decided to make the trip. That's all there is to it. You may send along a special adviser to accompany her."

"But—"

"I strongly advise you not to cross my will, Rashman. If I find the princess has been interfered with, you will be replaced within twenty-four hours. While His Majesty is sick, I am regent. Not to put too fine a point on it," Jaber smiled, thinly, "my word is law. Do I make myself clear?"

He heard the official swallowing. "The princess's wish stands. Yes, Your Royal Highness. Please do forgive my—"

"Good-bye, Excellency," Jaber said firmly. He hung up.

Haya was standing there, in the archway to his private apartments.

"Excuse me—I heard most of that."

"I hope you know what you're doing," he said heavily. "The king is sinking, Haya."

"When I go, I will go as a princess," she promised him. "No informality; I will wear the circlet. They will see a modern woman of Ghada who bears herself with dignity."

"Hurry back," he said. Uncomfortable, still. How much dignity could she have with those dogs of photographers ready to tear her to shreds?

⌐

Jane wanted to be sick. Her hands physically shook, when she read those papers. They were saying Sally was right. That anybody could manage the finances. That once they went public, she would shortly be replaced.

She had to perform at that meeting. She had to give the performance of her life. The only way to survive was to get her hands on one of the other girls' shares.

She wondered how Craig Levin, financial genius, would have handled this, and then hated herself for her need, for her ache for him.

No, damn it, no! No Cinderella fantasies. There was no white knight ready to ride and save her this time. Craig had been there at the start. At the end, it was going to be up to her.

⌐

Sally stepped out of the shower and reached for a toweling robe. She had these brought in direct from GLAMOUR, and they were the softest, fluffiest things this side of the Regent Beverly Wilshire Hotel. Perfect, in fact, for moments like this, when she barely had the energy to towel herself off.

Chris was out at the ball park, playing catch with a bunch of disabled kids. She was so proud of him; the only work he did these days was for charity.

She hadn't complained to Chris. In fact, she'd ordered the maid to sweep away the papers and keep the TVs permanently tuned to ESPN. This fight was her deal, no need to involve her husband. Pay her off? Bribe her with a salary? Those male writers thought she was the bimbo, but they'd somehow failed to see that she had more money than God. And when GLAMOUR went public, forget it, she'd be able to buy her own country. . . .

She didn't want money. Didn't they get that? It was all about control, about self-esteem.

Right now, she was gonna take care of herself. Go sit on the terrace and watch the sun set over her lawn; that big lawn where the tents had been pitched for her party, all those years ago; Jane Morgan's social debut.

Sally found herself sighing, with nostalgia, and bitter regret. She thought of the long, spiraling staircase the three of them had walked down together, beautiful, *beyond* beautiful, sixteen years old and with the world at their feet. . . .

At Sally's feet, anyway; she had spread the blanket of her popularity across them for protection; that dazzling night, it had worked.

Maybe those things didn't count for much now. Maybe it was time to grow up, to put the past behind her.

Jane and Haya evidently had.

She was walking out the door when something caught her eye. There, in the bathroom trash basket. The little stick she had tossed.

No *way*.

But yes—there was something different about it, something half-covered with a tissue, that had caught her peripheral vision . . .

Sally picked it up. She'd been too fast to throw it out. She hadn't waited the full three minutes.

There was a second line. Faint, but distinct. She reached out one manicured hand and steadied herself against the wall of her walk-in marble wet room.

She was pregnant.

~

There had been no socializing. No small talk. None of the girls was up for it. They shook hands; their lawyers shook hands. Nobody curtsied to Haya; she had not been expecting it.

"The meeting will come to order," Jane said loudly.

The lawyers shut up. When Jane Morgan spoke, people tended to listen.

"We're here to sign off on the exact terms of the IPO. I take it you all have the documents?"

Haya raised her hand. "Madam Chairman, if I may?"

Jane sat down immediately.

"Of course, Your Royal Highness," she said, with studied politeness.

"The company has aggressively pursued ethical commerce. As you know, ethical trade in the Middle East, with a remit to expand into Europe and Asia, has been my focus as a director. What guarantees can you give me this will continue?"

"I can't. A public company can make no such arrangements."

"That's unacceptable," Haya said instantly. "We made commitments, and I intend to honor your word."

That stung.

"May I say something?"

"Mrs. Nelson has the floor," Jane said crisply.

"My lawyers have discovered that Lassiter makeup and Lassiter-designed clothes have accounted for twenty-five percent of total merchandise sales. Further to this, we estimate that at least a third of the goodwill value of the chain comes from my personal image."

"You're hardly unbiased," Jane said. "Haya would contest that."

"Princess Haya," Haya snapped.

Jane inclined her head. "Forgive me, ma'am. *Princess* Haya. I think you'll find that my figures for the total real estate, staffing, distribution, funding, inventory management, analyst presentations, and general costs come to over fifty percent of the total value of this company."

There was a long silence. The three women around the table glared at each other.

"Well, ladies." Kent Green, the head of the firm of Sally's lawyers, spoke up, a touch smugly. "Perhaps it's time to let the professionals take over—otherwise this meeting could go on all day. And we *do* have a deadline."

"Just a second." Sally spoke up. "I'd like y'all to give us the room, please. I want to speak to my partners alone."

"I don't think that's wise, Sally," Kent said, paternalistically.

"I can't allow Her Royal Highness to be unrepresented in the room," piped up Ahmed al-Jamir, the special adviser. Babysitter, as Haya thought of him.

"I won't let my client go to bat by herself." Jane's lawyer, Rachel Frohman, spoke clearly and authoritatively. "Sorry, Ms. Nelson, but we're staying."

Jane was looking over at Sally; then she glanced at Haya.

"No—you're not. Give me the room, please, Rachel."

"But Ms. Morgan—"

"Now, please."

"Mr. Al-Jamir, you, too." Haya nodded at the diplomat, then backed it up in Arabic.

There was a creak and a shift, and with great reluctance the small army of lawyers, assistants, advisers, and accountants left the room.

As soon as the door shut Sally smiled.

"Girls, what the hell are we doing?" she said.

"What we have to," Jane replied, with a heavy heart.

"Bull*shit,* girlfriend. We're doing what we think we have to. We're cornered into this. Nobody wants to be here." Sally looked at her two friends—determined they would stay that way. "Y'all want to know what happened to me today? I found out I was pregnant."

Haya beamed, shocked out of her reserve. "Sally!"

"Really." She shook her head, tears in her eyes. "You guys remember that day in the playground, the first day Haya turned up? Nobody wanted to talk to her. I figured we'd look out for her. Why? Because I was pretty and Jane was smart. We filled the gaps with each other. Don't see why life has to get complicated. Don't see why we still can't do that."

"But GLAMOUR is everything we've worked for," Jane said. "It's everything I am."

"The hell it is. You were doing just fine before we started. And you'll do great after this. I want the company. We all do. But I was an only child, you two were practically my sisters." Sally passed one hand over her belly. "I've started Sally Lassiter

Cosmetics. Jane's got Morgana now. Haya, looks like that crown you're wearing's gonna get a bit bigger, no? *This is just a store.*"

Jane jumped up from the table and went to the window; not before they saw the tears streaming down her face.

She had lost Craig. And now she would lose these two?

"You're a hundred percent right." She turned round. "But we have different ideas. This store is something special. Let's not put it on the market and let men chew it up. Let's just decide who's going to run it."

Haya said, "I owe you both an apology. I got caught up in my husband. I haven't talked enough to you." She blushed, richly. "Sally, I dumped you in my wedding without bothering to explain a damn thing. I'm sorry."

"Me, too, Haya." Sally came over and gave her a hug; Haya stood up and went and rubbed Jane's back.

"You guys will guarantee the livelihoods of all the poor women supplying us, right?"

Sally and Jane both nodded.

"Then you can have my shares. Fifty-fifty. I'll give the money to charity."

As soon as she said it, a smile broke out on her face; something lifted, almost physically, from her heart.

"What a relief," she said. "It's been great, you know? But nobody needs this kind of pressure." Haya cocked her head, looked at Sally. "You're going to have a baby. If you want my two cents, let Jane have it. She's been the most driven of all of us."

Sally exhaled, then shrugged. "Yes. All right, then. Jane."

"No." Jane turned around; her eyes were red, but, like Haya, she was smiling; she rubbed the tears away from her eyes. "Sally, you said it. All these years, I've been fighting the fact I had nobody to love me. No father, no mother. But that was wrong. I had you two. I just couldn't see it." She paused. "I have succeeded in everything I've done. Why does it have to be the thing I started out in? Maybe I'll go into real estate. It hardly matters. But GLAMOUR . . . GLAMOUR is special. There can only be one choice. It's you, Sally. You who looked after both of us. You who taught us how to use being beautiful. There are a lot of skeptics out there, a lot of analysts sneering. You take it, and you show them all that being a woman isn't some kind of choice between beauty and brains." She grinned. "Besides, I want to trade stocks. I could use all that liquid cash."

Sally could hardly believe it. She clapped her hands, like a kid at a birthday party. "Really? It's mine?"

"It's all yours," Jane replied, and shook her hand.

The three girls came together and gave each other a hug.

"Shall we let them back in?" Haya asked, with a wink. "There are gonna be some pretty sad lawyers. All those billable hours down the drain."

"Let's." Jane grinned. "Can't wait to see the press when we announce this. What are they going to say now?"

Sally nodded, and Jane flung open the doors; the large knot of hangers-on raced back in and sat around the table.

"Don't get too comfortable," Jane said, smiling. "The deal's off. No public stock."

There was uproar.

"We have arranged a private sale. Ladies and gentlemen, I give you the new chairman and CEO of GLAMOUR. Ms. Sally Nelson."

Jane got up from the head of the table and surrendered her position to her friend; as she went and sat at Sally's seat, she felt no pain, no regret; just an open sense of joy and possibility. The future was hers; no limits, no ties.

She looked across at Haya, and saw that she felt the same way.

Sally shook out her long, glossy hair, in a delicious shimmer of gold, leaned back confidently in her chair, and glanced over the table full of dumbstruck investment advisers.

"I'm in charge, gentlemen," she said. "So let's get to work."

EPILOGUE

K ing Nazir died a day after Haya touched down in Ghada
City. Jaber led the mourning, and Haya found herself a
queen, mingling with royalty and heads of state at the
funeral. She didn't have much time to stand around and wonder;
a week later, just before the coronation, she discovered she, too,
was pregnant.

She decided to make her new role her full-time job. Haya
never let a day go past without visiting some charity, and the
people loved her. She founded girls' schools across the kingdom,
and worked with Jaber as a full partner on drawing up new laws
to promote democracy.

She and Noor were often seen, at weekends, dropping in to
the new GLAMOUR being built in Ghada City. It became the
hottest store in the country.

~

Sally continued work up until one day before her church
wedding ceremony, which was the social event of the year, and
two days before she gave birth. Queen Haya attended the wedding, and was Sally's matron of honor; Jane preferred to sit quietly in the front row. But at the birth, Jane was there, holding
Sally's hand as Chris Junior came shrieking into the world. His
dad, the toughest guy in sports, had refused to come in and

watch Sally moaning in pain he could do nothing to spare her from.

Sally took two months off. When she came back, she instituted flexible working hours and staffed day-care centers at every GLAMOUR store around the world. Women loved it, and the global sales soared.

"See? It's always the good guys who finish first," Haya told her friend.

Jane Morgan had believed that. She left the meeting at GLAMOUR smiling; for the first time in her life, it felt good to lose. She posed for pictures with Haya and Sally, Sally in the middle, the boss, the winner, and Jane didn't mind at all.

She had other things to think about. Like starting over. And mending her heart.

When the press finally melted away, Jane headed back to her limo. She got in the backseat, slipped her sunglasses on, and sighed, a deep, personal sigh of release.

"LAX, please."

The driver tipped his cap. "Yes, ma'am."

She checked in, in no particular hurry. First class meant you could take the first flight that became available.

"I'm afraid we only have seat 1B available, miss. Is that okay for you?"

"That's fine," said Jane, even though she usually chose her own seat. She shrugged. "Everything's fine."

"Great," said the flight attendant, glancing at her colleague with a sly look. "Then you're all set. Have a great flight."

When she boarded, Jane looked around the first-class cabin; it was empty. She spoke to the stewardess.

"I was told there was only seat 1B. . . ."

"That's right, ma'am, all these seats are booked. Can I show you to your . . ."

But Jane was already marching up the cabin. Great, they were going to be really late, all these last-minute boarders. But she wouldn't let something like that spoil her mood. Not now; not today . . .

At least there was one passenger . . . the back of a man's head in seat 1A. So much for a peaceful flight. Jane grabbed her case and lifted it . . .

"Let me get that," he said, standing and walking into the aisle.

Jane gasped; it was Craig Levin.

He took it from her, just like that first day, and hoisted it easily into the overhead rack.

"I'm not sitting here," she said, looking wildly around for the stewardess. But the woman had melted away, smiling discreetly.

"You are if you want to fly in this cabin. There are no more seats."

"Look around you."

"I bought all of them."

Jane blinked. "What? You bought an entire first-class cabin?"

"Just so you had to sit next to me. I think you'll agree that a gesture like that is worthy of respect, at least. Sit down."

"Craig . . ."

"I said sit."

She sat.

He leaned over and kissed her, softly, possessively, on the lips.

"I saw what you did today. That was brave, Jane. That was good."

"She's right for it."

"And you're right for me," he said. "I want to see if I can soften you up a little more." Jane stared as he reached into his pocket and drew out a ring case; she put her hands over her mouth; he flipped it open, showed her the small circlet of gold set with emeralds. "It was my mother's." He took her trembling hand, and gently slipped the ring onto it. "It's a simple fact; you were made to be my woman, nobody else's. I can't sleep without you. And the thought of another man so much as touching you is more than I can bear. So there's only one way to get you to myself. Preemptive strike." Levin kissed her again, much harder, wanting her urgently, hating that they had to wait five hours.

"That's a hell of a proposal."

"I'm not asking you. I'm claiming you. You're mine; my woman. My wife."

"Yes," she said, melting with happiness, and lust, and the sheer exhilaration of it. "Your wife."

They kissed, hard, then slower; then his arms snaked around her.

"Damn," Jane said, grinning, when she came up for air. "This is going to be fun."